FERAL AGENT

CALM ACT FERAL AMERICA BOOK 2

GINGER BOOTH

❀ Created with Vellum

MAPS

CANADA
QUEBEC
Montreal
ONTARIO
Ottawa
Lake Huron
MAINE
(Canada)
VERMONT
Toronto
ADIRONDACKS
NEW
HAMPSHIRE
Lake Ontario
Buffalo
HUDSON
FINGER LAKES
BERKSHIRE
Boston
Detroit
Elmira
Binghamton
MASS.
Erie
West
Point
CONN.
Lake Erie
Scranton
NARRAGANSETT
Cleveland
Apple
LONG ISLAND
PENNSYLVANIA
Pittsburgh
Trenton
Atlantic Ocean
OHIO
Philadelphia
JERSEY
Columbus
MD
Morgantown
Baltimore
DC
DE
WEST
VIRGINIA
Delmarva
Peninsula
Charlottesville
VA
Richmond
KEN-TENN
CAROLINA
(Norfolk)
Evolving Borders
State / Province
State - defunct line
National

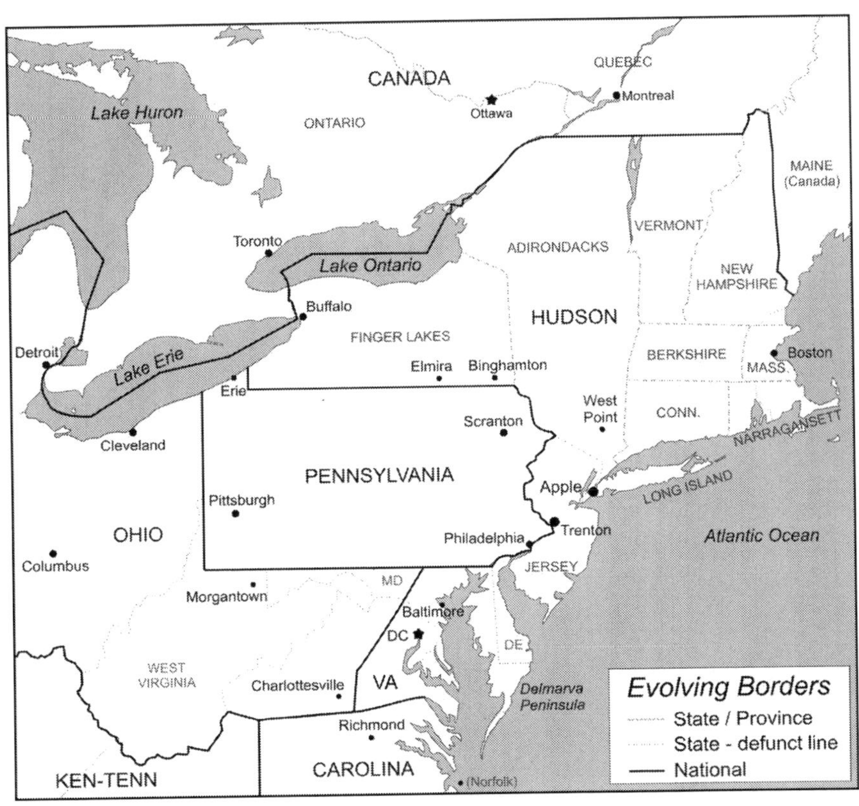

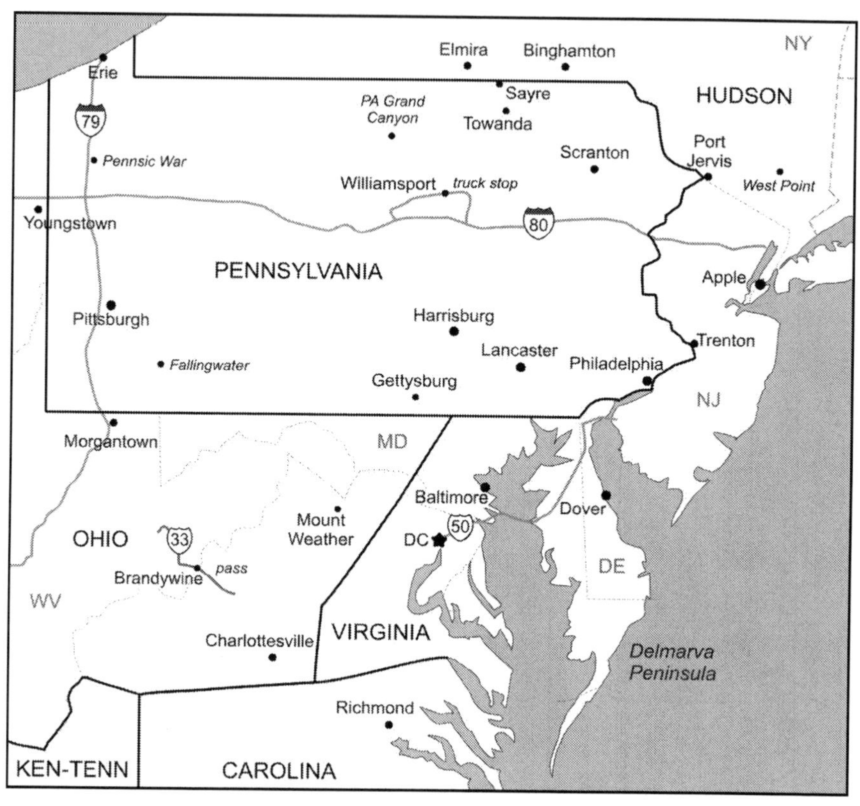

NY
HUDSON
Elmira
Binghamton
Sayre
PA Grand Canyon
Towanda
Scranton
Port Jervis
West Point
Erie
79
Pennsic War
Williamsport
truck stop
80
Apple
Youngstown
PENNSYLVANIA
Harrisburg
Pittsburgh
Lancaster
Trenton
Fallingwater
Philadelphia
Gettysburg
NJ
Morgantown
MD
Baltimore
Dover
OHIO
33
Mount Weather
DC
50
DE
Brandywine
pass
WV
VIRGINIA
Charlottesville
Delmarva Peninsula
Richmond
KEN-TENN
CAROLINA

PROLOGUE
THE CALM ACT

Climate change accelerated.
The tipping point came too hard, too fast.
Earth could no longer feed its billions.
America fared better than most.
Under a secret plan — the Calm Act.
Only half its citizens needed to die.

Life taught strange lessons to teenage Ava Panic.
She survived the culling of New York City.
She ruled in the gangs of the Starve.
She reveled in Army Basic.
And she opted to join the enemy.
The death angels.

1

––––––––––

Interesting fact: Pennsylvania grew 64% of the mushrooms in the United States, in small family-owned farms. Needing no sun, mushrooms were among the first commercial indoor crops.

Her first official act as a secret agent caught Ava Panic daydreaming, gazing out the passenger window at an endless sea of April-bare trees.

"I'm Ben. What's your name?" Cade Snowdon asked her, her boyfriend of two and a half years. "Pick one that begins with 'C.'"

"What?" Ava asked. She pulled herself upright in the vast leather bucket seat. Their SUV was perfectly proportioned for a family of tall 300-pounders. Ava was barely over 5 feet and 100 pounds. Cade's question caught her lying sideways, high-top red sneakers crossed at the ankle on the broad middle console. They rounded a bend to see a hostile orange traffic sign: *ROAD CLOSED – Penn. Border 1 Mile.*

Past the sign, the 2-lane rural highway broadened into a plaza, providing room for a dozen semi tractor-trailers to turn back north into Upstate New York. Or Finger Lakes, Hudson, as western New York was now known. The young nation of Hudson recently split Upstate into 'Finger Lakes' and 'Adirondacks.' The Governor-General favored natural place-names. Ava favored the new nicknames 'Up Finger' and 'Up Jacks.'

Cade didn't slow. But Ava's training as an army scout quickly picked up clues around the verge. This was a staging area, not a handy spot to turn around before the border.

"Did we invade through here, during the Penn War?" she asked.

"Since we're from *PA*, we call it the *Tolliver* War," Cade corrected her, in his usual cool even tone. "And yeah, Hudson did invade us through here. All a misunderstanding."

Cade slowed the SUV as they approached a traffic pileup at the armed crossing. He repeated, "I'm Ben. You are…?" He glanced at Ava and flicked a brief smile. "I use six personas in PA. Alphabetical to keep them easier to remember. Since we're traveling together, you also pick six. You choose one letter beyond mine. So when I change to Connor, you automatically switch to Donna or whatever."

"Got it," Ava murmured. Her mind automatically flashed to all the girls she disliked whose names began with 'C.' Most of them were New York City gang handles, as well. She cast further back in memory, to classmates before her family moved to the city of the damned. "Cheyenne," she picked.

Cade pursed his lips, then shrugged. "Pretty. Darcy, add to notebook, Ben Davis. Girlfriend Cheyenne Fields. Darcy, end."

"Noted," a phone replied, plugged into the SUV's elaborate dashboard.

Ava hadn't heard Cade speak to the car before. Her brow furrowed, daunted. "I need to learn how to use this stuff, don't I."

"That's your job for the next few weeks," Cade agreed. "New field agent training. Darcy, play notebook, Ben Davis."

"Ben Davis, Pennsylvania native," Darcy replied. Rather than replay Cade's voice, it seemed to read a transcript, in a voice reminiscent of the computer in *Star Trek*. "Northeast Pennsylvania counties Susquehanna, Lackawanna, Wyoming, Wayne, Pike, Bradford, Sullivan, Tioga, and Lycoming. Occupation trader. Girlfriend Cheyenne Fields. Last exited Bradford County, January. Shall I play mission notes?"

"No thanks," Cade murmured. "Darcy, go dark."

The traffic queue advanced quickly. Only one pickup truck remained between them and the sovereign nation of Pennsylvania. About twenty troops, well-armed, visibly milled around the road at this checkpoint. Trees were cleared to either side, to make room for a pair of machine gun platforms about 20 feet high, plus their sight lines. Four soldiers apiece were up there, too.

Hudson troops, Ava realized, studying their disposition with interest. Hudson controlled Pennsylvania's northern border. She was glad she wasn't one of them. That's what she expected, before she graduated from Army Basic Training at West Point a week ago. *Border garrison duty. What a dull job.* But she took an honorable discharge instead, and joined Cade to see the world.

So far the world involved a deluxe vacation campground in Up Finger, a whole lot of trees, and a huge SUV named Darcy, with unsuspected depths.

"Who's Darcy?" she asked.

"Ex-girlfriend," Cade said quellingly. "There's a cigarette pack in the glove compartment, green. Grab that for me."

"You didn't name it after me?" Ava quipped. She popped the box open. A green packet was right in front, among several others. She handed it to Cade. "Should I feel hurt?"

Cade went colder. "Darcy was over. Not now, Cheyenne."

The pickup ahead of them finished, and Cade pulled up for their turn at border inspection. "Don't reach for anything," he cautioned. "Makes them jumpy."

He rolled down his window. "Morning, Sergeant Bruckner," he greeted the soldier closest to the car.

Ava couldn't tell if Cade knew Bruckner. Like all troops, the man was labeled above his breast pocket. Four other soldiers ringed the car from a few paces back, carbines at the ready. Sergeant Bruckner's own rifle was slung on his shoulder, a tablet in his hands.

Cade continued, "Ben Davis, returning home with my girlfriend, Cheyenne Fields. Major Sullivan sends his regards." In his lap, visible to Bruckner and Ava but not the others, Cade flipped open the cigarette pack to display that it was packed with marijuana joints. He passed the gift underhand to the sergeant, who tucked it in a pocket.

"Transporting anything?" Bruckner inquired.

Cade shrugged. "Trade goods. The usual."

Bruckner stepped back and ran his eye along the extended cargo hold and storage box up top. The green SUV was 19 feet long and 7 feet tall, with tinted windows. He could barely glimpse inside. The vehicle could – and did – contain all sorts of dangerous things.

"Alright, you're free to go."

A soldier behind Bruckner shook his head in disgust. But Cade nodded and gently pulled away.

"He didn't even look inside?" Ava asked in wonder.

"Most do," Cade said. "But what do they care. They're Hudson. We're entering PA. What we bring in, is the next guy's problem. If we were entering Hudson, he'd have to inspect the back."

As they rounded another bend, Ava saw that there was indeed a next guy, or a next woman at least. The Penn – PA – troops looked like their Hudson counterparts. Though their road installation was more casual. Police SUVs parked on the shoulders to form a bottleneck, with orange traffic cones down the middle. None of the four militia held guns at the ready, Ava noted.

"Are they this casual on the Jersey side?" Ava asked.

"Hell, no," Cade confirmed. "The borders PA runs are hard core. This is lax for the farm market. Let's try the pink cigarette pack."

The pink packet was heavier. Ava peeked inside to see glass vials, insulin. In Hudson, this much insulin would make a hefty bribe.

There was no wait here. They pulled up to a stop sign. A single woman corporal bore a clipboard, her paperwork clearly not backed by a database.

"Names," she barked.

Again Cade supplied their names, and Major Sullivan's, and flicked open the pink packet to preview his offering. Corporal Schenck – her uniform was labeled, too – froze and pursed her lips. Ava watched with interest through her peripheral vision. The cop struggled, caught between moral imperatives.

"Good haul of electronics from Hudson," Ben-Cade shared. "Looking to sell at Sayre market. Traders."

"Smugglers," Schenck said. "I should throw you in jail right now."

Ava noted that she didn't say it loudly enough for her compatriots to hear. Schenck was torn.

"Filling a need," Ben-Cade countered, his eyes on the dashboard. "That's why we hold the Sayre fair, right? Bring in goods we need, but can't get from PA." He held up the packet by a corner, just below the window's edge, easy for her to pluck, then lowered it back to his lap.

"Give it to me," Schenck hissed.

He did so, eyes still not challenging hers.

"Get out of here."

And they were across the closed national border. Ava watched Hudson fall away behind them, as Cade brought the car up to speed again. "Oh my God. It's that easy? Cade, we actually escaped from New York!"

Her lips parted in delight. For two years, they'd been caught behind the Apple Zone epidemic borders, locked into a starving city, fighting for their lives. Nine out of ten around them died. Ebola. Violence. Typhus. Starvation. Cholera. Or the many who just gave up. They'd both escaped the city itself at Thanksgiving, Cade to this secret agent life, and Ava to Army Basic. But this suddenly felt real. They were free, and together, and outside Hudson!

"Who?" Cade replied coldly. "Where?"

"Ben. Hudson. Sorry."

He unbent slightly. "This is the easiest border crossing I know. And we almost lost it there. Darcy, wake up. Add to notebook, problems. Corporal Schenck, female cop, Sayre border crossing, PA side. Almost turned down a bribe of insulin and put us in jail. Darcy, end."

"Noted. You have a message."

"Darcy, play message."

Ava recognized Skull's voice – Major Sullivan, their boss. "Hey, Ben, updates. New PA-side border cop. Guess you're finding that out now. Check at the cheese shop for your allowance. Remember not to baby Cheyenne, alright? If she's as good as we think she is, she doesn't need it. Just like we talked about. You're set for the Sixers on Monday. Stay smart and stay safe."

Cade smirked. Ava missed that smirk in the eight months they were apart. It set off Cade's blond and icy good looks. With a start, she realized that Skull had used her new name of Cheyenne. *He monitors Cade's notes?*

"Darcy, reply message." His voice changed to address Skull. "Gee, Dad, thanks for the allowance! Man, you have *got* to hire someone for the scut work. We got all these newbies, and you're my handler for a trip to the farm market? I'll talk to the mayor about the border cop. Understood, on Cheyenne. Talk to you after the Sixers. Take care of yourself." Through this, his tone progressed from teasing, to down-to-business, to honest caring at the end. "Darcy, send."

At the insulting suggestion that anyone might need to baby her, Ava had popped open the glove compartment to inspect the other cigarette packs. There were repeats of marijuana and insulin, one pack of actual cigarettes, and some 54 mg strength nicotine e-liquid. The bribe cupboard also offered several small bottles of amoxicillin and doxycycline antibiotics, minus the cigarette pack wrappers.

If this was just the petty cash, they were rich. Ava couldn't help wondering what kept them from slipping their leash, and setting off into the sunset. That made her suddenly wonder how her friends from boot camp were faring. She pulled out her phone. She hadn't been allowed to contact them from their safe house, the campground they left this morning.

"Put that away," Cade said sharply. "We're outside Hudson. And you're not allowed comms during training."

"Good thing I work for my boyfriend instead of a hard-ass," Ava commented.

"Your boyfriend is a hard-ass, Cheyenne. He's also your training agent for the next few weeks. No comms."

"When can I text my friends again?"

"We should be back in Hudson in a month or so. Maybe we'll pass through the city on the way home."

Home. Ava blinked. Cade meant the campground north of Elmira, not the city they'd lived in for years. They'd lived in the Apple together until August, when she walked out on him. No, not him. Frosty. His original alter ego, Frosty the Snowman, gang leader of White Supreme in the Chelsea district of Manhattan. But she'd dated Cade Snowdon, the original one, for a few months before Ebola broke out. They lived in the same apartment building in Greenwich Village. They studied karate at the same dojo in Chelsea.

Home doesn't mean anything, she had to concede. *Except for the friends.* But Cade considered Skull a friend, not just a boss. They were close.

OK, no driving off into the sunset. Yet.

Ava replied slowly, "Can't just pop back across the border to Binghamton and visit Daneel?" One of her friends from boot camp had also joined 'the company.' They dropped him off in Binghamton on their way to Elmira.

"Border's open today for the Sayre farm market," Cade confirmed. "Twice a month. They make a big deal out of it to draw in traders from Hudson."

"So that's why you're training me in PA instead of Hudson?" Ava was glad she caught herself before saying 'Penn' again. Hudsons started calling it 'Penn' during the war, as a pejorative. Before the war, she didn't recall anyone bothering to mention Penn. Philly, maybe. That old poster showing the New Yorker's view of the continent – Jersey, a couple cows, some mountains, and then California – was only funny because it was true.

Cade nodded a so-so. "Questions later. For now, you're Cheyenne. We met last week, so you don't know me too well. We're shopping for food. Mostly. You need a hunting jacket. Red plaid."

"Ick." Actually, she could use other clothes, too, she realized. She hadn't brought many civvies with her to boot camp.

Cade's own tacky jacket was hung on the back of his seat. "Dress to fit in. So look around."

They'd arrived, it seemed. Only a few blocks from the edge of town, they reached the center, with a large town green. Ava was impressed by the three-story brick buildings of Sayre's downtown, until she realized they were all boarded up at street level, vacant. Still, there were quite a few cars parked on the streets. A throng focused on the large striped market tents erected in the square, snapping in the cold dry wind. Cade caught a parking spot right by the fair, as a pickup truck pulled out.

Apparently Darcy knew how to parallel-park herself, too. Ava was grateful she didn't know how to drive. The SUV was starting to intimidate her.

Cade supplied them each with a few cloth shopping bags, and handed her half his wad of cash. She pursed her lips rather than comment on the paper money. Cheyenne couldn't ask Ben questions on this busy street. She did briefly examine the Liberty Bell artwork, though.

She had no idea what the fifty-three Pennsylvania dollars were worth. In Hudson they used electronic currency now. The basic unit was ten Hudson dollars, a day's rations, which cost slightly less than a day's wages, until she joined the Army. In boot camp she drew half salary, five dollars, but used it for nothing at all. She hadn't held paper money since Ebola broke out. And that currency bore the seal of the defunct United States of America.

Her last purchase of cheap pea soup mix cost twenty-odd U.S. dollars apiece. Though she only had her grandfather's credit card with her that day. When the store suddenly went cash-only as the banks crashed, she ran out with her food without paying.

"I'll have more cash after my transaction," Ben-Cade said. "I might wander off. I'll find you again." He locked the car, adding some additional unexplained button-presses on his key chain remote. "You'll love the food tent here, Cheyenne." He shot her a quick warning glance. "Let's grab enough for about a week, OK?"

Cheyenne-Ava wasn't clear on what the warning was about.

They arrived at the food tent, and she forgot to breathe for a few heartbeats. The smell of fresh-baked wheat bread alone was enough to stop her like a body blow.

They fed Ava well in the Army. They really did. But years of starvation burned deep into her psyche. And even now, nowhere in the Apple could she see this much food. In April, no less – harvest was six months ago. The new season hadn't yet begun. Yet brilliantly colored vegetables of every description were heaped on tables. Breads. Eggs. Cheeses, milk, cream. Cereals. Meat. It went on and on, dozens of tables mounded with food, with extra crates in reserve.

And anyone could walk up and buy them. *In bulk. With cash! No rationing?* Ava swallowed, feeling a prick of tears for the friends she'd watched starve to death. While these people, only a couple hundred miles away, had all this? And *attacked* Hudson? Refused Hudson and New England their fair share of the Northeast strategic food reserves? She blinked and frowned to control the memory.

Ben-Cade squeezed her hand. "Let's get mushrooms. I'm thinking beef kebabs tonight. We need eggs, too. Bread. Snacks. Cheese. The works."

The mushrooms cost one dollar a pound, or three pounds for two dollars. Three pounds of beef for five dollars. No wonder they crossed to PA before packing food for the trip.

Ava wondered what it took to earn a Pennsylvania dollar.

Ben-Cade whispered in her ear, "You're doing fine. I'll go find ice."

Cheyenne-Ava wanted to stop him and ask what she should be looking for, secret agent wise. But on reflection, she realized that her lesson of the hour was simply to act as Cheyenne Fields, shopping for food.

For a week. Hmm. Actually, that took some planning. She got out her phone and puzzled out a week's generous meals and snacks for two, with unknown kitchen equipment. No, they had a camp stove and ice cooler. She caught some funny looks from passers-by, but screw them. She'd never done a week's food shopping before. She intended to enjoy it to the hilt.

What was it Cade called this job? *Orgasmic.*

2

———————

Interesting fact: Pennsylvania was a lead producer of dairy, corn, wheat, livestock feed, and potatoes. It also ranked high in apple and grape production, though lower than New York.

"**G**ood job on the food, Cheyenne," Ben-Cade praised her, as they finished stowing it. Ava's estimation of Darcy the SUV rose another notch as she learned Cade's food storage arrangements. She particularly liked his pantry picnic basket, a large wicker box which unfolded into handy stepped shelves when he lifted the lid. The vegetables Cade simply hung in shopping bags from the ceiling. He separated out some snacks for the cab. "Need crackers."

"Are we staying?" Ava said. "I'm out of cash. I was a few bucks short on the last stall. She let me walk away with the stuff. 'Just come back with the money later, sweetie.' Can you believe that?"

Cade handed her a couple empty shopping bags and his remaining cash. "Better go pay her, then. Yeah, let's stay a few hours. No rush. Don't forget the jacket."

Oops. Her tight black leather jacket, replete with brass zippers, looked cool. No one else looked cool. So far, rural PA looked old and frumpy in the extreme. Her eyes weren't used to so many people aged thirty to sixty. Back in the city, most from the middle age brackets were dead. The children were gone from the city, too, evacuated out to the country. Before they left, they didn't have the energy to play much. Here, children raced around laughing.

Cade tagged along back to the baker's stall. Ava paid up. Cade charmed a few extra free oatmeal cookies out of the middle-aged woman, and got pointers on where to buy crackers and clothes. Judging from the baker's glance at Cheyenne-Ava, a dowdy jacket would be an improvement. *Hussy,* the woman's look seemed to comment.

Fair enough. Ava had dressed like this to turn tricks in Chinatown more than once. Not that she'd admit that to Frosty-Cade-Ben. *Don't ask. Don't tell.* They did what they had to do.

"Ooh!" Ava said. She stopped at a craft stall, entranced. A hundred silk scarves flapped in the wind, marbled in brilliant colors and patterns. The artisan was doing a demonstration in a long shallow water trough, raised on trestles to waist-height. Most people saw the sign – $20 to dye your own – and scurried right past.

"Go ahead," Ben-Cade encouraged.

Cheyenne-Ava grinned at him and bellied up to the trough.

"We could use some gifts. And one for you," he continued.

"Gifts?" she asked, brow furrowing.

"I still owe Puño a wedding gift, and his wife Cantora. We have friends," Ben-Cade said. "They get married at our age. Need cash. I'll be back."

They get married at our age. Eighteen and twenty. It was true, her army buddy Puño was married. His wife Cantora was only sixteen. In Ava's mind, this had more to do with crappy career opportunities than being mature enough to get married. *Well, I'm not ready to marry Cade, anyway.*

That concern vanished as Ava watched the water marbling. The man squirted drops of dye onto the the water, which dispersed outward into polka dots of floating color. Then he drew a stick through the blobs, systematically criss-crossing, to mingle the colors sideways. Then he inserted a wire comb and drew it slowly down the length of the tray, creating a fairly regular texture. Ava helped him lay a brilliant white silk scarf squarely on top. The dye instantly soaked through in a gorgeous pattern.

After only moments, he drew the scarf through squeegee-rollers at the end of the trough, to push off the excess pigment. Then he plunged the masterpiece into a bucket of cold water, explaining that this set the dye. A quick rinse, and he tacked the scarf up to dry, snapping in the wind like the others.

"Your turn," the artisan invited with a smile. "I'm Jerry. Look through the scarves to pick out the texture you want." Meanwhile he cleaned the trough, ready to start again with a clean water canvas. A second trough stood unused beside it.

When Cade returned, Ava was dripping dye for her second scarf, a study in desert camouflage, with rare drops of melon. He took one look and requested permission to use the second trough. She glanced over a few times as he worked. Instead of a consistent smattering of color blobs, he seemed to have an image in mind, heavy on greens and black on one half, then blues, repeated with greens for a margin at the other end. In between he used white and orange, sandwiched with more black.

"Ben, what are you doing?" she asked, as she began the systematic comb-dipping to smear her camouflage.

"You'll see. If it works." He huddled secretively with Jerry the craftsman to explain what he was trying to accomplish, flashing a few grins her way.

Ava's camouflage came out perfect. She pinned it up and joined Cade's trough for the great scarf-settling.

"You're looking at it upside-down," Ben-Cade advised.

She tilted her head. "A water tiger!" she breathed in delight. That was the emblem of their karate dojo. Since they ran the gang from the dojo, it was their gang emblem as well. This made no sense to the neighboring gangs, a tiger pawing a puddle. As gang leader, Frosty didn't give a damn what made sense to anyone else. That was his Frosty persona. He was a third degree karate black belt. His black karate gi had a water tiger on it. *Deal with it.*

The scarf didn't really look like a water tiger, stalking to a jungle pool, just an out-of-focus marbling of color and drama. But the young couple could see the tiger, even if no one else could. And Ava felt that blurred and broken blobs of color and drama represented their memories together fairly well.

"I love it, Ben," she breathed, and plastered herself against him for a kiss.

"Good," he mouthed unvoiced, pleased. "I have another one in mind."

"Can we afford this?" Ava asked, alarmed.

"Five for eighty," Jerry interjected promptly. They'd attracted attention. People were stopping to watch and shop, with one waiting for a turn at the trough.

"Yes, Cheyenne," Ben-Cade said. "We can afford this." His ice-blue eyes lit with amusement.

Of course they could afford this. Food, travel, housing, clothes, were all paid for by 'the company.' If they spent PA dollars, it probably never touched their salaries back in Hudson. *Orgasmic.*

"I think I like PA," Ava said with a grin, as they left with their wet scarves.

Ben-Cade frowned. "Out of character," he murmured in her ear.

The clothes department was in the flea market section of the fair, near the gazebo center of the green. Ava settled in to refresh her wardrobe. She hated how the boxy hunting plaids felt when she tried a jab-cross punch in them, her standard test of outerwear. She attracted some alarmed looks while she did it, too, including from Ben-Cade, who drifted to another tent. She settled on a red plaid down vest and a black hoodie, then picked out pants and tops and extra underwear.

The proprietor grew ever more solicitous as Ava's pile grew. She assured Ava that any used underwear was washed in bleach. Ava attempted to look concerned and relieved at this news.

She took the lady up on her offer of a shower-curtain style enclosure to try on the jeans and tops. In deference to local fashion sense, Ava even selected one pair of non-stretch low-slung Levi's, nicely bleached and broken in. They paired nicely with a pretty periwinkle pin-tuck blouse. Which both looked hideous with a red plaid vest, but those were her instructions from her 'trainer.' The rest of her jeans selections were stretch denim that moved with her, to augment the black skinny jeans and leggings she favored.

Ava haggled successfully on the total, she thought. The shopkeeper seemed only mildly dismayed. Prices were definitely different here. In the Apple, among millions of dead, clothes cost virtually nothing, and food prices were high. Here, her week's worth of clothes rang up more than the week of food. And both were cheaper than their extravagant custom scarves.

"Did you look at the dresses?" the shopkeeper urged, in a last bid to increase her take. "If you like this lavender pin-tuck, I have a dress your size you might like…"

About half the women around her were wearing skirts. Ava bought the dress, and some low grey heels to wear with it. At least it would go with Cade's second scarf. He'd devised an orange, grey, and lavender confection with a few strawberry splashes, to invoke the memory of a romantic summer day they spent once on the Staten Island ferry. Now her clothes haul was no longer cheaper than the scarves.

"All set," she reported brightly, sidling up to Ben in a junk emporium tent, redolent of mildew from attics and garages. A grey-haired man with deep-hollowed grey cheeks glowered from a camp chair. Ben was contemplating a pile of bent metal painted green, with a baggie of hardware.

"Did you find crackers?" Ava asked.

"Yeah. I'm thinking of getting this hammock stand for Darcy. How much for the stand?" Ben asked.

"Hundred," the grey man growled.

Ben snorted. "I'll give you five. After you wash it." He ran a finger pointedly along the dusty tubular steel. "Have a hammock? Clean."

Making clear that this was a grave imposition, the junk dealer rose and slowly produced a hammock from another pile of junk, wrapped in a trash bag. "Clean," he spat. "Fifty for both."

"Fifteen," Ben countered. "Rusty steel, stained hammock."

"Where you get all your money, boy? You think I ain't seen? Your girl here with a new wardrobe in her bag?"

"Ten," Ben countered. "'Cause it's none of your damned business."

"Why you little…" The grey man shoved him.

Ben-Frosty slapped his hand away, eyes glittering. "I have a fourth-degree black belt in karate. Don't touch me again."

"Fuck. You," the man replied, poking Ben in the chest to underline each syllable.

Frosty grabbed his wrist, spun the man, and bent his arm painfully up across his back. "Keep your shit." He shoved the man away, hard enough to make him stumble into a pile of boxes and knock them over. "Let's go, Cheyenne."

"Militia!" the man screamed. "That punk assaulted me!"

They spent a tedious 15 minutes with a local cop, as they and witnesses explained the altercation. Ben was advised to mind his temper. Cheyenne was glad he kept his eyes down, because they still glittered dangerously. He managed to mutter apologies meekly enough to be let off with a warning.

"Blow this place?" Cheyenne-Ava suggested.

"Not done here," Ben-Frosty growled. "Need to talk to the mayor about the bitch at the border."

"Let's eat first," Cheyenne-Ava urged. Tigers must be kept fed.

He turned cold blue eyes on her, but relented. "Brats. This way."

Ava managed not to ask, until 'brats' turned out to be 'bratwurst,' a fat hot dog with optional repulsive trimmings, like sauerkraut and chili. *They put beef chili on a hot dog?* Her sausage and ketchup were good, though, and the bread was made with white wheat flour, an extravagance in Hudson.

As she suspected, the food lifted Frosty's mood. He got his Ben on straight again, and was smooth-talking by the time they collared the mayor. Ben argued well that the moralizing border cop jeopardized what Sayre was trying to achieve with this excellent fair. Not that Ben himself would stop coming by. But she might inhibit others. If she actually jailed someone coming across to trade for Major Sullivan, like she threatened Ben –

The mayor blanched nicely at that point. He was fulsome in his assurances that Ben needn't bother the Hudson-side Resco. The mayor could and would solve this by end of day. Ben thanked him warmly and they shook on it.

"Now we're done," Ben told Cheyenne.

Once they were safely back in Darcy, she asked, "Were you threatening the border cop? To the mayor."

Cade shrugged. "Interfering with a Resco is punishable by death. Most likely he'd demand that she be reassigned, and he'd get his way."

"Can we just invoke Skull like that any time?"

"Major Sullivan," Cade corrected on automatic, as he pulled out into traffic. Skull ran 'the company.' His public persona of Major Sullivan was a Hudson Resource Coordinator, the martial law chief administrator for the counties around Elmira.

Cade continued, "And no, that only works here. I did it because the boss mentioned the border cop. She must have hassled the agent who brought my allowance."

"How did that work? The allowance."

"Not on today's lesson plan, or I would have brought you along. No big deal. He brought over some goods. Someone else fenced them. Part of the proceeds were waiting for me. Normally I'd do all that myself. But, not today's lesson plan."

"OK. What's next on the lesson plan?"

"Darcy, where did I camp here last time?"

"State Game Lands 36. On map."

No wonder a red plaid hunting jacket was a necessity.

"So what did you learn?" Ben-Cade pressed. "Observe?"

"They grow a lot of food here. In greenhouses, I guess. But they're desperate for trade. Other than food, new goods are hard to get. I didn't see anything but crafts." Ava considered. "I need to stop thinking of you as Frosty, or Cade, while you're being Ben. Makes it hard for you to stay Ben. Hard for me to stay Cheyenne."

Ben nodded sharply. "Bad place to be Frosty. Probably shouldn't have done those scarves. You looked happy, though."

"I was happy," she murmured, then sighed. "About Cheyenne. I can't act like one of them. So Cheyenne is a wayward misfit here. Bit of a wild child. I think that works. People understood me. Girl who ran off with a handsome guy with money, for some fun."

"Makes sense," he agreed.

"The border, I was surprised that was so easy. But it's a long border. Not many people. They're negotiable?"

Ben shrugged. "Everything is negotiable. But like I said. Easiest border crossing I've seen. Anything else?"

"They're worried about this talk of PA joining Hudson, like New England did. Overheard people arguing about it, pro and con. That's a big deal to them. Some said they'd pay even more in taxes. How bad are the taxes?"

"On food production? Army takes most. Same as Hudson. Different rate, applied differently. Net effect, about the same. Freedom, or lack thereof, goods, or lack thereof – about the same."

Ava paused to think about that. "The Apple Zone is nothing like the rest of Hudson, is it."

"Nope. And to be fair, Philly and Pittsburgh are nothing like the rest of PA. And Boston is nothing like the rest of Mass."

"D.C.?"

Ben paused long enough to cause Cheyenne concern. "Haven't been to D.C.," he eventually replied. "Training first. Greater Virginia later."

"But that's where we're headed, isn't it?"

"Probably. We'll get details on our assignment later."

No, it wasn't her imagination. That sounded ominous.

"What if I hadn't taken this job?" Ava asked. "Would you go down there now?"

"I would have trained someone else. Boss won't send me in alone."

3
———————

Interesting fact: Pennsylvania set aside 1.5 million acres in over 300 State Game Lands for hunting, trapping, and fishing. Recreational use was secondary, but some SGLs offered public shooting ranges, and trails for horses, bikes, and snowmobiles.

Ava's next agent training lesson appeared to be camp craft. They left fallow farms and scattered houses behind, and climbed a rolling forested mountain.

Occasionally a clearing appeared by the side of the road, a hunter's parking spot. Ben chose a broad one, and parked to block it off from the road. Facilities were non-existent.

He ordered Ava to unpack the SUV, taking note of where everything belonged. Except the food hamper and cooler and stuff in the cab – Ben's fastidiousness could not abide those touching the ground. Most of the rest she arrayed neatly on the dry rutted dirt.

Ben worked on a tablet, using the car's hood as a standing desk. He wore his red hunting jacket with a Glock pistol in a holster on his hip, and faced the dirt access road. No one passed by.

When she asked what he was up to, he told her to focus on her own task. He'd show her later.

"I could have done this in Elmira," she groused.

"Context," he replied. "Have you dug a latrine yet? Figure out how you'll stow your clothes."

"So I'm ready to put things back in?"

"Storage box." He pointed to the large nylon luggage attached to the top rails behind the moon roof.

Ava blew out a put-upon sigh. Easier said than done for someone only 5-foot-1. *This is hazing!* But she figured out how to stand on the tailgate, shimmy around the flip-up door, pull herself onto the roof, and untie the thing. She checked for fragile contents before dumping it overboard, as the easiest way to get it down.

He snickered. Yes, he was watching.

Ava positioned the roof box neatly for inspection. Latrines dug. Festive scarves and dress-up clothes brightened up the place from a clothesline. *Check.* "I'm done."

Ben tossed his tablet on the driver's seat, and inspected the clearing. "Nice. Now for the concealed storage."

She wasn't expecting that. *There was a point to emptying Darcy?*

She followed him into the cargo hold – he crawled, she walked bent over double. And he showed her all the secret storage compartments. The driver and passenger seat upholstery concealed thousands of PA dollars.

The back was supposed to hold six seats, all retractable into the floor, of which only one in the second row was erected for normal use. But the carpeted-over seat wells held only one of the missing five seats. The rest held pharmaceuticals, an assortment of ammo (Ava approved), toilet paper, and high-value, small-volume trade goods. A false panel by the bed concealed a second Glock handgun and ammo. More was tucked under the driver and passenger seats.

Ben even had small stuff stowed in the unused overhead seatbelt holders, like a mending kit. He kept petty cash and his toiletry things in his sun visor.

"I use the rear-view mirrors to shave," he explained. "You can keep your bathroom items in yours, if you want."

Ben demonstrated how to manually remove the single second row seat from the car altogether. How to put it back. How to stow it in the floor. How to restore the two real second-row seats for use.

He got out and stretched. "OK, put it all back. Exactly how it was, so I can find it. You can leave the camp stove out."

Ava was hoping he'd teach her how to use the electronics next. "Could you please help me with the roof rack?"

"Not this time." He relented enough to explain. "Cheyenne, I could have told you all this. But you wouldn't remember. When you've done it, you know it. If you need something in a hurry, it's not your first time figuring out how to get at it. Isn't that how they drilled you in the Army?"

"Yeah," she admitted. Sergeant Calderon would've had her clambering on the roof like a monkey for hours, no matter how many tall guys were available to help. Calderon would have stood watching, too, to make sure she used proper lifting technique on the 5-gallon, 40-pound water bottles. The cad. At least Ben let her screw up and repair her mistakes by herself.

She had to admit, after this exercise, she knew what equipment they had on hand and where to lay her hands on it. And she was impressed. Cade was quite the housekeeper with his tiny home on wheels. From sharing their cozy studio in Manhattan, this surprised her not a bit. He was a neat freak. Shame about the hammock. That would be nice for summer. If summer ever came this year. In mid-April, so far spring was a no-show.

"Done," she reported tiredly. "Darcy holds a lot of stuff. What next?"

"Take a break. Run if you want. I'll start dinner. Sorry, that took longer than I expected. I can show you how to do what I'm doing tomorrow. Or, wait. Just a preview."

She joined him by the hood to see his tablet.

"I'm reviewing dashcam footage – the camera pointing forward. Looking for new features. Agricultural progress." He tapped through to show her a list of greenhouses, among other sublists of landscape features. He fast-forwarded through a few seconds of traffic near the fair, as well. "Some of this intel you can get from satellites. But the woods hide a lot. And you can't see people from the air, just roofs. Can't even tell what the structure beneath the roof is, usually. "

Ben caught and held her eye, face completely neutral, for a full second. Cheyenne-Ava acknowledged the familiar old warning with a blink. "There's an interior dashcam, too." He demonstrated a few seconds of Ava stowing boxes. "Our handlers review that footage."

We're being spied on all the time, Ava thought sourly. *I bet that includes audio, too.*

Freshly irritable, she took him up on the offer of a run, while he set up to chop vegetables for supper kebabs. She'd guessed right. The narrow folding banquet table served as his kitchen, holding cook stove, cutting block, and counter space.

The vestiges of a trail led into the woods, overgrown from years of neglect. She opted to run on the dirt road instead, with her M4 rifle along for company.

A single bend in the road, and Ava was completely alone. Thick bare trees blocked any view, including most of the hazy sky. No birds sang. The stream beds were dry. She slowed to a jog, then a walk. She still couldn't spot any wildlife.

After years of living in the Apple, and even more forced togetherness in boot camp, the loneliness had her spooked.

Ridiculous, she thought. During boot camp exercises in the woods, she'd laughed with the Upstate recruits when the city kids got nervous in the forest. She grinned, remembering how they got her friend Fox going about bears. Unlike many of her classmates, Ava had lived all over the States. She'd spent time in the woods in Minnesota. But the famed 10,000 lakes of the evergreen North Woods looked different, smelled different.

And she hadn't been alone in the big woods. And yes, there were bears. Back at the campground outside Elmira, feral pigs were the local menace. This was not a welcoming landscape. She walked past a burnt spot. It looked like trees had exploded out from a center. She had no idea what caused that.

Was this the next item on your training plan, Cade? she wondered, walking ever slower through the trees.

She wouldn't put it past him. He mentioned earlier that he'd brainstormed how to train her with Skull, their boss. Which suggested that her training was mostly up to Cade.

We're not free to run away. We have nowhere to hide that's a better deal than what we've got. For now. Ava thought that through. *Cade likes Skull, and likes his deal. The big expense account. Good salary, travel, fun car. If that changes... The big risk is Skull — if we get another boss, and aren't treated fairly. We already have a fall-back. At the end of our contracts, we can go back to the Apple.*

Looking around the endless ocean of bare trees, she sighed. *God, Cade must have been lonely. And scared without backup he could trust.*

Well, I'm here to fix that.

She tried to enjoy the illusory peace and freedom. But after fifteen minutes or so, she gave up and headed back, running all the way.

"YOU'RE OK WITH BEING SPIED ON," AVA-CHEYENNE OBSERVED. SHE leaned back against the car wall after a feast of beef kebabs and buttered bread. They dined perched on the tailgate. It wasn't really a tailgate — the hatch flipped up, not down — but there was a step and a foot or so of clear floor back there.

Cade-Ben was slow to rouse from gazing at a reddish beam of sunset that filtered through the trees. The Dust Bowl was getting worse again, making for spectacularly bloody sunsets.

"Monitored," he corrected her. He frowned. "Actually, I like it. It's lonely out here. Was." He smiled at her tentatively, then dropped it. "Not much for the handlers to see, when I was alone. It's security, Cheyenne. For them, but for us too."

"How many of them are there?"

"Not out here. Enjoy the sunset, then we police up the camp. We lock up to sleep, ready to drive away."

"You cooked. I'll clean. And bring in the scarves. Wouldn't want to leave without them."

His return smile bloomed for real, a rare full smile of the truly pleased. "God, I'm glad you're here. This, alone..." The smile drained from his face like the sunset dipping beneath the far shoulder of a mountain. "It's not so good for me, alone with my head."

"I know." She hopped up and pecked a kiss on his cheek.

He pulled her back into a hug, and murmured in her ear. "I need to be monitored, Cheyenne. I'm a monster. Them watching helps. Working for Skull is my chance to be a good monster. Not out of control. You watch me too. OK?"

She pulled back to lay hands on both sides of his face, and touched noses. "We're dangerous. We're not monsters."

"You're not," he agreed. "We kept you from that, Maz and I. You protected us. I handled the monster biz."

"Not buying it," Ava said breezily. She set to cleaning before she lost the light.

Disciplined to a fault, Cade declared that after dusk came school homework. They settled onto the air mattress under a camp light hung from Darcy's ceiling.

Cade reviewed algebra to finish his GED diploma. Now twenty, and never fond of math, he left algebra behind in middle school. His fancy prep school had provided him old-fashioned proof-based geometry, trigonometry for poets, spreadsheets for business scions, and a social studies-leaning AP Statistics course – unfinished – in high school. He'd completely bombed on the GED math section.

Ava read from the beginning of their hefty tome on Western Civilization. She needed to catch up to Cade in their joint distance-learning course for college credit. Sitting warm and dry in Darcy's cargo hold, she could freshly relate to what life must have been like in 10,000 B.C. Darcy was a starship compared to being naked outside, without modern tools or knowledge, alone and frightened by the dark.

AVA STARED INTO THE BLACKNESS THROUGH THE MOON ROOF ABOVE HER. Cade's air mattress was twin size, small even for him alone. His bed took up half of Darcy's cargo hold. There wasn't space for a bigger one. Ava reclined the single erected seat of the second row for her own bed.

She tried to review the day, all she'd learned. How to pass through the closed border. Tidbits from other fairgoers now merged with Cade's comments to coalesce into understanding. Yes, this area was rich in food. But not much else. There was little to do here, nowhere to go, no prospects, only food to grow and taxes to pay with it. They were comfortable serfs, but serfs nonetheless.

There's a big difference between a serf and a slave, she thought. Slaves were abused. Serfs had homes and families, and freedom within their towns and counties. Their lives were circumscribed, but rewarding.

Who am I to judge, anyway. Her life in Manhattan was a nightmare. She was free to starve, to kill or be killed. Her desire to live never faltered.

That isn't true. It faltered plenty. But they had a deal. Ava and Cade and his best friend Gary Mazurkiewicz. No, they were Panic and Frosty and Maz, then. It was Frosty's idea originally. It was hard to watch out for your own will to live. So they'd be brave for each other, drag each other through. There were two others in on that promise. They didn't make it. But the surviving trio wouldn't let each other off the hook. They had to live. Especially on the days they didn't want to.

And then they split ways. Panic left first, to escape Frosty and the gang. Later she left the city by joining the Army. Frosty left the city at the same time, to take this job. Maz stayed to reinvent the gang as a town. And they didn't have to think about each other anymore. They could stop remembering.

Now she was alone with Frosty, her life dependent on him again, and no one else. She was completely alone in PA, except for him. Not Frosty. Cade. No, Ben. Because she still trusted him, still loved him. Whoever he was. Or did she?

Maybe this job was a bad idea.

She didn't think she made a sound. But Frosty slept beside Panic for years. He recognized the caught breath. He sat up and took her hand. "Come to my bed." He tugged.

"The bed's too small."

"We've slept in it before."

"Slept? I remember sex, talking. Sleep, not so much."

He chuckled, and tugged her hand a few more times. She relented and crawled into the air mattress. He firmly turned her to face the other way, and spooned around her. They used to sleep like this, through the bitter New York winters without heat. Their bodies had filled out with muscle again since then. The sensation was a weird mix, familiar comfort, and anxiety from the old terror that the comfort was directed against. Ava tried to relax into his arms.

Then she exploded out of the bed, to crouch beside it, breathing out. *Just breathe out. Your body breathes in by itself.* "I need to move," she announced.

"Don't go anywhere," Ben said. "Stay by the car. I'll be out in a sec. Darcy, unbutton."

Ava was out the door before she realized she was in bare feet and one of Frosty's T-shirts. Ben's. The ground was frosty. Cade was lost and crying somewhere. She was losing it.

She erupted into burpee push-ups – squat, plank, push-up, squat, stand, repeat.

"Shoes," Ben offered. He'd pulled on sweat pants and sneakers over his boxers and sleep tee. He set an AK-47 on the hood, and started doing karate katas, movement sequence drills. She perched in the car door well to pull on socks and high-tops. The night air was cold on her bare legs. But she wasn't going into that car again just yet.

She followed Ben's lead and did her own martial arts warm-up, drawing on not the karate the couple shared, but the mishmash of traditions the Army taught.

"Warm up, not wear out," Ben advised. "Ready for a match? Darcy, headlights, high beams."

"We don't need to fight."

Ben picked her up, tossed her over his shoulder, walked into the headlights, and flipped her to the ground. She fell well, rolled, and came up crouched at the ready. She blocked two punches from him as they circled each other. She looked for a weakness, but dammit, he didn't have any. She could win fights by surprise – she did all the time. But no one surprised Cade. His ice-cold karate focus was what earned him the name Frosty the Snowman. She was good. He was better. And he was bigger.

"I can't win," she complained. "What do you want from me?"

"Hit me."

"I can't hit you."

"You haven't tried."

She tried. He blocked. She tried a combo, jab-cross, front kick. He grabbed her ankle and flipped her onto the ground. She swiveled on her forearms and tried to stomp sideways at his ankle with both of her feet. He hopped nimbly away, but at least had the grace to say, "Ow."

Then he stood straight, no guard. "Hit me. Take your best shot."

That would be poor sportsmanship. She paused. Then she front-kicked him straight in the gut.

He doubled over most gratifyingly. "I said hit me, not kick me."

Rather than pursue retribution, he settled onto the hood of the SUV, and pulled the AK-47 rifle onto his lap. Frosty-Ben was expert at the guerrilla's choice of weapon worldwide. He yawned mightily, and hugged his gut. "OK, get it out of your system."

"I'm sorry I kicked you."

"Me, too," he said sarcastically. "Hurry up and get over it," he said around another enormous yawn. "I wanna go to sleep."

He didn't invite her into his bed again after they locked up.

She asked into the dark, "How did I do today? Oh agent trainer."

The pause was long enough to make her suspect he'd fallen asleep. But apparently he was taking stock. "Eight out of ten. Not bad for the first day."

"What were the down-checks?"

"Stay in character as Cheyenne. Two points. Don't flip in and out of Cheyenne. Just be Cheyenne. And don't invoke Frosty. He's not here. Cade's not here. You're with Ben. No more talking."

Eight out of ten wasn't too bad, Ava reflected, for a new agent. But she took this job to be with Cade. She'd score the day about one out of ten on that front. Though as she reconsidered, the score kept going up. The scarves and dinner were magical.

4

———

Interesting fact: Before the Calm, Pennsylvania had only 65% of the population of New York. But by this time, its population was 16% larger. Both ex-states lost millions. New York lost more.

"Your panic attacks are kind of a problem," Ben-Cade observed mildly. "Want some Valium?"

Ava was behind the wheel on a straighter stretch of empty state highway. Her budding driving career had brought them about 30 yards so far. Ben insisted she needed to be able to drive Darcy. She blew out through the anxiety.

Just breathe out. Your body breathes in by itself. Cade's voice in her head. He'd taught her that.

"You want me to drive on Valium?" she countered.

"Not really," he agreed. "Flashback? Or just intimidated?"

"Intimidated," she decided. She wiped sweating palms down her thighs.

"OK. Turn it off." Ben got out of the car.

Eagerly, Ava killed the engine and hopped out. She hoped the driving lesson was over for the day. She should have known better. Ben arrested her before she made it three feet.

31

"Kick the tire. Do not kick Darcy's paint job."

She kicked, feeling silly.

"Tell her off. Tell Darcy she can't intimidate you."

Ava snickered. It took her a minute, but she gathered her nerve. "You're a tool, Darcy! A dumb machine!" She kicked the tire again. "I'm a second-degree black belt! OK, that's useless against three tons of steel. But if Ben wasn't here to protect you, I'd dent you! Scratch you! And I'm still smarter than you are!"

"Good. Climb back in. The driver's seat," Ben clarified.

"I can't do this, Ca– Ben."

"Fall off a bike, get back on the bike. Now, Cheyenne. Otherwise the fear wins. Never let the fear win."

Ava agreed with that in principle. Or at least, her head agreed. As she slid back in and buckled up, her heart started thudding again and her palms sweat. She blew out shakily.

"Turn on your hazard lights," Ben directed. "That tells other drivers to watch out."

She found and engaged them. "Aren't you getting in?"

"Nope. I'm going to walk beside you. You drive no faster than I walk."

That surprised a strangled laugh out of her. "You're kidding, right?"

"No. You need to feel in control of the car. See that big rock?" A short cliff lay a couple hundred yards up the road, its face sheared off with dynamite to get it out of the way. "Drive to that rock. Walking speed. Remember, the pedals are levers, not push buttons. Try to do it smoothly. At dead slow."

"What if I hit you?"

"Cars don't leap sideways. Quit stalling."

Prudently, he didn't touch the car, just strolled alongside. By the time they reached the rock, Ava had figured out that Darcy lumbered forward at Ben's slow pace if she just kept her feet off the pedals and didn't jar the wheel. She felt foolish as she came to a slow stop, and put Darcy back into park.

"Were you in control?" Ben asked.

"Yes," she decided.

"Good. Take a break. I'll find a big parking lot before the next lesson."

She surrendered the driver's seat eagerly. "What else do we do today?"

He pulled her into a hug. "This is it. You learn to drive."

"I was afraid of that."

"Cheyenne?"

"Yeah?"

"Never drive, unless you feel in control. Or in an emergency. Doesn't matter if you're on the effing Interstate. If the best you can do, is what you just did? Pull onto the shoulder of the highway. Put on your flashers. And go dead slow. You didn't fail here. You mastered level one. Got it?"

"Got it."

"And Cheyenne? You're really short."

"I really am."

"Darcy is too big for you." Ben dropped the hug and scratched his nose sheepishly. "Sorry about that. My turn. Hop in."

"Ben? You're a patient teacher. Thank you."

He smiled in surprise and squeezed her hand.

"Well, you're just a tiny thing, aren't you?" Ron Kaminski peered in through the driver's window at Cheyenne-Ava. "She needs blocks on those pedals, Ben."

The parking lot Ben-Cade found belonged to an empty school back in Sayre. This bored farmer was the second who'd stopped by to chat with Ben, who sat on a bench reading, and occasionally called out instructions. Maybe he hoped to bore Ava out of her anxiety. It was working.

"Yeah? Someplace open around here to buy pedal blocks?" Ben and Kaminski both chuckled.

Ava seized the excuse to turn off the SUV. "Maybe pillows?"

Kaminski shook his head. "Your legs are too short. But you're right. You want to sit up higher to see over the hood. Get in again, let me show you what I mean." He paced it out, to demonstrate how far he needed to walk in front of the vehicle before Ava could see his feet.

Apparently farmer Kaminski had happy memories of teaching his own daughter to drive years ago. And he had nothing better to do. He was ready for spring planting, but the weather wasn't. Before long, he was supervising Cheyenne's first real road driving, out to his farm. Ben followed with Kaminski's pickup at a cautious distance.

Before Kaminski headed for his workshop to fashion pedal blocks, he thought to ask Ben if he was sure the pedals weren't adjustable on the SUV. "Fancy car like that. She's a beaut. How long you had her?"

"Just a few months," Ben admitted, digging the manual out of the glove compartment. "I'll be. You're right." He circled round to the driver's side, and followed the instructions. While he had the book open, he checked. The seat could raise and lower as well. The guys put Ava back in the driver seat, and soon found settings that gave her a whole new perspective on driving Darcy – literally.

"Well, hell, Ron, thanks," Ben said. "Don't I feel the fool. Sorry to waste your time."

"Not at all," Kaminski purred, delighted to have proved so smart. "Now you can see the road and reach the pedals, little lady. Let's try once more around the block. Ben, you go introduce yourself to the missus. Cheyenne and I'll be back."

The farmer was even more insistent than Ben that Cheyenne go slow and make sure she felt in control every moment. Ava found that having to act as Cheyenne killed her anxiety attacks. She never suffered anxiety when she was guarded, even against the tiny danger of misspeaking.

Unlike Ben, who hadn't gotten to it yet, Kaminski reviewed all the rules of the road as though she'd never heard them before. She rolled her eyes to him, just a little, because she thought Cheyenne would. But in truth, Ava soaked some of this up before the epidemic. The last summer with her family, they rented a car for vacation, and started talking about teaching her to drive.

My parents wanted me to learn, Ava remembered. He was younger, but Ron Kaminski even reminded her of Deda a bit, her grandfather.

"What's wrong, Cheyenne?" Kaminski asked in concern.

Cheyenne shook off the sad thought, and smiled at him. "Just thinking of my grandfather. He'd be proud of me. He passed away a couple years ago. Been on my own since then." *Truth.*

"Ah, that's a shame. But he would indeed. Never drove before today, huh? Girl, you're a natural." It was Kaminski's turn to look sad.

"Where's your daughter now?" Cheyenne asked.

"She was in California," Kaminski said quietly. "No news isn't exactly good news. It's been a couple years."

"I'm sorry." They didn't hear much about California. The droughts and wildfires were bad enough, but then earthquakes took out San Diego, Los Angeles, and San Francisco.

Ava realized as they turned back toward the farmhouse, that she was being honest with him – emotionally honest, even though she was lying about who she was. *Strange.*

"Was she a natural?" Cheyenne asked. "Your daughter?"

Kaminski's smile was sad and warm at the same time. "That she was. Joined the Army at your age. We were so proud of her. Turn left up ahead. I think you're ready for a spin around downtown." He grinned as Ava quailed. "Take it slow. You'll do just fine."

In fact, downtown had little traffic to offer. Without the fair in progress, they only saw two other pickup trucks on the roads, and a parked police SUV. Ava slammed on the brakes as Darcy beeped at her.

"You came a little close to the cop," Kaminski said mildly. "That beep was Darcy's proximity warning, I think. This sure is a fancy car."

Cheyenne gulped and craned her neck to see the cop, who glared back. *Damn.* It was Corporal Schenck, the militia woman who'd threatened to jail them at the border.

The farmer chuckled. "Forward," he urged. "Try to hug the yellow line a little closer."

Cheyenne tried to do that, and glance in the rear-view mirrors at the same time, got flustered, and slammed on the brakes again. "The cop's coming after me."

"Don't stop unless she flashes you," Ron advised. "Turn right up ahead, then right again. Just drive carefully."

Schenck put on her flashers. Cheyenne gulped and pulled to the empty curb to stop. She drove a tire up onto it for a few inches, and winced as the SUV bounced back down. She pulled forward a little more trying to straighten out, but then she was angling out from the curb again. In frustration, she decided that was close enough, and put Darcy into park.

Cheyenne blew out slowly, as the bitchy cop arrived at the driver's door.

Kaminski patted her on the shoulder. "Let me do the talking." He opened her window from the central console.

"Afternoon, officer," he greeted the patrolwoman with a smile. "I'm teaching a brand new driver today. She's doing real well." He patted Cheyenne.

"You again," Schenck hissed at Cheyenne. "Where's the other one? Isn't this his car?"

"Ben?" Kaminski interrupted. "He's at my house. They're my guests. I'm just helping him teach Cheyenne. Ain't no problem here, Corporal Schenck."

"I didn't hit anything," Cheyenne objected. Kaminski squeezed her shoulder to shut her up. "Did I break a rule?" she asked him.

"No," he said. "You're doing just fine."

"I see two assault rifles behind your seat," Schenck differed.

And she didn't see the Glock tucked beside the driver's seat by Ava's thigh. Cheyenne reflected that it was probably a bad idea to shoot the militia woman dead where she stood. Fortunately Kaminski still had the ball.

"You're new around here, officer," he said, his tone less friendly. "Everyone drives with a gun for protection. We've broken no laws. Let us go. Have a nice day." He rolled up the window on her. "Drive now, Cheyenne. Slowly."

Screw slowly, Ava thought, and goosed Darcy up to 20 mph, the speed limit around the town square. With no oncoming traffic, she rode the middle yellow lines within an inch and got the hell out of there.

Kaminski laughed. "Not nervous at all when you're angry, are you?"

"Nope." She didn't slow for a 90-degree turn off the square, and bounced a little wide. But she straightened that out, and took the next right turn, performing it more smoothly. Then she practiced with a left turn, followed by an immediate right. Kaminski kept laughing. She pulled into the curb, climbed it again and bounced off. She pulled to the center, then pulled to the curb again, cleanly this time, but two feet away. Third try, she got Darcy parked almost parallel and a half foot away.

"I think I'm getting the hang of this," she declared.

"I think you're right! Let's head back to the farm." He started to point out the way, but Cheyenne knew exactly where she was. He settled back for the ride.

"That cop threatened to throw us in jail yesterday at the border," Cheyenne confided, then winced. *Too much information.*

Kaminski shook his head. "Schenck just moved here from the Jersey border by Trenton. Pretty hard-core, keeping out the Hudson ghetto there. She hasn't adjusted yet to how we do things here."

A Hudson ghetto rat is driving this car. "Big change of pace," she agreed.

"Free Penn," Kaminski said. He left it hanging there, like he was waiting for a counter-sign.

"Sylvania," Cheyenne hazarded. She had no idea what he was on about. Ben and Skull had simply been hammering it into her not to call the place Penn. That was a Hudson term.

Kaminski nodded, satisfied. "Thought you were one of us. There's my road."

Oops. Cheyenne had no idea how to follow this up. *So stop talking,* she concluded. Fortunately, Kaminski didn't press her.

Back at the house, Cheyenne flew into Ben's arms for an urgent hug. She whispered, "The lady border cop stopped me, and Kaminski thinks we're part of something called Free Penn."

"Aside from that, Mrs. Lincoln, how's the driving?" Ben asked with a silent chuckle.

"Great! I drove good, right, Mr. Kaminski?"

"Absolute natural!" he agreed, arm around his wife.

"Can't thank you enough," Ben said warmly, and stuck his hand out for a shake. "We ought to get out of your way now."

"Aren't you staying for dinner?" Mrs. Kaminski objected in disappointment.

"That new cop is a problem," her husband said, shaking Ben's hand. "I hope you'll drop by next time you're passing through."

"Sure will," Ben said. "Hey, can I offer you anything? You've been such a big help!"

Firm refusals and haggling eventually resulted in a couple rolls of Hudson toilet paper changing hands. No one refused a gift of soft toilet paper. Ava considered this surprise job perk nearly as orgasmic as the food shopping. Toilet paper wasn't even for sale in the Apple. No one could afford it. She adored using it again in the Army. But the good stuff was reserved for the luxury trade.

And Ben and Cheyenne rode out of Bradford County, PA.

"Do I rate ten out of ten today?" Cheyenne prompted, as they passed the sign welcoming them to Tioga County. She was pretty pleased with herself for her driving progress.

"You'd rate yourself a ten, huh?" Ben returned. "Alright. So far. Day's not over yet. I won't dock you a point. But don't get so chummy, OK? Kaminski was ready to adopt you."

He would have made a great dad for me, too! she thought, smug. "OK. But I liked him. And he thought we were allies. That's cool, isn't it?"

"Maybe. None of our business. If they're trying to 'free Pennsylvania,' that's not our fight. Sounds complicated. Avoid complications with the natives. We're just passing through."

"You can never have too many friends."

"Really. Frosty and Panic had what, twenty-eight hundred friends in the gang? At its peak. Because you can never have too many obligations."

That surprised a laugh out of her. "Um, yeah. When you put it that way." She lay her head back and gazed at him sideways. "Feels light as a feather. No gang. No army unit. No obligations. You were right. This job is orgasmic!"

His return smile faded. "We have obligations. Tonight, we camp in the Grand Canyon of Pennsylvania."

Ava eyed the rolling brown hills dubiously. "I'm guessing this won't look much like the Grand Canyon."

"No, it's a creek in a steep valley. Pretty, though. Another hour."

"Wow. We have fuel for that?" Ron Kaminski explained the empty roads to her. The farmer received a fuel allowance to support his work. But the average household received barely enough gas ration to carpool to Sayre Market twice a month. Clearly Ben wasn't concerned, though.

"Yeah, our range is about three hundred fifty miles. We're barely thirty miles from home yet. Need to fix that."

At Ben's suggestion, she took a nap to recover from the adrenaline of her anxiety attacks. She woke to sudden dark, as they plunged into shaded deep woods, on a looping path through a state park. Quaint and rustic wooden structures were dotted here and there, cabins and picnic pavilions, carved wooden signs and trail railings. A sign advised the park was built during the last Dust Bowl when the American economy collapsed, and the government hired the poor to build public works – a time like now.

Cheyenne felt closer to that era than the one she grew up in. Those migrating work crews were real. To her, the petty debates and materialism before the epidemic felt like a cruel lie.

They didn't spot another soul in the forest. Twice Ben stopped to haul fallen branches off the road before they could proceed. The third time a tangle of fallen trees blocked the road. Ben turned back to the last parking loop they passed.

This proved more appealing than she expected. A wide level parking area opened up a swatch of sky, sporting fast-scudding low clouds. A generous roofed pavilion over picnic tables and cooking grills, complete with a wooden outhouse, met a trail head promising a scenic overlook of the canyon. Ben parked Darcy alongside the pavilion, almost like a big house for the night.

Cheyenne alighted and stretched in delight. Mindful of her status as an agent trainee, and Ben's disciplined ways, she peeked into the outhouse and deemed it creepy. Instead she dug them a proper field latrine behind it. She stowed the shovel back into Darcy.

Ben leaned against the car, studying the clouds. As she passed him, he said frowning, "You know I love you. Right?"

He's in a mood, Ava thought, not sure what mood that might be. "You know I love you, too." He still looked distant, so she left him with a quick peck on the cheek. She waved their roll of toilet paper to suggest she still had business, and headed back to her newly dug latrine.

She was squatting when a shot rang out, and some fragments of bark hit her. On reflex, she pivoted on one foot and spun around the side of the latrine for cover, staying low, and pulled her pants back on. The toilet paper she shoved into her hunting vest pocket. Unbelieving, she carefully peeked around the farther edge of the outhouse.

Ben met her eye, right above the Glock he aimed straight at her.

5

Interesting fact: The Glock pistol is made of plastic. Most models fire from 10 to 17 rounds per magazine.

Another shot splintered the corner of the outhouse above her. Ava dove into the tree cover, heart pounding.

Cade wouldn't do this, she insisted to herself. Sure, he'd struck her now and then. Actually he hit her all the time in karate sparring matches, because they both practiced karate. He hit her last night, and she kicked him. And he hit her in front of the gang a couple times to make a disciplinary point. And a few times he'd slapped her around in private because he was pissed at her. Not lately or anything. Well, actually, he hit her the day before she walked out on him in August.

So you ignored all that and went back to him.

This isn't that, she told herself firmly. *This isn't Cade, mad at Ava. It's Ben training Cheyenne. I think.* The feeling of outraged betrayal was hard to shut up, though.

Furious, she beseeched herself to get her head in the game. *It doesn't matter why he's shooting at me! Would Cade sit here paralyzed, wondering what he'd done to deserve it?* She snorted silently. No. Cade would proceed directly to take her out. He might get sentimental after she was dead. Or not.

No, he'd care. He loves me.

STOP THAT! What the hell am I going to do about this?

With no one around and Ben on guard, Cheyenne had trustingly dug the latrine without a gun on hand. *Is that why he's doing this to me?*

STOP THAT! Think!

There was no crashing through the underbrush. Granted, he might have learned how to move silently through the woods. But it was quiet. And why would he bumble around after her? He held their strong point. Darcy had all their supplies, their transportation, their weapons. If there was a spare set of keys, she hadn't found it.

During a break from her driving lessons earlier, he set her up with an emergency way to enter Darcy when it was locked. The SUV had daunting screamer circuits, but they didn't go off at first touch. If she got to the driver's door and placed her hand above the lock for a long, then three short touches, Darcy would unlock and let her in.

Of course, if Ben was still in the mood to play gun-tag, that wouldn't do her much good. The Glock he'd aimed at her was the one tucked beside the driver's seat. Behind the driver's seat they stowed his AK-47 rifle and her shorter M-4 carbine.

She needed to slip into the car when he wasn't in it.

Why am I sitting here? Her current vantage point of pricker brambles and a double tree wasn't doing her any good. She needed a view of the parking lot. She removed her high-visibility red down hunting vest and balled it up under her far armpit. Her pale blue top underneath didn't blend into the woods, either, but it wouldn't stand out. The sun was dipping below the scudding clouds, with occasional fast-moving ruddy sunbeams stabbing through the forest gloom. She wouldn't be easy to see. She paused and pulled a scrunchy out of the vest pocket and quickly braided and tied her hair so it wouldn't catch on things. Doc, her room-mate and scout team leader back in Army Basic, had drummed that lesson into her. *Either cut it off, or keep it tied.*

Why couldn't I fall in love with someone nice, like Doc? Doc had survived the epidemic and the Starve just like Frosty and Panic. He held high rank in his Jamaican gang, the Rastafarians. And he rarely uttered a cross word. Then again, his nickname during the Starve was Raper. She'd never gotten that story out of him. She didn't really want to know. Frosty might know.

Stop that!

Staying low, and stepping as softly as she could, she made for the only immediately useful open ground she knew of, the hiking trail to the scenic overlook. She froze as she heard chopping. Then she realized Frosty – *Ben* – was making supper. Why wouldn't he, after all? He had the upper hand. She moved a little faster, with a little less care on the footing.

Snap! She'd stepped through a brittle twig, that rang out with its crack. The chopping halted. She didn't pause, only hurried along. Sure enough, a shot hit a tree only a few steps behind her. Then Ben resumed chopping vegetables.

Asshole.

She stumbled silently out of the bracken into the trail, and breathed a sigh of relief. Looking up the trail, she found she was right. He couldn't see her here. Of course, she couldn't see him, either. But she took a breather in safety, perched on a slight embankment.

What if this was for real? If her partner really had betrayed her, she supposed she could follow the winding road back to the tiny excuse for a town at Route 6. Her pockets included her phone and a few PA dollar bills. Her phone wouldn't have service, but it contained contact info for Skull back in Elmira. And she knew Ron Kaminski. Her best bet was to hitch-hike back to Sayre. The roads were pretty empty. She might need to ask the militia for help.

Of course, she could just go ahead and do that, and call this experiment in working with Cade a wash. She considered that a moment. But she was pretty sure this was just a training exercise. *I can trust Cade. Ben. Whoever the hell it may concern.* She wasn't ready to give up on her job on her second day in the field. *But yeah, if I believed he'd screw me over, that's what I'd do.*

That established, she rose to a crouch and advanced to the point where she could see Darcy. The back of the open-air picnic pavilion, for whatever reason, was solid. Ben was in there, hidden, making supper. She paused, listening, to make sure of that. *Yes.* Good, that meant she could cut to the back of the pavilion, only about fifty feet. In her best stealth, she made for the side by the outhouse.

The sky unleashed a spate of raindrops, that rattled everything. She took the opportunity to wade faster through the underbrush. She reached the wall just before the rain stopped. She waited until she heard the hiss of Ben splashing something on the grill, then silently stepped to her chosen corner.

The pavilion had a thigh-high stone wall on the adjacent sides, forming a base for the wooden posts supporting the roof. Cheyenne risked a glance. Ben had his camp stove on this side, with Darcy's back hatch open nearby. His Glock was on his hip, and the AK-47 an arm's reach away on a picnic table. She sighed. *Patience it is.* She could crawl behind the far stone wall and get into Darcy's other side. But her best chance was to disarm him when he passed this corner.

As boring minutes ticked past, she had plenty of leisure to reconsider. And time to salivate. His dinner smelled really good, the cad. He'd set chicken breast to marinate in some complicated sweet cream sauce after breakfast.

"Olly olly oxen free!" Ben called out, startling her. "Supper's ready."

She scowled, tempted to just stay put and mug him later. Maybe she'd even manage to make him worried. *Probably not,* she reflected sourly. Based on nearly three years' experience, so far as she could tell, Cade Snowdon really was cold-blooded. It wasn't an act. He might not be Frosty the Snowman right this minute. But that persona was ready to draw on whenever useful.

In a lower conversational tone, he added, "Ava, please. Chicken satay for supper. Over buttered noodles."

Is that the magic word? My real name?

"No coconut milk. I used cream and caramelized onions."

That's Cade alright, she allowed with a grin. She peered around the corner, shaking her head at him in amusement. He'd thrown a spare sheet over a table for a tablecloth, and set out candles and proper place settings.

"Come on, don't let it get cold," Cade wheedled. "You've got to taste this sauce." He set a small saucepan by the candles, apparently the cooked remainder of his marinade. "No more tricks. Day is done." He prudently placed the AK-47 on the bare picnic table behind him and sat on the bench facing her.

"Olly olly oxen free," she agreed. She stepped up and sat across from him at the table, shrugging her hunting vest back on to quit carrying it. "Should I grab the other Glock?"

"There was this great line in *Firefly*," Cade replied. "Something like, 'even petty criminals know that the small arms belong next to the butter knife in a place setting.'" He unholstered his Glock and clunked it down between the cream sauce and the green salad.

Ava grinned, and helped herself to buttered noodles. The satay smelled divine. They toasted each other silently in plain water, and settled in to savor everything slowly. Another couple rain spates came and went.

Cade waited until they were both happily finished eating, with delicious leftovers for tomorrow. Reluctantly he said, "Ben needs to talk to Cheyenne."

"Understood," she returned sourly.

"You go armed, unless there's a good reason not to. You're supposed to be my backup. Unarmed, what use were you as my backup?"

"Not a lot."

"What was your plan, by the way?"

"Jump you on the way to the latrine."

He shook his head. "This started at the latrine. Be aware of where your attention gets stuck. Latrine, latrine – brainstorm at least ten other plans before you go back to latrine. Your best bet was to approach Darcy from the far side."

She wobbled her head so-so to him, but mentally conceded he was right.

He shrugged that off. "Next. Stay aware of the worst thing that can happen. In your case, betrayal by your partner. I know you don't want to think about that. And *I* don't want you to think about that. I love you. But my agent trainer screwed me over. Then my next partner stranded me in Ohio. Do you know how hard it is to get to Elmira from frigging Cleveland these days? Felt like an idiot the whole way, too."

"How did he sucker you?" Ava asked quietly, in sympathy. The mellow candles and gourmet dinner, with secret confidences, were pretty romantic.

He unbent enough to hold her hand. "Never mind. Point is, just because they work for the company, don't trust them. But also, know what you know. I love you. You know that. If it looks like I'm attacking you, there is a reason. I know that's a contradiction. Don't trust anybody, especially not your partner. And trust me. But they're both true."

"I know," she agreed. "This isn't new for us, Cade."

"I don't like it any better than the first time, Ava," he murmured. "I hated doing this. I know you think I can do something like that cold. Shoot at you. Hit you. Not care who I'm hurting. It isn't true. It hurts. I do it anyway."

She gazed into his eyes and nodded ever so slightly. "A goal-directed monster," she said softly. "I know him well. I trust you, Cade. And my backup plan was to hitch back to Kaminski, then contact Skull for extraction."

"That'd work," he agreed.

"No. Because it would have left Cade behind. I'm here, because it wasn't OK to leave Cade behind. You know that. Right?"

"Sometimes I do," he allowed. "Other times, I think you made a mistake."

She smiled at the joke, but squeezed his hand. "It wasn't OK for Cade to leave Ava behind. Not once. I walked out on you. Didn't speak to you for months. You still couldn't leave that damned city until I did. I had a good crew back at West Point. They had my back. The Army made sure we learned that. But not like you and me, and Maz. Believe it. I've got your back. I won't forget the pistol again."

She released his hand and sat back, to contemplate the rain, which grew steadier as they talked. "Shall I rig the tarp?"

They collected rain that way back in the city. She'd left him in August before drinking water was restored to their compact Chelsea apartment.

But he shook his head. "No need."

"Think it's raining hard enough to wash my hair?"

"No need for that, either. You'll see."

This business of not telling her the plan was getting old. She sighed, and stuffed the Glock into her vest pocket to clean up after dinner. The rain didn't last long enough for a shower, so she washed the old-fashioned way from the bucket.

The candlelit table was awfully nice for homework.

After a huge deluxe omelet breakfast with home fries, Ava mentally steeled herself for her third day of training. Yesterday was brutal. If Cade – Ben – put the lessons in order, she was afraid to find out what he had in store for her today.

"Day off," he reported with a smile. "And on my day off, so long as no one else is around, I think I ought to practice being Cade."

Ava squealed in delight and threw her arms around him. "Why is it our day off?"

"PA is closed on Sunday. Kinda makes sense – not enough business to justify the other six days, really."

Ava blinked. Even now, with only small hamlets remaining, the Apple would still be the city that never slept aside from the 9 p.m. curfew. Chinatown had no curfew, to corner the party trade. Chelsea had no laws.

"Even in the cities?" she asked. "Philadelphia?"

Cade shook his head in disgust. "Philadelphia makes the Apple look lax. You've never seen martial law clamped down so tight. Pittsburgh is strict, too. They got out of control last fall. Hudson lent Colonel MacLaren to PA, to put the fear of God into them and install a new Resco. He called in the 101st Airborne out of Ken–Tenn and confiscated all the weapons."

Everyone knew MacLaren, the Savior of New York City. He was back running the Apple now after a few months of other assignments. It felt right to have him back where he belonged instead of mucking out Pennsylvania or Jersey. Ava and Cade had met the man. Ava was sorry they'd be on the road and miss MacLaren's wedding in a couple weeks. A circus of epic proportions was in the works. Ava's army buddies would likely be there on crowd control. They could have held a reunion.

Being constitutionally unfit to laze around, the couple indulged in a full workout, then decided to clear the downed trees from the road. Darcy was packed to go and never return, of course. Ava drove to the roadblock. She executed her first three-point turn to point the trailer hitch at the problem.

It was far from obvious how to apply Darcy to move a tree. Cade had rope, and block and tackle. But trees have big bushy bits on both ends. They were still trying to figure an angle on the problem – literally – when they heard a car coming.

Ava headed for Darcy's back door and opened it, putting the rifles at hand. Cade moseyed in front, seemingly empty-handed. Ava's first thought, that they were being overly cautious, vanished as a Jeep came around the bend.

Two guys stood, holding onto the roll-bar, rifles on their backs. The driver and passenger seats held another guy and a girlfriend of the blowzy variety. The guys wore off-the-shelf yellow blotchy camouflage, the kind worn by pre-Calm militia enthusiasts, not the authorized military.

They pulled to a stop about ten feet from Cade, in the middle of a road that had no shoulder.

"Howdy," Cade called. He waved a hand unnecessarily toward the downed trees. "Road's out."

The guys on top smirked at each other, one jostling the other, *Get the joke, huh?* Ava's estimate of their IQ proceeded rapidly downhill.

The driver hung out his window, possibly the leader. "You need a chainsaw for that. And gas." He looked pointedly at Darcy. "But I guess you got gas."

"No chainsaw, though," Cade returned agreeably. "We thought we'd apply block and tackle, maybe around that tree. Use the torque to roll the first one off."

"Say *what?*" The Neanderthals shoved each other some more in their laughter. The girl just looked blank, her head tilted.

Ava warned herself not to underestimate the girl. *There is no girl too smart to play dumb.* Ava often led with the dumb act herself.

"So, uh, we'll help you," the driver said, and started climbing out of the car.

Ava yanked out her M-4 and fired a warning shot into the trees. "We don't need help, thanks," she explained. "Just turn around and go."

The joyriders froze, their eyes narrowing. The driver focused on Cade's Glock, suddenly pointed between his eyes.

"You have to the count of three," Cade explained. "Before I kill her." He turned his gun on the girl. "Shooting you might slow down your exit. One."

Ava's caution proved wrong, as the girl started screaming and begging the driver to get back in the car and run away. Ava sighted both goons on top in turn. They visibly swallowed, and elbowed each other again.

"Two," Cade said calmly and clearly.

"Fuck this shit!" the driver said, clambering back into his seat. He'd wet his pants. Ava learned about that in combat training. Some percentage of people just messed their pants under combat stress.

Those weren't the people who survived the Apple.

The driver's coordination suffered badly. He half-shut the door on his own shoe, and dropped his keys.

"Three," Cade said.

Ava shot the roll-bar between the two guys on top, which made them screech in terror and fall on their butts. Cade took out the driver's rear-view mirror.

Then the Jeep was finally in reverse, the driver's door flapping open. He nearly rolled the car into a gully trying to do a three-point turn in a hurry. Eyes alight, Cade took out the passenger side mirror. And at last they peeled out.

Now that they were running away, one of the guys in the back raised his rifle for a parting shot. Ava's bullet caught him in the arm.

She was aiming for his heart. It was hard to get off a clean shot at a bouncing vehicle. Need to aim for the middle, and take what you can get.

And then their guests were beyond the bend.

"Let's move," Cade said. "They'll want revenge. Can't give them time to think."

Ava had already climbed in via the back door. She clambered through the middle console into the front passenger seat while Cade drove like hell after the Jeep. She brought the rifles with her.

"You planned this," she accused.

Cade grinned. "Some idiot always volunteers. PA is fun that way." He passed her the Glock to reload.

6

Interesting fact: Before the Calm, the term 'militia' in the U.S. referred to a private army, usually with right-wing convictions. But at this time, local defense forces were called militia, which also served a police role. The old-style militia were often enemies of the new.

Careening through the woods after the militants, Darcy chimed in. "Priority message."

Cade – Ben now – flipped his middle finger at the dash-cam. "Not now, Darcy."

"Priority override," replied the SUV.

Her Star Trek voice was replaced by Skull's. "Ben, stop and listen."

Ben sighed and brought Darcy to a safe stop. "That was self-defense," he protested. "And it's not over yet."

"Is this like a phone call?" Ava inquired. "I thought these were voice messages."

Ben pointed at the dashcam's eye.

Skull said, "Cheyenne, your handler notified me of the situation. I'm speaking to you directly, and watching your dashcam for responses."

Cheyenne-Ava tilted her head and shot a false smile and arc-like wave at the dashboard. She dropped the smile and resumed fishing for ammo under the seat.

Skull continued, "The Sixers asked for help with a local nuisance. The militia want them, too. I said no, but now you've run into them. So, these clowns are now part of your mission. Sort of a public relations stunt."

Ben looked pained. "Boss? Three dumb-asses and a bimbo. How is this a problem for Oelrich and the cops?"

"The Jeep you met was joyriders. Fred Oelrich estimates sixty in the band. But the locals don't know where they're camped. Since you've stumbled over them, get their location for Oelrich for cleanup. Up to you whether to join the party after that. Permission to kill on sight. But dead men don't talk, Ben."

"Got it. Visit the Sixers today, then? As needed."

"Call home first. Boss out."

Ben sat thinking a moment more.

Cheyenne handed him his reloaded pistol. "Wounded men talk fine," she pointed out. "Especially if they want first aid. Who's Oelrich?"

"You'll meet him soon enough." Ben resumed driving, more slowly. "I don't think this changes much. Except they might run to papa. Check the map."

Cheyenne looked over their prey's options. "They could take the loop we used last night. Just past that is a fork. Another fork a couple miles west – that's a slow road." She dropped markers on the map next to the intersections. "I bet this east fork is faster. We could exit that way, then west on route 6, and back in the other way and meet them head-on. Unless they bolt south at the west fork."

"Buckle up," Ben agreed, and hit the gas.

Veering right at the first fork, they careened across the 'canyon' wall, with glimpses of scenery through the tree-tops to their right. Cheyenne was peering down for a glimpse of the creek at the bottom, when suddenly Ben slapped an arm across her and hit the brakes hard. Darcy swerved and skidded to an angled stop before an old mud slide that blocked the narrow road.

Ben took a brief breather and looked at the dirt pile. "That was close. No tracks."

"Head back," Cheyenne agreed, heart pounding. Ben's eyes looked a bit glittery with adrenaline. She rummaged cheese and crackers from the middle console and offered them. "You react better when fed."

"You're not my mother." He took the turn to the other fork a little fast, running one of Darcy's wheels into the ditch by the side of the mountain road, but he righted it. After that he seemed to concede the point, and ate the snacks.

Cheyenne handed him water and a dried peach as well. "Slow down. Five hundred feet to the next fork."

Ben considered this. "They haven't had time to set up an ambush."

"Check the road to see which way they went," Cheyenne countered. "Two hundred feet. Stop, Ben."

As soon as Darcy came to a halt, Cheyenne jumped out the door. She ran to the fork, M-4 rifle at the ready, only slowing and hunching down when she could see the intersection. No Jeep. She hugged the gully on the right hand side to make herself harder to spot, until she could see both ways down the road. Clear. She stepped into the middle of the intersection and studied the road surface.

Ben brought Darcy up to the intersection and she jumped back in. "They went right," she reported. "Back to Route 6. Wait, no." She studied the map on the dashboard tablet, and dropped a marker. "Hairpin turn, half a mile. That would make a good ambush. Go."

Ben got driving again while Cheyenne considered what came next if they didn't catch the Jeep at the sharp curve. She dropped a marker at a road that joined theirs in a V, from some subdivision street complex, then another at a final possible ambush site before rejoining the thin civilization at Route 6. She was asleep when they left Route 6 on the way in, but wouldn't be surprised if it had a gas station or something.

Ben slowed at a sign warning of the impending hairpin turn. Cheyenne lowered the windows. Ben's side would have all the good angles. At that thought, she shifted to the second row seat behind him. "Your AK-47 is safed," she warned him, pointing her carbine out the window at the ready. "I've got leftmost."

With no opponent visible, coming down the shoulder of a mountain to turn before a stream, Ben started to take the hairpin turn at 5 mph. A shot rang out, and he reversed to protect Darcy.

Cheyenne was already out, rolling to the far gully. Once in that cover, she shot the leftmost shooter in the leg. Two returned fire, forcing her to keep her head low. She couldn't see the third man, but thought the girl was in the Jeep, just past the hairpin. She concentrated on suppressing fire, while Ben moved in on foot, under the better elevated cover on the right side of the road.

Cheyenne kicked herself for that. She should have stayed right instead of switching left. Ben was now in a better position, and he'd crossed from the left side of the vehicle to get there.

He looked to her. Cheyenne hesitated. She had signals to say what she needed, but they were army signals, nothing she used in the gang. She tried anyway, telling him she saw two shooters, one missing, one in the Jeep. He nodded.

Guess he does know army signals.

A shot hit the dirt only a foot away. A piece of gravel kicked at her face. She got busy again with the suppressing fire. But something niggled at the back of her mind.

"Drop it!" a man said, directly behind her.

Yeah, that. The third man would be in a crossfire position. She sighed, and 'dropped' the rifle. She was more-or-less lying with the rifle, so that didn't mean much. But she took her hands off it and raised them slightly.

He stepped forward and tried to kick her rifle away from her, with his own pointed at her head. She spun onto her back, grabbed his foot, and pulled it out from under him. And she kicked his rifle out of his hand.

"You little cunt!" he yelled, and lunged to pin her. But Cheyenne rolled sideways too fast. She grabbed his rifle and jabbed the back of his head with the stock because it was pointed the wrong way. Quarter-turn and she hit his head again with the side of the rifle barrel. Then it was pointed the right way. She slowly crouched down and picked up her own rifle to sling over her back.

"Get up," she ordered him. "Hands on your head or I'll shoot you."

She walked behind him toward the others, but Ben already had them on their knees, hands on their heads. Cheyenne escorted her captive, the Jeep driver, to kneel beside them.

"Out of the Jeep," Ben called to the woman.

She emerged, carrying a baby, maybe around 18 months. "I don't want any trouble," she called tremulously. She wore peasant top and skirt, and pull-on shoes over bare feet. The ragged quality and stains spoke more of burlap than fashion.

Cheyenne fired a shot into the air in a fit of pique. "What are you doing with that baby, fool!"

"She's my daughter!"

"You're an idiot!"

"Cheyenne," Ben interrupted, eyes alight in amusement. "Not now."

Cheyenne stepped back and covered them all with her rifle.

Ben continued, "Lady, kneel over there." Waving his Glock, he indicated a bit of gully ten feet left of the guys, away from the Jeep.

"I need her diaper bag!"

He reiterated his instructions with the pistol. He grabbed a bag out of the Jeep himself, a waterproof tote festooned with balloons and teddy bears. He lobbed it at the place she was supposed to go.

"Who the fuck are you people?" the woman with baby demanded.

"I have some duct tape," Ben replied. "Want it on your face? No? Then shut up. You." He stopped in front of the man who drove earlier, and ambushed Cheyenne. "Where's your camp?"

"What do you mean? There's just us –" He reflexively hid his head in his arms as Ben shot the dirt a foot in front of him.

"No camping equipment," Ben observed coolly. "Lie again, and I blow out your kneecap. You have a doctor who can fix a shattered knee? Bet not."

Ben stepped to the next man in line. This was the one Cheyenne shot during their first exchange of views.

"You should get that arm looked at, before you bleed out. I repeat. Where's your camp?"

"Don't say nothing, Joe Bob!" the third man piped up.

Ben shot his kneecap from point-blank range. That one commenced screams of agony and obscenity.

"I'll tell you!" the woman screeched. "Just don't shoot no more!"

Leaving Cheyenne to cover the men, one writhing on the ground, Ben walked over to the woman. "Before you say anything," he warned. "Be very careful it's the truth."

"The forest north of Route 6," she said. "End of Goodall Road, there's a fire tower. Turn left there on some dirt trails. Why you doing this?"

"Your group annoyed some business associates of mine," Ben replied. "Oelrich. Sixers. Know 'em?"

"You're no Sixers!" she scoffed.

"No," Ben agreed. "Hand me the baby. She goes with me. Do not make it hard for the baby. What's her name?"

"Lizbet."

"Alright, Lizbet," Ben crooned, taking her in his left arm to leave his shooting right free. "You want a treat? I have cheese and crackers. Mommy's going to wait with the noisy men, while we get treats. Won't that be fun?"

Lizbet sat frozen in his arm, little forehead creased, sucking hard on her pacifier in grave misgiving. But Ben continued his patter and headed for the SUV.

"He won't hurt her?" the mom begged Cheyenne.

"Ben likes babies," Cheyenne replied. "What's your name? I'm Cheyenne." A brief round of introductions supplied that the woman was Sallie Mae, the driver Strasbaugh. The man with the arm wound was Joe Bob, and the one busy whimpering was Doerr.

Sallie Mae glanced beyond Cheyenne, suggesting that Ben was returning. "Don't give us back to the Sixers!"

"Back?" Cheyenne reflected that it was high time someone explained to her what the 'Sixers' were.

Sallie Mae sucked her lower lip. "I left 'em, with Lizbet. Joined the Badgers to get away from 'em. You're not like them!"

"Shut up," Ben said. "Cheyenne, don't get chummy with the locals."

He handed Lizbet back to her mother, and applied a swatch of duct tape over Sallie Mae's mouth. "I'm leaving your hands free to take care of the baby. That changes if you annoy me. Got it?"

Sallie Mae nodded sullenly. Lizbet grabbed her nose to show mommy how her little hand smelled of cheese.

Ben moved on to duct-tape Strasbaugh's hands behind him. Then they switched, Ben covering everyone with the rifle. Cheyenne kneeled to see to the arm and knee shot, with the first aid kit Ben brought back.

The arm was just a graze. Cheyenne cut off Joe Bob's sleeve, and cleaned and bandaged his wound. The wound hadn't kept him from shooting, so she duct-taped his hands, too.

The knee injury was out of her league. But she cut off the pants leg, and used it to mop some blood out of the way. And she found what she'd hoped. Ben hadn't shot the kneecap, just the edge of the thigh above it. She found an exit hole, so the bullet was out. It was a nasty wound. But Doerr would walk again.

She didn't mention that to him. She rigged a tourniquet, and splashed some everclear around the area to cut the risk of infection.

That scream was ear-splitting, and frightened Lizbet into crying in sympathy.

Beyond that, Cheyenne was afraid she'd do more harm than good, so she rigged a compression bandage over the site. "Ben, this kit doesn't have anything stronger than ibuprofen. Shall I –?" She glanced toward the SUV. They had plenty of opiates in Darcy.

"Don't give him anything," he replied. At her skeptical glance, he elaborated. "There's a doctor where they're going."

"Where are we going?" Strasbaugh demanded.

"You want duct tape over the mouth, too?" Ben asked. Strasbaugh lowered his eyes and shook his head.

"I wouldn't mind an answer to that question," Cheyenne muttered on her way past him to Darcy. She stowed the medical kit and washed the blood off her hands and a couple spots on her top and jeans. She changed to another shirt and left the wet one to dry from a ceiling hook.

She rejoined Ben and the captives in the middle of a low-voiced debate between Ben and Sallie Mae. He'd let her remove the duct tape from her mouth.

"She needs me!" Sallie Mae said, clutching Lizbet.

"She needs a mother," Ben allowed. "Your call. Last chance." They could hear cars approaching now.

"I'm keeping her!"

Cheyenne couldn't help it. "Ben?" *What do you think you're doing? Take a baby from her mother?*

"Not now, Cheyenne." He indicated she was on guard duty with the spin of a finger. He walked past the Jeep to greet the new arrivals as a pair of military olive crew-cab pickup trucks pulled up. In the land of red hunting jackets, the dour bearded men who piled out were notable mostly for being drab. They weren't as beefy and overfed as the captive trio. The men conferred.

Most of them hung back, waiting for something. Ben returned, stone-faced, with their seeming leader. "Oelrich. My new partner, Cheyenne. Cheyenne, Oelrich is the leader of the Tioga Sixers."

Ben didn't introduce the younger man who accompanied them, maybe in his forties, who proceeded directly to Sallie Mae. He yanked her up by the arm.

"I can get up myself," she growled.

He slapped her across the face hard enough to draw blood from her lip. "Silence, whore!" Lizbet started to cry again. He dragged them toward the pickup trucks.

"Cheyenne," Ben prompted softly.

With difficulty, Ava-Cheyenne tamped her outrage and nodded jerkily at Oelrich. *Pleased to meet you,* was beyond her emotional range at present. "Oelrich," she acknowledged coldly.

Oelrich didn't look any too pleased to meet her, either. The senile looked to be around seventy, with grey-skinned features frozen in perpetual lemon-sucking disapproval.

"She is immodest," he stated, scowling at her crotch in its black leggings. "Put her in a skirt."

"Cheyenne is my partner, Oelrich," Ben said. "She is not one of your women."

The old man straightened in umbrage, the whites of his eyes showing. But Ben met his glare levelly. The impasse was broken by the sound of another vehicle arriving.

"We have business," Oelrich relented. "Let us be about it." He cast another glare at Cheyenne. "Do not speak to my men unless spoken to, whore."

Ben shook his head, without a glance at Cheyenne. The pair left her with the captives as they went to meet a newly-arriving pair of SUVs from the Tioga County sheriff. Like everyone else who had legal standing in enforcement these days, the brace of sheriffs wore the standard army forest camouflage.

Sallie Mae and Lizbet were already installed in middle-back of one of the Sixers' crew cabs. *Off the table,* Cheyenne realized. Who got the three men on the ground under her rifle was open to debate. But the Sixers claimed Sallie Mae.

It took a while, with the usual police penchant for red tape and taking statements. But eventually the tableau was cleared. A couple Sixers drove the Jeep away. The thigh-wounded Doerr left in the truck with Sallie Mae. The sheriffs claimed the other two, Strasbaugh and Joe Bob, and departed.

"Thou willst accompany us for the night," Oelrich said to Ben, as Cheyenne joined Ben by the last remaining pickup truck.

"Our appointment was tomorrow," Ben attempted to demur. "My instructions are not to participate in the assault on the Badgers."

Cheyenne knew that wasn't true. Skull said it was up to Ben whether to 'join the party' to clean out the militant Badger camp. Apparently Ben wanted no part of it. Cheyenne approved. She had yet to see anything here that she wanted to be a part of.

Oelrich waved off his objection as inconsequential. "My men can handle that without me. I insist. Thou must accept our hospitality."

Ben glanced pointedly at Cheyenne. "I wouldn't want my partner to be a distraction."

"Then control thy woman. I insist. We must break bread together, and thank thee properly for finding the Badgers. We can attend to business early tomorrow, and roll out by noon."

7

———————

Interesting fact: The Sixers apocalyptic sect went by different names in different regions. Their full range and membership was unknown. 'Sixers' referred to them carving '666' at the site of atrocities.

"**D**arcy, we're spending the night with the Sixers," Ben announced after they shut the doors on the SUV. Oelrich's truck was out of view, and his men out of hearing at last. "This is gonna suck. Cheyenne, um. Do you have any less sexy pants?"

"Levis," she replied sourly. "No stretch. And a nice dress. I'm not dressing up for these assholes."

"No," he agreed. "Just something that isn't skin-tight. Hurry up. We're not far from the compound."

As soon as she retrieved the pants and sat to change, he started driving. They were on Route 6 again by the time she rejoined him in the front row.

"Why did you want to take that woman's baby away?" Cheyenne demanded.

"You see how they treat women. Nobody asked about Lizbet. I offered to hide her, and slip her to the Tioga militia. They could have found her a foster family."

"What mother would give up a baby?" Cheyenne argued.

Ben sighed. "Yeah, well. Cheyenne, we don't have much time. The Sixers are one of our nightmare contractors. Oelrich is their business guy here in Tioga County."

"What are 'Sixers'?"

Ben slowed the SUV. "I'm trying to brief you. They're a lunatic fringe religious group. Trying to help God kill off the unworthy. So they're useful to the company. They doctor drugs for us. I drop by once in a while to make sure everything is going OK."

"Why?"

"That's what we do. We're agents. We represent the boss and the company. Go places, check things out, trouble-shoot."

"Oh. I thought it meant like secret agents. Spies."

Ben shrugged. "Our business is secret. Anyway, the Sixers want to hasten the Apocalypse. They hate women. Call them whores of Satan. They keep slaves. For work or sex or torture, doesn't matter. Everybody's tanked on the drugs. No scruples at all, that I can see. Vicious."

"Worse than MS-13?" That was the worst gang Cheyenne knew of, back in the Apple. MS-13 was a paramilitary Hispanic outfit that mostly stuck to Brooklyn, Queens, and Long Island. Martial law eradicated them fast.

"MS-13 didn't work for God." Ben pulled onto the highway shoulder. "We can take a few minutes. Point is, they're useful. I need to be here. And you need to watch yourself. Seriously, Cheyenne. Don't wander off. Don't use the latrine by yourself. Don't poke your nose where it doesn't belong. Don't argue with religious nut jobs. Stick close to me, and you should be safe enough. But these assholes consider women subhuman."

"You're not training me for this part of the job," Cheyenne gathered.

"No way," Ben agreed. "Couldn't send a black guy either. You'll see those in the slave pens."

"Slave. Pens. Why would the militia let these people live?" Ava couldn't imagine the Apple Zone Rescos tolerating slavers.

"I don't know." He sighed again. "Look, it's none of our business. It's not that I'm not curious. I just don't like these people enough to care. You know? We've seen worse. Hell, I've done worse. I don't want to be there anymore. But it's what makes me qualified for the job. I can deal with brutal."

"Why bring me?"

"You're my backup."

They stared at each other a moment with that beguiling thought.

"Sure, Ben. I'll protect you."

He cracked up laughing.

"What do you want me to say?"

He started up Darcy. "Nothing. That was perfect."

Cheyenne slipped into the back again to collect her more discreet knives and the spare Glock. "Hell of a day off," she muttered.

THEY BOUNCED UP A NARROW DIRT ROAD, UNMARKED, CLIMBING THE shoulder of yet another low mountain. Darcy's dashboard touchscreen showed only markers at the turn-off and destination, no road.

Cheyenne smelled the compound before she saw it. The familiar stench of open-air latrines and unwashed humans wafted in vile tendrils through the fresh smell of the forest, heightened by the rain spattering last night.

She didn't comment. If anyone hated bad sanitation worse than she did, it was Ben. Well, Frosty. Their gang expelled repeat offenders for sanitary infractions. Their death rates from dysentery remained lower than neighboring gangs.

There was no gate. A couple men with AK-47s sat on dead grass by the side of the road, looking stoned. Ben paused the car to identify themselves, then they continued on. Past another bend the trees retreated around a flat area, mostly grass, though it was shrubby for lack of mowing. The gravel drive appeared to loop through the field. A house and modest warehouse, or giant garage, stood off to the right, surrounded by a flock of trucks and camper trailers. Ben headed for those.

Cheyenne's eyes stayed glued to a fenced-in area, downslope and presumably downwind of the house, with people in it. Most of them seemed to sit or lay on the ground, staring into the sky. The high wire mesh fence was topped with razor concertina wire to discourage climbing.

"Slave pen," she breathed. "You meant that *literally?*"

"Repeat after me, 'none of my business,'" Ben murmured.

"None of my business," Cheyenne-Ava echoed faintly. From past experience, she had reason to wonder if she could keep that bargain. Some men were tying the woman from earlier, minus the baby, to the fence. "Sallie Mae."

Ben reached out and nudged her chin to face forward. "Forget her."

"She's a person, Ben."

"Not anymore. Seriously, Cheyenne. Get your head in the game. None of your business."

"None of my business," she growled.

Ben parked Darcy a good hundred feet from the nearest vehicle, facing the way out. "This is a bad, bad idea. I should go. Make excuses tomorrow. Another errand. Something."

"If I weren't along?"

He swallowed. "I'm here to maintain the relationship. You're here for training. As my bodyguard."

Decisively, he holstered his Glock and exited Darcy to make for the house. Ava had no experience or training as a bodyguard. But she'd watched others play the role in the gangs. She took up station a few paces behind and to his left. *Focus on threats, not content,* she thought.

Oelrich met them at the front porch with a similarly grey-drab old woman. "Ben. Martha, Ben's woman is Cheyenne."

"Welcome, Cheyenne," Martha said. "Come this way."

"Cheyenne stays with me," Ben said. He reiterated this simple statement pleasantly yet doggedly through a number of objections from Oelrich. Eventually Oelrich relented. Ben and Cheyenne were ushered into the large living room.

Ben sat in an armchair of honor, among half a dozen dour men over twice his age. Cheyenne took station against the wall behind him. Women in filthy house dresses – Martha's was clean, if just as ugly – cycled through bearing food and drink. Plastic bottles of prescription-strength drugs were also on offer from their serving trays. They didn't pass close enough to Cheyenne for her to identify what kinds, aside from the ubiquitous oxycontin, poisoned opiate of the masses.

The conversational topic of the moment was the Badgers. Cheyenne-Ava could live with that. The Sixers filled Ben in on their travails with the new militant group, who moved in on the Sixers' territory a couple months ago. They sought to liberate the Sixer slaves. They liked to liberate food and gas from everyone else in the vicinity, too, which explained why the sheriff was also eager to get rid of them.

Aside from the unfamiliar 'thees' and 'thous,' and the slaves, it sounded reasonable enough to Cheyenne. Which lulled her into the error of listening. It took her mind off the weird sensation of how her new used Levis felt in the crotch.

"Any impact to production?" Ben asked.

"Concernest thou not," Oelrich said with a wave. "The slaves stolen were few, and women. The Badgers are inspired by lust, not principle."

"The company will be pleased, as am I. So tomorrow we leave at noon, with the full shipments for the truck stop?"

"Perhaps not full," Oelrich hedged.

"Do we have a problem?" Ben asked, voice edged.

"Our expenses are increasing. There are concerns about gas and food shortages, and the prices. The Lord is nigh, and crops not sown." Oelrich sounded elevated by that last. No doubt the oxycontin helped.

Ben had claimed a pill as well, and visibly relaxed. Cheyenne trusted he palmed it. The home brew he was drinking for real, though.

"The full shipment is not available?" Ben pressed.

"It is available. But at the agreed price, the shipment is smaller."

"How much smaller?" Ben demanded. "It was supposed to increase twenty-five percent this month. Demand is high in Jersey and the city of Satan."

Increase poisoned oxycontin in the Apple and Jersey by a quarter? Ava swallowed. Real people took those drugs, seeking relief from failed lives. No one was sure what fraction of the opiates was poison. But to take them was playing Russian roulette.

No, she realized, Ben and Oelrich and Skull know the exact poison ratio. It must be specified in the contract.

Ben and Oelrich haggled at length on the price change, while Ava's blood boiled. Testament to her failure to play bodyguard well, the silent Martha, approaching barefoot in the April chill, startled her with a whisper.

"Is thy curse upon thee, child?"

Jarred, Ava-Cheyenne looked wide-eyed at Martha's creaky smile less than a foot from her own face. It took her a moment to puzzle out what Martha was saying. *Oh…* Maybe that wasn't a weird fit in the crotch. She squeezed her muscles down there and finally recognized the long-forgotten sensation of her period. Her body stopped that during the Starve, nearly two years ago. Athletic as Ava was, it hadn't come back yet.

Why does the timing always suck? Maybe that's why it's called the curse.

"Come with me," Martha urged.

Her periods used to come on slowly. But after so long away, Ava couldn't guess what would happen this time. If she didn't do something about it, she could be standing here dripping blood down her thighs. Apparently her predicament was already visible, to Martha at least.

She leaned down to Ben's ear. "Excuse me."

"What?" Ben stood abruptly, and spun on her. *What the hell?* his face said.

His negotiation with Oelrich had reached a testy phase. "Thou willst honor thy hosts, Ben! Speakest thou not with a whore in our presence!"

Cheyenne shot Ben an apologetic shrug and sidled out after Martha. The older woman, somewhere between age forty and seventy to Cheyenne's eyes, eddied them out in a corner of the formal dining room. The lower-ranked women used the table to stage the platters for serving the men. With Martha standing to block the others' view, Ava turned to the wall to examine the damage. Yes, even standing with legs pressed together, the spreading blood stain would be visible on the bleached blue Levis.

"I need to wash and… Martha, could you spare me a tampon?"

Martha shook her head, frowning censure. "I can loan thee cloths and proper skirt." She took Cheyenne's arm and led her to the kitchen to fetch bucket and soap. A linen closet for a few none-too-clean washcloths. A bedroom for a dumpy skirt with no pockets, sized for the girl's waist times two. Cheyenne stared in dismay at the sizing. The skirt would slip right over her hips. Martha added a ratty stained apron suitable for slaves to her pile. Last, Martha guided Cheyenne to a non-functioning bathroom to apply all this.

"Clean up after thy mess," Martha instructed as a parting shot, and closed the door on her, plunging Cheyenne into darkness. So the next step was to light a stubby candle, sitting with matches on the dry unused toilet tank.

Ben's going mental by now, she thought. But the two square feet of floor space, and unfamiliar tools and task, didn't speed her along. She didn't use either washcloth to wash herself, so she could keep a spare. But that wouldn't buy her much time. She'd need a stack of the things to avoid bleeding through her underwear again.

Dammit, dammit, dammit!

Cheyenne was trussing herself with the apron in lieu of a belt to keep the skirt on, when Martha returned. She held out a wad of lower-quality bloodstained rags, and some kind of rubberized panty cover for adult diapers, size large.

In her other arm, she carried the baby Lizbet.

"Thank you, Martha," Cheyenne breathed, and hastily pulled on the undergarment, trying not to dwell on their laundry standards.

"Thank *thee*," Martha corrected. "Thou mayest keep the bucket and hang washed rags to dry in here. But thy man is growing vexed. Thou must rejoin him."

"Yes, thank y– thee." Cheyenne guiltily toed the bucket back beside the toilet. She tried to straighten the wet Levi's on the towel bar, and gave it up as a bad job.

Don't ask, she implored herself.

She couldn't help it. "The baby – what will happen to her mother?"

"What dost thou know of these things?"

"We – Ben and I – caught Sallie Mae and Lizbet this afternoon, with the Badgers."

"That was ill done," Martha murmured. "But for relief from the Badgers, we thank thee." She seemed more resigned than sincere.

"And Sallie Mae?" Cheyenne whispered.

"Will be punished," Martha said. "Come." Grudgingly, Martha insisted Cheyenne pause again for a few swallows of beer on their way back through the dining room, and a single chunk of cheese. "The water is unclean."

As expected when Cheyenne finally regained the living room, Ben's cold blue eyes glittered with fury. She preferred not to think of how similar those eyes looked to the hatred in Oelrich's.

He thundered, "Ben, I must protest at this disrespect of our ways! Thy whore and her uncleanness thrust upon our deliberations!"

"I apologize abjectly," Ben returned. "I agree." He turned in his armchair to glare at Cheyenne, back against the wall. "This behavior was intolerable. It will not be repeated. Understood?"

Cheyenne attempted to duck her head meekly. She imagined her eyes said exactly what she felt.

Fuck you, too, Frosty.

Oelrich shook his head. "No. They are weak, and stupid, and understand only pain. Thou must whip her."

Ben sat and threw himself against the back upholstery of his chair. "Thy ways are not ours, Oelrich. I will deal with her fully, in private."

Ava believed that.

Oelrich leaned forward to shake a finger in Ben's face. "I insist!"

Bodyguard, was Ava's automatic thought. The blade of her hand came down on Oelrich's wrist with a karate chop. On the upstroke, she pivoted her hand and thrust him away at the shoulder.

A half dozen old men bounced to their feet in outrage. Ava's Glock was out to cover the leftmost three of them. Ben alone remained in his chair, his own pistol calmly pointed at Oelrich.

8

Interesting fact: Opiates like oxycodone are derived from the opium poppy. The United States spent trillions at war in Afghanistan, the world's leading opium producer. Yet legal pharmaceuticals used opium from legal growers in nineteen other nations overseas, including India, Australia, and Turkey. After the Calm, the ex-U.S. switched to Mexican or locally grown opium. The poppy grows in temperate climates as far north as Estonia.

"Well, that was awkward," Ava-Cheyenne quipped, as they strolled back to Darcy. She walked backward, gun at the ready. So far the men they left behind only glanced at them in disgust and went on their way. "Sorry."

Some kind of gathering seemed to coalesce in mid-field, between the house and the slave pen. A large crude wooden cross stood there, with '666' painted in drippy red paint. A gaunt man, black suit hanging off his frame, stood on some wooden shipping pallets stacked at the base of the cross. It was getting late. The last of the sun crawled up the mountainside above. Three flaming trash barrels stood in a semi-circle behind the cross, belching thick black smoke.

"Do not make me laugh," Ben replied in a low growl.

Cheyenne glanced at him. Indeed, his face was grim, but his eyes

69

danced in merriment. *Well, that's good.* She pursed her lips to avoid cracking a grin. She'd expected a royal chewing out, at best. She wouldn't have been too surprised if Ben acceded to Oelrich's demand and beat her right there in the living room. The cadaverous seniles might have felt entitled to offer suggestions on technique, though. Or they might have demanded their turn beating her. Fortunately Ben was too much of a control freak to permit any of that.

They slipped into the SUV. Cheyenne perched herself backward in the passenger seat, leaning against the glove box. She wanted a wider field of view behind them than her passenger mirror could offer.

She also wanted a better gun. She reached behind the driver's seat and pulled the M-4 across her skirted lap.

Ben leaned his head back on the driver's head-rest, and reviewed his mirrors. Satisfied that no one was launching an assault against them just this minute, he started chuckling.

"What the fuck, Ava?"

"Cheyenne," she corrected him primly. They traded grins, and both started laughing. "Um, it's embarrassing," she said, as the giggles died back. "I got my period."

This set off Ben laughing again for a moment. "Hum. Well. Congratulations. I don't suppose you brought supplies."

"After two years? No. It slipped my mind."

Ben wrinkled his nose in distaste. "I could spare you a sheet. Or a towel to cut up."

"Martha gave me stuff. Hey, could we never discuss this again? As long as I live?'

Ben's smile was calmer this time. He reached to squeeze her hand. "Deal. Congratulations, Ava. Really."

She bobbed her head and averted her gaze back to the tableau of fruitcakes on the field. "Thanks, Cade. Sorry I screwed up your negotiation."

"Nah. It was a good time to storm out in a huff. Resume tomorrow. Oelrich wanted seventy-five percent more payment. My starting position was twenty-five percent more payment for twenty-five percent more product. We'll settle at fifty."

"His demands are fair?"

"Fair enough. Food prices are skyrocketing. The business climate is dicey. Oelrich is skittish about whether PA will whitewash loose ends before joining Hudson. It's a valid concern."

"Hudson would wipe out these assholes," Cheyenne claimed with satisfaction. "Slavers? Drug dopers?"

"Hudson won't do squat to them," Ben said. "Won't change this part of PA. Look around. Deer outnumber people twenty to one. Plenty of Hudson is the same way. The 'Resco Raj' is concerned with concentrated populations. Tioga County PA can eat trees, for all the Raj cares. Might lean on them to produce more food. Open a free Internet cafe in the county seat. The last Resco here kept an eye on about a dozen counties."

"What happened to him?"

"He committed suicide. Skull's predecessor was the Resco here. Major Canton Bertovich. Now Skull is all they got. And he works for Hudson."

"Oh, yeah." This had been explained to Cheyenne before. She had more context to understand it now, though. "What are they doing over there? At the cross."

"Sunset Satanic service. They think they're Christian. I hope they don't sacrifice anybody on the altar."

Sallie Mae was being dragged to the cross. "You're kidding. Right?"

"Um. Sure."

Cheyenne stared at him.

Ben shrugged. "So. Trainee. Next moves. Now that we've offended our hosts. What next?"

"You don't want to flip 'em the bird and ride off into the sunset. You want to secure the shipment."

"That's what we're here for." Ben adjusted the central mirror. "Oh, good, it's an orgy."

Cheyenne considered the 'religious service' behind them. The preacher appeared to be mounting Sallie Mae. "Is that a turn on?"

"Not to me," Ben assured her. "Probably give me nightmares tonight. Trainee. Focus. Plans."

"Well, to butter up Oelrich, you could beat me. I'd rather you don't.

Oh, I know! We could have an exhibition match. Something showy and not too painful."

"I like it. 'Our ways are not yours,' kinda thing. And then?"

Cheyenne considered. "There's no reason to park here overnight. Or, I guess it's an insult to leave. 'We don't trust you.' We don't. But we're here to maintain a business relationship. Schmooze this guy Oelrich."

Ben remained studiously aloof.

Cheyenne considered the business relationships she'd watched Frosty navigate during the Starve. He might schmooze. He might draw blood or take hostages. He was flexible. "You don't care if we stay or go. You're not afraid of them. Because… Because we're their bread and butter. And it's not just this bunch. Skull has contracts with other Sixers, too. We might get hurt, if we interfere with them. But they won't kill us if we're fairly reasonable. So it's safe to spend the night. If we mind our own business."

Ben studied the left-hand mirror. "Get in the habit of calling him 'Boss,' not 'Skull.'"

"Boss," Cheyenne echoed. "Karate exhibition match. Supper. Homework. Bed. Never more than ten feet apart. Even visit the latrines together." She scratched her nose ruefully. "Um, that was the original plan, wasn't it."

He just forced her to think it through so she'd follow the plan better. She reflected that this would take some getting used to, after the micromanaging ways of the Army. But Frosty – Ben, Cade – was a leader, not a nanny. He was quite happy to let people screw up and learn from their mistakes. This conversation was his version of a productive chewing-out.

"A match before dinner sounds good," he agreed. He frowned at her ugly skirts.

"I'll go change, then," she said brightly, and scampered for the back.

After considering her options, she ended up in the same clothes she started the day with, complete with bloodstains from treating Joe Bob and Doerr. *Fitting.*

Ben chose to warm up in front of Darcy, letting the SUV block their view of the Sixer orgy beyond. She joined him and they worked up a sweat for 15 minutes before they squared off.

"Exhibition, not street fight," Ben specified, and then bowed.

"Punches and blocks first," Cheyenne agreed. The world contracted to only Cade as she circled round him. Four blocks in succession, both hands. Each style of punch singly, rising punch, jab, straight, cross, back-hand, scissors. Then double punch combos. Then triples. To the observer it might look like a fight, but to the couple, it was a dance done well. The acrid smoke from the coal fires burned her eyes and throat, but she saw only her lover. And he looked great. Watching his simple joy in motion, tuned her into enjoying her own muscles flex.

Cade escalated to elbows and punches and knees, telegraphing each move so she'd bring the perfect counter. She dodged the wrong way on one, and he simply aborted his punch to push her back at the shoulder.

"Company," he breathed. He grinned in pleasure when she didn't let the comment distract her from blocking a knee to her thigh with her own. Then he broke the dance with a flurry of silly slaps. She slapped him back, including high-fives, until they were both laughing out loud.

He stepped back and bowed to close the match. Then he turned to nod to their host. "Oelrich. My wife and I like to spar in the evening."

"Wife! I did not realize. Ben, thou shouldst have told me. We treat wives very differently."

Ben returned a casual throwaway gesture. "A misunderstanding. Cheyenne and I have been together for years. She is new to field work. Not new to me."

"I see that," Oelrich agreed. "I came to tell thee that the men are assembling to attack the Badgers. Thou willst join them?"

"I think not. Thank you, though."

"Only the wives and slaves will remain," Oelrich warned.

"Would you prefer we leave?"

Ben wasn't bothering any further with the 'thee' crap. Cheyenne recognized the subtle shift in power. Ben remained cool and courteous, but refused to play by Oelrich's rules.

"If we stay, we'll keep to ourselves," Ben said. "We won't trouble your womenfolk. But we're happy to leave and return in the morning."

"No, no, thou offered before, and I insisted thou comest. Stay, please, and rest thy selves. Ben…I truly cannot accept twenty-five percent…"

Clearly it was time for the men to inch along a little further in their haggling. Cheyenne would have preferred to sit for some cool-down stretches, but not spread-eagled in front of a creepy person. She secured the keys from Ben and started digging for supper behind Darcy. Ben subtly herded Oelrich thataway, so the SUV didn't lie between them.

With a nod of approval from Ben, Cheyenne slapped up their kitchen cooking table and got the grill warming on the camp stove. Ben's forehead looked pained, but she slapped burgers on, with a splash of Worcestershire for added flavor. She wasn't the gourmet cook he was.

Deal with it, she thought. *Or suck up your masculine pride and admit you do the cooking in front of Oelrich. Heh.* She decided to savor the moment by throwing sliced tomatoes on the grill, and letting cheese and sliced mushrooms heat on them instead of on the burgers. Ben's wincing expression registered a score.

The men reached new positions of thirty-five and sixty percent in their bargaining. Then Oelrich shoved off to join the Badger hunt. Ben and Cheyenne settled on the tailgate to enjoy the worst supper they'd had in a week, and watch the trucks roll out.

Martha fetched Cheyenne her damp Levi's and wash bucket after they left.

The couple studied as usual, though more focused on doing rather than reading. It was harder to ignore the screams outside while reading. Sallie Mae was tied to the slave pen again, and crying for water or mercy or her daughter. That set Cheyenne's nerves on edge. She nestling into Ben's arm for feedback on her neolithic mini-essays. She held his hand while she stepped him through an algebra problem he was stuck on.

For the first time since Elmira, she slept spooned in Ben's arms for comfort. They didn't trouble themselves with watches. If anyone touched Darcy, the SUV would scream bloody murder.

THE MORNING INSPECTION WAS MORE INTERESTING THAN CHEYENNE expected. Well, aside from Ben and Oelrich's glacial haggling toward settling at fifty-five percent. She wished Ben would just give in and settle at sixty like Skull advised when Ben called for authorization.

But Ben brought a hand-held ultraviolet light to the warehouse, as did Oelrich. Oelrich walked them through the marking and doping supplies. Ben observed the procedures the slaves used. To Cheyenne's consternation, the slaves seemed perfectly happy in their tasks, clean and fresh. They bathed and donned fresh clean clothes before entering the work area. They wore sterile gloves. Their tables were well-lit, with giant magnifying glasses on swing-arms so they could see the pills clearly.

They observed as one slave extracted three pills from a bottle of oxycontin, on a clean tray. He used a pipette to deposit three drops of poison onto each tablet. Turned them with tiny tongs. Then doped the other side. He tilted the tray to slide the pills to the side. There was one wayward drop, so he added one more drop to each pill. Satisfied, he transferred the pills back into the bottle. He shook the bottle gently to mix the three with the other 47 uncontaminated pills. Next to the pipette, was a marker. In invisible ink, he jotted a '3' on the cap. Then he placed the completed bottle in an 'out' tray for resealing.

The tables to the left of him were for unsealing bottles, the tables to the right for re-sealing. Ben gave a fair impression of being engrossed and impressed by their system. Cheyenne figured she only needed to appear attentive and scan for possible threats. Of which there were none.

"Question," she said. Oelrich scowled. Ben motioned for her to go ahead. "How do you keep the workers from sampling?"

Oelrich waved them along to watch in the next area. The re-sealer's first step was to dump a pill bottle into a counting machine. Only then did she pour them back in and begin sealing.

"The slaves receive librium on duty," Oelrich explained. "They will be rewarded with oxycontin for the night when their labors are done."

Ben nodded matter-of-factly to Oelrich, and to Cheyenne to indicate that this explained much.

It's important to Skull, she thought, *that everyone is a volunteer for his schemes. However sick, these people chose to do what they're doing. The addicts choose to take the poisoned drugs, too.* She had no idea how they became pill-doping slaves. Maybe the addiction came first. That wasn't a question she considered wise to ask.

Moving on to the shipments, Ben used his black light to verify the boxes for today's shipment were as specified, a few cartons of the powerful sedatives librium and valium, and fifty times as much of the opiates oxycontin and percodan. In normal light, the recycled boxes were labeled as ramen noodles or vitamins or whatnot. Using a random number generator on his phone, Ben selected cartons to unseal and open to verify the correct number of bottles and invisible bottle labeling. Then he likewise selected six individual vials at random.

Oelrich led him to a quality control workstation. Ben dutifully opened each vial to verify that its seals and cotton batting and desiccant packet were of factory-quality credibility. He ran each bottle's contents through a pill counter to verify the quantity.

Then he spread the pills across a paper blotter on the table surface. He spritzed them with a pungent reagent. After that, three pills glowed under his UV light, bright pink instead of the sickly greenish yellow of the label markings.

The pills also dissolved into a mess. The six sample bottles were destroyed in the testing.

That's the trick, Cheyenne thought. People could tell which drug bottles were doped, yes. But the only way to find out *which pills,* would destroy all the pills. And people took the pills anyway. They wanted the high badly enough to play Russian roulette.

Oelrich fetched another six vials to replace the ones destroyed by testing, and they resealed the cartons. Referring to some electronic paperwork on his phone, with Cheyenne assisting, Ben divided the boxes ready for shipment into twenty-eight larger boxes. He taped them closed, then affixed shipping labels with tape, and routing instructions with jotted post-it notes. The latter bore non-incriminating names such as 'Clarence' or 'John K.' The shipping labels gave addresses across Jersey and the Apple. Cheyenne assumed the post-its specified who would carry them there.

"I can fit four in my car," Ben murmured, as he attended to the last big box.

"Do not trouble thyself," Oelrich said. "The trucks need gas, anyway."

Ben nodded. "Fifty-five percent. For thirty percent more." They'd already packed that thirty percent into the shipment. "With the understanding that the company can and will provide advance notice of difficult changes. You know you can trust us on that. We have your back. Like with the Badgers. We value your continuing service. We will keep you in business."

Oelrich sighed. "Agreed." They shook on it.

"Gas?" Cheyenne inquired brightly, as she strode with Ben back to Darcy to depart, feeling better already.

"You'll like our next stop. Once the book-keeping is done. Promise."

9

Interesting fact: Ken–Tenn was a leader in marijuana growing even before the Calm, as Kentucky and Tennessee.

Cheyenne laughed out loud. "This is the gas station?" The diesel fumes made that clear.

Ben grinned. "Yup. Seediest truck stop in PA. We rent a room tonight. Hot and cold running water. Laundromat, shopping, king-sized bed. The works." He pulled into a motel parking spot at the edge of the broad truck plaza. "We can top up the tanks on the way out."

Cheyenne was relieved to hear that. After a boring hour and half drive south to Interstate 180 – a bypass north of I-80 – they spent another couple hours on tedious rendezvous, transshipping the boxes of drugs from the Sixers to the twenty-odd truckers who would carry them to points east on the PA-Jersey border. A large chunk of Ben's 'allowance' was handed over to the Sixers when they were done. The truckers would be paid at the border on delivery. By now the sun was angling low again.

A familiar Sixer pickup pulled up a few parking spots away. Cheyenne held up a hand to wave.

"You don't know them," Ben corrected her. "Anyone you met today, you were Cheyenne. Now I'm Connor. And you are?"

"Donna works."

Connor made a note of it with Darcy. Since they were checking into a motel, they were married this time.

Donna said, "I didn't think places like this still existed."

"They have to. There's a railroad, but most of PA can only be reached by truck. Most of the truck stops are run by the Army. This one's independent. Specializes in civilian traders."

"Like us," she agreed.

"Any more questions? You're Donna the second I open a door."

"I'm set. Oh wait, one question. Do we have rations for gas?"

Connor snorted. "We have cash." He peeled off a hundred PA dollars for her, to underscore the point. "Go grab the supplies you need. I'll check us in."

Donna set off with a shopping bag to the low building at the center of the fueling facility. Inside, it almost looked like a small shopping mall. Rows of seating in the middle offered TV's and someplace to sit and eat takeout. One end of the hall offered four competing fast food joints, the other end sit-down restaurants and bars. Rest rooms and rent-a-shower facilities, an Internet cafe, and convenience stores both large and small completed the offerings.

Tactful signs advised that sleeping was not permitted in the concourse.

She hadn't seen anything like this in years. It was hard to believe such a place still existed. Mesmerized, she couldn't help drifting by the fast food counters. The international chains were defunct, of course, but one still offered burgers and fries, another fried chicken, the third submarine sandwiches, and the last a hot bar, with banquet trays of macaroni and cheese, beef stew, and chicken tetrazzini. They even offered soda fountains, though not the brand-name beverages.

Cheyenne wondered what kombucha and elderflower soda tasted like, and whether they were carbonated and flavored corn syrup water, like the sodas of old. The Army certainly didn't feed its troops such things, and neither did Skull. She couldn't remember whether PA was one of the states that called the drinks 'pop' instead of 'soda.'

She yanked herself from her reverie, and hit the large convenience store. This was well-stocked. That was no surprise, since the truck stop was a crossroads for traders. But she had three varieties of tampons and four of pads to choose from. The condom department was even better stocked.

One of the aisles was dedicated to handcrafts. Most of it was junk, decorative knick-knacks and dust-catchers for the cluttered living room. If Ava ever wanted a cluttered home, she'd need to revise her choice of man first. Some of the little carvings were cute, though. She picked up an affable-looking dog that made her think of Doc, her room-mate and scout team leader back at West Point. Doc dreamed of having a dog. The smooth finish and heft of the piece felt good in her hand. She added it to her bag.

Half the store was dedicated to groceries. Connor planned to do all that tomorrow. But she couldn't help picking up potato chips, tortilla chips, and a jar of nacho sauce.

Because she could. And that was amazing to her. *What a colossal waste of precious oil and nutrition. Orgasmic.*

The prices turned out to be eye-watering. *Oh, yeah. That other thing about truck stops.* Her little bag of necessaries and treats came to over $50 PA. That much had bought her a week's food for two at the Sayre farm market, eating high on the hog.

"What the hell did you buy?" Connor asked, echoing her thoughts. He'd slipped in behind her at the checkout, since she took so long. He laughed when he rifled the contents of her bag.

Back at the room – Donna was pleased that she got her own key for once – she called first dibs on the bathroom. After five days washing from a pail, a leisurely shower with hot water felt divine. She'd just put shampoo on her hair when Cade slipped in to join her.

"Hey!" she objected.

"You're done washing the private bits," he argued. "I know you. You did that first. And I like washing your hair. And I like you washing mine. Turn around, so I can catch up."

The shower took longer that way, but they enjoyed it.

"You know," Ava said, soaping his back. "In Hudson now, all it takes to be married is to announce it in public. We're now married twice over."

"We're not in Hudson," Cade said. "Besides, I didn't say Cade and Ava were married. Just Connor and Donna. And Ben and Cheyenne. But only to the Sixers. I forgot to tell Darcy that. Who cares. Ben lied." He turned to soap her front, which didn't need it again.

"Ava. I'm not ready to marry. If I were, it would be you. You know that. It's not you I doubt. It's me."

She kissed him on the nose. "You doubt yourself too much. Calling yourself a monster." She shook her head and scowled at him. "You make the right choices, Cade. Look at that kneecap yesterday. The one you didn't shoot. Because you didn't need to. You just made them think you had. Man, you even had Doerr convinced, and it was his knee."

"That's a low bar. But thanks." He swallowed uncomfortably. "Hey. Congratulations. On your period back. That's a big deal. I don't know if you remember. When I could, um, again. A year ago now."

"Of course I remember. You um very well."

He enfolded her in slippery arms and kissed her. "Not quite the same. But sorta. I'm glad for you."

"We're not going to um now, are we?"

"No. I can wait a few days, thanks. We work tonight."

"We've been working since dawn!"

He slipped out to give her privacy to finish up with the bathroom. Every ghastly thread from the Sixers went into the trash. She even tied off the bag and started a fresh bag on top of it in the wastebasket.

THE SUN WAS DOWN AND THE BAR WAS PACKED. AVA – DONNA – WAS delighted to wear her sexiest skimpy black top over black skinny jeans, with makeup and opalescent jewelry, her light ash brown hair hanging smooth and loose. Her signature high-top red sneakers were a quirky choice for the ensemble, but she loved to feel her feet ready for traction, not wobbling on stilts. She didn't have any high heels with her.

She hadn't been out on the town in ages, not since she gained the weight back to show off some curves. The appreciative attention from fellow bar-goers was most gratifying. From Connor, too, though she suspected he stopped caring how she looked years ago. He knew the magic words to keep a girl from hitting him.

Once upon a time, truckers embraced the night for the light traffic. These days, the highways were unlit and rife with potholes, blown tires, and motley surprise hazards. The roads were plenty empty in daylight, and driving them then was a whole lot safer.

Donna split a Philly cheese steak with Connor, along with a mountain of fries and some side salads, completely filling their tiny cocktail table. The establishment had six beers on tap to choose from. Hers was a tall pint of pale amber lager. Connor elected a half pint of something dark and chewy, with a tall glass of ice water.

In social mode, Connor twisted on his bar stool toward the guy behind him. "Did I overhear you been down the VA border? What's the word? I'm Connor. Donna."

"Benson. Maryland. Yeah, I was down around Gettysburg. Didn't cross. Ohio's holding that border now." Benson was a beefy guy in his forties, with thin brown hair and a big beard, in unbuttoned green plaid flannel over T-shirt and jeans.

"Ohio. That far east?" Connor asked.

A half dozen other patrons overheard the exchange and pressed around to eavesdrop.

Benson shook his head in disgust. "The vultures are circling. Yeah, Ohio's claimed the southern border to just south of Gettysburg. They're making themselves known south of the border, too. Pushing back on refugees from the coast."

"Making a play for Gaithersburg? Rockville?" Connor suggested.

"No way, man," another trucker cut in, who could pass for Benson's younger brother, though they weren't together. "Too close to D.C. They'll stop at Frederick."

"What do you know?" demanded another. "You're full of it."

Shoves were exchanged.

"What I want to know is, what's PA get out of this? Right?" Benson said. "Why are we just hanging tight at the border instead of claiming some land?"

"Land comes with people," Connor suggested. "Problems to solve. You want to own Baltimore? D.C.?"

"Fit right in with Philly," another redneck growled. "Buncha pinko welfare illegal immigrants."

Connor turned his back on that one. "There's still a government in VA, though, right?" he asked Benson. "Like, it's still going in D.C.?"

Benson shook his head. "Nobody's listening to 'em. They never owned their borders the way we do."

Acrimony ensued as to what extent PA owned its borders, what with Hudson garrisoning the north, and Ohio the west and and south all the way east to Gettysburg. PA only controlled its southeast corner.

Feelings on this were mixed among the traders and truckers. Apparently borders under Hudson and Ohio management were more permeable than PA's own. Connor had mentioned that already to Donna. Before the war, PA had dumped its prisoners and malcontents into Jersey. PA didn't dare let that border go slack now. Jersey was more than happy to send PA's rejects back. Although from what Donna heard, Jersey used the rout after the February tsunami as a golden opportunity to execute or extradite a lot of them.

A newcomer shoved next to Donna. She recognized him from this afternoon, a courier carrying drugs to the Jersey border for them. He leaned down to whisper in her ear. "Get him for me? Problem."

"Connor!" Donna flagged him over. Now that she looked around, she recognized many of the truckers they'd transferred boxes to this afternoon.

"Thought you'd like to know," the trucker told Connor, making no effort to keep his voice down. "Cops put up a roadblock at the I-80 interchange. Suspect drugs coming in via I-180. East and west inter-changes." I-180 both began and ended at I-80, as a northern bypass.

"That right? Thanks, man." Connor shook hands with him. He dropped a kiss on Donna's head. "I'll be back, ten minutes or so."

"Shouldn't I go with you?"

Connor laughed. "No. Watch my beer."

Donna tried to listen and learn more about Greater Virginia's state of decay. But without Connor steering the conversation, it devolved into uneducated opinions and broke apart. She let the waiter cart away the wreckage of supper. She tried swapping chairs to get a conversation going again with Benson, but he shrugged her off.

Another girl plonked down in the chair across from Donna. Her black camisole, with pink ribbon trim, definitely crossed the line into lingerie. Tousled black curls sported another pink ribbon. She wore extreme spike heels and fishnet stockings below laced leather tight shorts, and pancaked makeup. Ava didn't know what Donna knew of such things. But the girl was clearly working.

"You're new here, honey," the hooker said. She blew a bubble-gum bubble, and smacked it loudly. "Closed shop. No freelancers." She crossed a long leg and bounced her calf toward Benson for display purposes.

"That a fact," said Donna, twirling a dangly earring. *What could I learn from a whore? What couldn't I learn from a whore?* Regretfully, she added, "I'm not working tonight. My guy's just running an errand."

"That a fact," the whore echoed, dubiously. "You're just a baby. You want some drugs? Got some pills that'll make him happy and get it over quick."

Donna shook her head. "Thanks, anyway. How long have you been working here? I'll buy you a drink."

The whore shrugged elaborate amusement. "I'm available for threesomes."

Donna waved down the waiter. Her guest – Angie – asked for top-shelf bourbon, at six dollars. Donna rolled her eyes, but paid it, plus one dollar for another lager for herself.

"I can satisfy my man myself," Donna told Angie firmly. "Just curious about the life here. You know?"

"You really want to know?" Angie leaned in, pressing ample bosom over bangle-clad arms. "Yeah, I worked here since the December. I'm from Jersey." She flourished a hand. "Stuck on the wrong side of the border. I guess. Didn't like it at home anyway. Runaway. But the owner here, he's my pimp. Takes care of us good." She blew a bubble. "A dozen girls. We got a big house. It's nice."

"You ever think of moving on?"

Angie shrugged and took a swig of bourbon. "Move on where? To do what? Here's good as anyplace. And *that,* is all you get for one bourbon." She wagged a finger in Donna's face. "No turning tricks, little sister."

"I'll be good," Donna promised, tilting her beer in a toast.

Angie downed the rest of her glass. "Don't go that far."

Guess this outfit is a little too sexy for a truck stop, Donna surmised. *Good to know.* She wondered if any women anywhere were satisfied with their lives and their options, after the Calm. Angie winked at her as she led a heavy trucker out of the bar.

"Haven't seen you here before, sweetheart," a man said, sliding into the seat Angie had vacated. "Buy you a drink?"

"No. My husband will be back in a minute."

"Nah, don't be that way. You're a fucking whore, just like Angie. I seen ya."

"I'm sorry. You're mistaken. Please leave me alone."

He grabbed for her breast. She slammed her sharp elbow down in the middle of his forearm, in a jab she knew was agonizing. Then she slapped his arm away.

"You bitch from hell!" He grabbed for her in anger now.

She swiped his feet out from under him, and stomped his shin once he was down. Then she poured the rest of her new beer on him.

"I said I'm not available. Buzz off."

"Ma'am, you need to leave." The bouncer's vast hand circled her biceps. She stared at it until it was withdrawn.

Donna attempted, "This man grabbed me. I already told him I wasn't interested. I'm here with my husband. He'll be back shortly."

"Yeah, I don't give a rat's ass, lady. You're not welcome here. Get out."

She considered arguing further, but his mind was made up. She sighed and headed for the door. *Great. The only women here my age are whores, and I have to walk back to the motel alone.*

Or do I?

She decided she had a perfectly good view of the mall from the Internet cafe. She'd spot Ben – Connor – when he returned. Hopefully Internet cafes weren't the pickup spot of choice. She pulled out her phone to ask him for backup.

But she was in an Internet cafe. She could contact anyone she pleased. Connor was busy. She could entertain herself for five minutes. She paid five bucks for a password good for an hour unlimited usage, and a cup of herbal tea.

With a pang of homesickness, she realized that contacting her friends from West Point was off-limits. Puño and Doc especially would pick right up on the fact that the text came from outside Hudson. Though not as fast as her meshnet programmer buddy Daneel.

Daneel! Daneel joined the company, like she did!

TAILPANIC: Daneel! I'm homesick! Talk to me! Any word from WP friends?

DANTHEEEL: LOL! You're so busted. Who? Got Foxfyre.

TAILPANIC: news?

DANTHEEEL: Foxfyre says your x plat housed E Harlem

DANTHEEEL: Calderon leads, LT green & shaky

DANTHEEEL: action in NJ

DANTHEEEL: mine in CLI, corps eng, sea incursion, hush

Wow, he types fast. Ava supposed that made sense. He was probably sitting at a keyboard all day. But he typed faster than Ava could decipher what he said.

'Foxfyre' was the meshnet handle for their mutual friend Fox. She was in GED prep class with Ava and Daneel at West Point, the young and brainy club from Basic Combat Training. The Apple lead Resco, Lt. Col. MacLaren, chose to keep Ava's training platoon intact and assign them to Apple Garrison – she knew that. And her squad sergeant Calderon was their platoon sergeant, along with some lieutenant who recently received a field commission from sergeant. It made sense the new LT would be green at the job. Seeing action in North Jersey was a given.

She hadn't realized Daneel's Basic platoon was likewise kept intact and sent to CLI, Central Long Island, that was once western Suffolk County.

TAILPANIC: sea what?

DANTHEEEL: Apple h2o from Catskills, LI ground

DANTHEEEL: hush hush

Ava frowned at her phone. *Why hush-hush? Oh!* After the tsunami, sea level rose like 9 feet. If Long Island relied on groundwater, and the ground water was getting salty, *ouch.* Her eyes widened. There were 2 million people on Long Island, rebuilt on ecotopian ideals, environmental zealots. LI was the rehabilitation star of the Apple Zone. But if LI lost its fresh water supply, Hudson would lose like 100 by 20 miles of prime agricultural island. And have 2 million refugees to either cull or resettle.

TAILPANIC: OUCH!

TAILPANIC: ur talking to them?

DANTHEEEL: against rooolz. intercept

TAILPANIC: spy on meshtexts? how rude

DANTHEEEL: mesh never private

DANTHEEEL: hint hint :)

Point taken, Ava thought ruefully. She knew that, in theory. The Hudson Constitution even stated that communications were not private. The government reserved the right to monitor, censor, or shut down the nets as needed to maintain order and curb troublemakers. Apples casually assumed that now they had their phones back, their mesh text conversations were private, like before the Calm Act. The rest of Hudson never lost phones and Internet during those years. They knew better.

TAILPANIC: u? training good?

DANTHEEEL: fun lotta work, u?

TAILPANIC: orgasmic

DANTHEEEL: sleeping with boss!

Connor plucked the phone from her hands. *Oops.* She was so thrilled to talk with a friend from West Point, she forgot to watch for him.

"Off limits," Connor murmured, scrolling through to read the interchange. "Both of you."

10

_Interesting fact: Indoor marijuana growing accounted for an estimated 1.3%
of the energy consumed in the U.S. Yet marijuana grew perfectly well
outdoors, as witnessed by plantations sprinkled through the national park
system._

"Can't I say good-bye?" Donna wheedled.

"No." But Connor seemed satisfied by what he read, and simply powered off the phone and pocketed it. "Why aren't you in the bar?"

"Got kicked out for fighting," Donna admitted. "Guy thought I was a hooker. Wouldn't take no for an answer. I messed him up. The bouncer was unreasonable."

Connor snickered. "That's what bouncers do, dumb-ass. Come on."

Smarting from the dumb-ass comment, Donna followed him back to the bar, where he simply strode in. The bouncer moved to argue. Connor raised an arm and called out first, "Barkeep! Round of beer on me!"

Ava was impressed. That move certainly scotched the bouncer's plans to bounce them out. The human tank just yelled at her over the applause. "No more fighting!" He left it at that.

Nearly a hundred people got their beers. Connor and the bouncer helped pull pitchers. Then a man Cheyenne hadn't met called out, "What are we toasting?"

"PA's finest!" Connor called out, pint held high. "Inspection road-block closed at the I-80 interchange!" The cheers and beer-glass thumping in response were deafening. As that calmed down, Connor added, "But they'll be back in business at six a.m."

"So you get us drunk first!" another yelled out. Cheyenne recognized him.

Connor shrugged with a grin, alongside the laughter. "Can't drive on one beer? What a wuss!"

"That was my fifth beer!"

"So sleep it off til four a.m.!" Connor returned. They exchanged cheerful middle fingers.

Men liked to bond that way, Donna reflected, and settled down with her lager. Connor perched beside her, but rose repeatedly to shake hands and exchange a few words with truckers who stopped by their table. Some she recognized. Most she didn't. But it made sense that many of the truckers here carried some contraband, whether for Connor or not.

"How did you get rid of the cops?" Donna asked during a lull in the well-wishers.

Connor shrugged. "Fire in a warehouse. No traffic to stop overnight. A word in the ear. Like that. Sorry, took a while. Rigged it myself this time instead of calling in the boss."

She nodded, impressed. "You're good."

"I know." Happily flushed with beer, Connor grinned. "I love this stuff."

Donna's happy return smile morphed into a scowl. She spotted Angie in the crowd, limping toward the bouncer. Someone had roughed her up. Her lip was bleeding, as well as her knees through torn stockings. She held her corset together with her bruised arm. There was nothing else wrong with her legs. Donna suspected the limp favored damage between the thighs. From where she sat, it looked like the bouncer just shrugged and told Angie to get lost. In tears, the prostitute begged him to reconsider.

"None of our business," Connor remarked, following her gaze.

"Sallie Mae was none of our business because we had business," Donna countered.

Connor sighed. "Hookers have pimps to protect them."

"Malfunction on the pimp," Donna observed. "I do not like that guy. Angie was cool."

"You chatted up a whore while I was gone?" Connor looked amused.

"See any other girls my age in here? We could relate." Donna took a pull on her beer. "I want to do something. This world kinda sucks, for women."

Connor shrugged. "I hear you. Got your back."

Ava shot him a very pleased smile. Cade was great that way. As Frosty, he ran possibly the most feminist gang in New York City during the Starve. Other gang royalty had harems and treated women like dirt. Frosty's queen bee, Ava Panic, was in charge of the home front, including keeping the guys from abusing the girls and children. It was a brutal time, but not as brutal in their gang as most.

Connor simply picked up his beer and stepped behind her as Donna threaded her way through the crowd toward Angie, now slumped on a cocktail table, crying alone.

"Who did it?" Donna demanded.

"Your fault," Angie accused, through her tears. "That guy you messed up, he took it out on me!"

"Where is he?"

"Sleeping it off in his rig."

"Show me."

Angie looked tempted, but glanced sideways at the bouncer. "I'll get it worse then."

Connor stepped in. "Want to blow this town?"

"Got nowhere to go. My kid's at the house."

Donna wanted to argue. But Connor took a slow pull on his beer and looked away. He waited for Angie to think it through.

He's right, Donna thought. *We don't have a life to offer Angie. Just a ride out of here, if she has the guts to take it.*

"Sorry this happened to you, Angie." Donna put a hand on hers on the table briefly. "Men suck. Not all of them." She glanced at Connor.

Angie sniffled. "I'll be alright."

"Green Ford Expedition XL. By the motel," Connor said. "If you change your mind. We leave mid-morning. Ma'am." He nodded respect, and tugged Donna away.

"She won't leave," Connor murmured in Donna's ear, as they made their way back to their table. "We offered."

THE NEXT MORNING, DONNA WAS BRAVING MESOPOTAMIA IN HER Western Civilization textbook, while an industrial strength three-load dryer had its way with their wardrobe. When suddenly Darcy sounded off in all her glory just outside the ground-floor laundromat. Connor's SUV had not one, but three ear-splitting car alarms – the standard flat scream, a police siren, and another that warbled up a scale and repeated.

She peeled out to see what was the matter, only to find Angie trying to soothe a two-year-old. Her battered suitcase and a package duct-taped out of brown shopping bags lay dumped to the curb.

Donna didn't have the electronic key fob. But she still had the emergency access Ben set up for her. She laid her hand on the driver's door in the correct long-short-short-short caress. The car shut up. It also unlocked, but she ignored that for the moment.

Angie looked ten years older in the morning light, with minimal sober makeup. The black eye and split lip didn't help much either. She wore a beige knee-length hounds-tooth straight skirt, suitable for business attire, below a sedate olive fuzzy sweater. Her heels were still black stilettos, but she'd tried. The mixed-racial toddler bawled, but Angie had a handle on that.

"Your car alarm sucks eggs," Angie greeted Donna.

"It does the job," Donna said. "So you want a ride?" She hadn't really considered what would happen in the unlikely event Angie took them up on their offer. Given Darcy's contents, Donna couldn't very well offer to let her wait in the car. "Do you have someplace to go?"

Connor bounced off the SUV as he arrived at a run, summoned from the store. Donna noted he'd need to go back for their groceries. He didn't carry any bags. He took in the tableau silently and waited for Angie to answer the question.

"Guy last night, gave me this." Angie handed out a scrap of paper to Connor, not Donna. She was more polite to him.

Connor read it, paused to purse his lips, and handed it back. "I know them. You're better off here."

"What, now?" she shrieked at him. "You know what will happen if I go back there now?"

"Fair idea," Connor admitted. "Still. They're bad news. Slavers."

"What do you think this is, Sherlock?"

"Still," Connor repeated. "Sixers," he added for Donna's benefit.

"Don't go there, Angie," Donna pleaded. "He's right. You're better off here in the truck stop. Make friends, find a way out sometime. Steer clear of the Sixers."

"Guy said they'd give me drugs. Work. Three meals a day. Feed the baby, too. I can't do without the drugs. That's why I'm stuck here."

"I won't take you there," Connor said. "Can't. Business. You want a ride to a mainstream church or something, that's fine. Not the Sixers. Look, I got to go pay for my groceries. Be here when I get back. Or not."

"Can't you reason with him?" Angie demanded of Donna.

"I agree with him," Donna returned. "Seriously, Angie. We know what those people are. Stay here."

"*Fuh-uh-uh-ck you!!!!*" Angie went off on a screaming, swearing tear, the true hooker shining right through her secretarial disguise. She didn't touch Donna, though. The motel front desk manager came out, arms crossed, and glared at her. Apparently he called the bar first, because some other beefy bouncer – the morning shift – came across the parking lot at a lumbering jog.

Angie was still screaming as he dragged her and her kid and her stuff away.

The dryer beeped. Donna remembered to reach inside and re-lock Darcy before she returned to their laundry. Connor could re-arm the alarms when he returned with the groceries. She tried to focus on the first code of law in history, pressed into clay tablets in cuneiform. She found it hard to relate.

Ava felt like a cad about Angie. But she didn't have any better option to offer. If she'd taken that militia job back in Soho Ville, working as a beat cop in Manhattan, that's the sort of thing Ava would be doing now. She'd handle domestic abuse calls most days, she imagined. She'd know the options available. Maybe some of them were even good options. The democratic town meeting set up a respite shelter. But not here. She wasn't equipped to be an amateur social worker to Pennsylvania. *Just passing through.*

Cade was right. Ben. Connor. It was better to mind her own business in the first place. She was glad he let her learn that for herself. Maybe she could find lesser blessings to bestow. Who was she to try to solve someone else's life? She wasn't queen bee anymore. This wasn't her tribe.

Another half hour of chores, and they were fueled up and back on the road.

To Donna's bemusement, she was Cheyenne again. Not only that, but they were parked in a small dead-grassy field in State Game Lands 219. Which, aside from the grassy bit, looked a great deal like State Game Lands 36. Which was unsurprising, given that their first night's camp was about 10 miles southwest as the crow flies. Sayre was 6 miles west of them.

Which left Cheyenne with the burning question – *why are we back on the Hudson border?* But Ben was a stickler for his rule against warning her what was coming next. She needed to keep on her toes and be ready for anything.

So far, 'anything' included a nice long workout, and the rest of the chapter on early Mesopotamia. Ben seemed determined to make *really good* Philly cheese steaks for supper, to compensate for the greasy bar grub last night. Cheyenne would have preferred to compensate with something other than fatty red meat two nights running.

"Finally," Ben muttered.

She looked up from her textbook to see two figures trudging out of the woods. "D–!" She caught herself. It was indeed her friend Daneel from West Point, but he wouldn't be called that. "You rat!" she told Ben. "What's his name here?"

"No idea." He turned to greet the newcomers as they dragged up to the encampment. "Aw hell. You again. I'm Ben. My girlfriend Cheyenne."

Cheyenne noted that she'd been demoted back to girlfriend. Apparently Ben decided that their marriage of convenience only applied to the Sixers.

"Mike!" Daneel's older companion belted out with gusto. He was indeed older, somewhere north of forty, with grey-specked hair and a bald spot, and thick eye-distorting glasses in heavy black frames. A generous gut strained the buttons on his beige button-down shirt, worn with phone, pens, and pocket protector, over khaki chinos. Hiking boots and a neon orange down vest, much like Cheyenne's only uglier, were his concessions to the fact that he was outdoors hiking on a mountain. He didn't carry anything but a walking staff. Not a stick he picked up along the trail, but rather an actual, much-polished, Renaissance-Faire quality staff. The pewter knob on the top resembled a dragon head from a Viking long-ship.

Daneel carried all their gear, in a huge backpack. Half-black perhaps, with jaw-length smooth dark curls tacked back with pink barrettes today, Ava's old classmate lost no time dumping the pack. He flopped onto Darcy's tailgate hard enough to jounce the SUV on the diagonal. Ben winced. Daneel pulled off hiking boots and socks as fast as he could, tossing them at random.

"Jamal. Nice to meet you," he muttered.

"It's so great to see you again, Jamal!" Cheyenne finally got to say. She walked up to hug him to her chest. Hot and bothered as he was, that cheered him up. The familiar boyish grin beamed up at her.

Ben pursed his lips. "John."

"John," Mike agreed.

"How very white bread," John acknowledged sourly. "I've heard about your white gang, *Ben.*"

Mike scratched his butt. "John, I forgot to warn you. Ben's a bit of a neat freak."

"Yeah?" said Daneel-Jamal-John. "We all have our crosses to bear. Also tents. Couple computers. *Textbooks.* This cocksucker made me hump forty pounds over a fucking mountain. *Mike.*" Daneel proceeded to strip off his red wool plaid flannel shirt, whose arms were already torn off, then his T-shirt as well.

"Ben could do with less swearing, too," Ben mentioned. "My home. My rules."

John nodded at him. "You may kiss my ankle, Ben. Got anything to drink, Cheyenne?"

"I'll get you water."

John continued to strip down to boxers, which bore a cheerful Monopoly board print. "Got anything stronger?"

Mike chuckled. "No drinking! You're in the field now!" He looked very much like a computer science professor who thought this was all great fun. He probably was. Daneel was a wizard with computers and the meshnet.

"It's a field. I noticed," John said. "Mike? I'm a gavi, from Lawn Guyland. Remember? I spent two years *camping* during the Starve. Next time, I pack. You want to bring rocks? Then you carry the goldfish rocks. This is so unreasonable."

Cheyenne provided glasses of water to the newcomers. Then she set out her chips and dip within Daneel-John's reach.

Outsiders tended to think of the city gang rats and Long Island gavis – short for *gaviotas,* seagulls – as being the same. At West Point, she learned differently. The gangs of New York were highly organized, reaching into thousands of members. They lived in apartments. The gavis tended toward small nomadic bands, twenty at most, with people drifting in and out. They camped outdoors half the time.

"Oh, that's good!" Mike said with gusto, after a generously laden chip, dripping nacho sauce onto Darcy's tailgate. "See, John? This is why we didn't pack food from Hudson. Food coming out of their ears in PA. And Ben is like a gourmet cook. What's for dinner, Ben?" He rubbed his hands in happy anticipation.

Ben sighed, and set about it. "You have your own car lined up, Mike?"

"No. Your car is huge! And this is a joint training op."

"I was afraid of that."

"Cheyenne, got a bucket of water and some baby butt?" John requested.

"Yeah, sure." She wriggled into Darcy's hold again. Two men and snacks on the tailgate were in the way. Both frankly admired the view as her posterior passed their faces.

"Mind getting off my tailgate, Mike?" Ben suggested.

"Camp chairs? Hammock?" Mike asked. "My pants will get dirty on the ground."

Ben leveled a look at him. Mike got off the tailgate and remained standing. "You briefing, or me?" Ben asked.

"You're the senior agent in the field!" Mike assured him.

"Yeah? How long you been at this, Ben?" John inquired. He accepted Vitamin A&D lotion and a water bucket from Cheyenne with a happy smile, for her only.

"December under this boss. Few months under the old management, but the job was different. Mostly Apple ops."

"Outstanding," John muttered, unimpressed. He applied lotion to chafe spots on his torso. One sore foot took its turn in the bucket. "What did you do in the Apple?"

"Hey, some ground rules," Ben returned. "Outside the car, we stay in role. I'm a trader in PA. Never been to the Apple."

"Go teach your grandma to knit, man," John shot back.

Mike added, "Ah, John has an unusual degree of experience, Ben. I think you'll be impressed."

John dropped his boxers to apply lotion to his chafed privates.

"Hey, could you not flash my girlfriend?" Ben demanded.

John turned to moon him, bending down to attend to the rash between his thighs. "She's seen it before. Roomed with two guys at the Point. One blacker than me." John shot him a glare, upside-down past his thigh. The pink barrettes kept it less ferocious than it could have been. "Neo-Nazi prick."

Cheyenne pursed her lips to quell incipient laughter. "I am used to it," she told Ben.

With a few months rooming together, she and Doc and Cookie flashed each other all the time, and laughed about it. Those West Point dorm rooms were small. Her conscience twinged a bit, though. She loved Cade, she thought. But she still wasn't reconciled to his racist and anti-immigrant leanings. At West Point, what little sympathy she had for those views got stamped out pretty thoroughly. She lived and worked with blacks and Muslims and Hispanics in the Army. She honestly liked them these days, and appreciated their cultural differences.

"I'm not used to it, though." John sighed, pulling up his shorts and plonking back on the tailgate to rock Darcy hard. The other blistered foot got a turn in the bucket. "No chicks in my platoon. Sergeant Zapple got 'em all from my company," he confided to Cheyenne. "The guy sergeants couldn't deal with the girls coming on to them. Female men, sorry. Humping like bunnies! In the dorm rooms, showers, tack rooms, everywhere. It was fun while it lasted. Then off to the nunnery they went.

"One time, they mouthed off to Zapple about like, what were they supposed to do? A girl gets horny! So Zapple – you know how Zapple gets, so sincere. She puts together this formal training on masturbation for chicks. Diagrams, video, bullet points, X-rated movie clips. Earnest big sisterly advice, about how learning to get yourself off makes you a better lover with a man, too. Oh, to be a fly on that wall!"

Cheyenne and John clung together laughing out loud. Mike grinned from ear to ear.

Ben shook his head, arms crossed.

Still chuckling, John asked, "She never showed that presentation to other chicks in the brigade, huh? Wonder why!"

"No!" Cheyenne said, wiping tears of laughter from her eyes. "And you know damned well why! I bet that went well." It felt great to talk about old Hogwarts-on-Hudson again! She tried to tamp down her mirth under Ben's less than amused eye.

"You've never been to West Point. You're from PA," Ben reminded her. "Now, here's the training op."

11

Interesting fact: The months following the great Atlantic tsunami saw a historic drought in the Northeast, with scarcely a half inch of rain per month, compared to over 4 inches per month in a normal spring.

Ben eyed the open field, ringed by trees, in disfavor. "No, I don't want to discuss this outside. Into Darcy. You need to police up all your crap, John."

"Yeah, before it gets dark," Mike added.

"Mike? It's like an hour to dark," John returned. "I can tell that by the light on the dog-cursed mountain you just made me climb. You see how there's a low saddle to either side of that peak? You walk there. Idiot."

"I didn't want to get us lost," Mike defended. "We stayed on the compass bearing."

"Hell of a lot easier to follow a trail, knuckle-dragger. Even a game trail. I know orienteering. You don't. Next time I –"

"Stop," Ben interrupted. "Into Darcy, I said. Now. Police the camp after supper."

Cheyenne took a minute to erect the second seat in the second row. She sat back there with John-Daneel, to Ben's displeasure. She got the impression that Ben and Mike had been in the field together before, and she wasn't sure Ben liked him. She hoped Mike wasn't the agent who trained Ben in PA. She didn't know details, except that the trip had gone badly.

From the driver's seat, Ben said, "Alright. In here, and only in here, locked up tight. We can talk about stuff outside our cover identities. But stick to our current names. Makes it easier to stay in character."

Mike in the front passenger seat nodded sagely. John rolled his eyes and grinned at Cheyenne.

Ben continued. "John is training as a boffin, like Mike. Crypto… What is it you do, Mike?"

"Cryptography." Mike turned in the passenger seat to explain to Cheyenne behind him. "Computer science. Tapping communications, deciphering codes. Electronic surveillance and counter-surveillance –" He was warming to his subject.

"Mike's a top hacker," Ben summarized. "John's his new apprentice. Anyway, John, as an agent, you go into the field too."

"I'd kinda have to," John said unnecessarily. "To do my job."

Ben shot him a quelling glance in the rear-view mirror.

"Why would hackers need to go into the field?" Cheyenne asked.

John replied, "Military communications are hardened. They don't use mesh texts to launch nukes. You don't break in through the Internet and back doors. You tap directly into their closed networks, get their decryption keys, stuff like that."

"The keys especially," Mike said, nodding. "The actual orders don't go out hard-wired. But to listen in, we need to decrypt them. Get their magic decoder ring." He waggled his eyebrows, bouncing his glasses up and down.

"Got it. Thanks," Cheyenne said.

"So, Cheyenne, in an op like that," Ben said, "we might go in with them as protection. Or if it's less challenging, maybe back up one of them."

John bristled.

Ben held up a placating hand. "John, I know you're trained with a gun. But you can't do both at the same time, focus on the computer and watch for hostile natives. You're more valuable to us cracking codes. Cheyenne and I can't do the computer work. So we get you in and keep you safe while you make love to your keyboard or whatever."

John nodded a grudging fair-enough. "So what are we cracking?"

"This time out, we're not cracking anything," Ben said. "Probably. This is an easy training exercise, to give you a little experience in the field. You've been caught in the Apple Zone for years, right?"

"Yeah, except for West Point and Binghamton. Man, what a dull town."

"I love Binghamton," Mike said. "A lovely college community, Cheyenne. You'd like it there."

Ben sighed. "Point is, when you go out on the real thing, you want to have the basics down first. Like, not boggling at PA paper money. Don't say 'Penn' when a native would say 'PA.' Don't get weirded out because the women wear skirts, or thrown by the gas rationing system. Just simple orientation. So when you go into the field for real, you're not tripped up by simple stuff. You can focus on your hacking."

"Cool," John acknowledged.

"And it's an awful lot of fun," Mike added.

"You're such a dork, Mike," John replied.

"Well, yes."

Ben cleared his throat. "Last week, while I was teaching Cheyenne to drive –"

John brightened. "Oh, sweet! He let you drive this barge? Can I drive?"

"No. Focus, please. I'm trying to give you a briefing." Ben paused to underscore the point.

"Last week we ran into a farmer, Ron Kaminski, who gave Cheyenne a sign for something called 'Free Penn.' She guessed the countersign, 'Sylvania.' So we've got some kind of an 'in' on some resistance group. We want to know what they are. How big they are. What they want. How we can use them. Potential allies. Mind you, we don't greatly care. For all we know, it's a handful of old farmers bitching into their beer. So it works as a training op."

"Basic sting," John said. "Say we're Free Hudson. Fellow travelers from across the border. Trader Ben doesn't want to hear the details. Just introducing people who might want to know each other."

Ben's ice blue eyes narrowed in the rear-view mirror. Cheyenne got the impression he was taking John-Daneel's measure seriously for the first time. She was impressed herself.

"You've run stings before?" Ben asked.

John smiled sweetly. "A time or two."

"Really?" Cheyenne asked. At the Point, she could have sworn Daneel was the most bubbly, guileless, strangely innocent Apple recruit there. He was the first guy since Cade she felt attracted to. She even kissed him once. Not that she'd tell Ben that. She hoped Daneel wouldn't either. But he seemed rather contrary today.

John-Daneel grinned and squeezed her hand. "I'd never con you, baby."

Cheyenne frowned. Of the recruits at West Point, she alone had data access to the nets, paid for as a personal gift from Guzman, her community coordinator and personal friend back in Soho Village in Manhattan. The others could only send brief texts and postcards. She could attach files, even video if she wanted. Daneel hit her up to borrow her access all the time.

Ben asked Mike, "And we trust this weasel because?"

"Trust is such a relative term," said Mike.

"I'm more valuable than you are, Ben," John suggested.

"Modest, too," Ben said.

"He's in a bad mood," Mike allowed. "Maybe I shouldn't have made him 'hump a ruck' in here over the mountain." He chuckled.

"Yeah, and maybe you should stop lusting after my pretty mocha butt. Perv."

"Maybe you should stop getting naked and flashing your pretty mocha butt at me," Mike returned cordially. "Don't blame me for admiring the view."

"He's not gay?" Ben inquired. "Could have sworn you both were."

Cheyenne blinked. She hadn't realized either of them were gay.

"Why, are you two-timing sweet Cheyenne?" John asked. "I'm flexible. Charge extra for fascists and lard-belly leches. Cheyenne, doesn't

Mike remind you of that sergeant we got sacked back at the Point? Lard-Belly Burton."

She primly pressed her lips together. Only Mike's modest gut reminded her of the expelled sergeant. Mike seemed a bit gross and dorky, but human enough as scniles went. More pleasant than some Sixers, Badgers, hookers and bouncers she'd met since her arrival in PA.

She counted back, to her consternation. Had it only been five days? "Is it Tuesday?"

"It is," John agreed. "I know. Time flies. So much to learn on a new job."

"OK, con man," Ben said. "That's the specific op. The general objectives are to show you around, get us used to working together. We might go into VA together after orientation." He looked dejected at that prospect. "I can only spare you a few days. Cheyenne, you've learned a lot in PA. Why don't you bring John up to speed."

Cheyenne frowned. Was that the hint of a smirk she saw in Ben's eyes? He turned away again too fast for her to catch it. He hadn't eaten in a while, and Daneel – *John* – was deliberately provoking him. Maybe Ben was getting glittery again, her mental term for his fey cold-eyed mood.

"We should eat soon," she suggested.

"Are we all sleeping in Darcy?" Mike asked brightly.

"No," Ben said with finality. "You pitch a tent." He climbed out to make supper.

"Oh, awesome, me too!" John cried after dinner, when Cheyenne shared that she and Ben were taking Western Civ for college credit. "I mean, aside from all the computer science. We can take a break for a few days, right, Mike? Numerical analysis can wait."

"That would be wonderful!" Mike said with enthusiasm. "Like a seminar."

Cheyenne noted with amusement that Mike seemed to greet almost everything with enthusiasm. He'd given up on keeping his khaki trousers clean, to embrace the outdoor experience. He sat happily cross-legged on the ground, streaks of cheese steak grease and salad dressing crossing his thighs.

Because it would annoy Ben, John waited until the last possible minute, plus two, before setting up their tent. But true to his Long Island ecotopian roots, the structure went up lightning-fast, gear stowed, ready to pass the most exacting sergeant's inspection. He lined up their boots precisely outside. Because there would be no outdoor lighting, he squared the opening of the tent with the driver's door on Darcy, fifteen paces away. He washed face, hands, and armpits, and donned fresh white T-shirt and boxers – baby blue with puppies this time – all before presenting himself for evening seminar.

Ben cast a flashlight around the encampment. Aside from the obvious tent, and the toilet paper in a waterproof box by the latrine trench, not a thing was left loose outside Darcy, should they need to cut and run in a hurry. He nodded in satisfaction. "Good job, John."

"I brushed my teeth, too, Dad," John said, and showed off his clean teeth.

Ben smiled crookedly. "But I want you to stow your pack in the SUV. Anything you don't need overnight. You said computers and textbooks. In an emergency, we can ditch the tent, but not those. You have a gun in there?"

They didn't, so Cheyenne loaned them her M-4 carbine. John was well-trained with it in boot camp. John swapped the rifle into their tent and retrieved the deflated backpack. It was significantly smaller without the tent and sleeping bags.

For seminar, the three youths shared the air bed and their single copy of the textbook, with pictures. Ben methodically led off with a question from the back of chapter one, about the Great Flood. For John's turn, he led a discussion about a beer-based diet, and how that made people different in the ancient Near East.

Mike, sitting squeezed between the front seats facing backward, surprised them by knowing this stuff.

"General knowledge," he said with a wave. "I am a college professor. Was." They'd spent a while on the beer, so he turned to her. "Cheyenne? Your topic next."

She ruefully realized she should have been expecting that. She could always punt and pick the next discussion item from the book. But then she thought of something. "I guess, relate that, society in the Neolithic and ancient Near East, to now. With technology kind of falling apart. If it is. And what that means for women. If that made sense?"

Mike beamed approval. "Wonderful! John, how do you see the role of women changing?"

The eighteen, nineteen, and twenty year olds did a lot of head-scratching and brainstorming and flipping through pages. But it was a fascinating topic. Ben was regretful when he kicked out the geeks for bed at 10 o'clock, later than they usually called it a night.

It was pitch black out, and the wind was fierce. Heavy clouds had rolled in. Cheyenne thought it smelled of rain and ozone, but that was probably just a tease. There had been precious little rain since the tsunami.

～

AVA JUMPED OUT OF HER SEAT-TURNED-BED IN THE SECOND ROW, FROM sound asleep to high adrenaline, heart pounding, in an instant. Darcy's three alarms were tolling, and rain hit the side of the SUV in sheets. Was that the wind knocking the car?

No. Mike's face appeared pressed to her window in panic. She opened the door to let him in, while Ben persuaded Darcy to shut up.

"Where's John?" Ava-Cheyenne asked, as the dripping Mike clambered past her. He couldn't have been more wet if he'd jumped into a swimming pool.

"He dove under the car." Mike stuck his head out the door again, cautiously opened only a crack to keep the rain out. "John? Come on out!"

No response. Ben gave Mike a towel to strip into. Cheyenne grabbed a flashlight and hopped into the rain. Their guests' tent was pancaked, sleeping bags trailing out. She squatted down by the driver's door and shone the light underneath, hand shielding her eyes from the deluge.

John lay curled in a fetal position behind the front wheel, hands over his ears. *Crisis,* she thought. She reached out a tentative hand and lay it gently on his muddy ankle. He immediately jerked it away, and retreated farther under the SUV, beside the far wheel.

"Daneel? It's me, Panic." *Screw Ben's rules. Daneel needs the familiar.* "It's OK, Daneel. Come inside where it's safe." She sighed. He couldn't hear her, freaked out like this. She lay the flashlight on the ground, pointing under the car, and shimmied down through the mud to reach him. She placed her hand over his, over his ear, gently but firmly. "Daneel. You're OK. You're with me."

He lurched, but grabbed her hand. He was shaking all over. *Definitely in crisis.* Lightning flashed, and then thunder almost immediately. *That one was close.* Cheyenne could smell the ozone, almost hear the sizzle of electricity vaporizing sheets of rain. Daneel reacted by grabbing her around the shoulders, his whole body heaving.

Dammit. From this position, there was no way she could pull him out from under the car. She had to get him to cooperate. "Shh, you're alright," she soothed, stroking his face and hair. "You're safe. Just come inside the car with me. Daneel? Please? I'm cold out here." Indeed, their teeth were chattering. The temperature had fallen to around 45 degrees and they were sopping wet.

Gradually Daneel allowed himself to be coaxed. They rolled out of cover together, and piled in through the right passenger doors. Daneel curled up into a ball again instantly. Cheyenne never stopped moving. She stripped out of her sopping t-shirt and shorts and panties, ignoring Mike. Ben passed her a couple towels, dry panties, and one of his sweatshirts to warm up in. While she changed, he found some of his clothes to lend John. They were close enough to the same size. Ben ducked out and retrieved their flashlight as well.

Half dry and much warmer, Cheyenne slipped onto the middle console between the front seats. From there she ministered to Daneel, getting him out of his wet things and into Ben's dry sweats. His teeth stopped chattering, but the shudders didn't subside, and he still hadn't spoken.

Mike, hesitant to interrupt, handed her an inhaler. "He's asthmatic," he explained. "So am I. I needed it myself."

Cheyenne didn't know how to work the inhaler, so Mike demonstrated. Then she helped Daneel apply a dose. His catching breaths seemed to ease almost instantly. As instructed, she waited out a minute, stroking his face for calm, then applied the inhaler again. Mike said it took two rounds for one dosing. The first opened the airways enough that the second inhale could reach deeper into the lungs. After that, his shudders seemed to ease off a little.

She tucked a blanket around him that Mike passed up from her bedding. And she launched into some soft-voiced stories from West Point, featuring Ava's friends Fox and Sauce, people Daneel knew from their GED prep class.

Ben got Mike settled on a second-row seat, and stowed all the wet things away. He gave Cheyenne a quick good-night peck, and withdrew back to his own bed.

Eventually she fell asleep in the driver's seat, still holding Daneel's hand. He didn't volunteer why the car alarm set him off. She didn't ask.

12

Interesting fact: Temperatures that spring were cool but not record-breaking.
Unfortunately, the season brought many late frosts and hard freezes.

"This is why I hate tents," Ben muttered in the morning. The muddy clothes and bedding they'd rinsed and hung up on a clothesline. The prospect of it all hung to dry inside his orderly beloved car wasn't improving his outlook.

He decided to hang the tent and sleeping bags to dry on some trees, and just leave them. Cheyenne helped him do it. The camping gear would still be here when they got back, or it wouldn't. It would dry, or it could stay here forever. John couldn't hike out of here carrying all that wet fabric. It was too heavy.

Cheyenne didn't think she could manage his pack even dry. But he assured her he kept it under 30 pounds. And it was only three miles to their car on the other side of the border. She could manage that. She'd managed 35 pounds and 6 miles in basic training, minus the mountain. Though she took a lot of painkillers afterward. She pressed a few more on John, who took them in sad resignation. He was subdued and moved stiffly this morning.

Ben waited until after morning workouts and breakfast to broach difficult subjects, softly. "John? Last night. Was it the thunder, or the car alarms?"

"I have trouble with both," John admitted bitterly. "Don't usually lose it like that. Sorry."

"Sorry isn't what this is about," Ben assured him. "No damage, no blame. Just wonder if we should run the car alarms now. Desensitize you."

John's back straightened. He was breathing raggedly just thinking about it.

"Give me the key," Cheyenne requested. Ben tossed it to her. "In your control, John. See?" She placed the key fob in his hand. She showed him the button presses that would turn the alarms on, then off, without generating any actual noise.

John swallowed nervously, but she stroked his lower back and stayed beside him. Ben and Mike remained quiet, and kept their eyes averted to let her handle this.

"Need your inhaler first?" she offered. He nodded jerkily, so she fetched it from the backpack and let him get more comfortable.

"I get panic attacks," she shared. "Fr – Ben taught me to control them. Breathe out, your lungs breathe in by themselves. Learned a lot of other techniques at West Point. Still sucks, but I deal. I had it real bad the other day, when Ben taught me to drive." She prattled on, about how Ben was such a patient teacher, and strolled next to the car, to make sure she had a win.

John squeezed her thigh. "It's OK, Pan – Cheyenne. You've talked me down enough. On three. One, two, three." Darcy squealed for less than a second before he cut her off.

"See? You're in control," Cheyenne pointed out. She winced in sympathy as he wiped sweaty palms on his jeans.

"Not by much," he muttered.

"Good, John," Ben said. "This next time, leave the alarm on for the count of two alligators. Then cut it off. Two seconds."

John did it again. Cheyenne supposed it was possible to say *alligator* that fast. She was freshly impressed with Ben's patience as a teacher, as he made John alternate between two seconds, and one second, of blaring noise, working up to ten seconds, for ten minutes.

"How much longer do I need to do this?" John complained.

"Are you bored yet?" Ben replied. "Bored isn't panic. Bored isn't in crisis. Bored is a major improvement. Congratulations. You're getting past this. Really."

John tossed him the electronic dongle with key. "Sure. If you say so." He looked disgusted enough with himself to cry if no one was watching.

"John, criticizing yourself makes it worse," Cheyenne said gently.

"Yeah, well, you're brave and strong," John argued. "I'm nineteen and crippled for life. A survivalist world, and I'm only suited for a desk job. Never know whether the next inhaler will kill me."

"Oh, I can show you that," Cheyenne said. She hopped up and retrieved a black light and invisible marker from Darcy. She wrote 'John' on his inhaler and showed it to him. "The doctored drugs are marked somewhere, like this."

Mike crowded in to see. He didn't say anything. But everyone worried when they took medication these days.

"I don't think we doctor asthma meds," Ben said. "But yeah. Any poisoned drugs would be marked. John? Take another couple jogs around the clearing to clear the adrenaline. Cheyenne, pace him. Then let's pack up and move out." He glumly contemplated the clothesline again.

Cheyenne figured it was a 50-50 chance Ben would ditch his plans for the day in favor of a laundromat. She gave him a peck on the forehead and grinned at his answering glower.

"What happened the other day?" John-Daneel asked, while they stretched before their jog. "I got you more info on your platoon. But you stopped responding."

"Not supposed to communicate with anyone during training," Cheyenne said. "We were in the middle of something anyway." As they started jogging, Cheyenne told him what she'd been up to since crossing the border, in rich detail.

"Wow," John said, after she finished telling him about Angie and the truck stop. "My life's been pretty dull in Binghamton. I live and work with Mike. End story. Well, his computer setup is pretty cool. Learning a lot. But you wouldn't be interested."

They both laughed. Back at the Point, Daneel tried to explain to Panic what he was doing and how the meshnet worked. Usually she begged him to stop. She loved electronics, but the communications protocols seemed endlessly intricate and boring, rich in fidgety details.

"Had enough?" she asked. They'd run 25 minutes and her endorphins were singing nicely. They stopped for a cool-down at the farthest point in the field away from Darcy. "So what else about my platoon? Ben still has my phone."

"Your boyfriend is pretty high-handed," John said.

Cheyenne bristled. "He had to be."

He held his hands out in surrender. "Sorry. Not my place to judge. Uh, your squad. Puño, Cookie, and Doc are team leaders, and a guy from Midtown. Marquis, that his name? He's kind of assistant paper-pusher for the sarge. Like a squad exec, if there is such a thing. Fox says the new squad sergeants need breaking in with a baseball bat. They're regular Army. Have trouble fitting in. But your old sergeant, Calderon? He's cluing them in, and the LT. Getting it from all sides. I don't envy him. Uh, a couple of them have wives. The wives chose to stay in their villes. And Yoda claims to be deliriously happy back home in Tribeca. Monday was supposed to be his first day walking a militia beat."

Through her familiar army stomach crunches, Cheyenne drank it all in, homesick for her friends from West Point. She lived and worked with her room-mates Cookie and Doc 24/7 for months. Most of the rest sat at her 'home table,' sharing three meals a day together, plus the day's exercises. Being back with Cade was great. But she sorely missed her unit at the Point.

"Awful quiet over there," John prodded, with a grin.

"Thanks, John," she replied with a smile. "And your old crew? You homesick for them, like I miss mine?"

He shook his head. "Not really. It's tough for them to be back on the Island. So close to home, but in uniform. Gavis look at them different, you know? They joined the enemy."

"We joined the enemy, too," Cheyenne breathed.

"Our enemy pays better."

"Doesn't bother you? What we're doing?"

He looked at her in surprise, and laughed. "I hack communications. Believe me, I've done worse. Why? Big Bad Ben leading you into evil deeds?"

Cheyenne flipped over to start her push-ups. John didn't bother. He sat cross-legged waiting for her to finish. Unlike her, he had no plans to maintain a boot camp level of fitness. He was done with that.

She replied, "No. Don't call him names. You don't know him."

"Yeah. Sorry. Seriously, though, Cheyenne. What you've done since you've been here? I wouldn't lose sleep over it. Even poisoned oxycontin. I mean, the drugs were poisoned Before. The drug cartels benefited. It wouldn't work, except people choose to take them. So the company causes order instead of chaos, and the junkies still get their fix."

She considered that, brushing dirt off her hands. "I don't feel good about it," she concluded. She rose decisively, and reached a hand down to pull John up. "But there would have been bad compromises in the Soho militia, too. And here, I'm with Ben." She met his eye, lips pursed.

John laughed. "OK, OK. No more criticizing your guy."

~

CHEYENNE CRACKED A POOL CUE ACROSS THE NOSE ON ONE OF HER attackers. Literally cracked – it was a cheap pool cue. She tossed it aside and leapt onto the pool table. Her feet made better weapons. Unfortunately one of the heftier rednecks heaved onto the table to grab at her. The pool table legs collapsed under his onslaught.

I could use Big Bad Ben right about now. But after they arrived in somnolent Towanda PA, Ben insisted they make their own way around town. He settled on his bed to review geometry, while they set off to persuade someone to lend them their washer and dryer. There was no laundromat.

She dove over the man's head and somersaulted down his back, pressing him into the wreckage. On the floor, she snatched up Mike's broken glasses, which he was helplessly patting around the floor to find.

"We need to get out of here!" she told him. She grabbed his elbow to guide him. A chair's legs came at them. She kicked them back into an attacker's face. The chair leg splintered, too. *This bar sure uses lousy wood,* she thought.

Daneel – John – finally made it around the pool table to cover Mike's other side. They had their backs to booths set along the front windows. So far the booth patrons seemed inclined to shrink back from the fight and protect their beers.

What would Ben do? Cheyenne wondered. She decided the bar was too hostile for buying a round of beers to work. Alas, after supper in a park alongside the scenic Susquehanna River, Ben settled onto his bed again and dispatched them to check out the bar for some fun. Where some rednecks decided to take exception to the sort-of-black John escorting the lily-white Cheyenne.

No one paid much attention to Mike.

The bartender held the door open to speed her group on their way. "Wimpy fruitcakes," he commented toward the guys. "Good thing you had your little lady to protect you."

John flipped him the bird. Mike didn't register that someone was trying to insult him.

"Fun little dive you have here," Cheyenne replied. "Invest in better furniture, man."

"Nah, just gets broken." He slammed the door behind them.

Cheyenne peered through the door to see if anyone was piling out after them to continue the argument. So far the barkeep was blocking the doorway.

"We better get gone," she said, pulling Mike along the downtown street. What passed for a downtown in Towanda, PA, at least. According to Ben, this little burgh was county seat and third largest 'borough' in Bradford County, though it was half the size of tiny Sayre. Cheyenne forgot to ask what the difference was between a 'borough' and a 'town.' She'd only ever heard the six huge wards of the Apple called 'boroughs' before. They had populations around two million apiece before the epidemic.

She turned the corner and pulled up short. Then she thought better of stopping here and continued to mid-block. She put a building behind her in case they had visitors. Mike and John followed her lead willingly enough.

"How much further to the car?" Mike asked. By the light of a pocket flashlight, he was trying to put his glasses together more by feel than sight.

John caught on and took the glasses away from him. He guided Mike's hand to point the light at the right place. "I thought Ben was parked on this block," he murmured.

"Yeah. Me, too," Cheyenne agreed. *Is this another test?* she wondered.

The door behind them opened a crack, still chained. A gruff voice called out, "What are you doing in my doorway? Get lost! Vagrants!"

"Yes, excuse us," she said politely. "My friend is repairing some glasses. My other friend can't see without them."

"Ask for some duct tape," John suggested. He kept his back to the door, hunched over the glasses. Which Cheyenne figured was just as well, since his lip was bleeding.

"Would you happen to have any tape?" Cheyenne asked sweetly, with what she hoped was an appealing smile. Unlike the others, she had no blood on her face or clothes. On second thought, she tucked her knuckles into her hunting vest pockets.

"Get lost! Before I call the cops!" the local replied, and shut the door.

"Just another minute," John muttered. "Got a hair band? Anything?"

Cheyenne unfastened a pony-tail elastic from her French braided hair and handed it to him. "There's glue in the car. We need to move."

No one had come around the corner from the bar yet. Unfortunately, Darcy was nowhere in sight either.

"We ought to stay where Ben can find us," Mike said worriedly.

"Mm, no," Cheyenne said. "He's not expecting us at any particular time. Maybe it's the next block."

"It was this block," John said. He handed the glasses to Mike. "Be careful, the left lens is chipped in the corner. The other left. Right."

"Ow," Mike said, and sucked blood from his cut finger. "No wonder you can't pass the English section on the GED exam."

"Kiss my butt, Mike," John returned. "I fixed your glasses. You're welcome."

Mike tried to find a way to get the brown hair band from crossing the exact center of his left-right lens.

"Let us stroll, gentlemen," Cheyenne insisted, dragging Mike along.

"It's a progressive lens," Mike objected. "I only have a prescription through the center."

"Use your other eye," Cheyenne growled. "Or I'll pop the lens out and put it in my pocket."

"I –" Mike conceded defeat in mid-word and relied on her to lead him.

"He doesn't see as well out of the other eye," John supplied on his behalf.

Cheyenne spotted three bruisers from the bar coming around the corner. "Jog now, Mike." They took a left around the corner and kept jogging. John and Cheyenne frequently had to save Mike from falling. Cheyenne almost went down herself on the uneven sidewalk in the pitch-dark street. Here, a block back from the single-story brick downtown drag, they were already into old two-story wood-frame houses, set back in their lawns. No doubt it was charming in daylight. At the moment, it was just dark, with rare gleams of dull light from curtained second-floor windows.

Mike flicked on his pocket light.

Cheyenne snatched it and stuffed it into her pocket. "We're trying to be inconspicuous."

"That's going well," John said.

Indeed, they'd been about as conspicuous as it was possible to be, all day long. Asking a police officer for directions to the laundromat. Knocking on doors offering to pay for a load of laundry. After a few doors, Cheyenne decided to try knocking on a door solo, which worked. The locals didn't respond so well to John and Mike asking to invade their homes. She suspected Ben would have called that cheating. She was supposed to be their backup, not their front woman.

"Shut up, John," she said.

"So if you were your boyfriend, where would you hide?" he retorted.

She turned left on the next street, back toward the main drag. "If Ben's hiding, we won't find him."

"Ben wouldn't leave without telling me," Mike said. "I hope we didn't miss him at the bar."

Cheyenne stopped short again. No bar toughs were in sight for the moment, and they were almost back to the main street. "Damn. I'm doing this wrong. I'm only along for protection. You guys are supposed to figure this out."

"John?" Mike prompted his trainee.

"I got nothing," John replied. "The river walk is back there. Might have benches to sleep on."

"No," Mike said. "Something's gone wrong. Ben would have made rendezvous. Could we be on the wrong street?"

John sighed. "Wait here." He walked stealthily up to the brick-clad boarded storefront corner and peeked around in both directions. He did this a few times. Cheyenne watched the other direction.

John rejoined them. "There's one car on the street that could be Darcy. Two blocks that way." He pointed away from the pool hall. "It's dark. No lights inside."

"Cheyenne, as our backup, I'm asking your opinion," Mike said. "Can we walk directly to that car?"

"Don't see why not," she said. "If someone comes out of the bar, they're a block behind us."

"Let's go, then," John decided. "You watch our back, Cheyenne? I'll take Mike and front."

As they strolled a downtown block of a tiny sleeping town, Cheyenne felt downright silly. She dutifully kept glancing back toward the bar for would-be pursuers. *I used to be a gang queen bee, honest. I ran the most dangerous streets in America, even though I was starving then. This podunk town is nothing.* Then again, those rednecks were by no means underfed. She was awfully small to protect two grown men against a half dozen big bruisers. Stealth was prudent. She still felt like an idiot. *What next? Scurry up to the police station and beg the nice officer to protect me? It's 9 p.m. They're probably asleep.*

"Hello," John said softly.

Cheyenne glanced forward to see their target vehicle on the move, without headlights. *What the hell, Frosty? Ben.* That seemed unlike her fastidious boyfriend, to drive without lights. Belatedly, the low beams came on, flashed to high once, and down again.

The car pulled to a stop across from them, and cut the lights again. It was indeed Darcy. Ben put the window down a crack, and called in a voice that barely reached across the road, "Get in. Silently."

That's weird, she thought. Belatedly, she recalled her bodyguard assignment. "Careful here, guys," she murmured. "This is way off."

She decided to claim the front passenger seat, and let John make sure Mike got through the back door. She slid in easily, and didn't realize anything was wrong until she heard a gurgling noise behind her.

She looked back between the seats. A guy buffed like special ops had his hand over John's mouth and a knife at his throat, between the seats. Mike sat very still behind Ben. She caught the glint of other eyes among the mounded darkness in the back.

"Hi, there," she said to the guy who held John. "Honey, who are your new friends?" she asked Ben.

13

Interesting fact: Beer was more discovered than invented. Grain ferments spontaneously from wild airborne yeast. Chinese peasants were brewing by 7000 B.C.

"Drive," the man holding John instructed.

"Alright," Ben said. He turned on the headlights and drove placidly out of the tiny town. "Where to? State Game Land on the border suit you?"

Cheyenne blinked. *Since when did car-jackers take suggestions from the victim?*

"Is that close?" John's captor asked.

"Ten miles," Ben said.

"Alright. There, then."

Cheyenne craned around to frown at John in concern. "You know, those guys are both asthmatic. They need their inhalers." She flipped open the glove compartment to rummage, surreptitiously retrieving a Glock. During the day, they kept both pistols up front now. "It's not up here. Must be in their backpack."

Ben rolled down his window an inch. "It's getting kinda close in here, with seven people," he remarked apologetically.

Cheyenne nodded agreement. *Three assailants in the back. Don't shoot in the car,* she readily interpreted Ben's message.

"This car seats eight," the goon countered.

"We removed four seats for cargo space," Cheyenne explained. "Please. Let John go. And pass me up the big backpack. You ever seen an apple go into crisis?"

"Huh?"

Huh, what? Cheyenne wondered. *Not from around here? I can test that.* "An apple is a survivor of New York City. Crisis is when something sets off his PTSD."

"Huh. Alright, pass it up."

Someone from Hudson or eastern PA should have said he knew that. Where are you guys from?

Cheyenne let John hold the backpack for her. He shifted it around. She hoped he found a knife or something while she stuck an arm in to fish out his medicine.

John was indeed breathing shallowly, as his captor removed the hand from his mouth so John could apply his breathing treatment. After his second lungful, Cheyenne met his eye and traded nods. He handed off the inhaler to Mike, who also gratefully took a couple doses.

Ben suggested, "I could drive a little faster, if everyone could take a seat."

John was shoved into the seat behind Cheyenne. "Buckle up," his captor growled. "We're good back here. Drive faster."

"I didn't catch your name?" Cheyenne attempted again. "I'm Cheyenne. That's Ben, John, and Mike."

The guy snorted.

Ben answered quietly, "He's Garcia. Jamal and KT are in the back. Just met them tonight. Drove down to the river to take a leak —"

"Shut up and drive," Garcia said.

Cheyenne reached across and gave Ben's thigh a reassuring squeeze. He squeezed her hand in return, then suddenly veered the car badly, both hands back on the wheel.

"Sorry. Deer," Ben said. "Getting tough to drive at night."

Garcia grudgingly gave up crouching and applied his butt to the floor. The unseen men behind him appeared to be seated as well.

After a few minutes, Mike said anxiously, "I need a potty break. Or I'll soil my pants."

Ben slowed to a stop on the shoulder of the state highway. Any paved road through the wooded hills here qualified as a state highway. Cheyenne noted that all signs of the slight population of Towanda had fallen behind them. They were alone on the road.

Mike jumped out and crossed the street to see to his bio needs.

"I didn't give you permission to stop," Garcia groused.

Ben returned, "Not letting him do it in my car." He got out, taking his key, and Cheyenne followed his lead.

"Hey!" Garcia barked.

"Stretching," Ben said.

The goon trio piled out and split up to cover their victims. A white guy, presumably KT, followed Mike to supervise. Mike crashed mostly blind, downslope through underbrush, seeking some privacy.

John quietly opened his door as well, on the shoulder side, and kept it ajar. Cheyenne tried to pass him the Glock before any captors made it to them, but he declined.

A half moon in a clear sky provided the only light. That cast crisp black shadows and prevented eyes from adjusting to the dark.

Ben stepped around off the highway to envelop Cheyenne in a hug. "Don't injure them," he murmured in her ear. "Much."

"Break it up!" Garcia demanded, following him around the front fender. The black guy, Jamal, approached from the back.

"Now," Ben said mildly, releasing Cheyenne from the clutch with a faint smile. They pushed off each other and spun.

Cheyenne moved wide to the left. Following the side of the car, Jamal didn't see John's door. John slammed it into his hip.

"Oh, wow, man, sorry!" John cried, closing the door partway again. "I didn't mean it! Don't hurt me!" He shoved the door open again into the man.

Cheyenne caught Jamal with a roundhouse to the back of the knee while he was distracted. He went down to the other knee, swearing. Cheyenne hopped up and gave him a straight kick to the back of his shoulder, sending him into the door again. Then she climbed onto his back and tried to throttle him.

This was no amateur opponent, though, but a 180-pound skilled fighter in great training, all muscle. He growled and easily rose with her. He threw himself backwards at the car to try to dislodge her. But he didn't think to hold onto her legs. Cheyenne happily stepped on his head as she climbed him onto Darcy's roof.

"You little b–" Jamal stopped speaking abruptly as she aimed her Glock between his eyes. He tried to dance away.

She shot two bullets past his ears. "Stop moving," she suggested. "All set, Ben?" she inquired. She'd heard a few thunks and grunts from that direction, but hadn't been free to observe.

"Yeah."

She heard another kick, and a gun skittered on the road.

"I've got this one hostage!" KT called, stumbling with difficulty out of the trees. That side dropped precipitously from the road bed. He was trying to hold Mike, aim a gun, push Mike up a wooded embankment, and climb the bluff himself, simultaneously.

"Give it up," Ben said. He swooped to the ground and plucked up Garcia's pistol. Ben was tidy that way. Without pausing in the movement, he strode across the street still talking. "You're not going to kill my egghead. So drop the gun before I reach you."

KT didn't, so Ben rushed him, faking a kick, then dodged left and caught the guy with a straight karate chop across the gun-wielding wrist. KT loosed his hold on Mike, who promptly curled to the ground and rolled back downhill to escape the fray.

Then Ben kicked KT, a full-powered front kick straight to the sternum, which due to the slope, was at Ben's waist height. KT staggered down the embankment as well, though several feet to Mike's left. Ben collected another gun, and gave Mike a hand up.

"Is he…?" Mike asked, jerking his chin toward KT.

"Don't worry. He can't breathe right now," Ben assured him.

"Enough, ha-ha!" Garcia called out, now struggling to his feet. "You did alright, kid. Game over."

Ben shot three bullets at him, without pausing his stride. The first was a foot in front, spraying asphalt at Garcia, the others to each side, much the same way Cheyenne had bracketed Jamal.

"I need to discuss this with my boss," Ben said calmly. "You'll wait outside the car. Everyone who's with me, get in. Jamal, go stand with Garcia."

"Hey, kid –" Garcia started to argue. He stepped forward.

Ben shot the road again exactly where he had before. This time, Garcia's foot was only an inch from the hole. Garcia raised his hands and backed up. He signaled Jamal to join him, since Jamal's ears weren't working quite yet.

Mike clambered into the car. John was already in. Cheyenne fired another shot to encourage Jamal to hurry up and follow instructions. Once he was past her, she dropped from the roof and climbed in. Ben had opened the driver's door and stood in it, using the doorframe to steady his aim. Once Cheyenne was in, he jumped in as well.

He stuck the key in the ignition. As fast as Darcy could start moving, he drove straight at Garcia and Jamal They dove for the upslope side of the road, and Ben swerved to miss them. He hit the gas.

"Game over?" Cheyenne inquired.

"We should probably talk to the boss," Ben conceded. He made no move to do so. He continued driving as fast as the winding frost-heaved night-dark deer-infested road would permit, maybe 45 mph.

Darcy pinged an incoming message. Ben scowled at the console. She pinged again. He flipped the bird at the dash camera.

"So, Skull sent us goons to play with?" Cheyenne hazarded.

"That's what they said," Ben agreed.

"Incoming message –" Darcy announced pleasantly.

Skull started talking before Darcy finished. "Ben. Go back and get them. Exercise over. Time to talk."

Ben considered that, not slowing. "I'll feel more chatty in the morning. Maybe in a public place. Sayre town square."

"You left them without transportation," Skull noted. "Weapons? Gear?"

"They said they were ex-Navy SEALs. They can deal," Ben claimed.

"Ben, I can see you're still driving away," Skull said. "Stop. And go back for them. That's an order."

Grudgingly, Ben slowed the SUV to a stop on the shoulder.

Cheyenne decided to barge into this conversation. "Boss? I'm confused. Why did Navy deserters car-jack Ben while we were in the bar?"

"You weren't with him?" Skull asked in concern. "Ben, they got the drop on you alone?"

"Yes."

"Oh…"

"Jamal keyed my car," Ben said. "Right by the driver's door. So I can see his scratch on Darcy's paint job every day. They already had me immobilized. What kind of asshole keys a guy's car right in front of him?"

"Your car?" John said in disbelief. "You're not worried about Cheyenne, for instance. Or us!"

"Cheyenne can take care of herself," Ben growled. "Darcy was an innocent bystander."

Cheyenne interrupted again stubbornly. "Boss? Who were these goons? They weren't Hudson."

Skull sighed. "I'm trying to put together a team for…ah, an operation in VA. These ex-SEALS were available. They had doubts about teaming up with gaunt kids. So I sent them to meet you."

"This is why I wanted backup," Ben muttered. "Someone to have my back. So I can take a leak safely. In the middle of town."

"If they were testing you," Skull agreed, "waiting til you were alone and then jumping you three on one, wasn't very sporting."

"I don't want to team with them," Ben said.

"They have skills," Skull said.

"John got one with a car door," Ben said. He belatedly turned and offered a hand-shake to John-Daneel. "Nice move, John."

"Thank you," John replied. "But Cheyenne got him under control. Didn't see what you did to Garcia. You took him down too fast."

"He assumed I was afraid of his gun," Ben explained. "I wasn't."

Cheyenne frowned. "Guys? We couldn't take down three SEALs. They were just testing us."

Ben nodded an annoyed true-enough.

"Boss?" Mike said. "I feel much safer with Ben than…them."

"Understood, Mike," Skull said. "This is a different op. After yours. Not a two-person job, Ben. I need you to go back and make nice. See if you can get past this and work with them." He paused.

Ben didn't respond, just stared into his rear-view mirror.

"Ben, that's an–" Skull started.

Cheyenne spoke at the same time, though. "Ben, were they that rude? Before they caught us? I mean, aside from keying the car. That was rude. But Darcy takes pings off the road all the time."

Head laid on the headrest, Ben rolled his face around to glare at her.

"They're hurt, Ben. I'm not," she pointed out. "You're not. John, Mike, you OK back there?"

They assured everyone they were fine.

"We'll each have a pistol," she continued. "John and I can take the carbines onto Darcy's roof while we chat. Stand them in front of the car again. Car bowling." She grinned.

Ben cracked a reluctant half-smile at that.

"Car bowling?" Skull inquired.

"It's all good, boss," Cheyenne assured him. "We'll go back and chat with them. Might toss their gear off a bluff."

"You'll talk to me," Cheyenne asserted, lying on top of Darcy beside John, with Ben's AK-47 pointed at the car-jackers standing obediently in the headlights. "Ben is still cranky about Jamal keying his car." She sighted Jamal down her rifle. "That was an asshole move, Jamal."

"That mother can kick," Jamal defended. "He got me in the nerve plexus of my thigh."

"Garcia?" Cheyenne said. "Could you please kick Jamal in the thigh? Or his nuts. It would make Ben feel better."

KT moved first, and got Jamal's thigh plexus with a sharp knee.

"Thank you, KT," Cheyenne purred. "So tell me. Who are you people?"

"Need to know," replied Garcia.

"Yes. I do need to know," Cheyenne agreed. "Tell me. Or we'll throw your gear down the bluff and be done with you."

"Skull said –"

"Ben leads this team. We came back to chat, because Skull wants us to chat. Start chatting, or we're done."

Garcia relented. "We were Navy SEALs. After the tsunami, the Navy bugged out for Hudson. We stayed behind, loyal to VA. We've been rethinking that. Now we're freelance."

"How long have you been freelance?" Cheyenne asked. The Eastern Navy agreed to make its new home in Hudson a month ago. The tsunami was two months back.

"This would be our first job," Garcia admitted.

"And in the meantime?"

"We worked for Admiral O'Hara out of D.C. But we lost faith in her. She had us do some bad stuff. Our unit. So the three of us peeled off."

Cheyenne knew that O'Hara was the Governor-Admiral of Greater Virginia, analogous to Governor-General Cullen, ruler of Hudson, and Taibbi in Pennsylvania. Except Penn and Hudson were well managed. O'Hara refused to take climate change seriously. She posed Greater VA as the rightful successor to the United States. Instead of restructuring to face new conditions, she tried to play business as usual. Poor VA didn't stand a chance against the tsunami. It practically washed over the Delmarva Peninsula, drowned Norfolk and Virginia Beach forever, and barreled up Chesapeake Bay, flattening cities and nuclear plants. Even with martial law firmly established, Cheyenne knew Jersey lost 50,000 civilians to violence after the tsunami, as people fled the coast, before order was restored.

Virginia never had that order in the first place. Once 12 million panicked civilians were on the rampage, it was a bit too late to institute control.

"In Hudson, they say O'Hara was a fool," Cheyenne acknowledged.

"We were patriots," Garcia said bitterly. "Loyal to the United States."

"And you're trying to join the company?" Cheyenne wasn't sure what to call their company in this context. *Does he know he's working for the death angels?*

"Just a contract, for starters. Help you navigate VA. Perform an extraction."

"Alright. I don't know anything about that job. This is a training unit. Half of us are new hires. What do you want from us tonight?"

"You're a new hire?" KT blurted.

"New to the company," Cheyenne agreed. "My second week. This is an orientation field trip. And you mugged my trainer three on one. Big bad scary jerks." In irritation, she shot a round over their heads. "Ben is my boyfriend."

"We didn't realize you'd split up at first," Garcia said. "Then we decided it would be a demonstration. We'd keep the upper hand so nobody got hurt."

"And did we learn anything?" Cheyenne inquired sourly.

"You're better than we thought," Garcia conceded. "Look, could we just go camp for the night together? Get to know each other without guns pointed at each other. Start over."

"I'm not feeling warm and fuzzy. How about you, John? Would you sleep well with them?"

"Sooner shoot them," John agreed beside her.

"Look, you've got our gear and our guns," Garcia argued. "Our car is back in Towanda. We behave, and we get a ride back into town and our gear back. We're just looking for a job. We have every reason to behave."

"You're deserters," John pointed out.

Cheyenne sighed. "But we're only the trainees." She thumped three times on the roof. "Ben? What do you want to do?"

He cut the headlights. "Get in," he growled. "Cheyenne, John, keep them covered while they're in the car."

The three muscle-bound SEALs looked ridiculous seated together on the floor, their backs to Ben's air mattress, leaning on edge against the wall. Cheyenne was afraid their bulk would pop it if they sat on it.

Any extra guns were stowed in the front passenger seat with Mike. She and John sat backwards in the second row seats keeping the SEALs covered with pistols, which no one wanted to go off inside Darcy, least of all the driver.

Ben drove them back to last night's camping spot in State Game Lands 219.

14

Interesting fact: The ancient Near Eastern beers were thick and porridge-like. The oldest surviving recipe used barley bread.

Cade's scream was ear-splitting in the night, loud enough to set off Darcy's car alarms. Ava wouldn't have dared approach, but she was already touching him, cuddled on his air mattress while John and Mike slept on the reclined second row seats. Cade sat bolt upright, sweating and shaking, mouth hanging open, staring at Darcy's back hatch in horror.

Ava knew what he saw. She still saw it herself some nights. She held on around his waist, under his arm, cheek to his side ribs, while she patted around for the keys stuck between the air mattress and the wheel well. Once located, she tossed the fob to John, who was well versed in how to shut Darcy up.

"Shh," she crooned, once Cade could hear her again. "I'm right here. We're safe, Frosty." Slowly, she placed her hand below his navel and left it there, still. His heart was pounding, his breath ragged, his stomach shuddering. "That was long ago and far away. They can never touch us again. You want to lie down? Or move?"

He made a move to lie down, then jerked back upright. "Move."

"I'll get the hatch for you."

John scurried out of his seat and pulled a carbine out of the front. "Use my door. Bring a gun, Cheyenne."

She blinked. *Oh, yeah. Cheyenne is me.*

"Sorry," Ben muttered, as they clambered out. "Sorry, Mike. I–"

"No worries, Ben," Mike assured him.

"No problem, man," John added.

Cheyenne lagged behind to grab a leftover egg salad sandwich from the cooler. *Keep the tiger fed.* She touched Mike and John gratefully on the shoulder as she followed Ben out the door. "Re-arm the alarms," she murmured to John. He nodded.

By the light of the half moon, she could see the SEALs sticking their heads out the damp tent, their scant accommodation for the night. "Just a nightmare," she explained to them. "Give us space?"

Garcia said, "Happens all the time, man. Flashbacks. Have a good night." The others nodded with him. They closed themselves back in the tent.

"Brushed my teeth," Frosty objected, as Panic handed him the sandwich.

"You can brush them again," Panic insisted. "Eat. It'll help ground you." She set a slow walking pace around the field and drew him along. "The moonlight is pretty."

He handed her a half sandwich. She nibbled on it companionably, then handed it back to him to finish once he ate his half. "Not hungry. Drank a beer in the bar," she explained. He nodded and finished the sandwich.

"Same old dream?" she asked when he was finished.

"Memory," he breathed.

"Katas? Match?"

"I don't dare fight you. No control."

"Finish the lap, then. And katas."

After running through the familiar karate sequences in silence, Cheyenne squatted down and slapped his shin lightly. He stepped away twice, but finally gave in. The aim of this mock slapping 'chicken fight' was to knock each other over. Her balance was terrible squatting down and slapping his arms, between her knees sticking out to both sides. It was almost impossible to take a step that way, or right herself if he pushed her off balance. They both toppled twice.

The last time he grabbed her and lay his head in her lap. "Enough." After a few minutes his breath slowed. "When you left me. I thought maybe they'd go away. Maybe being around each other brought back the nightmare."

She'd wondered the same. That maybe the two of them kept each other frozen back in the Starve in their minds. Maybe by leaving him, she could leave it all behind. "Didn't work for me."

That wasn't entirely true. Being away from him had loosened the grip of those memories.

"Me neither," he said. "Just didn't have anyone to hold. Or chicken-fight." They both chuckled softly. "Missed you worst of all then. Cried my heart out. Like I needed to see you, touch you. Check that you were really OK."

She couldn't truthfully say the same. So she smoothed his hair away from his face, and petted him quietly. She had years of experience taming this tiger. He hadn't worn a T-shirt to bed, because it was too hot with both of them under the blankets. She gently touched his scars, silvery in the moonlight. He hadn't added to the collection. She'd been there to tend each one when the wound was fresh. He rolled onto his side to place his face against her stomach, his top arm around her hip, holding on for dear life.

"I'm really OK," she murmured eventually. "You're really OK too, Cade." But her pretty tiger had fallen asleep. She didn't wake him. The sky was already lightening toward dawn. Instead she reviewed the things she once thought she could solve by leaving him, as though Cade was the scapegoat carrying her memories and sins, instead of herself.

No. It isn't that easy. No one else will ever really understand.

But it was worth a try.

As dawn's bright sunbeam struck them, Cade growled and drew them back inside Darcy to get another couple hours sleep. Ava tried to peel off to sleep in the passenger seat, but he pulled her to the air mattress. He went back to sleep with his face between her breasts.

～

Over breakfast, the SEALs tried to tell the team from Hudson their life stories. Cheyenne interrupted them.

"Outside Darcy, we stay in character. Ben is a trader from Bradford County. I'm his girlfriend, learning the ropes. We met a couple weeks ago."

At her gesture of invitation, John continued. "Mike and I are with Free Hudson, a group protesting martial law. We're here to hook up with Free Pennsylvania. Ben and Cheyenne are going to introduce us. Is that today, Ben?"

"Decide that after we drop the SEALs at their car." Ben rose. At his kitchen table, he dumped his garbage bowl into the compost bag. True apples, they didn't let food scraps go to waste.

Garcia objected, "Our goal was to get to know you."

"You know me fine," Ben countered, catching and holding Garcia's eye firmly. "And I know you. Let's work out. Cheyenne, why don't you take the fishy dudes for a morning run. The rest of us don't run."

That wasn't quite true. Ben could almost keep up with John. Mike could jog once around the clearing without too much trouble. But they didn't enjoy running. Surely the SEALs were real runners.

"Sure." Cheyenne popped to her feet and started stretching. "Maybe Jamal could stay behind and hit the bags with you."

Ben glowered at her. She grinned back.

"Bags? Like punching bags?" John inquired, looking toward Darcy.

Cheyenne pulled out a mat with straps, and four rolled hand wraps. She had to pull out her M4 rifle, anyway. "Buckle it to a tree," she explained. Then she set off running with KT and Garcia.

She was tired of running in circles around this field. They veered onto the road to parts unknown to her. Not that it looked any different from all the other wooded hills, but at least there was a chance of novelty.

Once they were out of earshot, KT inquired, "Why single out Jamal?"

"Ben's holding a grudge over Jamal keying his car."

"Dumb move," KT agreed. "Where did you –" He amended the question in mid-stride. "How long you been fighting?"

"Started karate when I was six," Cheyenne replied. "Met Ben at a dojo, actually. We both have black belts. He's four dan. I'm two dan, working on three. Shouldn't take long, practicing with Ben every day. You know karate?"

She wasn't surprised to hear the Navy trained SEALs in a hodge-podge of martial arts traditions, just like the Army trained her. Hand to hand combat was her second favorite subject in Basic at West Point. Her favorite was blowing stuff up, but the instructors didn't let her practice very often. Between sprints, they kept the conversation going, comparing martial skills minus any context.

KT got into the spirit of it more easily than Garcia, who kept slipping in countries and wars, ships and ranks by mistake. Cheyenne liked KT, who lacked the wedding ring Garcia wore. He was attractive for a senile, with wavy long light brown hair. They were twice her age, though, maybe mid-thirties, so not all that attractive. KT kept the flirting minimal. She carried the only gun.

"Bear," KT said softly, and blocked her with an arm. The trio slowed to a stop. A full grown bear stood on all fours by the edge of the road. He slowly turned his head to regard them.

Cheyenne frowned. "Do I need to shoot it?" She didn't want to. The bear was huge, maybe 500 pounds. But if it didn't hurt her, she didn't want to hurt him. Her. Whatever.

"No. Black bear," Garcia supplied. "Just stand still a minute. Don't make eye contact. We're no threat."

The bear wasn't so sure of that. He lumbered into the roadway and came toward them, sniffing.

"You just let me know when to shoot," Cheyenne murmured, as the bear came within ten yards, then five.

"Nobody's angry yet," Garcia assured her.

Just then the bear rose onto its rear legs and sniffed. He thought about it a minute, then fell back to his forefeet and clicked his jaw.

"Now let's walk backward, nice and slow and calm," Garcia suggested.

"Wish I had a camera," Cheyenne said.

"Bad idea to stick a camera into a predator's face," Garcia assured her.

Still walking backwards, they made it around a bend, and a little farther for good measure. "Really bad idea to run from a predator," Garcia explained.

"Long way back to camp walking the whole way," KT mentioned. He didn't seem much more studied up on bears than Cheyenne was.

"Just giving him a little distance and respect," Garcia assured him, turning but maintaining a walking pace. "Guy might have family in the neighborhood. Wouldn't want him to feel he needs to defend them."

"That is so cool," KT said. Cheyenne agreed, and bopped fists and grins with him.

"Boar!" Cheyenne squealed. Her gun was level in an instant, looking for a shot. Garcia jumped one way, KT rolled another. Cheyenne stayed in the middle, staring down the feral pig through her rifle sight. "Watch out for his tusks. Boar isn't friendly like the bear."

Garcia found a fallen branch, half rotten. KT yanked up a sapling, and joined Garcia on the same side of the boar, to Cheyenne's right.

Garcia said, "We'll try to scare him away. Cheyenne, stay put."

"Stay clear of my shot," she said mildly. "But sure, give him a chance."

The boar stayed put at the edge of the woods, glowering now at the men, who waved their branch-laden staffs and slowly crowded toward him.

"A warning shot wouldn't come amiss," Garcia suggested.

Cheyenne aimed a foot to her right of the boar, between him and the SEALs. The bullet grazed a sapling and sent some bark flying. That was enough for the boar. He turned tail and ran off into the woods. She whooped.

"Gentlemen, I believe we work well together," Cheyenne said. They traded high-fives all around. "Ready to run back to camp?"

Once they got jogging, KT asked, "Think Jamal and Ben have bonded?"

"Not a snowball's chance in hell," Cheyenne returned. "Guys, Ben won't do well with black men today. That nightmare last night. Something that happened in a previous life."

"They were black?" Garcia guessed.

"A dozen of them," Cheyenne agreed. "The rest is personal."

"What kind of personal?" KT asked.

"If I told you, he'd knock me ten feet, kind of personal," Cheyenne said. "Don't take it personally. I don't."

"Got it." After a moment KT added, "I hope that wasn't literal, Cheyenne. Not OK for him to hit you. Ever."

But we're both fighters, she quibbled to herself. *We hit each other all the time. Sometimes it crosses the line. We both regret it.*

"That's personal, too," she said aloud.

KT let it go.

When they reached the clearing, Ben was whaling on his punching tree. Jamal had prudently settled in with the geeks, giving them workout pointers John didn't need and Mike resented. John and Jamal seemed to be trading insults cheerfully enough. Cheyenne decided that was about as good as the group bonding was likely to get today.

She settled in to regale them with stories of bear and boar. John and Mike and Jamal were delighted.

Ben met her eye searchingly. He seemed satisfied with what he saw there, that she was OK. He turned away to take his turn first washing in a bucket.

Left to their own devices, the others probably would have faced the day sweaty. Body odor didn't carry the stigma it once did. But Ben's standards were high. Without a word from him, everyone else followed suit.

Ava always admired that about him.

15

───────

Interesting fact: Navy SEAL training takes a year. Only 6% of applicants pass pre-selection, and then only 1 in 4 succeed in training, for an overall success rate of just 1.5%.

"We're in the car," Cheyenne pointed out, as they hit the road back to Towanda to drop off the SEALs. She sat in the second row with John, to facilitate discussion while Ben drove. He was feeling too rough today to handle this.

They hadn't discussed it. Cheyenne had been his queen bitch for years. She stepped in on automatic.

She continued, "Meaning, we can discuss things we couldn't outdoors. Ben, any questions?"

"Yeah," he agreed. "Navy dudes. If Skull hires you, and we're on an op together. That means you're a temporary contract, and I'm Skull's agent. Just wanted to point out, that kinda means you'd have to take direction from me. I'd make the judgment calls. Question is, can you guys live with that? Not asking for an answer. Just think it over."

Cheyenne nodded. "Excellent point." Garcia looked like he wanted to respond, but she got in her own question first. "I think John and I need to know why you deserted." She didn't choose to explain why she and John were the ones who might hold that concern.

John-Daneel looked a bit dubious about why he should care. It wasn't like the Army had been loyal to him. But he'd certainly been indoctrinated enough that the question did leap out at him, even if his gavi roots and discharge left him ambivalent.

The SEALs looked at each other grimly. Garcia spoke for them. "Our orders weren't coming from principle anymore. Assassinate innocent people. Snatch a leader because he disagreed with O'Hara. Kidnap children to control their parents. That's not who we are."

Cheyenne nodded. "But you walked out on your unit."

"No," Garcia said. "We're representatives. The team sent us to meet Skull, and you. Decide whether we can do business. The team is split. A couple platoons and the HQ are still trying to compromise with O'Hara's command. Our platoon is actively looking for another boss. Possibly two other platoons."

"How many is that? Three SEAL platoons," John asked.

"Full platoon is sixteen," Garcia said. "Ours aren't full. Maybe a dozen left in mine, bit more in the other two."

"Good to know," Cheyenne acknowledged, nodding thanks to John.

Mike was next. "You're equipped? Like, you took your gear with you when you left?"

"We took some," Garcia replied. "The other two platoons are still embedded. They can bring out some more equipment when they desert."

Cheyenne pursed her lips, picturing this. Chances were, what and who they actually managed to walk away with, would be something less than they hoped for. It might not even be worth the risk of asking for them. Last minute conscience checks could result in pursuit instead of help.

"My turn," Garcia said. "Mike, John, what's your mobile EW capability? Couldn't ask that outside."

Ben answered first. "Electronic warfare? None. Cheyenne and I don't do EW. John and Mike aren't part of this."

Garcia said, "Your boss is thinking of including them."

"I don't even know what op we're talking about," Mike said.

"Different job," Ben told him. "May not be needed. Still a few weeks out yet. Hopefully yours will be done, and you'll be extracted first. Garcia, Cheyenne and John are new hires in training. No details."

Mike nodded. John looked vexed. Cheyenne sympathized – no one was telling them what they expected to do in VA. Adding three SEAL platoons to the outing tended to suggest a whole new league of scary scenario. But as new hires, Ben was right. They weren't entitled to ops details this week. They were still on baby steps. Like how to do laundry in tiny Towanda PA.

"I have a question," KT asked. "Who are you people? I don't mean your boss. I mean, where do you come from?"

Mike replied, "Ex computer science professor. From Chicago originally. Here and there since then."

John shrugged. "Apple survivor, Long Island."

Ben remained silent.

Cheyenne said, "Ben and I are apples from Manhattan. Ran a gang there." Because the numbers seemed to blow people's minds, she elaborated, "About twenty-eight hundred at its peak. White kids. The more established criminal gangs were minority. We taught white kids to fight to survive. Our niche."

John added, "Cheyenne and I graduated Hudson Army Basic a couple weeks ago. They dropped the lowest twenty percent of the class. We didn't make the cut. She's small. I've got asthma. So we were recruited into the company."

"What does 'apple' mean?" KT asked.

Cheyenne stared at him in wonder. "We survived the New York epidemic zone. Only ten percent made it."

"Jesus," KT said.

"You didn't know about that, in VA?" Cheyenne asked.

"The news isn't trustworthy in VA," Garcia said. "Especially not on a Navy base."

"Never know what to believe," KT said. "There were rumors, New York City was penned up to die. I didn't buy it. That's like the siege of Leningrad. Americans couldn't do that to their own people."

Cheyenne stared at him coldly, until he dropped his eyes. "Well. They did."

"Makes you wonder what else they lied to us about," Jamal said.

"Damn near everything," Garcia concurred.

Following directions from Garcia, Ben pulled up to the SEALs' modest SUV. They'd left it by a defunct supermarket across the Susquehanna from the river park where the SEALs abducted Ben. The store must have been derelict years before the Calm. Grass and shrubs made good headway against the parking lot asphalt. No one was around to watch them transfer gear and weapons.

They lined up for good-byes, three SEALs along their SUV, and Ben's four slouching on Darcy. Garcia put forward a hand to shake with Ben.

To Cheyenne's surprise, Ben shook his hand, though coldly. That made sense, she figured. No matter how much apples disliked touching hands – most were germophobes for life – that was a quirk Ben the PA trader wouldn't share. So he got over it.

"I think we could work together," Garcia said.

Ben nodded curtly. "Happy trails." He turned his back and got into his car.

Cheyenne smiled. "Nice to meet you all. I have no idea whether I hope to see you again or not. Enjoy your visit in PA."

KT and Garcia grinned at that and waved a salute. She and Jamal left it at a wary nod, not even trying to part friends, though John and Mike traded farewells with him.

"Took you long enough," Skull groused.

John and Mike had been playing with the car's electronics. Skull's voice now boomed at them in God-like surround sound from all the car's speakers, instead of from the one little phone stuck in the dashboard. Cheyenne shot John a dirty look. She trusted the change was reversible.

"Needed a nap to start my day over," Ben replied.

Finding the decrepit supermarket lot unappealing, he'd shifted them to the pretty Towanda riverfront park, where Cheyenne and the geeks amused themselves while Ben caught another hour's sleep. That was interrupted by a police officer dropping by. The cop was a bit hostile toward John's coloring, and mentioned complaints about a fight in the pool hall last night. But he melted like butter under Ben's handling. They even got a lead from the cop on a fun place for supper tonight.

"So what's the word?" Skull asked. "Garcia says they can work with you."

Ben didn't answer immediately. "Cheyenne?" he eventually asked.

"We'd work fine with the SEALs," she said. "No problem." Ben and Jamal would never be friends. But she knew Ben – or Frosty, at least – well enough to know that he could deal professionally and coldly with anyone he just couldn't like.

"Why is Cheyenne answering instead of Ben?" Skull asked.

"I trust her judgment," Ben said. "More than mine, today."

Cheyenne said, "Of course, I don't know what the job is in VA. Getting awfully curious about that. Oh, and they seemed to think Mike and John might be in on the SEAL project? Ben and Mike were surprised. John and I have no opinion. Because no one's telling us what we're doing with SEALs in VA."

Skull said, "Extraction is still a weak point in the plan."

Ben sighed. "SEALs do boats."

"That's an advantage," Skull agreed.

"A boat won't carry Darcy."

"Ben? If you need to leave Darcy behind, I'll buy you another car."

Cheyenne intervened again. "I'm sure Ben will do whatever is necessary, boss. But let's not contemplate leaving Darcy behind right now."

"This'll take some getting used to," Skull said. "Cheyenne speaking for Ben. When Ben is the team leader." His point sharpened as he went along.

"I'm good with it," Ben said. "Can we return to our training op now? The plan?"

"Mike? You're good to continue?" Skull inquired.

"The training exercise? Sure. A plan that needs three platoons of SEALs? I have misgivings."

Actually Mike looked horrified. At least they'd found time to glue his glasses back together. This morning, Jamal tried to talk him into having laser eye surgery before going into VA. With only one eye correctable even with lenses, Cheyenne couldn't blame him for resisting the prospect. If the surgery went wrong, he'd be effectively blind. Medical care wasn't what it used to be, these days.

Mike concluded, "I'd prefer not to see the SEALs again as long as I live."

"OK," Skull agreed. "Have fun. Call me for pickup." He clicked off.

"John?" Cheyenne demanded. "How do I turn off the God sound on boss?" Ben snickered.

John wriggled between the front seats and made a quick adjustment. "So you're vice team leader now, Cheyenne? Speaking for Ben?"

Ben reached over and squeezed her hand. "Partner."

"I just know him," Cheyenne told John. "Ben didn't like the SEALs. But he doesn't really care. He'll be over it by tomorrow. Maybe the next day."

"Except the one who keyed Darcy," Ben quibbled. "Jamal is toast."

"The fact that he's black and attacked me doesn't have anything to do with it," Cheyenne twigged him with a smile.

"Didn't help," Ben allowed. He shot a glower at the too-brown John still leaning over his shoulder.

John beat a retreat into his seat.

"We've all got triggers, John," Cheyenne reminded him. "Nothing personal."

"Got it," John agreed. "No problem."

"It's a problem," Ben differed. "But not with you. Sorry."

"Definitely!" John-Daneel agreed with Ron Kaminski's latest political pronouncement. He slid another chunk of wood into the chimenea-style outdoor stove. For authenticity, he shivered as though he were cold.

Frosty, Panic, and Daneel had survived two New York winters without heat. The pot-belly fireplace was charming for ambiance, but mid-fifties with a stiff breeze wasn't cold. The sun was shining in early afternoon. The Kaminskis' little bricked patio tried to be stylish. But it fell well short of elegance, furnished with mismatched cheap resin chairs. Bits of stray farm equipment crowded round.

Cheyenne nodded sympathetically. She wasn't paying attention and couldn't care less what John was agreeing to. Politics was boring enough in the democratic town meetings of Hudson. She couldn't imagine how people found it interesting as a spectator sport.

"– And then they pushed Apple refugees on us," Kaminski continued. Cheyenne's attention was suddenly riveted. He raised his hands to forestall objections. "I know. You can't feed them all in Hudson. But they can't just force communities to take in strangers. They don't fit in here. Are you a farmer, John?"

John shook his head in apparent unconcern. "Little gardening here and there. I'm more the suburban type."

"Well, they dumped six hundred on Bradford County. Inner-city types from the Bronx. Don't know how to farm. Don't have any jobs. What are we supposed to do with them? But the Army just stuck us with them."

"Where did you put them?" Mike asked in interest.

"We call it the Colony." Ron waved his hand vaguely southwest. "*They* get fed for free. *They* even have Internet. So they can call the Army and complain if they're mistreated. What happened to freedom and liberty, you know?"

John nodded sagely and matched his wave. "You're lucky you only got six hundred. And then people look at me, you know? Like I'm brown, so I must be one of *them*." He shook his head in disgust.

Cheyenne was impressed. John was pretty convincing.

Ron unconsciously mimicked the head-shake. "Social engineering, that's what it is. East Coast city folk with their bleeding heart liberal values. Instead of respecting people's freedom."

"PA should give them the freedom to starve!" Cheyenne attempted to play along.

All four guys swung heads toward her, frowning. Ron was kind enough to laugh it off, shaking his head. "They're people, Cheyenne, just like us. Down on their luck, sure. But."

"I almost forgot," Ben interrupted. "Do you compost, Ron? I've got food scraps in the car."

"Sure, thanks," Ron agreed. "Mandatory now." He turned back to John. "What next? Garbage inspection?" The guys chuckled companionably.

Ben drew Cheyenne with him to visit the car. As soon as they were out of anyone's earshot, he asked, "What was that?"

"I was trying to play along."

"Yeah? Don't." Ben shook his head. "Just watch and learn, OK?" He popped the back of Darcy. "This is cross-training. Let John and Mike handle the sting."

"Sting?"

"Con. John's trying to get Ron to keep Free Hudson informed of Free Pennsylvania's plans. And hopefully give John his contacts deeper into PA."

"OK. But what did I do wrong?"

Ben sighed. "You went farther than your mark. Way farther, like out of left field. First you have to track him. Especially body language. That hits him in the subconscious. That's like the training phase, where you convince your mark you're on the same wavelength. Then when you veer the conversation to a new place – slowly – he follows along."

"Interpolate, don't extrapolate," Cheyenne suggested. Actually, now that she thought about it, her comment wasn't even an extrapolation of Ron's points. *I guess I did go too far.*

"Extrapolate. Is that on the GED math test, too?"

"No," she said penitently. "It's like whether a point is –"

"I know what it means, Cheyenne. I passed AP Statistics." Ben considered, and added, "Also, you're a girl. Nice girls don't say mean things."

Cheyenne waggled her eyebrows. "Now you want me to be a nice girl?"

"No. Ron does." Food scraps acquired, Ben shut the tailgate. "He wants you to be the daughter he'll never see again. The good parts, anyway. Not the wise-ass parts."

"I can't pretend to be her. I don't know anything about her."

"Just don't say much." He dropped a quick kiss on her forehead. "Try it. Keep your mouth shut. Nod a bit. People think you're smarter."

Cheyenne bit back her retort because the other guys were coming around the corner of the house.

"Road trip!" Ron called out happily. "John and Mike want to see the Colony. Cheyenne, let's see how your driving is shaping up!"

Ben handed her the key with a crooked smile, and trotted up the porch steps to hand off the scraps to Mrs. Kaminski. Cheyenne beamed her best attempt at a proud-papa smile toward Ron. Her palms were already sweating.

16

———————

Interesting fact: Freedom of religion was a sticking point in Pennsylvania joining Hudson. Hudson guaranteed freedom of private religion, but required regulatory training and a license to preach in public. After Pittsburgh devolved into interfaith armed conflict, a Hudson Resco intervened. Pittsburgh's religious freedoms were severely curtailed for a cooling off period. These two news items got mistakenly conflated in people's minds. Religion was thriving in Hudson, not outlawed. A sect like the Sixers, however, could never secure a license.

"You need to take it less personally," Ron advised her, as Cheyenne stumbled out of the car, wishing to drop to her knees and kiss the solid ground. "People honk, just pull over."

"Flip them the bird as they go by," John added, grinning at her.

"That's maybe more a New York thing," Ron joked back.

They made her drive on the highway. Every time she got up to 40 mph, her panic rose out of control, and she had to pull over to calm down. But if she drove slowly, someone would tailgate her, and start honking. Then she had to pull over to let them pass and calm down.

She'd driven ten miles with the emergency flashers on, and must have pulled over twenty times.

Ben laid a hand on her shoulder. "I'll drive on the way back." He'd spent the whole ride in the cargo hold on his air mattress, practicing what he preached. He didn't say a word.

"No, she's doing great!" Ron objected.

Ben laughed. "She needs a break, Ron. Without anything hanging over her head." He tucked Cheyenne under his arm and hugged her, and kissed the crown of her head. "All done driving for today."

"Thank you," Cheyenne breathed.

"Ben knows how to make you feel better," Ron said, with a proud papa smile.

Cheyenne nodded gamely. *Also how to make me cringe, grovel, fight, and dance, like a puppet on strings,* she thought. *But Cheyenne hasn't known Ben that long.*

Mike and John had already stepped toward the 'Colony.' They eyed it dubiously. "So they built their own shelters?" Mike hazarded a guess.

"If you call that building," Ron agreed.

The sloping field sported a haphazard collection of lean-to's, corrugated metal and scrappy plywood, looking like something out of a South American slum. A few women and old men eyed them suspiciously, and shooed curious children back among the huts. Their bellies were still distended from the Starve, arms and faces bony-thin.

"In the Bronx, they were probably tenants," Cheyenne said. She stopped as Ben squeezed her to remind her to stay quiet.

But Mike seemed to think it a valid point. "Yeah, maybe no experience in the construction trades. Where is everybody? Or do they not like visitors?"

"Well, some work," Ron said. "I don't know anyone here."

John stepped forward again with a flashing grin. "Well, shall we…?"

The rest of them followed his lead, as the most color-coordinated. Ava didn't see any whites in the camp, and didn't expect to. Pennsylvania came late to the party for Project Reunion, after Hudson's victory. They took in Apple survivors as part of their war reparations.

They got dregs, people Hudson would have left in the city to sink or swim. New England and Upstate, Long Island and Jersey, could only absorb so many.

Of course, Hudson left Ava and Cade in the city, too. Even loser Pennsylvania wasn't foisted with the Apple's dangerous juvenile delinquents. Cheyenne didn't have any first-hand experience with the resettlement. White Supreme, her gang, surrendered their kids under 12. Navy sailors took them away to quarantine. She never heard from them again.

Come to think of it, Frosty held her under his arm like this on that day, too. That was hard for her, to let the young ones go. They were her responsibility through the Starve. She was terrified they'd be taken to some kind of concentration camp, forced to work until they died of cold and starvation. The nightmare barracks she envisioned then looked rather better than the flimsy shantytown before her. There were no guards or barbed wire. She wouldn't care to face the Pennsylvania winter snow in a shack built for Rio, though. This poverty was extreme even by her standards.

"Is this good farmland, Ron?" Mike asked. "Doesn't look rutted like a farm field."

Ron considered. "Too steep for a combine." He frowned at the sky. "Northeastern slope. No. I doubt anyone's ever farmed here. Grass. Probably means the soil is too shallow for trees. Stone." He looked around some more in misgiving, as though seeing the place for the first time. "No. This land's not good for much. Grazing, maybe."

Fifth time was a charm. John finally found a woman who spoke English and allowed them into her hut. Ben held Cheyenne back to enter last and let Mike and John have their fun. The plywood walls broke the wind, but the chinks let in enough light to see by.

They'd have their pick of apartments back in the Bronx, Ava thought. She wondered if they had a choice, whether to go back. Two men sat in the hut on a dirt-strewn nubby bathroom rug, one old, one maybe middle aged. They stared into space without registering the guests.

"I watch them, and a couple kids," the woman was saying, Qwanisha. "While the others go off to work. Mushroom farm, over the hill.

My knee don't work too good. But I can lug them to the bathrooms. I earn my keep."

"They your family?" John asked.

"I ain't got no family. Them neither. Kids either. Just a job I can do, and people who need watching."

"Do you get what you need here? Enough food and…" John eyed the walls. There was nothing in here. No pots and pans, furniture, clothes, tiny treasures. It wasn't clear why they chose to sit in this box, except to keep the wind off.

Qwanisha followed his glance with a cynical eye. "We don't live here. Barracks in the schoolhouse. Cafeteria."

"Oh!" John shot her a million-dollar smile. "I didn't realize. Could we see that?"

Qwanisha plonked down on the ground to sit beside the men. "Go ahead." After a brief staring contest, she deigned to point a direction.

"Thank you. You've been most kind," John assured her.

"No I haven't."

"If I could ask one more question, Qwanisha? Why the huts, if you live in the schoolhouse?"

Qwanisha shrugged.

THE 'SCHOOL' WAS LOW PINK BRICK, WITH A FLAT ROOF. LOCATED IN THE middle of nowhere, Cheyenne couldn't immediately work out why anyone built an elementary school on this particular hill. Then she noted the grating on the windows.

Ah. That kind of school. A defunct state penitentiary for wayward teens, perhaps, or a mental hospital. The shantytown gave it a wide berth, by a set radius it seemed. A few dirty white vans parked along the loop of driveway in front, eschewing the parking lot off to the right.

Ron Kaminski scowled at the religious billboards painted on their flanks. *Embrace the End of Days! Good Samaritans Evangelical Congregation. Meet Your Maker with Good Works!*

The advertising slogans didn't do much for Cheyenne. But she couldn't see why they bothered Ron. Religious loons ran rampant these days. The Hudson Constitution put strict limits on their proselytizing as a nuisance. In misgiving, she realized that PA probably hadn't done that yet. Or perhaps they never would, unless they joined Hudson. Religious freedom was a big deal to some people. In Hudson, the Rescos decreed that the balance of freedoms required the religious to quit shoving it in other people's faces. Like most apples, Cheyenne was vastly relieved.

John tried the main door and found it locked. He banged on it a bit and peered inside. Eventually a pastor came, judging by his collar, and opened it from within.

"Hi!" John greeted him warmly, and proceeded to introduce their group.

"This is most irregular," the middle-aged reverend said, who styled himself Pastor Tom. He still stood in the door, which sought to shut itself on him. "We don't have visitors."

"Tom Allen," Ron Kaminski addressed him. "Concerned citizens, checking up on our new neighbors. The Colony came up in conversation. My friends here wanted to see it. And I realized I didn't know much about it, either."

"Let us in! Show us around!" John encouraged.

"Well, try not to be disruptive," Pastor Tom conceded uncomfortably.

That was invitation enough for John. He pushed the door wide open and held it for the rest of them to stroll in.

Mike asked, "Why do you keep the door locked, Pastor Tom?"

"Just basic security." Ben and Cheyenne passed the nervous minister at that point, as though to underscore his concerns. *Dangerous people might drop by.* "We're a bit isolated here. We have afternoon classes right now."

"Does your church have a contract to administer this facility?" Mike asked. He drew Pastor Tom toward the security office, getting him out of John's way.

"Let's," John invited the rest of them with a fey grin. Pastor Tom tried to direct him uncertainly, but Mike kept distracting him with questions. John simply hung a right, and strolled down the long hallway, peering into door windows.

No one was wandering the halls. The first few rooms Cheyenne peeked into were paved with bedding, with some bunks and cots, but mostly floor pallets. One had a corner devoted to building new wooden bunk beds, though construction wasn't in progress right now. A few old people were laying around in the third room. The door advised that *Jesus Loves the Incontinent.*

"Kids," Ben said, beckoning her to the next door with a smile.

"Let us disrupt," John said, yanking the door open. "Well, hello, hello! How is everyone today?" Ignoring the teacher at the front of the room, he waded toward a scant dozen kids, aged 5 to 10, seated cross-legged on floor mats.

To Pennsylvanian eyes, the kids probably looked younger. But Cheyenne knew what stunted growth looked like.

"What –" the middle-aged woman in the front objected.

"Sheila?" Ron Kaminski interrupted her. He looked aghast. "What are you doing with them?"

"Ron..." Sheila looked embarrassed. "I left the Church, after Tony left me..." And teacher Sheila was conveniently sidelined like Pastor Tom, to defend her choice to leave the Catholic Church and take up with the Evangelicals, to a deeply offended Ron.

From their argument, Cheyenne gathered that priests were in short supply in the area. Ron argued that good Catholics needed to stick together and maintain their community in Christ. Sheila looked mortified.

John, delighted to kick over a bee's nest, plopped down on the mats with the kids. "What are we studying?"

"Bible reading," a boy said, and shoved a tattered Sunday school newsprint at him.

"Oh, it's Sunday!" John declared. "Did I make a mistake? Is it Sunday? No?" The kids crowded round the clown on their knees to correct him. Today was *Friday!*

One boy, white with red hair, hung back as though not included. Ben squatted down to chat with him. Another girl, this one black, also hung back, biting her lip and looking nervously between John the clown and the teacher up front. She looked about six, but Cheyenne figured she was closer to nine.

"I'm Cheyenne. What's your name?"

"Tamasin," she lisped shyly. "We're supposed to be praying."

"Yeah? What are you praying for, Tamasin?" Cheyenne gently tapped the cross dangling from Tamasin's neck. "That's a pretty necklace."

"That's Jesus Christ. Mommy's with him. She'll be back soon."

"Is that what you pray for?" Cheyenne asked. "That Mommy will come back soon?"

Tamasin pursed her lips and looked away, with an exaggerated nod.

Cheyenne was confident mommy was never coming back. Mommy had probably been dead a couple years. But little kids never gave up that story.

"I wonder what mommy prays for," Cheyenne said. "I bet mommy prays that Tamasin is happy, and healthy. And learns a lot in school. And grows up, and falls in love, and has lots of fat happy babies."

Tamasin grinned bad teeth, and shook her head.

"Tamasin, I'm new here. Could you show me around?"

The smile fled in panic, and her head-shake turned violent. "Mommy's with Jesus. I have to do what teacher says and pray. Or I won't see mommy again."

Sheila waved her hands in negation, and attempted feebly, "Tamasin, that's not quite what I meant –"

"Sheila, how could you?" Ron Kaminski demanded. The two of them returned to their low-voiced theological dispute in anguish.

"God is confusing," Ben declared. "Terry, I think Cheyenne had the right idea. Show us around?" Terry was apparently his lonely red-head's name.

Ben rose, tossing the giggling child over his shoulder. "What, you don't want to ride this way? Maybe upside down?" He hung the laughing kid upside-down from his waist. "Maybe ride my shoulders? Well, it's boring, but we can do it that way if you want."

"Come on, Tamasin." Cheyenne whispered in the girl's ear. "I could carry you, too, if you want."

Tamasin looked deeply torn. She shook her head and looked anxiously to teacher Sheila, still wilting under a barrage of catechism from Ron.

"Mommy's praying that you're happy. So come play." Cheyenne grasped her hand and pulled her up. Never, not even during typhus or cholera outbreaks, had Ava shrunk from holding hands with a child, no matter how grubby. "Show me around your place!"

"We're not supposed to walk in the halls."

"This hall?" Cheyenne pulled her out and hammed it up, looking both ways. "Are you sure? Looks safe enough. Are there goblins? No? Gang-bangers? Drug dealers? Black cats? Black cats are bad luck."

Ben was already halfway down the hall, past the turnoff to Pastor Tom, holding Terry under the armpits and swinging him side to side.

"We need to keep orderly," Tamasin explained.

"Sounds dull. Let's follow Ben and Terry."

"That's why everybody's outside," Tamasin said. "They're not *orderly*."

"Maybe they don't want to be in, because everybody is too *orderly*," Cheyenne countered. "Do you have recess?"

"Yeah. That's my favorite subject."

"Mine, too! Race you to Ben and Terry?"

"We're not allowed to run in the halls."

"Live a little, Tamasin," Cheyenne urged. "We'll run together. You can't get in trouble if a grownup does it with you. On three. One, two, three!" At a gentle jog, she pulled the girl along.

Tamasin hid her mouth behind her free hand to stifle her guilty giggles.

"Cafeteria," Ben proudly proclaimed when they reached him, indicating the double doors with a flourished wave. A few refugees sat around backward, elbows propped behind them on the bolted down tables, ignoring a nearby collection of wet mop gear. Apparently they were the after-lunch janitors.

"What was for lunch, Terry?" Cheyenne asked.

"Applesauce and bologna sandwiches."

"And milk," Tamasin added. "We have to drink milk every meal, or the preachers get cross. The grown-ups don't drink milk."

Cheyenne nodded sagely. "Do you get snacks too?"

Terry looked at her wide-eyed and shook his head. "You have snacks?"

"We have snacks," Ben agreed magnanimously. "Maybe you could show me your room on the way, Terry. And we'll get snacks."

Tamasin looked scandalized. Cheyenne wondered what all they'd told the poor kid that God would punish her for. She doubted Tamasin had managed to scrape together a single sin yet worth mentioning.

Terry didn't have that problem. Ben had him going like a wind-up toy. He zoomed down the hall arms outspread, bouncing wall to wall, with sound effects. "This is our room!" He jumped up and down in place waiting for them to catch up.

He opened the door and pointed side to side. "Girls. Boys. This is my bed." He hopped over to a pallet and started jumping on it.

The large converted classroom held beds for about forty. Cheyenne guessed that all the kids in the camp shared the one room. Tamasin had a pallet on a top bunk sized for four girls to share. She shyly showed off a blond Barbie doll who stood vigil at her pillow, dressed for the Florida beach. A cross hung above the beds, too, but that didn't belong to her personally.

Cheyenne thought it was a shame the girl didn't have a black Barbie to match her own mahogany skin tone. A tomboy herself, and a karate student from first grade, she never had any use for Barbies. Her hard-working Serbian nurse mother despised the things. Ava received them as gifts at birthday parties, but then promptly traded them in at the toy store for something fun like a standing kick bag, or new swim goggles. That was long before they moved to the city.

Amidst much teasing and rough-housing, Terry showed Ben where he kept his clothes. Each of the kids had a toy bin in a shelving system under the windows. Outerwear was apparently stowed closer to a door to the outside.

Cheyenne and Ben declared themselves massively impressed with the fine accommodations. Tamasin shyly admitted that she missed the Bronx. Terry didn't want to talk about that. The very thought set him back to zooming in the hall.

"Hold the door," Ben told Cheyenne solemnly, as he exited with

Terry to procure snacks from Darcy. She saluted him back with matching sternness, then frowned at Tamasin.

Cheyenne jerked her head slightly outdoors. Tamasin shook her head vehemently. Cheyenne sighed and looked outdoors wistfully. Tamasin grinned and ran out after the boys.

"See here!" Pastor Tom said, finally catching on. "You can't do that!"

"Can't do what?" Cheyenne asked. "The kids are helping my boyfriend fetch a treat."

Mike latched onto the pastor again doggedly. "Are you the legal guardian of that child? You personally? Of that child, Pastor Tom? Seems to me this is their home. And you've penned them up like prisoners!"

Fighting a grin, Cheyenne tuned them back out. She figured out how to jigger the lock, and set off after Ben. If the lock engaged, Mike would doubtless still be here to open the door.

17

Interesting fact: Community commitment was crucial to rehabilitating resettled 'apple' survivors from New York City. 'Apple trauma' was more than a psychological effect. Prolonged starvation could cause brain damage and dementia, especially in children. Most communities rose to the challenge. Some did not.

"See ya, Terry!" Cheyenne called, as Ben swung the boy upside-down by his knees one last time. Terry liked that. She hoped he'd be happy with the Kaminskis. She suspected the farm couple had no idea what they were in for, fostering an Apple survivor.

Ron Kaminski and his wife took turns enfolding her in a last hug, insisting that she and Ben drop by again. And they'd have that Colony straightened out starting tomorrow! Saint Elizabeth's would teach Good Samaritans Evangelical a thing or two about freedom! She wished them luck with that.

After Ron patted her door paternally, he hung on John's window behind her for a few last words. Ben relinquished his red-head play-mate to his new foster grandma.

Terry didn't have any ties to the group at the Colony, aside from having been born in the Bronx. Some senile latched onto him as her ticket into quarantine at Camp Upstate. He didn't like her and didn't know where she ended up. When Ron offered to bring Terry home with them and see how it worked, the boy jumped at the chance. Ron promised to bring him back to the Colony if Terry wasn't happy with them.

Cheyenne was sure the Kaminskis would bend over backwards to make this work.

At last, stuffed to the gills from the wonderful supper spread Mrs. Kaminski laid out for them, they were back on the road.

"So what's our score, John?" Mike asked.

John referred to notes on his phone. "Twenty-seven names, Free Penn in Bradford County. Thirteen in Tioga County, fifty-three in Lackawanna. He gave me their entire membership spreadsheets. Someone needs to teach Free Penn about cell structure and security. And – ta-da! I've got contacts in Scranton, Philadelphia, Harrisburg, Gettysburg – is that right? I thought Gettysburg was in Virginia."

"Nope. PA," Ben confirmed. He reached back a hand for a high-five, though he kept his eyes on the pitch-dark road. "Well done, my man!"

John slapped his hand and continued. "There's more! Williamsport, Wilkes-Barre –" Mike interrupted to correct his pronunciation. John slapped him off in irritation. "Lancaster, State College, Allentown, Altoona. I love that town's name. This guy has no sense of self-preservation."

"You played him alright," Ben agreed.

"He was easy," John said. "Have a little fun together, do a little project, and we're all best buddies. That was a blast!"

He hung on Cheyenne's seat back. "Uncle Ben? I'm all manic and psyched. Please, sir, can we play some more? I don't want to go home. School is bo-ring."

Ben tilted his head. "What do you think, Cheyenne? Back to the border, or keep these turkeys another day?"

"We have time?" Cheyenne confirmed. "Keep them! Can we visit the truck stop? You guys would love it!"

"Mike?" Ben asked.

"Having the time of my life! As always, Ben. I'm with Cheyenne on the truck stop idea."

"I'm game if the boss is," Ben decided. "Darcy, record message to boss. Hey. Mission accomplished with Free Penn. I'm keeping John and Mike til Sunday noon-ish. Darcy, send message."

Mike said, "You don't ask. You just tell him. I love it."

"If he doesn't like the plan, he'll let me know. It's too late for the truck stop tonight. Navigator, pick us a forest."

A fresh State Game Lands was nearby, deserted and dull, and perfectly suited for Western Civ seminar and an uneventful night's sleep. After full morning workouts – the fresh mountain air even inspired Mike and Ben to jog – John found them a farm market in Williamsport, near the I-180 truck stop. Feeding the three SEALs for a night, plus the two geeks for days, had depleted their food stocks.

Ben and Cheyenne turned back into Connor and Donna. John and Mike advanced to Liam and Nate.

While not much of a city to Donna's eyes, Williamsport and its cluster of related townships formed the biggest settlement she'd seen yet in PA, with over 100,000 souls. Williamsport itself only held about 30,000 of them. A study of the map made clear that the I-180 bypass was not to avoid congestion down on I-80, but to serve this population clump without I-80 veering off its east-west course.

The farm market was even larger than the one in Sayre, taking up three giant tents. Liam-Daneel's wide eyes and deliriously happy grin were worth the trip. The spacious tents weren't even crowded. He helped Donna-Ava select a week's worth of breads first.

Their delight came to a crashing halt when they tried to pay.

Alas, the locals required ration coupons here. Connor pursed his lips in displeasure when the baker's cashier quoted prices double what they paid at Sayre Market.

"Tell me there's a way around that, B– Connor," Nate-Mike prompted softly.

Connor contemplated the militia at the tent opening, checking bags and canceled ration coupons, then sized up the bakery counter woman. "Do they take bribes?" he asked her. A slight tilt of his head indicated the checkout line.

She looked uncertain.

Donna started returning their bread selections to the table.

Liam leaned in and gave her a high-octane smile. "We'd rather not use all our ration coupons, you see. If you know of another venue…" He peeled off a five Liberty dollar bill.

The sales clerk looked offended. He peeled off another. She held out her hand, then ducked behind Liam for cover while she tucked the bills into her bra.

"There's an after party," she confided, low-voiced. "Some get tired and head home. But our bakery is there. William Street by the highway, tucked in between the hotels. Everyone sells there." She handed him a card with her name scribbled on the back – Hannah. "That'll get you in."

"Need to wait a few hours?" Liam asked.

"Already open," Hannah said. She turned to another customer.

Donna noted that Connor was still watching Hannah thoughtfully. "You don't believe her?"

He shrugged. "You guys decide what you want to do. I've never shopped here before."

Liam decided. "We can check out her story at another table. Not too close by."

They drifted into another tent. The guy at a butcher's table gave them the same location and a signed card for free, but said the after-market wouldn't open until the main market closed. He also advised that it was a black market, so most prices were higher. The exceptions were fresh vegetables and bread, with a shorter shelf life.

They pulled away to discuss. Liam said, "So she took my ten bucks and tried to sucker us. Wonder what kind of reception we'd meet over at the hotels now."

Connor weighed in. "There might be a reward for turning in a black marketeer."

Liam's mind was still on losing ten bucks for a bad lead. That was more than their entire shopping bag of bread was worth, before they returned it. And it went to Hannah's personal gain instead of to the bakery. "I want to screw Hannah back."

Connor pursed his lips. Nate ventured, "Maybe you could turn that into a discount, get the bread cheaper."

"Donna?" Connor prompted.

She was as incensed as Liam over the bad actor at the bakery table. "I'm in for revenge on Hannah. You can't just let people screw you over."

Nate was pursing his lips, too, and traded a glance with Connor. "Maybe we should hang back," the older man suggested. "Just in case."

~

"What took you so long?" Donna demanded of Connor, as they exited the Williamsport police station. She and Liam had languished in jail for a couple hours after the militia carted them away from the farm market.

"Ingrate," Connor replied. "Try 'thank you for bailing us out, Connor.' Or, 'sorry for getting thrown in jail, Connor.'"

It wasn't actually bail. He paid fifty PA bucks apiece in fines for their 'black marketing' offense. As he could have predicted, Hannah screwed them over again. They were on her turf, and she had allies.

"Fork you, Connor," Liam grumbled. "This is so unreasonable."

Donna's women's pen was significantly more pleasant than Liam's. Late morning in suburban PA, she was the only female in custody. Liam had a dozen room-mates in the men's lockup across the corridor, most of them unpleasant. Donna had nothing better to do than watch him operate through the cell bars. She was impressed at how well Liam navigated the social scene. Practice, no doubt. She'd never been incarcerated before, herself.

"Hey, where's Nate? And our stuff?" Donna asked.

They arrived at Darcy to find her nearly empty. Their clothes and food hampers were still in the back, but the boxes and bedding were missing. She climbed in and popped the glove box. Even their guns and petty drug bribes were missing.

"Donna? Think," Connor said shortly.

"Wow, this land yacht is huge," Liam commented, swimming in space in the second row.

Donna hazarded, "You couldn't go to the police with all our contraband in the car? Oh. So Nate is guarding our goods. And money. And guns…" She suppressed a grin, picturing the computer science professor guarding all that with an AK-47. "Was he OK with that?"

"He'll be happy to see us," Connor confirmed, eyes alight.

On the outskirts of town, they turned into a self-storage facility, and wound through rows of cinder block garages stepping up a hill, woods to either side. PA's cheap land was evident, as the long warehouses were single-story, lined with car-sized doors.

In the Apple, self-storage places rented by the cubic foot. Drive-up access cost extra. When they first moved to the city, Ava's parents rented space to keep their Texas household worth of furniture out in Queens, since it wouldn't shoehorn into a Manhattan apartment. When they decided to stay for Ava to attend high school, they liquidated it all rather than pay the steep fees.

Connor backed in to garage door #37-F in mid-building, in mid-lot.

"Did it have bullet holes when you left?" Donna asked, studying the door. There were three holes in it now. No blood or wet spots were evident on the pavement, though. It looked to her like the bullets had come out, not in. She studied the warehouse across from it, but couldn't spot any secondary damage.

"No." Connor got out to use a key to open the garage. He thought better of it, and knocked first. "Nate? Connor. Coming in."

"Thank God!" came the muffled response from inside. As soon as the automated overhead door opened enough to allow it, Nate-Mike threw himself at Connor for a hug. "Thank God you're back!"

Donna and Liam, still in the SUV, exchanged grins.

"Good job, man," Connor assured Nate, patting his back. "You're alright. Donna, Liam! Pack up the truck." He tossed the keys in to Donna. "You can back in."

She clambered across to the driver's seat, and started the car. Connor gave her a minute to realize her own mistake, then pounded on the back fender. "Donna? Don't run over the rifles."

She looked in the rear mirrors and saw nothing. She hadn't bothered to raise the seat and pedals, just to back up twenty feet. Now she did so, and still couldn't see behind Darcy. Sighing, she asked Liam to go out and clear the way and direct her in. Connor prudently claimed the pistols for himself and Nate, and stood well out of the way, outside.

At dead slow, after several false starts and corrections, Donna fit the 20-foot car into the garage, with only inches to spare, Liam plastered against the wall.

Connor turned the key to close the garage doors on them. "Let us know when you're done."

"Aw, man!" Liam complained. "This is so unreasonable."

Donna sighed. "It's actually pretty interesting. A lot of work, but interesting. Everything has to fit back in exactly where it came out."

"Because Connor is anal retentive," Liam growled.

"Because we need to be able to find stuff in a hurry," Donna returned, clambering out the back. She noticed in passing that Connor, the rat, had completed the grocery shopping. Replenished bags of mushrooms, bread, and other produce hung from Darcy's ceiling. No doubt the cooler was packed with fresh meat and ice, though she didn't check. "We start with the under-seat stuff. That pile." At least Connor hadn't bothered to remove the clothing box on the roof, she was happy to see.

They cranked up some tunes on Liam's phone, and got to work. With him to fetch and pass her whatever she asked for next, Donna had Darcy re-packed in under an hour. She especially appreciated his help with the 5-gallon water bottles, though they were running low. After a final round of the garage checking for oversights, they collapsed onto the tailgate for a breather.

"He is anal retentive," Liam said. "But damn, he's good."

Donna sighed with a smile, and nodded.

Liam smiled back, setting off a dimple. "I'm better, though," he whispered. "We're all alone in here. Up for a little nookie?"

"No!"

He shrugged. "Can't blame a guy for trying. He doesn't know what a good thing he's got."

Donna decisively hopped off the tailgate, and shoved Liam off, too. She closed up Darcy and told Connor they were done.

~

"Now you thrash the water to make bubbles, and catch them in your pants," Connor instructed, high and dry on a public boat ramp.

He stood a ways back from the trio in the water. The lack of spring rain had left the lake level low. But the water filled a deep hollow, so the falloff into deeper water was steep. The lack of snow melt hadn't kept the water any warmer. Donna noticed that Liam and Nate's lips were turning blue. Her own teeth were chattering.

They'd taken off their pants in the water. Under Connor's direction, they tied the ends of the pant legs together, and hung that knot behind their necks, with the zipped waists of the pants lying on their chests. The goal was to create a buoyant life preserver out of heavy pants that would otherwise weigh them down. Better to keep the pants for when they escaped the water.

Unlike every other water safety instructor Ava had known, her boyfriend also insisted that they wanted to keep their shoes. If they got caught in a flash flood, they needed shoes on their feet and pointing downstream. Shoes were their best protection to fend off obstacles in the water. Since she was a strong swimmer, Connor insisted she do all of this while treading water, out too deep for her to stand. He let the geeks practice chest-deep. They were only about ten feet from her, though.

She supposed Connor's difference in lessons made sense. In her pool classes in middle school, or in Army Basic, the assumption was that you were surrounded by people who could pull you out. Connor assumed it was up to you, not only to save yourself, but possibly bring along someone unconscious or injured or panicking. Context changed the rules. You didn't want to jettison your assets. You had to make them work for you.

Donna couldn't for the life of her imagine how thrashing the water would inflate her pants legs. She was also hampered by needing at least one of her arms still sculling to keep her head above water. Lean and muscular, her body found neutral buoyancy a foot under water. Going under had worked for skimming her pants off one shoe at a time. It certainly wouldn't fill anything with air, though, and she was wearing herself out.

"Holy sugar. This works!" Liam reported in surprise.

Donna looked. Liam's makeshift life preserver was starting to look a bit puffy. She also caught Connor frowning at her. She grimaced and got back to thrashing.

"Donna, move in!" Connor called. "Next to Liam."

"I got this!" she insisted, and thrashed some more. She was working about four times harder than the guys, for a quarter the effect. Even if her black skinny jeans could magically inflate themselves, their volume was laughably small compared to Nate's chinos or Liam's baggy jeans. And they weren't inflating at all so far as she could tell.

"Donna, swim in! Now!" Connor insisted.

18

Interesting fact: Climate change caused severe droughts. But it also increased the incidence of torrential rains and floods. Warmer oceans evaporate faster, and warmer air holds more moisture.

Donna shook her head, determined, and tried harder to inflate her pants by thrashing water. Her feet were going numb in the icy lake, though.

"Liam! Grab her," Connor ordered from shore.

Carefully holding onto his inflated pants so the air didn't escape, Liam-Daneel swam the few strokes to Donna. Then he was stuck. He needed one arm for locomotion, one to hold the pants, and one to grab the girl.

"Come on, Donna," Liam urged. "Swim in." His lips were distinctly purple now. "Or hold my, um..." He had no idea how to do this.

"If you can do this, I can do this!" Donna argued through chattering teeth, still splashing. The pants inflated a little, but then she messed up and let the air escape.

Connor sliced through the water with a shallow dive, and came up right beside her. He grabbed her, dunked her to turn her around, and then she was clamped firmly under his arm. His powerful scissor kicks brought them to waist deep water in three strokes. He held her there without looking at her, and yelled to Liam and Nate. "Everybody out of the water! Liam, you need help?"

Connor watched carefully until Liam was waist deep and making good progress. Then he dragged Donna, still held firmly across the chest, out of the water. He stooped to grab his electronic key fob along the way.

Leave it to Frosty to protect the car dongle, Donna thought uncharitably. "I've got it," she grumbled. "Let me go."

He ignored that and kept her clamped to his side all the way to the car. "Get in. Get dressed," he ordered coldly. He started to strip standing by the car door.

Feeling one of those marital moments, Nate and Liam hung back. Dripping and shivering in their underwear, they faced the lake and untied their pants legs with numb fingers. Noting that Connor was stripping, they reluctantly followed suit.

As soon as his clothes were off, Connor popped open the back of the SUV. He pulled out towels, clothes for himself, and the other guys' backpack.

Donna noted that he only paused to tie a towel around his own waist before delivering towels to the other guys. He spoke briefly to them, then came back to pull on his own dry pants, still waiting on the tailgate.

Ava huddled with her wet hair in a towel turban. With grave diffi-culty, and fingers that moved like winter molasses, she'd managed to get partly changed. Skinning out of the skin-tight wet sports bra had been a particular trial. Her dry replacement was a pretty cotton peri-winkle bra that Connor – Frosty – had given her as a gift. So far it was still unhooked, because she couldn't get her pants fastened. She'd only donned the bra for modesty.

Frosty clambered through the hold. Businesslike, he hooked her bra, then made her stand so he could handle the zipper and button on her Levis. Before she could pull on the stomach-skimming half-sleeve top she'd picked out for herself, he took it away and came back with a grey sweatshirt, emblazoned 'PROPERTY U.S. ARMY.'

"You're pissed," she finally said.

"Yeah."

"Sorry –"

"You do the laundry." He met her eye with icy fury. "And you apologize to *them*. You can swim. They can't."

"Liam can –"

"Shut up, Panic."

He left to finally beckon Liam and Nate into the SUV, out of the chill wind. Then he set up the camp stove to boil water before he got around to putting on a T-shirt, socks and soccer sandals himself. His usual sneakers were in the wet laundry bag.

Ava – Donna – apologized to the geeks, mortified and near tears.

"He ripped you a new one, huh?" Liam said sympathetically. "Man, can he swim!"

Ava knew Cade wasn't as good a swimmer as she was, though maybe better than Liam. He just never let anything faze him. She didn't answer. Cade's mug of hot tea helped, too. When he handed it to her, she immediately rose to put away the camp stove. But he insisted she stay inside and warm up.

She thawed well enough, laughing at Liam clowning around in the SUV. Frosty stayed frozen like a block of ice.

~

"You had your hot shower yet?" Nate-Mike asked Donna-Ava, sauntering into the truck stop motel laundry.

"No, I wanted to get this done. So I didn't hold everybody up for dinner."

Nate plonked down beside her onto a hard orange plastic chair. He contemplated the three washing machines she had running. "Must be nice to have washing machines again."

"Orgasmic!" Donna agreed. "That was hard work, during the Starve. Cleaning. Cooking." The glee quickly drained from her face. "I shouldn't have said that," she whispered. "Sorry."

"My bad," Nate corrected her. "When Connor let us stay an extra day, I expected playtime. Rough day." He swallowed uncomfortably.

Donna noted his freshly washed graying hair and partially-repaired glasses. They made the older man look especially seedy and tired tonight. Not even night yet. Beyond the parking lot, the setting sun found a break in the overcast to bathe them in bloody light. *Atmospheric dirt from the Dust Bowl,* she thought. Such a little thing, to bring down an empire. Some dust in the air. Though of course, it was more than that.

She grasped his hand for a squeeze. "Hey, you never told me what happened to the garage door. Someone tried to break in?"

Nate's fingers dug into her hand. Then he realized what he was doing and released her. "They had a key. The management came snooping, I guess. All I saw were their feet. I shot above their heads. Then the garage door closed again. That's all I knew." He flashed her a quick haunted smile, and swallowed. "Not much of a story. Bet you and Connor have much more hair-raising adventures all the time." He wiped his palms on chinos of yet another hue of neutral.

Donna's imagination could fill in the rest. Shut in that garage alone, she would have been climbing the walls. No idea who would be coming back or when. Nate needed a silliness break, in her opinion.

"You know what I like about being a girl? Wearing bright colors. I mean, Connor likes it when I wear gaudy colors. So why can't he wear them?"

Nate smiled at her gratefully. "Hasn't always been that way, you know. Fashions change. Take what guys wore in the Renaissance – Never mind. I can watch the laundry, while you take a shower."

"This is my penance for being stubborn in the lake."

"For disobeying Connor?"

"For putting you and Liam at risk." She wobbled her head. "For scaring Connor. And you had a rough day. Thank you, though. I'm gonna miss you guys. You're a lot of fun."

He beamed. "Thank you. I don't hear that too often."

She patted his hand. "That's settled, then. Tonight, you get to be fun. Sorry I can't offer you any gaudy clothes. Connor's idea of wild and crazy is a single ear stud. Repressed."

"I could borrow Liam's pink barrettes." He ran a hand ruefully through hair too short and thin to hold a barrette.

"Oh, I have scarves! Wait here!" She scampered to the SUV and returned with their painted scarves from Sayre market. She handed Nate the two she painted, desert camouflage with melon blobs, and a brilliant marbled abstract in navy with peacock blues and greens.

Nate hung them both around his neck until he could pass one to Liam.

They migrated the laundry to the giant drum dryers, chatting away. Donna perched on a washing machine, Nate leaning on his elbows on the next one, when Connor appeared, and froze in the doorway.

Donna swallowed. "We're wearing scarves to dinner. You don't have to. If you don't want."

Face inscrutable, Connor waded in and plucked his Staten Island Ferry scarf from the pair around Donna's neck, and hung it around his own. He handed her a room key. "Go grab a shower. I'll bring up the laundry."

"Cool. See you soon, Nate!" she said brightly, and slipped off the washing machine. She pecked a kiss on Nate's cheek on the way out, but not Connor's.

By the time she finished her shower and dried her hair, Connor was back in the room, lying across one of their two queen-sized beds, arm across his eyes.

Draped in a towel, Donna sat next to him.

"Um," she said. "Sorry for scaring you at the lake."

"Sorry for getting so angry," he whispered. "I get so angry..."

"I'm not scared of you, Cade Snowdon," she whispered back. That wasn't entirely true, she reflected. But she insisted, nevertheless.

Then she remembered something one of her teachers at West Point told her. She'd already told Cade about her. Gever was a 'resource aide,' sent from Long Island to help with the traumatized apple trainees in lieu of psychiatric staff. "Gever said angry felt better than sad, or scared. More powerful, instead of weak. So I don't get scared. I get angry. Like that."

She wished Cade had the opportunities she had in the Army to work through some of her lingering issues from the Starve. Maybe he was thinking the same thing.

"My shrinks weren't that useful. I got a scrip." He waved his hand vaguely toward the spare bed, where his toiletry bag lay neatly among their gear and folded laundry. "I don't take it. Leaves my head feeling woolly."

"What is the scrip for? I mean, what was the shrink's diagnosis?"

"Borderline. Bipolar. Schizophrenia. Not sure."

"Cade, that's bullshit. You've got PTSD. We *all* have PTSD. The whole Apple Zone."

"Stop." Cade waited to make sure she stopped talking. "My mother was borderline, Ava. That's what broke up their marriage."

She never knew that. She waited a moment to make sure he was done speaking. "She couldn't have been too bad. Or you would have lived with your father."

"The court awarded custody to Dad. I demanded to stay with Mom, to take care of her."

Ava frowned. "Wow. You were what, twelve?"

"She started having breakdowns when I was seven or so. I was used to it."

"No wonder," she said.

"Huh?"

"Your personality, it's so different." Ava was thinking out loud. "Other people go nuts, you go cool. Sometimes in the gang, you'd lead crazy. But it was like someone cool and calculating decided, 'Now I shall act crazy.' Scary how much control you have."

"Dissociated, is the word," Cade murmured.

She turned to lay next to him, propped up on her elbow in her towel. She poked his chest. "Stop talking like it's a disease. It's your personality, not a symptom."

"Not so sure of that."

"I am. You do have a problem. Hypoglycemia. How long has it been since you ate? Do we have any snacks up here?"

"Hypo – what?"

"Low blood sugar. You get edgy when you haven't eaten. Moody, quick to anger. Dangerous. Glittery, I call it."

Her backpack was on the bed. She still had a protein bar in there, left over from Basic. She retrieved it, and handed it to him.

"That'll spoil my dinner," he objected.

"Just take a couple bites. Please. I'm trying to explain something."

Irritably, he tore the wrapper and bit off the end of the bar. "How long does this take?"

"Couple minutes." She returned to the other bed, and pulled on underwear fresh from the dryer, discarding the towel neatly in the bathroom. "You want the ferry scarf, or the tiger?"

"Your clubbing clothes are black. You wear the tiger."

"I can go either way."

"So can I."

"How are you feeling?"

Connor levered himself up on his elbows, and frowned. "Better. I like your black for evening. You're with three guys. You can dress sexy."

She shot him a smile. "Black and tiger it is."

"Blood sugar."

"Hard to handle when we were starving."

"Damn."

"You've still got PTSD. Worse than mine." She shot him a sympathetic glance. "You went out and fought more. I stayed to protect the hood. That's not so bad. Scary, but. Nothing like stealing from Jersey. I don't know how you could bear it, going with Chet on those raids. *Chet* was psycho."

"We were all psycho." Cade sat up and rubbed his face. "Scared, huh?"

"And hungry. And sick and tired, then. But now we're good. Let's have fun tonight, instead of work."

"Ava."

"Hm?" she turned to face him. He reeled her in between his knees, and planted his face in her still-bare midriff, hands on her lower back and butt. She lightly hugged him around the head and shoulders, and planted a kiss on his crown. She felt his deep sigh, when his shoulders unclenched.

She let him cling a minute longer, then kissed his head again. "You're OK, Cade. Safe."

He sighed deeply. "No. I'm not. But at least I'm with you." He released her to finish dressing. To go with his whimsical ferry scarf, he opened a garment bag on the bed. He changed into perfectly fitted grey wool trousers and a crisp button-down lilac shirt. And he wore his one ear stud. He left the bespoke suit jacket and tie in the bag.

He studied himself in the mirror and started to pull off the scarf. "I look ridiculous."

Ava wrapped arms around him from behind, and stayed his hand on the scarf with her own. "You look good enough to eat. Fun. Remember?"

"Fun," he repeated. He posed a gleeful smile in the mirror. It looked so stilted that Ava laughed out loud. He unbent and smiled, too – a soft and rare real one this time.

THE TRUCK STOP'S SIT-DOWN RESTAURANT HAD THE AMBIANCE OF A 'family' chain restaurant from before the Calm – golden light from hanging faux Tiffany lamps, dark orange vinyl benches in the booths, and walnut grain on the formica table. The menu was pure steakhouse, with 'light' options for dieters.

Ava wondered if there was a restaurant left in Hudson that needed to offer light options for dieters. She went for the four-ounce petit filet mignon drowned in mushrooms and wine sauce, with side salad and baked potato, feeling positively gluttonous. The guys ordered bigger steaks.

Cade – Connor – intended to nurse a single beer as his limit for the night. But Donna insisted this was her night as the designated driver. He needed to cut loose, in her opinion. She was too full to finish a beer anyway.

Liam-Daneel led the dinner conversation, making up topics out of thin air. They couldn't discuss anything real. In the quiet restaurant, it was too easy for bored truckers to eavesdrop. So he made up hilarious stories about imaginary relatives in Mifflin, another PA town whose name he enjoyed, like Altoona.

To Donna's surprise, Connor and Nate played along. Connor claimed Liam as his first cousin. Nate was Connor's uncle by marriage. Imaginary cousins and their complex love lives were invented with reckless abandon. They moved the pepper shaker in front of any of them who missed a beat and said something that contradicted what was said before.

Donna didn't even try to compete, just laughed along.

The tab was seventy Liberty dollars, higher than their first week's groceries. The waiter apologetically explained that prices were skyrocketing all over. "This weather."

Connor just nodded and paid. He left a twenty percent tip. "Always tip well," he murmured as they left. "Goodwill is valuable."

To Donna's delight, music was booming in the truck stop bar on a Saturday night. There were more women, too, besides the working girls. Apparently some of the market traffic stopped here for the night before heading home. She spotted truckers she'd met before on the Sixers drug run, too, but they did no more than tip a drink in Connor's direction.

She pulled Connor onto the dance floor first, then Nate, before allowing herself one dance with the young hacker Liam. By the time they made it back to the table, Connor and Nate were deep in a conversation about the collapse of Virginia with a neighboring table, so she danced a couple more songs with Liam.

"We make a good team," he whispered during a slow dance, beery breath tickling her ear. "Little bird tells me he hit you."

Donna shook her head. "Don't go there. I'm with him."

"I'm more fun..." Liam pulled back to show off his flashing eyes and dimple. He was awfully cute – and he knew it. He ended up with the blue scarf, over an armless torn brown sweatshirt, over brown skin, that said 'BROWN.' It showed off his Army-buffed arms to perfection. He reeled her in again. "Anyone is more fun."

"Don't," she pleaded. It was a fun fantasy, to have a fling with Daneel. But it would destroy Cade. Her reverie was interrupted.

"You again." The bouncer's familiar meaty hand pulled Donna away. "You're not welcome here. And no mixed dancing." He glared at Liam.

"Mixed?" Liam asked. "What does that mean, exactly?"

"You know damned well what it means," the bouncer said. "Upsets the clientele."

"They're with me, sir," Connor said, arriving to drape an arm around Liam and Donna both. "My cousin. My girlfriend. No problem here. Hey, sweetie, let's all dance together!" Connor swung them around until the bouncer was at his back instead of theirs, and started dancing. Nate waded in, clicking fingers above his head, like a waiter at a Greek restaurant. Ignored, the disgruntled bouncer gave it up.

When they got tired enough to return to their mini cocktail table, Donna waited until Connor sat on a stool. Then she parked herself between his knees, sometimes with his arm around her, sometimes not. The guys explored the beers while she sampled her way through unfamiliar soft drink offerings. The non-alcoholic birch beer wasn't bad.

"I want to get laid," Nate abruptly announced to the table.

Donna pointed out Angie to him. The hooker studiously avoided them, though she shot them frequent dirty looks. Any bruises on her face were cloaked by thick Goth makeup. Nate gave a solemn drunken nod, and headed off to negotiate.

"I'm in a truck stop," Liam announced. "I don't need to pay for it. They have restrooms."

"Really?" Donna asked, incredulous.

Liam flashed her another grin and a little finger-wave over his shoulder, as he did indeed head for the lavatories.

"Really?" she asked Connor.

"I'm not going in there wearing a scarf," he confirmed, with a laugh. "Truckers get lonely. I get propositioned enough. And you, missy, better stick with me."

She turned and draped her hands around his neck. "Yes. I think I will."

He pulled her close. "Thank you. Fun."

"Fun," she agreed.

"What a concept. So tell me. Are you over that…situation?" He glanced toward her crotch as politely and briefly as possible.

"I am," she said, with an exaggerated nod.

"Outstanding. But we have guests."

"You weren't thinking that we shouldn't do, um, when we're here?" Donna inquired. She hadn't expected this trip to be platonic. But so far, it had been.

"No," he confirmed. "Circumstances. Mood. But tonight we're having fun."

"Fun," she agreed with a laugh.

They couldn't leave the bar without their tech wizard charges. But once the geeks were safely escorted back to their motel room, having had their fun, Cade and Ava had time for theirs.

19

Interesting fact: One surprise effect of climate change was new 'blocking patterns' that held weather in place longer. Basically, the Arctic Ocean warmed faster than anticipated, with odd effects on the northern jet stream. These blocking patterns exacerbated the record-sized Hurricane Sandy in 2012 (New York and New Jersey), the record-shattering rainfall of Hurricane Harvey in 2017 (Houston floods), and the California drought of 2011-2017.

"I see you wore a long-sleeved shirt," John-Daneel quipped to Ben, as they settled into Darcy's four seats to debrief. "Prudent. I suppose a ski mask would be overkill. To protect you from her nails."

They were back at State Game Lands 219. John and Mike's belongings were extricated from Ben and Cheyenne's, and the camping gear retrieved from the trees. All packed again, John's ruck lay on the dead grass beside Mike's wizard staff, ready for their hike back to Hudson. Around the mountain instead of over it this time – a cranky and hungover John-Daneel had hammered on that point.

Ben shot a sour look at John, in the seat behind Cheyenne, and returned to fidgeting with knobs on the dashboard. "Your debrief, agent John."

Cheyenne frowned a question at Ben across the console. He didn't look at her. She sat reversed in her seat, back against the glove compartment, for their final group chat. Ben sat sideways against the door, one knee up by the steering wheel.

"Thank you, agent Ben," John said. "Well, the Free Penn con was a success. Mike, I don't think you could have pulled it off yourself. But your interference at the Colony was great. Good job."

"Gee, thanks," growled Mike.

"Extra bonus points to Mike for not losing it when his glasses were broken," John continued. "For VA, Mike, you need to bring a couple spare pairs of glasses. Did great in the lake. Schmoozed the girl. Ben, what am I missing?"

Ben replied, "Escape and evasion on the roadside. Mike dealt with the SEALs well. And guarding my stuff, shut in the storage garage. Even went out on your own last night with a hooker, Mike, and came back safe. I was impressed. You did a lot better than last time. Much more comfortable in the field."

Ben reached through to shake Mike's hand behind him. Cheyenne, lips pursed, noted that he did this without meeting her eyes, though she sat beside him. *What the hell?*

"Thank you, Ben," Mike murmured sincerely.

John continued, "Ben, I tried to stick a wedge between Cheyenne and you. Didn't get anywhere. I didn't try too hard."

"Gee, thanks," Ben said.

"Ben, what's going on?" Cheyenne demanded.

"Debrief, Cheyenne," John said. "I'm the senior field agent, giving feedback. Not that I'm very senior to Ben. Technicality. So. Cheyenne."

Ben's eyes winced shut.

"What do you mean, you're senior to Ben? You started the company with me, um…" Frustrated, Cheyenne counted backwards on her fingers.

"Time flies," John sympathized, echoing his words of Tuesday, the day he joined them. Now it was Sunday. "West Point graduation was two weeks ago, sweetie. But I joined the company in July, a couple weeks before Ben. I was our inside man at West Point."

Cheyenne held her breath as a couple heartbeats thudded in her ears. She hadn't put two and two together, that Frosty was already working for the company when she broke up with him last August. And that Daneel was a con artist, not a fellow recruit.

"You knew this?" Cheyenne breathed to Ben.

He nodded slightly, still not meeting her eye.

"Cheyenne," Mike said, "John gave us the meshnet code base as his way into the company. Lock, stock, and barrel! The security protocols, back doors, encryption keys. Everything!" He grinned in admiration.

Cheyenne stared at him, appalled. "And you, Mike? You're a newer hire than them?"

"Oh, no! No, I've been in from the beginning." This time Mike broke eye contact. "They didn't give me much choice."

John explained, "Mike's not a field agent. Cheyenne, I really am studying under Mike. I don't have formal training in computer science. High school interrupted, like you. Though I was a year ahead of you. Learned to hack from hackers. I was undercover for half a year straight on the West Point operation. I earned a sabbatical. And I need some new tricks for Mount Weather."

"We're not discussing Mount Weather," Ben interjected.

Ava's mind was stuck on all the times she'd let Daneel borrow her unlimited, paid meshnet-and-Internet access back at West Point. He wasn't a charming fellow recruit. He was a black hat hacker embedded into her class by the death angels. With access paid for by Ava's friend and mentor Guzman, back in the city. Access she gave to Daneel. He was conning her all along?

"Why are we not discussing that op?" John asked Ben.

"Cheyenne isn't cleared yet," Ben said. "I don't know that she's going to VA."

John – Daneel – whoever the hell he was – tilted his head and considered Cheyenne. After a contemplative moment, he flashed a brilliant smile and dimple at her. "Of course she's coming! She's awesome! You're great, doll baby!" He glanced at Ben. "Might want to work a little on the gullibility." He laughed.

"Get out!" Cheyenne demanded. "How dare you?"

"Cheyenne, stop," Ben murmured. He finally met her eye. "John and Mike are fellow agents, getting field experience outside Hudson. This week's theme was con jobs. We told you that."

"You didn't tell me *I* was the target!" she shrieked. "Damn you!"

Ben scratched his neck. "Mike, John? Any other business? Maybe we should let you go."

"Any feedback for me?" John asked, serious for a moment.

Ben looked out the windshield, then back at John. "Don't do it again, with Cheyenne. I know you had to this time. But we're partners. Respect that, or you and I will have a problem. On my team, everyone needs to trust each other."

"Trust!" John said, delighted. "Among hardened criminals. You know, *Ben,* I think you might pull that off." Just for a moment, he dropped the carnival facade. "Truly. Thanks, man. About my break that night, with the sirens."

Ben nodded slightly. "Cheyenne handled that," he pointed out.

"You make a good team," John agreed, manic manner restored. "And with that, I think we're done. See ya, Panic!"

"Not if I see you first." She glared at him. The bastard even admitted to toying with her affections, just to see if he could get her to cheat on Cade. What a flaming –

John took in her demeanor and scooted forward to hang from her seat back, cheek intimately pressed to the leather upholstery between seats. "Hey, hey, Panic," he said softly. "Did you know 'con' was short for 'confidence'? That's how a con works. You gain someone's liking and trust. Then you use that to persuade them to do something that maybe isn't in their best interest. I know how you feel right now. Like everything I've ever said or done was a lie. You feel betrayed.

"But two things, girlfriend. One – did I lie? Am I not the person you thought I was? A goofball young hacker from Long Island? Sweetheart, that's exactly who I am. Granted, if Colonel Newsome back at the Point didn't have his head up his ass, I should have been discharged the first week. Because I really do have asthma. I didn't need to rig anything on that," he added as aside to Ben. "Command was just that stupid."

"Charmed life," Ben acknowledged.

John flashed a smile, and returned his attention to Cheyenne. "I really was a fellow recruit, Panic. I lived the life with you. You knew I was a hacker. You knew you shouldn't give me your phone. And that's point two. The downside of running a con, is when someone realizes you played them? Man, they feel betrayed. Just like you do right now."

He gazed at her with limpid, sympathetic eyes. He spoke to her like a lover past the seat back.

Cheyenne agreed with everything he was saying. Maybe she was being silly to hold it against him that he'd conned her.

Ben scowled and reached out stiff-fingered to push John's face back.

God damn it! Cheyenne thought. *He played me again!*

John withdrew merrily enough, hands in the air, and laughed out loud. "I'm just sayin'!"

"You said plenty," Ben growled. Then he extended a hand for a shake. "Good to work with you, John. Impressed as hell."

"Yeah, man. You have no idea how good you are. Seriously. Impressed as hell."

Ben shook his head and traded an aggrieved glance with Mike.

"I know," Mike said. "Just take the compliment at face value. It's true, after all. You're awesome in the field."

"Thank you," Ben said.

John spread his hands in entreaty. "And like I was just telling her. I *don't* lie. It *wouldn't work* if I were lying. That was my point." He grinned.

"I think we're done," Mike said. "Cheyenne, you're a delight. I hope to see you again soon!"

Ben climbed out of the car to see them off. Cheyenne stayed where she was, arms folded grumpily against her chest. Ben leaned on the SUV, hands in his pockets, until they vanished into the trees.

The world seemed lonelier without them. And that pissed Cheyenne off, too. She waited another minute, and banged her way out of the car. "I'm going for a run," she announced.

Three strides later, she stopped and threw her head back, mentally kicking herself. She returned to open the passenger door. She reached into the glove box to retrieve the Glock. She shoved it hard into the back of her waistband.

"Because if I didn't, you'd probably shoot at me again," she accused Ben. "Asshole!"

"Maybe not today," Ben murmured, eyes wincing.

Cheyenne wanted to wipe that wince off his face with a pistol whipping.

Reluctantly Ben added, "The wildlife is kinda dangerous here, though."

"*I know that!*" she yelled at him. "You stayed here *pouting* while I dealt with the bear, and the boar, and the effing hulking *SEALs!*"

Ben nodded jerkily. "Go take your fucking run. And get your head on straight." Cold blue eyes glared into hers. "We're on the road by three."

Great, just fucking great! Ava raged inside, breaking straight into a run without proper warm-up. *Now he's pissed at me, too. Way to go, Panic.*

Her first lap was around the dead-grassy field they parked in. This was the sort of landscape and aspirational lifestyle that years of TV commercials showed to sell the dream of a Ford Expedition like Darcy, to fat Americans who racked up the miles running errands in the city, or to visit relatives out of town. *Buy an SUV. Ride off into the wilderness to camp in the woods. Pretend no one's ever been here before.*

They've been here. They took one look and left. This land is useless.

From Ron Kaminski's appraisal of the Colony, Ava recognized the signs. The trees ringed the field because there was solid rock a few inches under the uneven turf she ran on.

When she came to the spot where John and Mike disappeared into the trees, she stopped. Legs planted wide, she dropped down for some belated hamstring stretches, blowing out rage.

I could follow them straight back into Hudson. Don't even need to follow them. Head north. Hudson's big, can't miss it.

The thought cooled her temper tantrum. *I didn't want Daneel. I wanted my friends back from boot camp. I thought Daneel was one of us. But he never was. I want Cookie and Doc, Yoda and Puño. I'm homesick. But they're not there anymore. We all moved on.*

Moving. Good idea. Ava Panic used to be good at thinking once, at least after a morning jog to jump start her hectic school day. There had been some changes made. The only time she thought well was when she was moving. And Calderon, her drill sergeant back at the Point, cast his doubts about that.

She considered veering off to run along the rutted dirt road that passed the field. Then she'd be out of Ben's sight. But as Ben – *Cade, dammit!* – pointed out, the SEALs were awfully handy last time facing down the wild predators. She didn't fancy her chances solo against a boar. And she was supposed to be here as Ben's backup. So another lap of the field it was.

Trust among hardened criminals. Trust your gang! Trust your unit! *Hardened criminals.* Trust a boyfriend who stood beside you through everything Ebola and the Starve could throw at you. *I'm pissed at him, too. Dammit!*

Don't try to think, Panic. You suck at it. Calderon again. *Just move your body smarter this time.*

Thirty minutes. No matter how pissed off she was, thirty minutes of aerobic exercise, and her endorphins would kick in.

Hell. Might as well do it right.

She stopped where she was and did a set of the running strength exercises Calderon taught them, back in 'fat camp' before Basic. Before the Calm, fat camp was to run off the weight. For the starved survivors of the Apple, they needed a six week head start to gain weight. Familiar movements took over. Gever, also at Basic, taught her to meditate by breathing into each muscle. Trying to empty her mind, or to focus on a serene imaginary setting, was hopeless when she was on a rage binge. But to focus on a flexing limb, that she could do.

I'm not a criminal.

OK, enough with the stretching. She alternated sprints and jogs with walks, until she was dripping with sweat. She was dressed for a 50-degree day, with gusty wind. To run, she should have stripped to boy shorts and tank.

They lied to me! I trusted them!

Alas, endorphins started to flow. After another lap around the field, she tried to tally up all the lies they told her. She stopped for a breather, and then set to crunches and stretches. She kept her skinny jeans on, but stripped to her bra for this part. There was no one to see but Cade.

Cade settled in to ignore her with his algebra textbook on Darcy's tailgate. *Self-disciplined to a fault.*

Neat freak. Control freak. Discipline freak. Freak –

That brought her up short. The last thing Cade Snowdon needed was for her to feed his fear that he was going insane. If his pesky rituals and tidy storage helped keep his inner demons at bay, she was all for it.

What did they lie to me about? Daneel... She reviewed Tuesday through Sunday, and couldn't find a single lie. *Well, he came on to me! Acted like he was interested!*

He flirted. Big deal. *He shouldn't have flirted with me with Cade right there.* Yeah, and he shouldn't have flirted with Cade right in front of her, either, but it was good for a laugh at the time.

The look on Cade's face when Daneel – Liam that night – explained that his band on Long Island was polyamorous – that was priceless. She laughed again just remembering. *'Yeah, we all slept with all the others.' 'All the girls, with all the guys?' 'You're making assumptions. I'm not hetero. All of us slept with all the others.'*

Well, maybe he'd lied then, maybe he hadn't. Ava chuckled. She'd bet on exaggeration.

Daneel lied, but he lied to the Army, not me. Cade didn't even lie about White Rule and how he joined the company. He told me he wasn't free to talk about it. If Mike lied to me about anything, I wouldn't know.

She flopped onto her back and stretched her feet up in the air to trace loops and scissors and generally goof around with her toes.

I don't like being called a criminal.

That doesn't mean it isn't true.

It is true. I am a criminal. There was a questionnaire. I filled it out in loving detail, itemizing my crimes for Skull. My kills and foreign languages, my weapons and past addresses, my sex work history, my drug dealing, and my grades in high school. He screened us well. He only hired stone cold killers and criminals.

Cade told her he was in the Hudson citizenship database as gang royalty – a leader in organized crime. She was right there beside him. The Governor granted amnesty for crimes committed during the Starve, understanding why they did it, allowing the apples a fresh start. But gang royalty had skills that wouldn't vanish when a little food turned up, and some crappy minimum wage job. And they were answerable for the crimes of thousands, not just their own. Gang royalty were forgiven, but not forgotten. And they were right.

What am I still angry about? She couldn't think of anything. She picked up her shirt and carried it back to the SUV. She plonked onto the tailgate, trying to bounce the vehicle on the diagonal like Daneel had. She didn't have the mass for it. Darcy scarcely dipped.

"How goes it?" Ben asked neutrally, eyes still on his graph paper, looking vexed.

"Tantrum over. How goes algebra?"

"It's like foreign languages. You study them when you're a kid and your brain is wired to learn them. I think my brain hardened against algebra."

"What an empowering thought, Ben. We could put it on the rear-view mirror like an affirmation. You dropped a sign on the second line." She stabbed a minus that should have canceled into a plus. "The rest of that was pure bullshit."

"Theme of the day. Pure hogwash."

"Hogwash. Pardon my French."

He smirked. "Wash up, little piggy."

"One thing. From now on, you to tell me what the plan is."

"Deal. We have business in Philadelphia Tuesday. Need more money first. We'll go around the state clockwise. Get money. Visit contractors. Spend money. And then it will be Sunday again. We kinda blew our Sunday off this week to play with Mike and John. And last Sunday was the Badgers."

"OK. What's the training agenda?"

"We're done with that. Now you practice. Ask questions, learn what comes. Gain confidence. Sound good?"

"Good." She rose to rock a 5-gallon jug out to the tailgate to wash. "Philadelphia sounds fun."

"Really?" Ben gazed around the lonely wooded hills that surrounded them. "I like it here. It's more fun with company. But even alone." He turned back to her with a rare soft smile. "You've changed. The Army was good for you."

"What do you mean?"

"I figured you'd take it out on me for days." He smiled after he said it to soften the comment.

She hit him anyway, but not hard. That led to karate practice, which segued into even more fun forms of wrestling. Ben gave plenty of positive reinforcement for mastering her temper.

Ben and Cheyenne became Ace and Bridget by half past four.

20

Interesting fact: Philadelphia was the sixth largest city in the U.S., with about 1.6 million people. Pittsburgh was number 63, with about 300,000. All cities lost population after the Calm Act, of course, but Pennsylvania's cities fared better than most.

It's amazing what people can get used to. Ava – or Bridget or Cheyenne, Donna or Ellen, Faye or Gwen – fell into the rhythm of their days. Aside from Cade's rituals, there wasn't much pattern to them. He usually sought to accomplish one major task or two lesser errands per day. Plus life maintenance, like fueling themselves and Darcy, and finding a safe place for the night.

Their next 'allowance' arrived in the form of a trailer of electronics that crossed the Delaware near a river island in State Game Lands 209. That was near Port Jervis, where the prior states of Pennsylvania, New Jersey, and New York met to PA's northeast. They helped the border soldiers heave the trailer from their boat to dry land after dark on Sunday, and spent the night.

In the morning, Cade-Ace told her to take point on fencing the goods. He'd play backup today.

"I have no idea how to do that," Ava-Bridget objected.

He pointed at the trailer, and she looked again. She laughed. A thick manila envelope with routing slip was taped to the side, just like they'd attached to the drug shipments bound for Jersey.

Ace crooked a smile. "It's a simple system."

"Hardly seems like they need us," Bridget said.

"Bridget? That's one hell of a lot of money."

"Ah. Point taken," she said thoughtfully. Finding the fence should be the safe and easy part. Getting out of there alive, with that much money, might take some assertiveness.

They drove I-84 into Scranton, the only real city Ava had seen yet in PA. They found the specified address in an industrial park. The counter man at the goods laundering facility was all too amused to deal with an 18-year-old 'little girl' who claimed to have business. He cracked up laughing when Bridget attempted to bolster her authority with her routing slip.

Ace gave her a few minutes, then leaned against the service counter beside Bridget. He pulled his gun on the jerk at at the cash register, carefully shielded from the store cameras with his body. "Is your name Clive? Bridget, our shipment is for Clive. Let's not waste time with the hired help. You. Get Clive. Tell him Ace and Bridget are here."

Bridget quietly fumed as the middle-aged cashier with the bouncer build hastily retreated. "I should have asked for Clive?" she asked Ace.

Ace shrugged unconcern. "Anyone who can fence this shipment? Same-day cash? Clive has better things to do than wait on customers at a pawn shop. Just tell the pretty receptionist you have business with the boss. She doesn't need details."

Bridget grinned at his casting the beefy male cashier as the pretty receptionist. "Got it."

They were soon ushered into Clive's sloppy office in the back. Ace stepped back to let her do the talking. Until the very end, when Clive said he'd take the shipment now and have cash tomorrow. Bridget frowned and looked to Ace.

He tilted his head to suggest she think it through.

"Do you have a quiet place where you can check the shipment?" she suggested. "You can inspect the goods. But you don't take possession until we're paid in full. Samples, maybe. But you have the itemized contents right here." She tapped the bill of lading. Clive had already gone through it and jotted bids in the margin, for what all of it was worth.

In fact the 'routing slip' envelope included two copies of the full inventory of the trailer box. At first, back at the trucker transshipment with the Sixers, she'd laughed. She thought it was cute that contents were fully specified, if vaguely worded, on the doped drugs, just like a legitimate warehouse business. She was beginning to realize that the reason some things didn't change was that they worked. If shipments and money were to trade hands, the contents needed to be clearly specified. Their operations might be considered crime, but it was still a business.

Clive threw up his hands in disgust. "I can't ask people to pay for goods before delivery!"

"Twenty percent on top. Your brokerage fee," Ace suggested.

"Thirty!"

"Twenty-five. But only if we're out of here by noon. After that, your cut drops one percent every half hour. And at two, we leave and find another dealer." Ace offered scarcely an hour before the penalties set in.

"And then you never see our business again." Bridget pursed her lips.

"You got balls," Clive said to both of them, eyeing them appraisingly.

"Don't try anything," Bridget said, staring him straight in the eye. "Sure, we're just agents. But the people behind us? Screw with us and they will end you."

Clive looked at his final figure for the shipment. That trailer of electronics was enough to pay the Sixers camp five times over. The most eye-popping figures were for critical replacement parts for cell phone towers. He blew out a long breath. "I believe that," he muttered. He plied his calculator, then scribbled a twenty-five-percent figure at the bottom, and subtracted it off. "Wait outside."

Clive may have meant out in the pawn shop. But Bridget chose to exit to the parking lot. She made herself comfortable perched atop the low trailer, with just the tip of her M4 carbine visible to the pawn shop side. Ace elected to wait in the driver's seat, key in the ignition. Bridget figured if she heard Darcy's engine start, she'd better hang on.

But wonder of wonders, Clive decided to play straight with them. He came outside, and made her open up the trailer for inspection. He did a perfunctory check to make sure he was receiving the specified inventory instead of an empty trailer. Five minutes was enough for that. The cell tower parts alone were worth half the value of the shipment.

He handed Bridget an envelope thick as a brick, and settled to watch her verify the cash. She bumbled through this for a few minutes. Clive scowled and grabbed the envelope back. He held the money down and behind the trailer, out of sight and out of the wind. He counted bills into her hands, with well-practiced swiftness, frequently licking thumb and finger for ease in separating the bills. With fifties the largest denomination, this took far longer than his cursory goods inspection.

Clive came up fifty short. Rather than recount, he peeled another two hundred liberty dollars, in twenties, out of a wad from his back pocket. "Close enough," he muttered.

"Absolutely," Bridget agreed. She shot a thumb's-up to Ace, who started the SUV. "Thank you for your business, Clive." She thrust out her hand to shake.

Clive frowned at her tiny hand and shook his head in disgust. He walked to the trailer hitch, stooped down to unfasten it, then stepped on the coupling. He pushed off Darcy to work the trailer apart.

Mission accomplished, Clive nodded to her. She snatched her M-4 from the top of the trailer and hastened to the passenger door. Ace gave the guy a neutral nod and a wave while waiting for Bridget's center of mass to hit the seat. Then he peeled out while she struggled to get the car door closed.

They didn't stop the SUV again in that county.

Bridget had plenty of time to stow the cash neatly, tucked into hidden pockets in the front leather seats in unequal-sized pre-counted portions, divided into white envelopes labeled with the amounts. Ace's fastidiousness in storing money now made perfect sense to her. Clive's finger-licking trick was too gross for a nurses' kid. But she poured some water on her jeans, and moistened thumb and finger on the damp spot to speed her cash counting.

Collecting money was a minor job. The day's second act was to drive to Philadelphia, about a four hour trip these days. The empty roads were better than average. But disrepair and bypassing checkpoints ate up time.

~

In Philadelphia, Cade as Dean Fuller checked them into an upscale hotel, with Ava now Eileen Bennington.

Before the woman at reception could assign them a room, Dean asked, "By the way, my partner needs a business suit for tomorrow. Can you recommend a store? Or a tailor. Might need both."

"Of course, sir," the front desk manager purred. Her name tag advised her name was Tracey. "The hotel has a relationship with a bespoke tailor who would be happy to send someone over. Their prices are quite reasonable." She shifted to address Eileen sympathetically. "For off the shelf, you'd be looking at used clothing. You're an unusual size for business attire. That could be very time-consuming. Hit or miss."

Eileen, dressed in her usual skinny jeans and red hunting plaid vest over a T-shirt, with red high-top sneakers, blinked stupidly. *What does 'bespoke' mean? I have a dress.* Though as she took in the hushed velvet elegance of the lobby, she began to suspect her lavender cotton dress was better for a summer picnic at Coney Island. *Ace – Dean – knows what my dress looks like. Hm.*

"The faster the better," Dean assured Tracey. "We're only here for two nights. I wouldn't mind a new suit myself. If they can really deliver that quickly."

"Oh, yes. And their prices are quite reasonable. So many people desperate for work, you know." Tracey lowered her voice tactfully on that last.

Dean nodded, oozing disinterest. The little people's problems, were not his problem. "That would be ideal. If you could arrange it?" He slipped her a twenty. He waved a hand at her terminal. "Are there room upgrades to consider, or…?"

Tracey bent over backwards to please him, ignoring Eileen completely after this. Eileen wondered what her commission was on the tailor. They received a 'free' upgrade to a room with jacuzzi. Unlimited broadband Internet was included, of course.

"I could get used to business hotels," Ava murmured happily, as they soaked in the jacuzzi sized for two before their appointment for fittings at 6:30. The room was as lush as the foyer, with deep garnet pile carpet, swagged brocades, heavy gilt mirrors, and red velvet patterning on tasteful metallic wallpaper. The walls and floors in the bath featured marble veneers. A glass wall isolated the shower stall. Before the soak, she scrubbed clean with luxury soap and washed her hair under its rainfall shower head.

Cade wriggled a foot to tease her ear with his toe. "Not a business hotel. I'd say nouveau riche poser hotel before the Calm."

"Ah," she said helplessly. For her family, the cheapest possible motel was the norm. Her mother rated vacation expenditures by her hourly wage after taxes. Her grandfather found them an even cheaper house to rent for their final vacation on Cape Cod, only an eight block walk from the dunes. It rained a lot.

"Who has money for a nice hotel these days, Eileen?" Dean pressed.

"Successful businessmen and criminals," she hazarded. "Like us. And Clive. Is all of Philadelphia like this? It seems so…old normal."

"Don't really know. It's broken down into neighborhoods, militia checks between them. This district is for business, no militia hassles. We come in on the freeway. We leave on the freeway. I've never seen the rest of the city."

The woman from the tailor's arrived at their room punctually. Nadezda had a Slavic accent, reminding Ava of her parents again. She made a conscious effort to pronounce the name in American.

Nadezda measured her in every possible dimension, several of which Eileen had never considered before. Ava could almost see her mother standing behind the seamstress. Her arms would be crossed, white rubber-soled nurse's shoe tapping. She'd dole out withering commentary on Ava's boyish figure, and the stupidity of dressing her up like a Wall Street parasite.

When Nadezda switched to measuring Dean, Eileen prudently turned to hide a smile among the fabric swatches and pattern book lying on the bed. Mama could be pretty funny. She and Ava's father traded caustic barbs as a sort of foreplay. Mama would have had great fun at Tata's expense, supervising his crotch measurements.

"Not suits," Nadezda called out to her. "You're too small. You'd look ridiculous. Look at dress patterns."

Eileen pinched her nose to stifle a laugh. Mama would have been less polite, but Nadezda channeled her intonation perfectly. "I was thinking a suit for a concealed carry. A pistol."

Nadezda left Dean waiting, and flipped the pattern book to another page. "That one. Carry the gun in the pocket. Or your purse." She resumed her squat at Dean's crotch.

Eileen studied the dress Nadezda recommended. The severe tailored coat-dress had asymmetric lines, with a single wide contrast lapel slashing from shoulder to hip, and a balancing slash pocket on the other side. The snug fit extended nearly to the knees, with a long back slit. *Wow. That would make me look old.* But that was probably the point.

The finished garments arrived by 9 a.m. as promised, complete with all the trimmings. Eileen's deep red dress, with navy contrast, came with navy thigh-high stockings and shoes, and a beige slip of the correct dimensions.

She layered her base makeup on thick, with only the slightest blush to warm the contours. One of her lighter red lipsticks was too garish for business, except it matched the red suit-dress. For her eyes, she stuck to black, grey and brown. She smoothed her hair into a severe bun, then skewered it with golden chopsticks in an X. For her ears she wore her simplest gold studs. They picked up reading glasses last night at a bookstore desperate for business. She perched them on her nose, the narrow heavy rim bisecting her eyes so she needed to peer over or under.

She straightened up from her detail work and stepped back to gauge the effect. "My God, I look thirty," she said.

Dean, done dressing, looked up from his notes and smiled. He rose to stand next to her in the big room mirror. "Well, maybe a law school student instead of high school. You still have the chopsticks." He happily extracted her sharp stabbing weapons from her bun. "They don't go with the outfit," he murmured in her ear, a hand at the small of her back.

She raked her eyes over his reflection. The wonders of bespoke tailoring – his new suit fit him like a glove. Its style was different. He already had a standard button-down suit and tie, which would have worked perfectly well. He just wanted to add a summer suit while they were at it. But Nadezda talked him into trying the latest in men's fashion. No tie, no collar, no lapels on his jacket, no pockets or fidgety bits, in a graphite jacket and slacks, with a pale blue shirt that brought out the color in his icy eyes. Done sloppily, he might have looked like a Puritan preacher. But his suit was of the finest materials and workmanship. His old-style suit would have provided distractions that hid an unfortunate build.

But Cade's figure was perfect.

He tried on his own narrow reading glasses. But then he discarded them on the bureau with Eileen's makeup. He preened a little, turning to and fro. He modeled a hand in the pocket, since she was staring.

"You look incredible," she breathed. "How can you look so natural in that getup?"

He caught her reflection in the eye for a moment, his expression unreadable. "Dean Fuller is more like Cade Snowdon than Frosty ever was."

That was wrong, somehow, but she couldn't put her finger on it. "Cade went through the Starve with Frosty and Panic. He grew up." That sounded more right to her. "Cade… You know, he was kind of superior and arrogant. No matter what happened, you would have grown out of that. Because you're better than that."

Still expressionless, he nodded slightly. "Yale might not have been the right place to grow out of that. But you would have helped."

She shook her head, and fidgeted with her eye shadow colors. "You wouldn't have belonged with me. I feel ridiculous in this suit."

"You need to get into Eileen's head," Dean critiqued, sitting on the bed behind her, still visible in the mirror, but smaller and shorter. "Say we started Yale together. Both socialized with the same crowd. Maybe crewed at Yale Corinthian Yacht Club for fun. Caught all the plays, the visiting lectures. Ate a few tons of pizza in our Gothic dorm rooms. Of course you had a sober dress or three. You had occasion to wear them. But that was years ago. You went into business consulting. You found you have a flair for money."

"I have a flair for money," she told herself archly in the mirror.

"And today you're my goon. The strong cool silent type, handling the cash. I do the talking. You don't have the background for these meetings. Listen and learn."

She thrust a hand in her pocket and made a finger pistol, aimed at Dean in the mirror. "Pow."

He grinned, but maintained Dean's perfect posture and arrogance.

Eileen said, "If you'd gone off to Yale, I never would have seen you again. That's so strange."

He shook his head solemnly. "I would have come back every few weeks, to visit Mom. It's only a couple hours on the train. You would have visited New Haven, too. Maybe we'd commute between New Haven and Boston after you started at MIT, or I'd transfer to be in the same town. You wouldn't have turned into Eileen. But you might have kept me from turning into Dean."

She scoffed. "You'd have broken up with me."

He shook his head again. "I don't leave people behind. People matter to me. We would have had some hard conversations along the way. You telling me you were Serbian. Me telling you my mother was nuts, and I was afraid... Afraid it was genetic. That I'll go crazy, too. But I wouldn't leave her behind. Or you."

He took a deep breath. "So, you would have had to break up with me. Because you realized that a Cantonese engineering geek was sexier and sillier than me. Eh, boring old Cade. So aloof and serious all the time. And I know how you love the sing-song sound of Cantonese."

She laughed. He knew how she loathed the clangor of Chinese languages. Mandarin, Cantonese, Taiwanese, Vietnamese, it didn't matter. They sounded like a bank of clanking washing machines torturing irate songbirds. A lot of Asian kids attended high school with her at Brooklyn Tech. She hated how they reformed their cliques the moment class was over, and broke back into their screeching gibberish.

If she were fair about it, she might have admitted it was the social angle she resented. Making friends in New York seemed impossible until she joined Cade's dojo. By age 12, it seemed the city kids had already cliqued up for life. But Cade was in the same boat, having moved to Greenwich Village from a posh Jersey suburb around the same age.

"It doesn't matter what might have happened, Ava. That Cade and Ava, they're gone. We had a lot in common then. We have more now. And our first appointment is in twenty minutes. Ready?"

"No?"

"Just don't say much. Listen attentively. Makes you look smarter."

THEIR FIRST MEETING WAS AN ARMS DEAL, A PRE-CALM MILITIA OUTFIT much like White Rule but classier, near the Delaware border. They would make themselves available for 'population control operations' on request, in exchange for arms and ammo.

The next pair, older men in business suits, represented an arms manufacturing consortium. They produced AK-47's and ammo. Eileen gave them a $10,000 down payment for 'samples' to be delivered to an address in Erie, at the opposite northwest corner of PA. She was no longer bemused by the carefully itemized receipt. She photographed it with Dean's phone, then filed it in his briefcase.

The next trio seemed to get on Dean's calendar by accident. Farmers, a father and two middle-aged sons, sought capital for a major greenhouse operation, producing potatoes with high-density hydroponic methods developed in the Netherlands. A fascinated Eileen studied their presentation. Dean heard them out, then asked them why they hadn't secured funding from the PA lead Resco right here in Philly. Father farmer complained of paperwork held up by the pending merger of PA and Hudson, and an army officer not knowledgeable about large-scale agriculture.

Dean said his company could put in a word for them with a Resco on the Jersey side of the border, who might help move their proposal forward. Eileen gave them $20,000 to get their nutrient orders off stall, and filed their proposal for followup.

A drug manufacturer's agent. A pair of enterprising young pot growers. A business rep from the southeast branch of the Sixers. A smuggling operation along the Maryland border, materiel only, no people. A specialist in 'personnel relocation' with a contract and payment complaint. Most of them received cash. Some, like the Sixer rep, quite a lot of cash.

Between appointments, in their private party back room of a dark restaurant with no front room customers, a closed-mouth middle-aged waiter refreshed water pitchers and trays of snacks. Eileen reminded Dean to graze regularly.

At last, by 4:00 p.m., Dean rose and stretched and yawned mightily. "That's it. Be sure to tip the waiter a hundred percent on the tab."

It was the smallest payout Eileen made all day.

"Playtime?" she asked hopefully.

"I'm gonna hit the gym," Dean said. "You have a meeting with the boss at 4:30. Video chat, while we've got the broadband connection." He tapped his briefcase. "You can report on today while you're at it."

21

———

Interesting fact: The martial governments did not intend socialism. They simply backed social enterprises, critical infrastructure, and priority industries. The private sector was less effective, as the collapse of pre-Calm currencies left them short on capital, long on instability, and reinventing the wheel. The public sector was larger by default.

"Wow, that's quite a makeover," Skull said, with a gratifying double-take at Eileen's appearance. His image and voice projected from the hotel room's wide screen TV. Cade arranged that for her with a simple cable to their tablet. The device sat propped against the TV for its camera.

Skull wore his workaday uniform, as Hudson Major Sullivan. In his late thirties, his military short brown haircut frosted lightly with grey, neither short nor tall, perfectly fit without making an especial point of it, Skull's bland appearance and expression were the camouflage of a model army officer.

"Hi, boss. Bye, boss." In workout attire now, Dean leaned into the camera angle for a quick wave.

"Thanks, Dean," Skull said, cracking a slight smile. "I'll talk to you later."

Eileen sat quietly waiting, as the room door closed behind Dean. "He's gone," she reported.

"Good. I wanted to check up on you. I have reports here from Dean, John, Mike, the SEALs. An unsolicited tirade from Oelrich with the Sixers. And a thank-you note from the Tioga County sheriff's office. They tell me you're doing great. Are you? Doing great?"

Eileen blinked. "I think I'm doing good."

Skull sat back and waved for her to expand on that.

"I've learned a lot, sir. I'd say today was a real eye-opener. But every day has been that. New skills. My driving is improving. PA – No, the world changed a lot since the epidemic locked me in the Apple. In the city, I still saw the outside world as it was Before. I guess I felt put-upon. But it's tough all over. Um, is that the sort of thing you wanted, sir?"

Skull rolled a pencil minutely on his desk. "Call me boss instead of sir."

"Yes, s– Boss."

He quirked a smile. "How are you getting along with Dean?"

"Great."

He outright grinned at that. "Expand on that please."

Their personal relationship was none of Skull's business. Eileen cast her eyes around the room, seeking some framework in which to answer. "I admire him. How he operates. How he handles people. His outlook. He's patient. A clever trainer. He doesn't just tell me stuff. He sets me up to learn for myself. I'm learning a ton. He's comfortable here, always poised for whatever comes next."

"How's his equilibrium these days? Emotionally."

"I'd like to think it's getting better. I think he's happy I'm here. Not being alone."

"You'd like to think," Skull repeated. "Interesting wording. Do you believe he's stable?"

"Stable," Eileen echoed in turn. "I don't know what that means for an apple, sir. We both have PTSD. We help each other. We've come a long way this year. How'd he put it… I don't remember. We were like porcupines with big red buttons all over. 'Push me, make my day, asshole!' We're not prickly like that anymore. Not so much, anyway.

We can deal reasonably with people. Even when they piss us off. He always was better at that than I was."

"You say 'we' a lot," Skull observed. "Seems like you've bonded as partners again."

"I'd like to think so," she said. Then she winced at having repeated the same phrase the boss had called her out on a minute ago. "Our relationship is…good."

Skull grinned. "Impressed as hell, Agent Panic. I've interviewed captains who couldn't have handled those questions so smoothly. Debriefed D– John the other today. 'Um,' 'huh,' 'you know…'"

"'This is so unreasonable,'" Ava quipped.

He chuckled. "Yes. His signature. Let's get into the weeds a bit."

Skull reviewed their operations since arriving in PA and asked easy-to-answer detail questions for the most part. Because Dean asked her to, she also reported on their business meetings today.

Skull promised to get Lt. Colonel Washington in Trenton to follow up on the potato venture. As an afterthought, he said he'd talk to General Hoffman, top Resco for all Hudson, about making sure the PA Rescos weren't waiting on Hudson to secure the agricultural base. That would be foolhardy.

Ava was a bit over-awed at the thought she'd played a part in setting policy for the Resco Raj.

"Just a bunch of men doing their jobs, Panic," Skull assured her. "Stuff falls through the cracks. Pete Hoffman will appreciate a word to the wise."

Skull clasped his hands and looked her in the camera. "So. Agent trainee Panic. The reason for this meeting today is to decide whether to confirm your contract. As a favor to Cade, I held off confirming your hire. Neither of us was sure whether you wanted the job, or just to be with him."

"Both," Ava said.

"If you keep this job," Skull continued, "I will send you into VA in about a week. This is not a safe assignment, Panic. You could die there ten times over. Cade, too. I know that's hard to think about, but if Cade were gone, you would still be bound by the company. You're smart enough to realize by now, that the more you know, the less you're free to go."

"I think I'm already past that point, sir." She didn't correct herself. They weren't bothering to correct names anymore. "Cade said this job was a one-way street. I thought he meant the company wouldn't let him leave. But to be honest, Skull, Cade and me, we're more devious than that. If we left, you'd never find us."

Skull raised an eyebrow. "Yet here we are. Why?"

"My life is bigger with this job. I can't go back to the Army, or to Soho Ville. I'd have to get smaller. I never want to be a small cog in the machine again. I mean, I don't want to put down my platoon mates. Or Guzman, my Coco back in Soho. But I felt pretty cog-like. Like I needed to break out. This job is awesome! I'm free! I travel around and everyone else is penned in. But I'm not." She pursed her lips and added, "Though, we worry if someone else was our boss, instead of you."

Skull listened to all this intently, and nodded slightly now. "The way to handle that isn't a bolt-hole, Panic. You need an alternate patron to fall back on. Like the Raj."

"The company doesn't control the Raj?" she asked, not expecting an answer.

"Let's say there are good old American checks and balances," Skull replied. "But back to my main concern. What happens if Cade dies next week? Or you two break up? Panic, he could end up as your boss."

"We've worked together before," Ava automatically defended. "Nothing killed us yet, and plenty tried."

"Panic? I'm asking you to really look at it."

She frowned at him. "I haven't seen this job without Cade. How would I know?"

"What would have happened in the gang? If you and Cade broke up."

Ava felt an echo of the old clawing terror, once so familiar, and blew out between her lips. "That wasn't an issue between Cade and me."

"You did break up," Skull pointed out, misunderstanding her.

"No. I meant, what happens to a fallen queen bee. Frosty wasn't the problem with that scenario. The other girls were. If Frosty stopped protecting me. That doesn't matter here."

Skull shook his head. "You're not going to look at it, are you."

Look at breaking up with Cade? Or losing him? *No!* Maybe it wasn't a death sentence anymore. She still couldn't bear to look at it.

"Alright, Panic. Your contract is confirmed. You are now a full agent of the company. Congratulations, and welcome aboard. And you're headed for VA. Enjoy your last week in Pennsylvania."

She breathed out in relief. *Safe!*

After they signed off, Eileen hurried to shed her fancy outfit and makeup. She soon caught up with Dean, playing with a little punching bag in the hotel gym. Full of gleaming white and chrome exercise machines and surrounded by mirrors, he had the place to himself.

Eileen strutted in with street attitude. "I'm in. Contract confirmed. I am now a real agent of the company." She blew on her fingernails and buffed them on her grey workout bra. Her ghastly army shorts were lighter grey with neon yellow-green waistband, sure to be visibly ugly through the grayest of days.

Dean paused the speed bag with his hand and looked sad. He schooled his face and returned her a smile. "Congratulations. I think. We should go out for a fancy dinner to celebrate."

"We have a fancy dinner every night."

"True. Courtesy of the company."

"Do you mind?" She sidled up to him at the bag, so they could speak more privately.

"Feel a little selfish," he admitted. "Tough job for a girl. Not easy to get respect. Sorry. I get a little protective."

She leaned into his ear. "I noticed." She licked his earlobe. "But I'm not as helpless as you think."

"I think we're both kinda crazy."

"You say that like it's a bad thing. C'mon, I've been sitting all day. Time to work up a sweat!"

～

After dinner out, Eileen hit the hot tub, expecting Dean to be right behind her. Instead, she heard voices from the living room.

She listened hard enough to figure out that he was talking to Skull, but couldn't hear details over the bubbles. And she probably shouldn't be eavesdropping anyway. Dean gave her privacy for her appointment with the boss. After 20 minutes and several bouts of laughter from the bedroom, she decided she was waterlogged. She wrapped herself in a towel and headed out to join the party.

Dean had availed himself of the room's mini-bar. A couple miniature bourbon bottles lay spent under the TV. "Ah, Eileen's out of the tub," he hastily told Skull, and they signed off.

Eileen picked up a mini-bourbon bottle quizzically. "What was that about?"

Dean shrugged. "Just cheering him up."

"About me?"

His averted eyes said yes.

"Funny kind of congratulations," she mused. "You passed probation. You're hired. Let's have a drink – but not with me?" She wasn't angry, just confused.

Dean pulled her over by her hips, to gaze up her towel to her face. "Skull feels guilty. He's a dad. He's got kids not much younger than you. Feels like he's contributing to the delinquency of a minor. Or whatever. His conscience hurts. I knew he'd get drunk tonight. A few didn't pass probation. The exit interviews sucked. The rest of your batch of new hires passed, and he feels guilty. I called to remind him I love this job, and you're having a blast, too. Have some laughs. Not let him drink alone."

"You feel guilty too," she said. "About me."

"VA is dangerous," he admitted. He stood abruptly. "Did you drain the hot tub?"

"Nope. Hey, Dean, I mentioned to Skull that I didn't think the company could keep us if we wanted to leave. That he was great. But my biggest doubt was what happened to us if he was replaced."

He gave her a quick peck on the forehead, and wouldn't discuss it further.

AND THAT WAS TUESDAY. WEDNESDAY WAS ANOTHER SIXERS CAMP AND drug delivery to supervise. That went well, so they had time to cruise along the southern borders with Delaware and Maryland.

Refugee camps had sprung up, despite the extreme security of the PA-controlled borders. Dean pointed out PA machine gun emplacements along the Delaware River. They veered back north to King of Prussia to find a tank of off-ration gas. For grins, they camped the night in the Valley Forge National Historic Park, where Washington apparently crossed the Schuylkill River, since they were miles from the Delaware. There were no ticket-takers or fellow tourists. There were plenty of trails and signs labeling where the troops made camp and the Founding Father billeted.

Thursday's task was travel from the southeast to the southwest corner of PA. They started early for plenty of time to ogle the Amish near Lancaster. They dropped off some money and schmoozed a bit with a Sixer camp near Gettysburg. They detoured to take a grinning selfie in front of a sign for the infamous Raven Rock ark complex. There the final President of the United States made his terminal speech to justify Penn's invasion of Hudson. They sent the photo to Mike and John.

The night's choice of nature preserve featured a fancy house by Frank Lloyd Wright named Fallingwater, which incorporated a beautiful stone waterfall into its levels. The lonely caretaker was more than happy to take their money for a tour. The old man looked so sad to see them go that Cade – now Ed – suggested they stay and have dinner together. Then the caretaker still wouldn't let them go. They ended up sleeping the night in a room designed by the greatest American architect of the twentieth century (Ed's opinion).

Friday featured complicated business dealings among the arks of PA's southwest corner. Three years into the Calm, their once-gleaming geodesic domes were looking rather rusty. Ava – now Faye – remembered how her parents scoffed at people hustling after 'good jobs' to win a place in the arks. She'd never felt more free in her life than to leave the ark-holes in their prisons and head north. They camped in

Raccoon Creek State Park, giving Pittsburgh as wide a berth as possible.

The border here was controlled by Ohio forces. On Saturday, they stopped in to speak with an Ohio captain to arrange release of a few drug couriers caught by overzealous border guards, and their impounded trucks. Some Sixers in the neighborhood required increased payment, so they dropped off money and shared a meal. The Sixers called themselves Judgment in this area. But they were chapters of the same organization, more or less.

"No one's shot at us in days," Faye complained to Ed as they left. "I feel unloved."

He laughed. "And we're done for the week. Time for our day off!"

They headed for a proper campground for the night. Faye chose one used by the Society for Creative Anachronism to stage their imaginary Pennsic War.

The map didn't warn her that they were war-gaming *today*.

And they weren't. The full-blown event was held for a week in summer. But a few dozen modern campers and period tents were already at the campground as they drove in, supporting a throng of people in medieval costume. Bales of hay abounded, archery targets, and other paraphernalia.

Ed's eyes lit in delighted amusement. He paused the SUV before they intruded. "Would you rather be alone together?"

"Is that a crossbow?" Faye replied. They traded grins, and drove in.

The SCA folk asked that they park Darcy well away from the period area. But they welcomed the newbies into the fold to play. None of the SCA craftsmen came stocked to sell clothing this weekend. So the newcomers were tolerated dressed as they were, though Faye changed into her lavender dress for the first time. They both wore gaudy scarves to get into the spirit of the thing.

Faye tried all the bows, including the crossbow, and the smaller edged weapons besides. Ed shunned the European swords in favor of a guy with a full collection of Japanese weapons. He got pretty good at throwing stars. Faye fetched their own nunchucks from Darcy. The martial arts lovers bonded.

As night came on, gourmet Ed got sidetracked into the feast preparation. A number of haunches were being roasted and smoked. After a deep conversation with an SCA herbalist, he couldn't resist experimenting with pan-seared mushrooms glazed with some of her verjuice, a sour medieval concoction pressed from unripe grapes and apples, used instead of vinegars that spoiled the palate. He did insist on fresh-ground black pepper with them, whether it was authentic or not. His mushrooms were a hit, and earned them a share of the excellent smoked meats and roast vegetables.

As the medieval musicians brought out harps and lutes and drums, the young couple leaned back against a hay bale and quaffed ale until their eyelids drooped. They shook hands warmly all around in farewell, not willing to commit to being here for the next day.

Not once did any of the SCA mention their real lives, or inquire into theirs.

"Thank you, Ed," said Faye. "That was fun!"

Ed tucked his prize new bottle of verjuice away in the pantry basket. "Thank me? That was a blast!"

"When are you going to tell me what happens next week?"

"Monday morning we head north. Sunday we don't talk about work if we can help it."

"You want to stay for Sunday?" she wheedled.

"Nah. I'm overdue for some downtime. OK?"

For Sunday, they hit another farm market to restock, this one not staffed to enforce ration cards. Ed bought twice as much food as usual, but Faye thought nothing of it. They found another lake to laze around next to. They had time to get in full workouts, and bone-chilling dips in the lake.

Faye's Western Civ essays were eliciting fewer red marks from Ed for English infractions. Now he offered pointers on how to develop her arguments better. Predictably, their Sunday supper featured verjuice in every course, and it was excellent in all of them. Bodies tired and happy, they slept deep under hazy stars.

AVA WOKE TO A DISTANT COCK-CROW. THE ROOSTER HAILED SOME TRACE of the coming dawn too dim for her to see. The air mattress was still too narrow for the both of them, but they usually slept in it together now. She carefully extracted herself, to sit cross-legged on the spare second-row seat, and watch him sleep.

"What?" he asked muzzily, rolling onto his back. "Bad dream?"

"No. We're going to VA today, aren't we."

"It'll take a few days. But yeah. Point of no return comes tonight. No return for a while, anyway. Cold feet?"

"I don't know enough about it," Ava said. "But you have cold feet. That worries me."

She thought he'd fallen back to sleep before he answered. "We get our final orders tonight. Then we do the next thing. That's why I started you that way. Not warning you what comes next. When you know it's gonna be hairy? Don't let the future gang up on you. Take it one step at a time." With that, he yawned and rolled over.

Ava's heart was thudding, and her adrenaline coursing. She tried breathing out to control an incipient panic attack. But this wasn't anxiety. It was excited anticipation. She remembered the feeling from Basic, waiting for deployment orders.

Practice was over. Time to get real. The hard part was waiting for tonight, hours and hours away. She slipped out into the darkness to work it off.

22

Interesting fact: Ohio was paired with West Virginia to form a super-state, similar to New York–New Jersey. Its first acquisition was the western panhandle of Maryland tucked between Pennsylvania and West Virginia. By now, Ohio had annexed Indiana and the lower half of Michigan. Canada took Michigan's Upper Peninsula.

Dark drizzling fog rolled off Lake Erie onto Ava-Gwen and Cade-Frank while they waited on the pier. To the girl from New York City, freshwater fog smelled funky. The lake dock seemed new and flimsy, adding to Gwen's nerves.

A hectic day brought them there on time to meet the ferry at 8:15 p.m. But the ship kept them waiting past 9:00. Miserly with power, or maybe to cloak the furtive international commerce, the dock lights were barely sufficient to prevent travelers from tripping off the dock.

A shape quietly detached from the disembarking throng to envelop Gwen in a hug. "Hey, hey! Great to see you again!" Daneel murmured. Mike was right behind him to take his turn at a heartfelt silent embrace. Daneel moved on with a handshake-and-hug to greet Frank.

"Neal. Ike," Daneel introduced the two of them, low voiced.

Ava smiled. Neal for Daneel, Ike for Mike, should be easy to remember.

"Frank, Gwen," Cade reciprocated. "Not for long." He plucked up the handle of Neal's large duffel on wheels. The Long Islander was also encumbered by his hefty hiking backpack. Gwen took over one of Ike's generously sized pair of rolling suitcases. They melded back into the crowd's pace.

"How was the ferry?" Gwen asked.

"Lot of Canadian border patrol," Neal whispered back. "Tell me we're leaving."

Frank concurred. "And miles to go before I sleep."

Too many miles, Gwen thought. It was past their bedtime. Frank had shifted to sleeping later the past couple nights. But Gwen was too wired.

When they reached Darcy, Frank popped the back hatch, flipped his bed on edge, and heaved the first suitcase into its spot. He gestured the others to do the same and hurry it up. "Sort that out later."

Neal tapped the good-sized trailer hooked behind the SUV. "Tell me that's already loaded."

"No. And we're late. Climb in."

As soon as all the doors were closed, Ike asked, "How soon do we need new identities?"

"You can start that, thanks. Ohio IDs to go with the names. Ohio uses laminated plastic," Frank explained to Gwen, riding shotgun. "Darcy, what's my name in Ohio?"

Darcy replied, "Wheeling West Virginia, Abe. Youngstown, Akron, and Cleveland Ohio, Brad –"

"Darcy, stop." Frank interrupted the litany just when Gwen thought it was getting good. Cade hadn't told her much about his adventures in Ohio, a lack she suddenly regretted. "Never mind. Gwen, pick us two throwaway names. We'll only use them for crossing Ohio this time."

"Anna and Clay." It didn't obey Cade's naming convention, but she was in the mood to use their own initials for a change.

"You go first this time, huh?"

"Of course. For VA, too."

His pleased smile said he liked it. Ava loved that about Cade. Other guys paid lip service to respecting women. Her guy wanted her to stand up to him.

"Hanging a right for Youngstown?" Neal asked. "That's up near us, isn't it?"

"It is, and we're not going there," Frank said. "Unless you have other orders. Ike? Neal?"

Ike didn't answer. He was already in the back to retrieve his computer from the bags. "Up to you," Neal said. "You're in charge."

"Ike?" Frank called back. "You agree with that? I'm team leader on this jaunt?"

Ike slid back into his seat behind Frank. "We both recommended you, Frank. You're in charge."

"No one asked me." Gwen sniffed. "They just assumed."

Frank laughed softly, turning the SUV into an industrial park near the lake. "I think you're a little new for the job, Gwen. Maybe next month."

"I might have picked Neal. Or Ike. They like me."

"I like you, too." Frank squeezed her hand, then set to the awkward bit of backing the trailer up to a gaping black loading dock, industrially anonymous in the red-tinged gloom of reversing tail lights. "Get out and deal with the pissy natives for me."

Gwen exited while Darcy was still crawling backward. She did indeed get an earful from the pair of loading dock workers, who'd been waiting an hour for them to return.

"You get paid by the hour, just like we promised," she told them. "But now you need to hop to. We got places to be." She herded them further back into the warehouse to strategize how the rest of the arms shipment would pack into the trailer. Unlike with businessmen in fancy suits, or weird religious nuts, Gwen didn't doubt herself for an instant when it came to bossing a work crew around. She'd done that for years. She expected them to obey her, and they did.

Neal joined her. He took in the status at one glance, and opened up the now-parked trailer with a key from Frank. He located and quickly latched in the dock's old-fashioned steel loading ramp, replete with embossed stars for traction and worn painted stripes to direct feet on the gangway. Frank followed. He passed Gwen a battery-powered work light to hook from the ceiling inside.

With practiced ease from loading army trucks in Basic, Gwen supervised the packing inside the trailer, while Neal directed Frank and the hired help at hauling in crates of guns and ammo. Paranoia limited the work light to the single dim bulb inside the trailer. With an assist from Neal, Gwen took extra care on securing the final rear-most tier of boxes and crates – toilet paper and canned goods – to stand securely as though the whole trailer were packed with similar cargo. That was a tricky bit with ropes and bungee cords and thick mover's blankets, since the ranks of heavier boxes behind weren't as tall.

"It won't pass close inspection," she warned Frank. "And we should stop to check if it shifted before crossing any borders."

Frank leaned briefly, hands-first, against a chest-level box of toilet paper near the middle. "Good job, Gwen," he assured her. "Pay the dudes."

He didn't need to remind her to tip well. Cade's lessons tended to stick.

They drove away, threading through the dark sleeping city of Erie PA.

"Gwen," Frank prompted. "How far is Mount Weather from Morgantown, West Virginia?"

Gwen plied the map tablet, holding it below the glove box to spare Frank's night vision. "As the crow files, maybe a hundred twenty miles. As the roads go… Well, they don't go there. There's an interstate through Ohio-Maryland, then drop down. Otherwise, the roads are a spiderweb that don't go anywhere. That's all them hillbilly hollers, huh? Could be two hundred miles or more. National forests, mountains."

Neal asked, "How's your mileage towing all that weight back there?"

"Not great, but we're topped up," Frank said. "Gwen? Don't even try to speak hillbilly. That goes for all of you. No fake accents. Try to track people, like with the con job practice. But don't pretend to be someone you're not. Just talk less. Neal, Gwen, talk suburban instead of Brooklyn. Ike, you're fine. Chicago and hillbillies go way back. "

"Ah-yup," Ike confirmed. "In Up Finger too."

Frank grinned. "That catching on? Up Finger for Finger Lakes?" They'd missed the latest news from home.

"Like wildfire," Ike said. "Up Jacks is still hotly contested. The real Adirondacks hate it. The Hudson valley wants its old name back, but the country stole it. I predict we'll give up and call it Upstate again."

The conversation on news from Hudson ate up the miles. Neal and Ike snuck down to the Apple to see the Royal Wedding in person. Though of course they couldn't get into Central Park to see the exchange of vows. Gwen twisted to stick her head between the seats, and hung on every word.

The big wedding – Hudson officially frowned on the term Royal Wedding – was the spectacle of the year so far. And that was in a public calendar suddenly and strangely rich in spectacles and sporting events. Resco Lt. Col. Emmett MacLaren and his partner Dee Baker, queen of the Amenac and PR News media empire, jointly called the Saviors of New York City, and currently ruling the Apple Cities, were married in the biggest party yet. Nearly a million people saw the wedding in person, or the procession back to the Resco Mansion in Brooklyn. Millions more watched the event over the Internet.

And Gwen was out of town and missed it!

"They say it's a competition between MacLaren and Resco Margolis of Up Jacks," Ike said. "Margolis is still trying to top the Thanksgiving soup kitchen during Project Reunion, a hundred thousand served."

"Margolis will never top that," Gwen assured him. "That was Santa Claus, the tooth fairy, and God Almighty rolled into one. Frank and I ate that Thanksgiving at Chelsea Piers. We didn't see MacLaren and Baker, but they were there, on the ferry. If the Royal Wedding was bigger, it was because it was for *MacLaren and Baker*."

Ike shook his head at her. "You know, Margolis is a better Resco. He's an administrator."

"No!"

"MacLaren is a combat officer," Ike persisted. "Margolis led Project Rebuild."

Gwen put her hands over her ears and hummed. "Not listening!" She laughed. "MacLaren rules!"

Neal put in, "Neither of them can touch Good King Cam." Resco Lt. Col. Cameron presided over Long Island. By Long Island lights, MacLaren and Margolis were pansies. They mustered up a hundred thousand troops plus the Navy before they dared sink their tender toes into New York City. Cam and his husband gathered a handful of friends, and had the Coast Guard drop them and one little boatload of gear on the far end of Long Island. They worked their way up from there. Long Island even had more people than the city, by the end of the Starve.

"None of them are as good as Up Finger's Colonel Nasser," Ike argued. "You like electricity? You like enough heat to have running water? You like *food?* That's Upstate! Sorry. Up Finger." He laughed.

"Frank, tell them MacLaren's the best," Gwen pressed. "He's the Apple Savior! Come on, you've met him!"

Frank let them wait for it a few heartbeats. "And one king to rule them all. I think General Hoffman must be effing brilliant to run these lesser Rescos. Not to mention General Cullen!" he added more loudly over the mounting boos.

"He picked Jersey," Gwen said, melodramatically slapping her forehead. "Frank grew up in Jersey." She slapped his arm for good measure, and he laughed. General Hoffman, commander of all the others mentioned, was also lead Resco of Jersey.

"Skull's awfully good, too," Frank allowed. "And covers even more territory than Hoffman. Speaking of which, we need to talk to the boss."

Frank completed his maneuvers onto Interstate 79 southbound. He engaged the cruise control, breathed out, and relaxed a bit. He kept his eyes glued to the road surface, though, unlit except for their headlights.

"Darcy, record message. Hi boss! Picked up a couple friends and the package in Erie. Heading south now, looking to find someplace to crash for the night. If you're already in bed, good –"

Darcy interrupted. "Incoming message."

Skull spoke right over her. "Hey, hey, gang! And they're off! I don't need to tell you how important these missions are."

"I wish you would," Gwen muttered.

Skull asked, "What was that, Gwen?"

"I still don't know what the mission is, sir," she spoke up. Neal chuckled behind her.

"Ah. OK, back up," Skull said. "This group has two missions in VA. First we want to install a communications tap at Mount Weather. That's Ike and Neal's department. Mount Weather is a hardened bunker for continuity of government. The underground part is an ark now, command for Homeland Security and FEMA – Federal Emergency Management Agency. CDC, the Centers for Disease Control. We're not sure what else, especially since FEMA doesn't exist anymore. And HomeSec supposedly answers to the nation-states. But Mount Weather has broadcast and wired communications to most of the ex–United States after a nuclear catastrophe. And they're wired to the Pentagon. The company wants to listen in. Especially now the facility is about to change hands. Ohio is massing to invade."

"Invade Virginia–Del–Mar?" Gwen asked. "Ohio?"

Frank frowned at the highway before him. "Now? That's already begun?"

At his comment, Gwen frowned harder. Mount Weather was right smack on the Ohio–Virginia frontier.

Skull sighed. "Yeah. Ken–Tenn and Carolina jumped the gun. Ken–Tenn did a big push this week. They're already at I-77. Carolina's taken Norfolk and heading up the James for Richmond –"

Gwen snatched the map tablet from the dashboard again. Ike and Neal brought up maps on their laptop and phone.

But Frank had to watch for road debris. "Boss? I can't drive at night and follow along on a map."

"OK. Virginia's like a squashed triangle. The top point is up by Mount Weather, where Maryland, West Virginia, and Virginia meet, fifty miles south of PA. Virginia's snail tail wraps under West Virginia to stab into Kentucky. The eastern corner is at Norfolk and Virginia Beach, at the mouth of Chesapeake Bay. Basically cut it in half north-south, south of Charlottesville in the west, north of Richmond in the middle. Ken–Tenn and Carolina are advancing to take control of that southern half, and split it between them. To the northwest, Ohio plans to take the Shenandoah Valley, Blue Ridge Mountains, and east to

Charlottesville, at least. Then they're all supposed to halt and decide what to do next."

Gwen asked, "What about Washington D.C.? Maryland and Delaware?"

"Nobody wants D.C. and Baltimore," Skull replied. "The Delmarva Peninsula is where your second mission comes in. Delmarva is the eastern side of Chesapeake Bay. All of Delaware, plus bits of old Maryland and Virginia. It's the natural extension of Jersey and Philadelphia. Arguably. But Hudson doesn't want to take Delmarva by force. Because General Hoffman in Jersey thinks the lead Resco in Delmarva, Jack Ekstrom, would happily transfer his turf to Hudson without a shot fired. Problem is, Jack Ekstrom is missing. Admiral O'Hara recalled him to the Pentagon, and threw him in jail. We think. He might have been executed for mutiny." From his voice on that last, Skull cared about Ekstrom, the man, not just the military situation.

Frank added softly, "Lieutenant Colonel Ekstrom is an old friend of the boss."

"Yeah. A close friend. Other Hudson Rescos, too. Especially MacLaren, and Niedermeyer in the Coast Guard."

Gwen blinked. What a truly interesting friend list, especially with Hoffman, the top Resco of Hudson, also batting for Ekstrom. "Boss, how did you all know each other? Before the Calm."

"Not now, Gwen," Skull said. "OK, this is highly sensitive. Like, if O'Hara catches word that anyone is coming for Ekstrom, she might kill him. If she hasn't already. So let's refer to Ekstrom as Major MacGuffin. Your second mission is to spring the MacGuffin and bring him home. Note 'home' instead of 'Delmarva.' Or find out if he's dead."

"MacGuffin," Frank repeated with a grin.

"He'd love it," Skull assured him. "Jack was an English major back at West Point." He snorted a sad laugh. "What an idiot. Who goes to West Point for literature?"

Gwen had no idea what they were talking about.

"You two go way back," Frank murmured.

Skull sighed. "Yeah. Enough of that. Job 1, tap Mount Weather. Job 2, spring the MacGuffin and take him home. Travel could be insanely difficult. VA was already a basket case, and now three armies are advancing. A fourth is waiting in the wings. Maybe a fifth, but so far PA says they defer to Hudson. So before Mount Weather, you join a gran caravan to cross into Virginia. Travel with them for protection. Frank, rendezvous is no later than Wednesday evening, in or around Brandywine, West Virginia. Thursday they'll take route 33 across into the Shenandoah Valley, then fan out to cross the Blue Ridge Mountains."

"No SEALs?" Frank asked.

"Yes, SEALs. You'll have comms again with me from the caravan," Skull replied. "But expect to meet up with Garcia and crew on the way from Mount Weather to Arlington."

"Arlington?" Frank echoed.

"The Pentagon is in Arlington Virgina," Skull said neutrally. In the Army from age 18, Skull assumed that everyone knew where the Pentagon was. And they did, just not that specifically. "Across the river from D.C."

"And this MacGuffin is being held *inside* the Pentagon?" Frank asked.

And if so, what the hell do you expect us to do about it? Gwen thought. She pointed out a sign for a highway rest stop exit. Frank nodded gratefully.

"Current best intel is that he's in a civilian jail in Arlington," Skull said. "Again, the caravan can help you with that. And I'll contact you again."

Silence fell inside Darcy. Frank pulled into the rest area, just a loop off the interstate for tired travelers. The place was unlit and deserted. A few turquoise porta-potties stood sentinel by a dark building, locked and boarded.

"Frank?" Skull asked. "Got it?"

"Checking the map in just a moment, boss," Frank replied, bringing Darcy and the trailer to a halt spanning half a dozen parking spaces. "Sorry, I should have stopped somewhere before we called you."

Finally with the map in his hands, Frank frowned in consternation for a few moments. "Jesus, boss, are you nuts?"

23

Interesting fact: No one hyphenated Ohio, or its Governor-General. General Schwabacher claimed that the nation's name honored the mighty Ohio River, not the defunct state. He didn't explain his choice not to style himself Governor.

"What?" Skull bit out. The boss was usually laid back, a little sad. But he was a major in the Hudson Army. His reflexes didn't care for Frank's attitude.

"Excuse me, boss," Frank hastily backtracked. "I was…surprised. By route 33. That's… An army, you say, is massing in West Virginia."

Skull's voice remained clipped. "The Ohio Army. Yes."

Gwen had helpfully dropped markers and annotated distances on the map tablet. Visiting route 33 to cross that mountain range, by her estimate, would add about a 100 mile detour to their trip from Morgantown, West Virginia to Mount Weather. The path meandered through a spider web of country roads that didn't so much lead anywhere as daisy-chain hamlets in adjacent hollows through the Appalachians.

Morgantown was where they intended to cross out of PA. A more efficient route from there, on a perfectly good interstate highway, could take them east to Hagerstown ex-Maryland, then drop south to Mount Weather in 150 miles. If they weren't carrying a shipment of rifles and ammo, they might even cross the PA border a mere 75 miles from Mount Weather.

Gwen asked, "Who are the rifles for?"

"The gran caravan," Skull replied.

"So Skull," Frank resumed, "do we know where in West Virginia we might run across this army?"

Gwen considered, and pointed on the map for him. "They need to cross in north and south of the Shenandoah Valley. Silly to cross two mountain ranges in the middle when what they want is to envelop them. So they'd muster here in the south, then take I-64 and barrel into Charlottesville. In the north…" She tapped her teeth in thought, then drew an arc that pretty much covered her original 'more efficient' routes to Mt. Weather. "Oh."

Skull said, "Has Gwen pointed out why you're going south to route 33?"

"Maybe," Frank said. "This makes sense to you, Gwen?"

"Yeah. Though, I'd send some through the middle, too. If I were Ohio."

"More likely just barricade the middle," Skull contradicted her. "Block civilians trying to escape the net. Keep them in VA."

"Wouldn't –" Gwen stopped herself.

"Gwen? Complete your thought," Skull ordered.

"Yes, sir. I was thinking, if I were Ohio, I'd rather keep the civilians east of that mountain range. Not let them up route 33 to scatter into the mountains. Same for all the routes across the mountains."

"Ah. Yes, I see your point," Skull said thoughtfully.

Frank blew out a long breath, and rubbed his forehead as though to knead out an incipient headache.

Skull said, "Frank. You can do this."

Gwen glanced up at the dashcam, expression neutral, freshly reminded that Skull was watching them.

"Yes, boss," Frank said, his voice now clipped. "Can do. Anything else?"

"Don't be late. Wednesday night."

"Right. Sleep sweet, boss."

"Frank, maybe you and I should talk one on one. Take fifteen and call me back. Alone. Skull out."

In the following quiet, the overcast night blanketed them in black, with no light save the bluish cast under their chins from their screens. Gwen contemplated fishing a snack for Frank out of the console stash. She prudently elected to instead withdraw toward her window. He was staring at her, eyes glittering ice.

"Who knew?" Frank said, breaking the silence. "They teach you all those map tricks at West Point? Army movements? Road selection, to invade a country?"

"I was good at it," Gwen said defensively. "The captain held seminars with some of us. It was fun."

Neal muttered, "They didn't teach any of that to me. Your *captain?*"

At West Point, the average company captain commanded 250 recruits, and didn't say *boo* to any of them. Even Gwen's sergeant didn't talk to Captain Deluca, only her platoon sergeant. Deluca reported to the head of West Point, Major Thurston, who commanded the whole brigade in addition to their battalion.

Ike mused, "Maybe they were exploring training for baby officers."

Gwen shot him a sharp glare. "The Hudson Army doesn't want 'little girls' leading infantry. Believe me."

"Lack of imagination," Frank said, icy expression still inscrutable. "So Panic– Gwen. Excuse me. How would you get from Morgantown to route 33?"

"There's a map. I thought we'd drive. Don't be an ass, Frank." Gwen pulled open her door and stepped out decisively. "Pop the tailgate for me, would you? Let's have sandwiches before we get back on the road."

Frank breathed, "That's what I was afraid you'd say."

Neal and Ike eagerly jumped out of the car as well. Neal hung the handy homework lamp in mid-Darcy, spilling a faint glow radius out onto the parking lot.

"Gwen, I wasn't criticizing," Frank said lamely.

"Glad to hear it. Ham and cheese? With that... owie stuff you made. And spinach."

"Aioli," he corrected on automatic, then continued contrite. "Sounds delicious. Thank you." Frank scrubbed his face with his hands and alighted from the car, too.

"Crank some tunes, if you want," Frank directed, to no one in particular. For himself, he did a few rounds of yoga sun salutations, a graceful controlled progression from stretching upward, to plank, to hips in the air, and back. Then he launched into sets of side kicks, alternated with punch combos, to loosen his muscles from driving and wake himself up.

A semi roared by on the interstate. It laid on the horn in greeting, to outrage the quiet night. They all hid their eyes from its blinding headlights. Gwen didn't look away fast enough. She was left slathering Frank's gourmet mayo on onion rolls that crawled with bright green blobs from the afterimage. Neal and Ike helped set out the standing meal on the tailgate, and took turns at the porta-potties.

"You want to talk about it?" Gwen offered to Frank with a sandwich.

"Not right now," Frank replied, dropping his mini workout in favor of food. "Break time."

He joined the cluster at the tailgate, wedged between Darcy and the trailer. Most people would be awkward mixing back into the group, but not Frank. He was cheerful and refreshed, relaxed and friendly. He ignored the others' wariness, and set the tone for the meal. He proposed a toast in water. "To an awesome team!"

To go with 'Major MacGuffin,' Frank led a renaming contest for Mount Weather. Neal's suggestion of Cheeseburger Hill was the group favorite. They clowned around about a team name, too. But Frank's opinion won that round. Company. Boss. Team. The company preferred anonymous labels on who they were, and what they did.

Frank's fifteen minutes were up. Gwen and the geeks repacked Darcy and left him to his private conversation with Skull. By the boarded-up rest building, Gwen wheedled more details about the wedding in the city. Neal and Ike had caught the procession through the Lower East Side. Street vendors served *rice balls* for the occasion. Rice didn't grow in Hudson. But since the Navy had to abandon their ports in VA in favor of Hudson, all sorts of new foods poured through the Apple. Gwen was entranced.

Frank rejoined them.

"Boss tear you a new one?" Neal inquired.

"Not at all," Frank replied. "But we need to cross the border to Morgantown before dawn." His leadership skills held. One might think this was his own happy thought, a minor wrinkle in their plans. "Ike, can you drive?"

"I– no. In the daytime, maybe. I have no depth perception. My night vision is terrible."

"Cool, you'll get some practice tomorrow. Neal?"

Neal eyed the trailer dubiously. "Um. I've never driven an SUV. Or with a trailer."

"Right. So Gwen, you're up for a bit. Let's go."

The guys started for the car. Gwen's feet remained rooted to the concrete sidewalk. She blew out the rising panic.

Frank turned back to gather her under his arm, and pulled her to the driver's seat. "You can do this, baby. You did fine hauling the trailer last week. It's a little bigger this time, that's all."

She'd driven only a half hour with the little box trailer, in broad daylight. She drove on an empty state highway, not an interstate. That box hadn't blocked the rear-view mirror like this walk-in trailer did. She'd never driven Darcy at night. There wasn't a streetlight in the entire Commonwealth of Pennsylvania, and no one maintained the roads. Potholes, unmarked washouts, fallen branches, and blown tires abounded, along with dropped junk ranging from cardboard boxes to mattresses. With only the range of the headlights for warning, even Frank got rattled driving at night.

"Stay in the right lane," Frank encouraged, belting her in. "We'll start by getting you up to speed – whatever speed you want – then practice stopping on the shoulder."

"How far do we need to go tonight?" Neal inquired, leaning forward between the front seats.

"Not helpful, Neal," Frank clarified.

Point taken, Neal withdrew.

Frank continued, "Don't let the future gang up on you, Gwen. Get up to speed. Drive a minute. Coast to a stop. That's all. You've got this."

Gwen fidgeted with the seat as much as possible. She looked in her left mirror. She checked over her shoulder at the stygian blackness of the interstate, invisible beside her. She swallowed, turned the ignition, and let off the brake. Barely rolling, she steered to cast around with the headlights to find the ramp back onto the highway. That found, she stopped. Swallowed.

"Cade, I can't do this," she whispered.

"Ava, you can," he murmured back. "I'm right here. You have to try." He laid his hand palm-up on the console by her thigh, for her to grasp whenever she wanted.

"What did you talk to Skull about?"

"Stalling won't help, baby. Drive up the ramp now." He kept up a soft patter, talking her through, assuring her she was doing a good job.

Gwen spotted a blown tire in the road in time, and veered, but misjudged and clipped it. At the jolt and the horrible noise of tire thwacking Darcy from below, she jerked the wheel in reaction, and the trailer pulled one way, then the other. She managed to get the wheels all pointed the same direction again without jack-knifing. But by then she was panting out in short breaths like she was going into labor.

"Let's coast to a stop now," Frank crooned. "Use your lights… Hazard lights, too… You're doing fine. And stopped. Well done." He popped her seat buckle and hauled her into his lap. "Sh, baby. You're alright."

Gwen sobbed in his arms, mortified. "I'm sorry. I'm so sorry, I'm sorry…"

"It's alright," Frank said. "We'll make this work. Neal, ride shotgun, help me stay awake. Gwen, get some sleep. Lie down in my bed in the back. Hey, I love you." He gave her a quick kiss, and laid his nose and forehead to hers briefly. "It'll work out. Always does."

Gwen stumbled back to his air mattress in defeat. She contemplated some of the hellacious situations she'd faced with Cade over the years. Yeah, it worked out, if you counted still breathing. She didn't think she could sleep. But Ike nodded off quickly. Neal's voice droned from the front, telling Frank his life story – probably fictional – in tones too soft for her to follow. It took remedial instruction, but West Point eventually taught her to sleep under adverse circumstances. She drifted off in spite of herself.

GWEN CAME AWAKE IN AN INSTANT, AND REMAINED FROZEN. DARCY wasn't moving. The red strobe of police lights stabbed through the car. It was the car doors closing that woke her, though Ike had left his hanging open. Darcy's cabin lights were off, though the time shone from the dashboard, after 1:00 a.m. She couldn't make out the voices, but recognized the sound of the trailer lock opening.

She slunk low toward Ike's door, keeping below window level. Their pistols were both up front. She grabbed her M4 rifle instead, plus a wad of Liberty dollars. She peered out carefully but quickly. Everyone else was behind the trailer. Good.

She sidled barefoot and silent along the side of Darcy and the trailer, walking down the middle of the slow lane. Not that it mattered at this hour. She paused without taking a look, to mentally position the cops by their voices. She only heard one, on the other side of the trailer. They wouldn't dare in the Apple, but maybe police in the boonies soloed night and day.

"I said, haul that toilet paper out," the cop demanded. "I need to see what's behind it. Not you two. You stay on your knees!" His voice swung around on that last, as though he were covering all three men.

"Look," Frank urged. "Take the bribe. No one needs to die here tonight."

"Die? What the hell are you talking about? Get that box out! Now!"

Gwen didn't have an angle to shoot the cop without firing too close to Frank or the others. So she stayed in hiding and simply shot into the air, a three-bullet burst. By the time she could hear again, another fine Glock skated across the pavement to her. She picked it up and thrust it into her back waistband.

She stepped around the trailer. Frank was crouched by the cop, patting him down. He found a body cam and yanked that, pocketed some ammo. He tossed a walkie-talkie to Neal.

"Is he dead?" Gwen asked.

"I offered him a choice," Frank confirmed. "You slept deep, huh? Hope you're feeling better." He dropped a kiss on her forehead and turned to the geeks. "He wore a body cam."

"That records in the car," Ike offered. "I'll pull it. Can fry the electronics if you want."

"Good. Yes, please. Would that kill the low-jack?" Frank asked. A cop car had plenty of electronics to scream its whereabouts at all times.

Neal replied, "Hard to do that even in a car shop. Got a few hours?"

"Nope," Frank replied, yawning in spite of himself.

"Could ram it into the meridian," Gwen said. "Then back up so it's hanging into the fast lane. Put the cop in the driver's seat. You broke his neck, right?"

"Good plan, Gwen," Frank decided. "Neal, can you execute? After Ike's done. We'll bring the body. Wear gloves."

"Will do. Sounds fun."

They didn't even have to change the car plates, they realized. When they stopped, Frank got out immediately and walked back toward the police car. The cop never got a good look at Darcy, only the back of the trailer. That was painted white with no markings. Trailer plates were optional these days in PA. Indeed, all plates were optional. There was no Department of Motor Vehicles. Frank simply pulled the plate. Gwen checked the box arrangement in the trailer and locked up again. Frank engaged Darcy's hazard lights in case anyone came by while they were still arranging the scene.

Not risking whiplash himself, Neal's damage to the police car couldn't have killed a man except by astonishing bad luck. Unless someone came along and rammed it, the cause of death wasn't too credible. But if the cop hadn't called in a description on Darcy, Frank didn't much care.

"I'll drive a while," Neal offered. "I've been watching."

Frank looked sorely tempted. But he shook his head. "Coming up on the 76 interchange. Then Pittsburgh. I better do it."

"Short nap first?" Gwen suggested.

"What, here? Next to a dead cop?" A little sharpness snuck into Frank's voice on that. "Sorry. No. Time to take some speed."

"Oh, hell," Gwen said.

Frank shot her a crooked smile. "Ought to warn you guys. Speed does terrible things to my personality. Oh, and from here, we're Ed and Faye. Faye, go back to bed."

"Why am I the one sleeping?"

"Because one of us needs to negotiate with Sixers. I'm popping speed until dawn. You want me on public relations?"

Faye laughed out loud, picturing it. "No, honey."

Climbing back into the car, Neal asked her softly, "What happens when Ed takes speed, Faye?"

"During the Starve, he took speed before a gang battle," she replied. "Said it got him in the mood. Start killing, quit caring."

"Outstanding," Neal breathed. "Ike, want to ride shotgun?"

24

———

Interesting fact: If Michigan, Indiana, or anyone else complained about the high-handedness of Ohio and Canada, no one heard them. Hudson had the only news broadcast beyond its own borders, and it was heavily censored. Hudson was allied with Ohio and Canada. If Hudson's Governor-General Cullen had an issue with his allies, he spoke to them privately.

Ike's scream woke Faye next, after 2 a.m. by the dashboard. The jolt and clattering crash just afterward would have woken her anyway. She sat up to peer out the side window. A brief impression of orange-and-white-striped wreckage flashed by before they were back to barreling along dark pavement.

She made it to the front in time to help a rattled Ike climb across the console and retreat to the second row. She slid into place beside the driver, and rummaged in the console. "We need fresh snacks up here."

"Whatever," Ed growled. His brake foot was pulled back, knee up, other arm straight on the steering wheel, head back against the seat, tilted to the side. His body language screamed, 'I don't care. Screw with me, make my day.'

Faye could believe that. "Was that a barricade we just smashed through?"

"I-279 interchange," Ed said. "There was an open lane at I-76 a few miles back. But here the assholes closed the road after dark."

Faye applied her map. "They might take offense at you breaking their sawhorses."

He rolled his head on the headrest to glare at her. "Got to cross the Ohio River somewhere, Panic. It's a big river. It's in the way."

Faye shot out her arm to brace against the dashboard. Ed took the hint and looked back to the road just in time to swerve violently around an oil drum. It took him a couple more swerves to get the trailer to stop knifing.

"I kinda like it," he laughed. "Let's do that again."

"Let's not, Ed." Faye reassured herself, barely, that Ed was now tracking the road again as they sped along at 55 mph under adverse conditions. She detached the map tablet and studied the upcoming challenges. "If I were pissed off about you breaking my barricade, I think the best place to catch you is the bridge over the Ohio. But not a lot we can do about that."

"Nope."

"Well, I could give you a seven-mile detour."

"Nah."

"Then there's the I-376 interchange in about ten miles. This is Pittsburgh, Ed. We're not in the middle of nowhere. Lead Resco of western PA has this place under her thumb."

"Gosh, Panic. Who told you that?"

He had, of course. She sighed, and debated whether to make an issue of it. *Yes.* "I think a seven-mile detour would be prudent. And call me Faye."

"I think you're wrong, *Faye.* And I'm driving. So I choose." He gave that a moment to digest, and added, "I'm not as far gone as I look, Panic. Our best bet is to get through Resco Drumpeter's turf before she can mobilize her reaction. No detours. We splinter a barricade, we piss her off. We mow down her men, she'll hunt us and won't stop at the border. We don't have time to pussy-foot around. So we go fast. We go through."

Faye nodded sadly. He made sense. "Just remember, Ed, a lot of the bridges are broken around here. From the tornados. When we get to the river, you have to slow down. Some of those sawhorses might block off holes in the bridge. No swimming."

He frowned slowly. "Point. Grab your carbine."

She reached back to pull the gun from under Ike's feet. "Weren't we just saying Caroline Drumpeter would chase us to hell and back if we hurt her guys?"

"Shoot over their heads. Makes them move." Ed waved a hand, spread-fingered, to suggest people scattering. "I think it's disrespectful to call a woman by her first name, when we'd call a man by his last name."

"Good point, Ed," she returned to humor him. "I sit corrected. Drumpeter would kill us if she had to chase us to Ken–Tenn to do it."

He nodded. "Drumpeter."

"Would you be willing to bypass the giant pretzel in the sky at the next interchange? Tornado damage there, too."

"No. We can skip the I-70 interchange if it makes you feel better. Go to ground to find the Sixers."

"Right." Faye reflected that Ed knew this area by heart. "I'll get more food and water."

She returned from the pantry basket and fed him just in time, before they reached the I-79 bridges over the mighty Ohio. This was a double span in series, because of a township-sized island in mid-stream. Entrance and exit ramps flanked the highway before the first bridge. Faye spotted a couple sheriff SUVs pulling into position, strobe lights on with no sound.

"They made sure we didn't leave the highway," she decided aloud. That exit ramp led to the detour she'd promoted.

"That doesn't bode well," Ed agreed. He slowed way down to obey the orange forest of warning signs and lane closures. Yes, this was one of the bridges where whole sections of the roadbed had fallen into the Ohio River below.

Faye continued thinking aloud. "We are now bottled up on an island. If they want. The island's only about two blocks wide at this point. There are three other bridges south."

"Here's a trick you won't like," Ed replied.

The divider between north-bound and south-bound traffic was broken to allow emergency vehicles to pull a 180. Still going fairly slow, Ed used one of them to cross into the north-bound lanes, still driving south. Then almost immediately, he turned to exit onto the incoming entrance ramp.

Ed murmured, "When you said three other bridges, I wonder if you counted this one?" He stopped on the entrance ramp, reversed for a wobbly three-point turn with the large trailer behind, and drove through a break in another divider, to transfer onto yet another one-way road in the wrong direction.

Faye checked the map in amazement. This was a lesser bridge, one-way going the wrong way, alongside the bigger I-79 bridge. "Why is this here?"

"I don't know. But it's very handy," Ed said smugly. "Navigator, how do I rejoin I-79 southbound?"

"I think this whole bridge is an exit ramp from I-79 northbound to the island," Faye reported. "After we're back on I-79, just find a way back into the southbound lanes."

"Alrighty." And police being just as reluctant as Ed to go too far in the wrong direction, a turnaround break in the divider came along rather soon. And voila, they were past the Ohio River. If other forces had been massed on the island to trap them, Ed's route was too devious for Faye to have spotted them.

"Pretzel coming up for route 60," Faye reported. "Do you think we should do that again?"

"I think they want to keep me on the highway here," Ed shared. "And I concur. Check your map again, Panic. I can't switch from south-bound to northbound at the next pretzel. Separate roadbeds."

"Ah, yes. Sorry."

"Any other exits before I-376?"

"No." Faye studied the next elaborate pretzel interchange, promising swooping ramps in the sky. She barely looked up to see the first loop flash by. As Ed had predicted, there were indeed sheriff vehicles blocking the exit ramps, but not the roadway. "OK, we could just go through and hope they don't block us."

"They've had time to block us," Ed argued.

Faye agreed with that assessment. "Or, we take the exit for I-376 eastbound. Immediately cut across all lanes and enter the wrong way onto an exit ramp from I-79 northbound. Then go south on I-79 north-bound for two miles before we reach an entrance ramp to exit on. Then get back onto the highway on the right side of the road. Did you catch all that?"

"I do believe you're catching on, Faye. Cool."

"This is so unreasonable," Neal muttered from behind Faye. Clearly he'd been biting his tongue all this time.

"Everyone alright back there?" Faye called sweetly. "If you're not, please shut up about it."

"We're awesome," Neal replied.

"Just peachy," Ike concurred.

Ike still sounded a bit shaken from crashing through the first barri-cade, poor man. This sort of thing was hard on the heart for a senile, Faye reflected. It wasn't doing her nerves much good, either.

Ed, on the other hand, looked increasingly alert and amused, a fey gleam in his eye as he navigated a perfect figure-eight, looping high above the freeways twice to land up on I-79 north-bound, going south.

"Should be just a few minutes on the right for the entrance ramp we want to exit on."

"I caught that part," Ed agreed.

"From the ramp you go straight to cross West Main street. Hang a left onto Main, then you can just follow the signs for I-79 south-bound."

"Easy enough. And we believe the lovely and talented Colonel Drumpeter will not counter because…"

"Well, it's a stupid thing to do," Faye mused. "And we're not giving her much reaction time." Indeed, they began exiting the entrance ramp as she spoke. "Is she? Lovely? Colonel Drumpeter?"

"Kinda big and horsey for my taste," Ed replied, taking the left onto West Main with screeching tires and rocking trailer.

A sheriff's SUV, with lights flashing and sirens this time, had just taken the entrance ramp to I-79 north-bound not a hundred yards from them. He'd soon find a way to turn himself around.

"I favor pretty and petite myself. Brilliant and talented Drumpeter, let's say," Ed concluded. "Or whoever she has on graveyard shift. Her assets thin outside Pittsburgh, though. Navigator?"

By now they were committed on I-79 south-bound again, going south.

"Where are our Sixer pals?" Faye asked. "Judgment."

"Oh, yeah!" Ed said, breaking into a crazed smile. "South Park. We should be within ten miles by now, right?"

They were indeed. Faye bid him take the next exit ramp. She'd hoped the local authorities had no reason to foresee that move. And they didn't. But by now any ramp on or off I-79 headed any direction was clearly fair game for the renegade SUV and its intriguing white trailer.

"Don't kill a cop," Ed reminded her. His own hands were occupied coaxing Darcy and the trailer a touch too fast around the curving exit ramp. Faye and Neal were the ones with the semi-automatic rifles out the windows, one on each side. Ike prudently huddled in the back between boxes. "Never worth it to kill a cop. They just never stop coming for you. I like my beat in PA. It's restful. The food is outstanding. I love mushrooms."

"Yes, dear," Faye said. She sent one spray of bullets over the militia's heads to encourage them to hide or scatter. Then on closer approach, she carefully sprayed the two sheriff cars on her side with bullets centered on the back wheel, until that corner slumped to the ground, its tire exploded. She got both tires on the second car. In return, Darcy took one shot in the grille. Another few shots caught the trailer but mercifully missed the ammo.

And then they were past the intersection.

"Got the car, none of the cops on my side," Neal exulted.

"Two cars, no guys for me," Faye replied. They traded high-fives between the seats.

"Sweet shooting, team," Ed said. "Nobody's following. Navigator?"

Faye hurriedly stowed her rifle and got back to map strategy. She didn't want a merry chase. Her goal was no chase at all.

"Behind the dead Walmart," she directed. "Slow back here. We're hoping there's a…yes! Take that shortcut into the subdivision. And drive quietly."

They zigged and they zagged. Occasionally they did a placid stretch of quiet road across a mountainside. But Faye routed them through sleeping neighborhoods as much as possible.

Ike got their radio equipment from the cop up the road working, and found the Pittsburgh frequency to eavesdrop on. After that, cop avoidance got far easier, though they had to stop now and then to let them pass. Everyone's adrenaline calmed down a bit with the break from pursuit.

"Too bad we didn't get that done earlier," Neal groused.

Ed snapped at him. "Hey! It made no difference on the interstate. Darcy can off-road it. But not with the trailer in tow. Ike did good."

"The interstate was a constrained problem," Faye agreed soothingly. "Hey, Ed? You never did tell us about your conversation with the boss."

"My private, one-on-one conversation?" Ed verified.

She chuckled.

"He was concerned I was being a brat," Ed allowed. "I explained my grieving process. How I really wanted to sleep in a nice State Game Lands tonight. Take a placid drive south tomorrow. Today now. Meet up with Sixers in an orderly fashion. Judgment. For a quiet border crossing tomorrow before dawn."

"Grieving process?" Faye inquired.

"Because if I had to cross the border this morning instead? Because my Ohio rendezvous is too far south? There would be dead bodies. Drama. I mean, driving across PA wasn't supposed to be the dangerous part. That was a cake walk."

"And Darcy might get shot."

"Yeah, about that. I think they got the radiator."

Neal said, "You know there's stuff for that. You pour it in to plug the leak."

Ed cracked a smile, then burst out laughing.

Faye said, "Neal, I'm not a mechanic. But that might work better for a pinhole than a NATO round."

"Oh. Yeah." Neal grinned at himself.

Faye returned to Ed. "Boss was OK with drama?"

"He authorized up to a dozen bodies tonight, and a new SUV." Ed petted Darcy's dash. "Don't listen to the meanie, Darcy."

Amusement quenched, Faye asked, "Why? One day. What does it matter? Is this MacGuffin guy worth the lives of a dozen cops?"

"This MacGuffin guy is worth the lives of an estimated five thousand Hudson troops. Your pals from West Point would be the ones dying on the front lines. Not to mention what we're going to do about D.C. and Baltimore."

"What's Hudson going to do about D.C. and Baltimore?"

"Hudson won't do a damned thing. No stomach for it. Hudson did New York City. Cullen thinks Hudson cannot, will not, ever take down a city again. He doesn't have the will. If he did, his nation and army wouldn't follow him."

Ike interrupted. "This isn't our problem. Ed, you go too far."

"Right. You're right." Ed drove in silence for a while. Darcy's quiet voice took over to read him the turns from the map route Faye laid in.

"Blew it anyway," Ed said bitterly.

"Blew what?" Faye asked in concern, glancing at the hood.

"Blew a day. We need to fix the radiator. Find gas. Travel a hundred extra miles of Appalachia where we don't know a soul. Have no allies. And oh, the Ohio Army is in the way. By tomorrow night."

"There are Sixers in West VA. Judgment. Watch Tower," Faye said, correcting herself twice. And then she realized. "But you don't know any of them."

"Nope."

"Well that'll be time-consuming, won't it," Faye murmured.

"But you're very charming," Ed snarked.

Faye pictured herself standing up to Oelrich and demanding he sell gas to a whore. Faye pictured Ed, coming down from speed, being charming to anyone. Faye pictured relieving Ed of his Glock for the next couple days. She concluded she had no effective way to disarm him. She never did. "We'll figure it out."

"We always do," Ed agreed woodenly. "God knows how. Give me another hit of speed."

"No. You don't need more."

"I planned to take more now. It's three a.m. and I've still got to get us across the border. We're nowhere near the border. Give it to me."

"The border is only fifty miles from South Park."

"It's not on an interstate! Give me the speed, bitch, before I give you a fat lip and a black eye. You'll fit in much better with Judgment –"

"Fine! Wreck yourself! What do I care?" She lobbed the amphetamine bottle into his lap.

On that unhappy note, they found their way into Sleepy Hollow, a crease in the hills just south of the South Park playground complex. South Park featured a golf course, bath house, flashy gazebo and fair-grounds – quite a nice complex, reminiscent of the SCA war camp-ground they'd visited a couple nights ago. In contrast, the Sleepy Hollow annex featured yet another hundred thousand black trees with a creek at the bottom.

Darcy pulled alongside dull-colored pickup trucks and buses lined up by the side of the road, headed out. Ed popped the hood and tail-gate. He proceeded to investigate his radiator, corralling Neal into that effort. Faye brought Ike as her male spokesman and set out to find Kauffman, the Judgment business agent she'd met with Ed last week.

Conversation was awkward, with Kauffman speaking only to Ike, but Faye feeding Ike his lines. But they got through it. Kauffman was easily as cranky as Ed about having to pull their plans forward a day. But Skull had gotten word to them. They'd roll out on time.

Or at least, they'd expected to roll out on time, until Faye admitted they needed gas and they'd taken a bullet through the radiator. Kauffman yelled and fumed and nearly hit her. But a brace of black-clad stoned mechanics was summoned to pull up next to Darcy and see what could be done in twenty minutes.

Liking Kauffman even less than on their previous meeting, Faye walked back down the line of buses toward Darcy, sadly confident she'd just get yelled at again by Ed.

"Panic!" hissed a voice.

Faye looked up to see a black girl's face peer at her from a bus window. Faye drew a blank at first. But then she recognized a recruit who left West Point with her and Daneel. Cade dropped her off at a train station with directions to meet her trainer on the platform in Schenectady.

Judgment had a company new hire caught in their slave pen.

25

Interesting fact: Pittsburgh's Lt. Colonel Caroline Drumpeter was the highest-ranked woman Resco in the Northeast. Before Pittsburgh, she supervised the Erie section of northwestern PA, and cultivated the Great Lakes trade.

"Ed, I want to buy a slave," Faye announced. "Maybe two."

A pair of humorless Judgment men swarmed Darcy's hood around Ed and Neal. They constrained what she could say.

Ed reached out one stiff-fingered hand and pushed her face away. "Busy." Then he glanced at her and grinned. His fingertips left engine gunk on her cheeks, which she then proceeded to smear like war paint before she realized what it was.

Darcy's grimy guts were well-lit by the work lamp hanging above, as four men debated whether it was just the radiator hose, or if the radiator was also cracked, and if so, what they could do about it with no time left.

"Ed, I need to—"

Ed whirled on her. "Faye, you know what I need? I need you to pull your weight. You want a slave? Buy a fucking slave. But do it yourself. We leave in five. Shift change at six a.m. on the border." He shoved her out of the way.

Right. Faye grabbed a wad of cash and dragged Ike with her at a jog back to Kauffman. "We need to buy one of your slaves. Maybe two. And pay you for the gas and mechanics. That one. How much you want for her?"

Kauffman scowled and tried to talk to Ike instead. Faye shoved up into his face and slapped his nose with the wad of Liberty dollars. "You talk to me because I have the money. And we're pressed for time. That slave. Hey, you! Let her out! I'm buying her!"

The black ex-recruit, currently dressed in torn panties and bra suitable for street corner commerce, tripped out of a bus to land on her hands and face.

"Fifty?" Faye suggested to Kauffman. She had no idea how much a slave was worth. "Hey you. You had a partner, didn't you? He dead?"

The slave spit out dirt with a murderous look at Faye. She pointed to another bus. "Gorey."

Faye stomped up to the indicated bus and yelled out. "Gorey! On the double, send me out Gorey!" Kauffman waved an irritable hand to confirm that the bus driver and guard should humor the crazy whore and get this show on the road.

An older man, maybe thirty, maybe black, was thrown out of the second bus to land even less fluently than the first. He seemed rather the worse for wear. Maybe he was shielding a broken bone.

Faye, having studied karate from age six, was wholly unimpressed with two full-grown agents who didn't know how to take a fall. "Ten for him?" she suggested to Kauffman. "And four hundred for the gas? How about five hundred altogether." She peeled the bills off, and tacked on an extra two hundred to cover the sheer lunacy of the morning, plus duct tape or whatever was going to coax Darcy's radiator across the border. "In addition to whatever Ed owes you on the other side."

Kauffman took the money to wash his hands of her.

"You!" Faye pointed at her new black slave girl. "Grab your Gorey, and hurry up about it." She stomped imperiously back to Darcy.

Ike deigned to help the girl half-carry Gorey between them back to the car. Faye forced them into the cargo hold without sympathy, and sat them on a utility blanket thrown over Ed's bed.

"I'm Faye. Gorey," she whispered, pointing at him. Now that she got a closeup on him, he might be dark Mediterranean. "You?"

"Rahema for now."

"Can either of you drive an SUV with a heavy trailer?" Faye asked urgently. "Ed's been driving all night."

"I can drive anything," Rahema claimed. "Motor pool at Hogwarts."

Aha, Faye realized. That's where she'd seen 'Rahema' before graduation. Most of the trainees recruited into the company were in a GED prep class with Daneel and Ava. But Skull also screened recruits who'd finished high school before the epidemic. Her friends Puño and Marquis had started college Before. They filled out the same wonky crime questionnaire as Ava.

"Good to know." Faye eyed their condition and size, and considered Ed's presently warped sense of humor. *Not worth it, at first.* "Let's get you clean and dressed first."

The caravan was bouncing out, with Darcy embedded in midstream, by the time Faye started getting her new slaves squared away. Gorey's shoulder was dislocated. That would have to wait until they could get out of the car and yank at it without infuriating Ed. Ike's clothes fit Gorey well enough, except in style. He seemed pretty strung out, not tracking well enough to talk beyond monosyllables, with a possible concussion.

Rahema wasn't big, but still a good three sizes larger than Faye, who preferred her pants to fit like a glove. The best they could do was sponge off the dirt, safety-pin her bra back together, and put her in some of Neal's clothes. She ended up looking very butch, every inch the motor pool tough. Judging by the smeared makeup and bra, this didn't suit Rahema's fashion sense. *Tough.*

"Where are you headed?" Faye asked at last. Neal squatted beside her to check out their new riders. Ike observed from his seat behind Ed. There was no space left in the cargo hold.

"Ohio," Gorey replied muzzily.

Rahema pressed her lips together, and decided to speak for their duo. "Supposed to rendezvous with a gran caravan, too damn far south into West Virginia. Cross into VA."

"Cool, us too," Faye said. "Then where?"

Gorey shook his head in refusal. Rahema overruled him. "Richmond. We're supposed to watch the circus go by and report. Expedite operations and shipments in VA. You?"

"Not Richmond," Faye answered. "We have specific targets. Passing through. Can you proceed? Or do you need to abort? Like, should we kick you out before the border? Quickly now."

Gorey looked too ill to contemplate continuing. Rahema said, "We need transportation and currency and communications. If you can get us to the gran caravan, I think we're set. Right, Gorey?"

Gorey frowned, seemed to think hard, and then threw up on the utility blanket and Rahema's new outfit.

"The boss knows you as Rahema and Gorey?" Faye asked.

"Close enough," Rahema confirmed. She got busy cleaning up her agent trainer.

Neal stayed to help and get to know them better. Faye clambered into her seat beside Ed.

"I want to send a message to boss," she announced.

"Darcy, record message," Ed said. He'd programmed Darcy to take voice commands from Faye only in an emergency.

"Boss, we're nearing southern point for dawn," Faye said. "I just bought two slaves named Rahema and Gorey. No clothes or other accessories. Current plan is to carry them with us. Have maybe a half hour to change our minds and leave them behind. Advise if you want."

"Darcy, send message to boss," Ed concluded. "Good report, Faye." He sounded faintly surprised.

"Do you know them?" Faye asked. "Gorey, I mean. He's in bad shape."

Ed scowled and shook his head. "Darcy, record message to boss. P.S. Boss, Gorey is in 'bad shape.' Faye. Elaborate."

"Possible concussion, dislocated shoulder, bruises and contusions. He isn't tracking too well mentally. Rahema's been roughed up. But she seems intent to get where she's going."

"Darcy, send message," Ed said. "Yeah, I know Gorey. He's alright." Ed's verdict lacked enthusiasm. "Holdover from Canber. Well, so are we. Except you."

"How's Darcy?"

"Probably pull over once an hour to add water. When it gets to once every ten minutes, we're screwed." With that thought, he added his own P.S. message to Skull, but concluded that their team was still a go.

Meanwhile Faye tried to feed him something. Ed refused to eat. Speed left him completely without appetite, yet running on empty.

Darcy reported an incoming message. Skull replied, "Plans confirmed. Good work, and good luck today."

Faye blinked. "That wasn't what I was expecting."

Ed shrugged. "It's what I expected. Boss can't second-guess us in the field, Faye. We're doing the best we can. Plans hit reality and SNAFU. Situation normal, all fucked up. We have not yet achieved FUBAR. The day is young."

"Fucked up beyond all recognition," Faye concurred. "No. Not there yet."

Neal stuck his head between the front seats. "Asked them how they ended up as slaves. Sounds like Gorey wanted a bender last night. Um, Sunday night. Copped some Ecstasy and insisted Rahema do it with him. Next she knew she was in a Judgment slave pen. Probably raped a couple times while she was knocked out."

"Sounds about right," Ed acknowledged.

"Would you go on a bender before an op?" Neal retorted.

"No, obviously. I took speed and killed someone. What gets your rocks off, Neal?"

Darcy interrupted. "Warning. Engine overheating."

Ed poked the trip meter to zero it again. "Twenty-eight miles. That's a short leash."

They'd rejoined I-79 by that point. Ed pulled onto the shoulder. Rahema helped Neal top up the radiator, and they got going again. Ed sped up to overtake the slow six-vehicle Judgment caravan, and merged Darcy back into the middle.

"What's our status on the radiator?" Faye asked.

Neal replied. "Chunk out of the hose, wrapped in duct tape. The radiator itself has a hairline fracture, probably. Near the top. Also duct taped, with a patch."

"Ask Rahema if she can fix that?" Faye requested. "She worked in the motor pool during Basic. I don't think she was in fat camp."

"She's from Schenectady," Ed supplied. "That's why Gorey met her there. She left her kid brother in foster care to join the Army. She wanted to see him again before disappearing."

Faye blinked. "You know this much about all the new agents?"

"Helped the boss review the questionnaires. I liked her. Girl's got balls."

"Yeah. She seems to." Faye relayed Rahema's assignment in Richmond.

"She'd be good for that," Ed said. "I don't know about Gorey. Maybe if she stayed put while he went out looking for trouble. She'll get tired of reining him in. If she isn't tired of him already. Not our problem."

"You think he forces her to sleep with him?"

"I don't know about force. We don't have any female senior agents. She'll make her own choices. You're free to tell me that bed is off limits. I doubt we'd last very long that way. But you have the option. Another trainer might not see it that way."

"She has sex work experience?" Faye guessed. That could be used against her in a brush-off discussion.

Ed shrugged. "So do we."

A spate of rain hit the windshield. Due to the drought ever since the tsunami in February, three months ago, Ed didn't take it seriously at first. He hit the mist setting on the wipers once, and smeared dust across the windshield, tinged hot pink from the tail-lights on the bus in front of them. He followed up with a few swipes of washer fluid. But the splatter of drops recurred, then developed into a steady rain.

"This night just keeps getting better," Ed complained.

"You know what? You're awesome," Faye assured him. "And Rahema can drive after the border, and give you a break. Or Ike or Neal. We're almost there. Couple dried strawberries for luck?"

"No. I am in the right mood."

"You're in the mood to reach out and kill someone."

"Exactly. You do the talking."

"Damn! I forgot to check the trailer for settling at the Judgment camp! Should we stop?"

"Too late."

Ed coasted in to a stop. Empty-eyed slaves stared down at Faye from the rear window of the bus in front. They must have seen her take two of their number out of captivity. But perhaps they assumed that the sold slaves were no better off than they were themselves.

"Can't they escape?"

"Easily. They stay for the drugs." Ed rolled Darcy up another bus-length as the line advanced. "This isn't new, Av– Faye. West VA had an opiate problem even before the Calm Act. Leading cause of death. Practically a prototype for the company's program. Some towns, one in ten was a junkie." They advanced again.

"We're moving through quickly," Faye said optimistically.

"Yeah. Get me ten grand."

Faye boggled momentarily, but hurried up.

"Just in case," Ed said. "And get out your Glock. I have a bad feeling."

"That bad feeling is an amphetamine crash."

"That too."

Faye had some money pre-counted into ten-k servings. She retrieved the prescribed bribe in an open white business envelope. She nestled it between Ed's thighs, the bills peeking out to face her for the moment, not visible from the driver's window. Meanwhile, Ed asked Neal and Ike to pass up their crisp new Ohio ID's. Rahema and Gorey didn't have ID. They formed a quiet hump under the blanket in back.

Their turn next. The Judgment vehicles ahead were gone. Nothing stood between them and West Virginia but a simple orange-and-white striped boom gate, and the line of orange traffic cones that herded them into a single line for inspection. Beyond the gate, Ohio positioned two armored personnel carriers. Spillover light from Darcy's head-lights showed machine gunners perched on top, with the roadway already ranged.

Colonel Drumpeter in Pittsburgh called ahead to the border, of course.

Ed lowered his window and let Darcy roll forward nice and slow. *Kramer*, the Ohio Army uniform blouse proclaimed its owner, a corporal not much older than Ed.

No, Ed was Clay now. And Faye became Anna.

Another border guard stood only inches behind Kramer's shoulder, a corporal labeled Partridge.

"Good morning, officer –" Clay began.

Kramer spoke over him, indicating the coned-off right highway shoulder ahead. "Pull over there. Do not try to run. We will use lethal force."

Clay turned the bribe envelope so the bills showed. Kramer looked at it, then looked Clay straight in the eye. "Joyriding and a shooting spree up in Pittsburgh a few hours ago. Dead sheriff north of there."

"Take the bribe, Kramer," Clay advised. "Ten grand. No one needs to die here today."

"Threatening me, too?" Kramer reached for his gun.

A muffled shot caught Anna by surprise. Her gun hadn't made it up to aim yet. Kramer's eyes grew wide. The left side of his shirt grew darker and wetter than the rain could account for. As he slumped down, Anna glimpsed the pistol in Partridge's hand. He must have shot diagonally through Kramer's rib cage to the heart.

Partridge held his hand out for the bribe. He leafed through it, then held out his hand again, flapping his fingers, 'Hit me again.' Clay nodded minutely to Anna. She hastily produced another ten grand envelope.

"Take the body. Lose it," Partridge directed. "Don't drive this SUV into PA again." He spit on Kramer's body and stepped back. He strolled off toward the Judgment pickup truck behind them.

That was cold, Anna thought. But Kramer was a fool. His whole shift was on the take. Partridge wouldn't risk being exposed. Still, that hit looked personal.

Neal and Ike hastily hopped out and dragged the late corporal into Darcy. Rather than pile a corpse on top of their slaves, they propped him on Ike's seat and tried to plug the bloody leaks.

Clay slowly let his foot off the brake and rolled Darcy away. Only Anna saw him blow out through pursed lips. That was the way he taught her to do it, long ago, to control her anxiety attacks. *Just breathe out. Your body breathes in by itself.* Unlike her, anxiety attacks didn't immobilize him. He claimed he found driving soothing.

A mile or so further into West Virginia they veered into a welcome center, another no-exit rest loop off the interstate. Behind the abandoned building was a slight rise, tree tops visible from the other side.

Rahema hustled to feed the radiator.

Clay snatched the bloody and disgusting utility blanket off Gorey. He spread it on the pavement. Then they set Kramer's body on top. Neal quickly patted down the man's uniform to empty its pockets, insignia, name tag, and weapon. Then they rolled the body in the blanket. Clay and Anna, Neal and Ike, carried the bundle up the rise.

The far side was too steep to clamber down into the woods. So Clay and Neal swung the body three times and let fly. They couldn't see where it landed. The corpse cracked through tree branches on the way down.

"Go, go, go," Clay urged. "Sky's starting to lighten."

26

Interesting fact: Before the Calm, West Virginia ranked #49 among states in per capita income, beating only Mississippi. Neighboring Kentucky and Tennessee ranked 46th and 45th, and Maryland 1st. New Jersey, Connecticut, Massachusetts, New Hampshire, and Virginia were 2nd, 4th, 6th, 7th, and 8th.

"I don't care if he lives or dies," Clay complained, poking a sneakered toe into Gorey's side. "Get him off my bed."

"Clay, he's –" Anna attempted.

"I am *done!*" Clay yelled at her. *"Finished!* I can't deal with any more! Get this *problem* off my bed so I can sleep!"

The hope had been for Clay to stop driving the moment they reached West Virginia. The roads didn't cooperate. The only exits from I-79 led into downtown Morgantown, or I-68 eastbound, the inevitable route of the northern pincer of the Ohio invasion. Seeing no better options, Anna steered Clay onto I-68, just to cross the Monongahela River and the Morgantown conurbation as fast as possible. As dawn rose, she could see army transports parked everywhere. Soldiers mobilized for the day like an irritated ant hill. In the weak watery light,

Clay looked grayer than the sky. Finally, a good 20 miles past the border, Anna finally directed him into an abandoned boy scout camp.

Anna's intent was to find the camp center and commandeer a dormitory.

Clay's intent was to stop the damned car and collapse. Clay won.

"Got it," she agreed. Neal and Rahema helped Anna shift Gorey into the tailgate zone, with a folded blanket for a pillow. Clay immediately collapsed into his bed.

Anna didn't want to screw around with a tent they couldn't dry afterward. Instead she had Neal and Ike rig a tarp between Darcy and the trailer, for a bit of outdoor canopy out of the hard rain.

"Anybody ever fix a dislocated shoulder?" Anna asked. A chorus of shaking heads suggested she was the most experienced medic.

Ava had little training, but her parents were nurses. One time they were watching some doctor drama on TV. Her father was incensed at how the actors bungled a dislocation. He demonstrated on his daughter how it was done. That was years ago. Army Basic taught her no more than Rahema and Neal, mostly first aid for battle injuries. But her gang kept a few medical books for reference, instead of burning them to cook supper. During the Starve, she was one of the braver ones at daring to fix people. Most of Frosty's scars bore Ava's needlework.

Anna felt around Gorey's shoulder to visualize what had to happen. That should have hurt, but Gorey was unconscious. She thought it better to complete this operation before he woke. She hopped up on the tailgate, and took his wrist and elbow.

"Neal, anchor me around the waist," she directed. "Rahema, try to brace his torso. He's going to wake up screaming."

She rotated Gorey's arm the way she pictured, and jerked. He didn't scream. The shoulder didn't shift back into its socket, either.

Neal had watched carefully. He took a turn, yanking harder with his longer reach. Anna checked the shoulder – good, back together again.

Not so good, was that Gorey didn't rouse through two rounds of an excruciating procedure. Anna peeled back his eyelids to see mismatched pupils, eyeballs tracking in slightly different directions.

Concussion, bad one. Frosty had a concussion once, from one of his forays with Midtown into Jersey. She wasn't there, but one of Midtown's mounted cannons nearly hit him. She'd been terrified for him, that he'd suffered major brain damage. Despite the best she could do at home, his recovery was slow and dicey. Disoriented, Frosty flew into towering rages over nothing, then crumpled into sobs of agony from the splitting headaches. Brain injuries were serious. And there wasn't much she could do about one.

She bent and listened to a chest of raspy breathing and irregular heartbeat.

"We're losing him," she concluded.

She scampered through Darcy to the console. "Darcy, record emergency message. Boss, Gorey has a concussion. He's unconscious, maybe a coma. He can't wait for delivery. It's ten or fifteen miles back to Morgantown. Clay passed out and needs to sleep. Watch Tower doesn't use doctors. If I don't hear from you in ten, we need to ditch the trailer and find a hospital in Morgantown. Clay won't be happy. Please advise. Anna out. Darcy, send message to boss."

"Message sent," Darcy confirmed in unconcern.

Anna frog-marched back to the tailgate. "You heard that?" she asked the group. "What do you think?"

Ike summoned the courage to answer first. "I wouldn't make that move without consulting Clay. I don't care to let a fellow agent die, either."

Neal pursed his lips and shrugged.

"Rahema?" Anna prompted. "You know anything I don't?"

"They controlled the slaves with drugs," Rahema replied. "We don't know if this is concussion or drugs. Knowing Gorey, he might have overdosed by his own fool choice."

Neal asked, "Anna? If it were Clay's call, what input would you give him?"

Clay, who didn't ordinarily snore, took a strangled breath, rolled onto his back, and snored loudly.

Anna stared down at Gorey's bloody hair, and crouched down to smooth it. "The kind of company I want to work for stands by its people. That's the kind of team I choose to be. Gorey's best chance is in Morgantown. But we're burning daylight. And we paid heavy for –"

A crunching sound approached on the gravel drive. Anna crouched lower to peer through Darcy's window above Clay. A white compact sedan appeared, heading directly for them. She ducked forward through the SUV to grab her carbine. Neal stepped through the rain beside Darcy to meet her at the rifles behind the driver's seat.

The car stopped on Darcy's passenger side. Anna lowered the windows on that side. She and Neal leveled their rifles, pointed at the visitor.

A soldier in his twenties gently stepped out of his car. He raised his hands in the air as much as the process of exiting the car permitted. "Understand you guys are in trouble. Here to help. I'm First Lieutenant Tucson. Call me Tuck." He pronounced his name Tuck-sun, though his shirt spelled it like the town in Arizona.

Neal pointed his AK-47 at the man's shoulder patch, a green-rimmed white circle with a fat red bulls-eye in the middle. "That a buckeye?"

"Ohio." Tuck scratched his nose, then humored the kids by raising his hand again. "You are in Ohio, you know."

Ike hesitantly peeked out from behind Darcy. Tuck eagerly switched to the grown-up. "Sir, I understand you're trying to reach a rendezvous near Brandywine. Route 33."

"Don't know about that," Ike said. "But we have a sick man here. Looks like a concussion. We were discussing what to do about him."

Tuck slowly lowered his hands. Anna, then Neal, withdrew their rifles to exit the car doors and follow him. Neal held onto his gun. Anna traded hers for a Glock stuck in the back of her waistband. Tuck headed to the tailgate to look Gorey over. Before Anna made it out the door, Darcy pinged an incoming message.

Anna plugged in ear buds and played the message from Skull. "Anna, whoever you're talking to, get a photo of him. I didn't send him." The dashcam angle didn't provide Skull a clear view of the newcomer. He didn't mention Anna's previous message.

Annoyed, Anna pulled the tablet out of the dashboard and followed around to the group consulting over the unconscious Gorey. "Tuck," she said, getting him to look up. "Say cheese!"

"What?"

"Close enough," she said, and returned to the dashboard with her tablet photograph. "Neal, help me."

Tuck chuckled. "Wow, you've got a young team, agent –?"

"Ike," Ike supplied. "That's Gorey."

Tuck pointed to Clay, who no longer snored. "Another casualty?"

"Just sleeping," Ike continued. "The proposal, Tuck, was to back-track into Morgantown and find a hospital for Gorey."

"Just need to get him to the caravan," Tuck argued. But he checked Gorey's eyes and pulse, much the way Anna had. "Hell, he's not going to make it, is he."

Meanwhile, Neal took over from Anna to transmit the photo of Tuck to Skull. Anna returned to Gorey out through the cargo hold. She was thinking that she'd really like a response from Skull before making any further decisions, when her eyes lit on Darcy's extravagant first aid kit. She rummaged and found a few doses of naloxone, the opiate overdose antidote.

"We're sure he has opiates in his system?" she demanded of Rahema.

"Correct," Rahema confirmed.

That was good enough for Anna. She ripped the nasal syringe out of the package with her teeth and dosed Gorey. She and Tuck both grasped a wrist to monitor Gorey's pulse. The heartbeat strengthened, and then Gorey convulsed slightly and coughed up some phlegm. Tuck wiped it away with a corner of the blanket. He listened to Gorey's breathing again, and checked his eyes.

"Well, he's better," Tuck confirmed.

"Not better enough," Anna concluded. "Tuck, take him to a hospital in Morgantown. In your car." She folded the syringe wrapper and inserted it conspicuously in Gorey's breast pocket. "Rahema, go with him. See if you can find anything to help with the radiator. We leave here in one hour, max."

Offended at this tiny girl trying to give him orders, Tuck looked to Ike to intervene.

Ike nodded solemnly. "One hour."

"Hell! Alright."

They transfered Gorey into Tuck's back seat, his blanket pillow and head on Rahema's lap. Anna intended to leave Rahema to her own best judgment, to come back within the hour or not. But Neal pressed a phone on her. "Ike is agent one in the phone book. Send a snapshot of where you leave Gorey. Text if you're running late."

Anna and the hackers stood in the rain, waving good-bye, as Tuck tore out in a spray of gravel. They were back to their own proper team of four.

"I'm feeling better already," Neal quipped.

Anna smirked back at him. "So we leave in forty-five minutes unless ell-tee Tuck checks out. Thanks for backing me up, Ike."

Ike shrugged. "What next?"

Anna thought out loud. "Food ready to eat for the day. Any blood stains washed. I need to check the trailer. Top up the radiator now and later, to be on the safe side. If we need to peel out of here, who's driving?"

They considered each other unhappily, and contemplated the soaking rain. "I am," Neal concluded. "I sure hope Tuck is legit. Rahema would be better."

Anna nodded and soft-punched his shoulder. "Just a backup plan," she assured him.

Inside the trailer, she shifted the toilet paper cartons to wriggle into the back. She could see daylight through the bullet holes. She fetched the duct tape to seal the ammo and gun crates from the rain. She didn't spot an exit hole for either round, nor the bullets. But if they hadn't exploded anything yet, they weren't going to. Satisfied, she rigged the layer of innocent goods again, and locked the trailer.

Ike had already cleaned the blood by the time she rejoined them under the tarp. He rinsed rags while Neal made sandwiches. Anna washed her hands, then sliced a block of cheese, peppers, and mush-rooms for lighter snacks. Clay – Frank at the time – had made some hummus, too. All their water bottles got refilled and stowed back where they belonged. They even had time for a quick sponge bath and face wash to freshen up.

"Dammit," Anna concluded. She returned to the front console.

"Darcy record emergency message. Boss, really hope to hear from you soon on ID, one first louie Tucson of the Ohio Army. Spelled Too-sahn like in Arizona. Why do we have him." Belatedly, she realized the dashcam wouldn't have picked up what was going on. She hurriedly outlined their status. "Ten minutes until we rabbit and ditch Tuck and Rahema. But we'd rather have them if Tucson is legit. Please advise soonest. Anna out."

Ike received a text message. "Rahema found a radiator hose. They're headed back now. They dropped Gorey at an emergency room. She sent a photo."

"Do you know where they are?" Anna asked.

Ike switched to a live tracking map on his phone and showed her.

"Damn we're cutting it fine," she said. "Strike camp. All in." In minutes, the tarp was folded and stowed, the food hamper shoved back into its slot, radiator topped and hood closed. Neal slid into the driver seat and blew out unhappily. Anna studied the tablet map of West Virginia in dismay.

She didn't have a clue where to tell Neal to drive.

"Update," Ike reported. "They just turned onto this road."

"OK. Change of plans," Anna decided. "We take Rahema, and we take Tuck prisoner."

"Good call," Neal said. He'd already bonded with Rahema. He tried to find the driver's pistol but couldn't.

Anna still had the navigator's pistol in her waistband. She got out of the car and leaned against the passenger door. "Take the carbine on your side, Neal. Can you shoot to maim? Like graze his shoulder?"

"Um."

"OK. Shoot in the air."

"I can do that," Neal agreed. "Ike, stay low."

Keyed up and ready for action, Anna blew out, ignoring the slight jounce of Darcy at her back. A tap on the passenger window got her attention. Clay waved for her to move. He pushed the door wide open, and pulled her between his knees, sitting sideways in the passenger seat with his sock toes in the doorway.

"Good job, baby. But no," Clay said, kissing the crown of her head. "Neal, stand down."

He didn't have time to explain. Tuck's Toyota four-door appeared and pulled up beside them.

Rahema hopped out and brandished her radiator hose in triumph. She took in the pistol in Clay's hand, lying relaxed on Anna's lap, and frowned. "Is he safe out of bed yet?" she quipped.

Tuck climbed out of his car more slowly.

"No," Clay replied. "Lieutenant Tucson, good to meet you. Thank you for taking Gorey for medical attention. I'm Clay, team leader for this expedition."

Clay stuck out his right hand to shake, and found a Glock in it. He transferred the Glock to Ava, and stuck his hand out again.

Tuck accepted the hand-shake, lips pursed. "You're the team leader?"

"He is," Ike confirmed. "I'm a tech specialist."

"She's my second," Clay added, chin on Anna's head. "Because she knows what I would do. Mostly. Thing is, Tuck, our boss doesn't know who you are. So we're going to kick back for a minute or two and get to know each other."

"I'm a first lieutenant in the Ohio Army," Tuck began. "And unless you –"

"First louie?" Clay replied. "Cool. So you command a platoon, in combat? Have I got that right, Anna?"

"Could be a squad," Anna quibbled. "Or staff. All our ell-tees were staff."

"I commanded a squad," Tuck admitted. "As second louie. Since Detroit fell, I've been in the quartermaster corps. Reassigned to Char-lottesville."

Clay nodded. "Degree, experience – valuable to the company. Thing is, Tuck, I've commanded hundreds in combat. Trusted field agent with the company. Chosen leader by this team. You and Rahema, we'll part ways at Brandywine or whatever. So who told you to –"

Darcy beeped for attention. "Excuse me," Clay said pleasantly enough to Tuck. He banged open the glove compartment. "God damn it, Ava, where'd you put –"

She pointed to the ear buds jacked into the dashboard. "Clay needed some sleep," she apologized to Tuck. "He's cranky."

Clay bopped her lightly on the head with a fist, and listened to his message. Apparently it didn't require a response, because he just stowed the ear buds back in the glove box and turned back to report. "All copacetic. Our friends in Brandywine re-routed Tuck to expedite after hearing my concerns last night. Tuck, apologies if you want them. But I feel better now."

"I could have told you that if you'd asked," Tuck objected.

"We were getting to that," Clay allowed. "Is that a trailer hitch on your car?"

The quick subject change caught Tuck off-guard. "Um, yeah. I had a boat."

"Think you can haul this trailer? Thing is, we've pissed off all sorts of people lately with this Ford Expedition hauling a trailer. Besides, if you're stopped, you can say you're bringing arms to the front. Confiscated weapons, blah-blah, woof-woof. Ike, you can forge that order, right?"

Ike nodded confidently. Neal reached into Tuck's car and grabbed his tablet. "We'll have this back to you in a jiffy," he promised.

"Uh, my car's a hybrid," Tuck said. "In these mountains, I won't go very fast."

Clay assured him, "I've come to accept that this day will last an eternity. Night's likely to suck, too. Even with you hauling the trailer, I'll probably need gas before Brandywine. Radiator repair. Rahema, let's see you transfer the trailer onto Tuck's car." He tossed her the keys to Darcy.

Rahema caught them with a grin, delighted, her smile a bright spot in a rainy day.

"I screwed up. Sorry," Anna said. Maybe she should have woken Clay before pulling a gun on a suspected ally.

"Not at all. You did great," Clay assured her. "I was listening, mostly. Um, boss suggested, for next time? You might spell out the name. That Tuck-sun, too-sahn thing? Slowed things up." He pushed her off and closed the car door, then lowered the window. "Someone should ride with Tuck."

"I'll do it," Anna agreed. "Navigate for both cars from the lead. Ike and Neal's phones seem to work. Don't drop too far behind. If we get separated, I'll be really pissed at you."

Clay nodded. "Love you. Be safe." They traded a quick kiss before Rahema started Darcy moving to reposition the trailer.

An eternity was an exaggeration, perhaps. But as lead navigator, Anna tracked the trip meter and progress in detail from Tuck's passenger seat. Threading from Appalachian hill to hollow, trying to trend south-southwest. Up and down mountains, with the little Toyota struggling mightily against the trailer's weight. Avoiding Ohio forces here, stopping to let them pass there. They regrouped in a dead coal mine for lunch while a long column passed. Rahema took the opportunity to replace the radiator hose, so the Darcy contingent could stop for a refill less often. They were barely making 20 miles per hour, let alone 20 miles in the right direction.

Inside the Toyota, Anna let Tuck do the talking at first. He embroidered his military career to impress the inexperienced young girl. He'd never served outside the U.S., having graduated a couple weeks after the Calm Act was signed. After a while she concluded he was the sort of bounding idealist doomed to be a screw-up in the Army.

Anna could relate.

Eventually Tuck asked where her family was. Just for grins, she told him, and blew his mind. Tuck grew a lot more cautious around Clay after that, and didn't mistake Anna for an innocent girl again. Anna was glad to spike his flirting. Clay could get difficult about that today.

And the rain fell harder.

27

Interesting fact: In troubled combat veterans, it was difficult to tease apart the lingering effects from traumatic brain injury – TBI – versus post-traumatic stress disorder – PTSD. They often suffered from both. The symptoms were similar and synergistic.

Hell on earth nestled in the mountains west of the Monongahela Forest. Anna gazed in horror-struck awe the next day, open mouth hidden behind a rag rapidly turning grey.

Tarry black coated the ground. The skeletons of burned trees died back from the noxious poisons filling the hollow. Flames engulfed a tall boiler, thick belches of soot and red fire pouring into the sky. The heavy rain tried to beat the smoke back down to the ground. Bent and blasted pipes protruded like spider legs, carrying distillation fractions to lesser containers. Sulfurous fumes wafted over them in hot waves, reeking of demonic rotten eggs from the bowels of the Earth.

They'd found the outlaw oil refinery.

"You've got to be kidding me," Clay breathed. "Tuck, you're insane. Put this bootleg crap in my *car*? Darcy's *engine?*"

"You're awful squeamish for a cold-blooded killer," Tuck returned.

"The equipment is legit. Or was. Some of it. They stole it off a real, um, a legal refinery. So I'm told."

Clay didn't budge from Anna's side. Tuck sighed and stepped forward alone to approach a trio of blackened men about buying some gas. It was his idea, after all, to buy contraband instead of him risking his way into an Ohio Army encampment to procure it. Clay figured it would be even less safe to approach an unknown chapter of Watch Tower.

Neal, true to his Long Island environmentalist ideals, growled from Anna's other side. "We killed our planet for this? God, it's like a cattle feedlot. Lots of luck trying to eat a burger afterwards."

Anna nodded. "This is the most disgusting thing I've ever seen. And the *smell.*"

"Car's gonna run like hell," Rahema said. "Never mind the octane and impurities. Just think how much water is going to get into the fuel line. Clay, after using this gunk, don't run it below a quarter tank until you can drain it all off and start fresh."

That girl had a true vocation in vehicles. Last night she sealed the crack in Darcy's radiator with fiberglass and epoxy. She worked under a tarp to control the rain and hide the work light. This morning she made sure both cars and the trailers started the day with tires inflated to the proper pressure, and topped up the engine oil and washer fluid besides. She drove Darcy just as well as Clay, too. Anna had never seen Clay so utterly jettison his racism. He thought Rahema was great. Anna was almost jealous.

Rahema couldn't stop the rain, though. The trailer sank into the mud overnight. Tuck's little Toyota was helpless to rock it out this morning. Clay decreed that was the end of Tuck hauling the trailer. Darcy needed to pull it again, and that meant they needed gas. A last-chance appeal ahead to the caravan yielded no joy. Skull relayed the request that if they found fuel, they should bring extra to the rendezvous.

Tuck returned from his negotiations with a half gallon milk jug labeled with a scribbled 'K.' "For your camp stove. Kerosene," he told Clay, offering it as a gift.

Clay made no move to accept the dubious jug. Anna relieved Tuck of it, then stared at it, trying to figure out how they could safely stow the thing.

Tuck scowled at the team's lack of enthusiasm. "They can sell us two hundred seventy-five gallons of gas in a heating fuel tank, plus a trailer to carry it. That's maybe a ton. They want four thousand dollars. It's a good deal."

"Four thousand buckeye?" Clay asked, reluctantly engaging the problem. "I don't have Ohio cash. And a ton's too much for the Toyota to haul in this weather."

"Top our tanks, pull a hundred fifty gallons?" Anna suggested. "If it's for the caravan, maybe they'll take AK-47s in payment, some Liberty dollars, oxycontin."

Clay snorted. "Well, ammo anyway." His eye fell on the the milk jug of kerosene in disfavor. "We need a test drive. Let them fill your tank, Tuck. Let's see you drive a few miles and back first." Clay finally walked forward with Tuck to negotiate a road test and payment with the oil-dipped hillbillies.

One of the other locals rushed the fire around the boiler, hollering and pouring fuel on the flames. "Insane," Anna breathed. This ugly scene felt like her worst misgivings about her death angel job made manifest. They had descended into Hell to fuel their evil agenda.

Rahema roused her. "Bet we can siphon that kerosene into the camp stove tank. Come on."

Anna gratefully latched on to the project. *I've done worse,* she consoled herself. The crude oil that slathered the hollow was probably safer for her health than sewage in the city. It didn't smell any worse.

She kept Darcy closed tight as much as possible, so as not to fill with fumes. Ike emerged only once to vomit, and promptly retreated back inside.

Rahema was right. They were able to shoehorn most of the kerosene into the stove tank, which seemed safe enough. Distrusting the storage problem of explosive fumes in a flimsy plastic bottle, Anna returned the lees to the facility boss. He stood with Clay awaiting Tuck's return. Clay was still dickering on the price. He wondered aloud how exactly they measured octane rating for quality control. The hillbilly drew him away to tour the test lab, an oil-drenched shack as pathetic as anything else in the blackened clearing.

Anna was amazed that Tuck volunteered his Toyota – and his life – for this test drive. But she supposed once upon a time oil refining was done in such low-tech settings.

Neal echoed her thoughts. "I saw this story on the news once. Rebels in Africa. They had a river that just oozed this crap. They were pissed at the government for selling their oil without the locals getting paid. So they refined it like this in the swamps. Most disgusting thing I ever saw."

"I don't want the car to blow up," Anna said. "With us in it."

Rahema offered, "More likely it would just gunk up the engine so bad it would quit running. Clay's on it, though. If he decides it's safe, I believe him. Don't you?"

Put on the spot, Anna hastily agreed. "Yeah. You can trust Clay."

Neal chuckled. "Yeah, that was convincing."

Tuck's car returned, saving Anna from having to respond. Rahema was more interested in the sound of his engine, and wandered over to listen. Her pose struck Anna as a macabre reprise of how she checked Gorey's breathing and heart the day before. Clay joined Tuck and Rahema in a huddle at the Toyota's hood to make the final determination.

The verdict was yes. Neal and Anna paid the oil bootleggers six cases of ammo. Anna cobbled together a nice tip out of Pennsylvania produce, Liberty dollars, and some pharmaceuticals. The fresh mushrooms were a hit. And they took to the road again with full tanks and a half-ton of extra gas for the caravan. Darcy didn't run as smoothly on the new stuff. Even Ava could hear the difference.

But the SUV ran. They were still in business.

❧

"WE FOUND THEM!" ANNA CRIED OUT.

Everyone in Darcy broke into a cheer, fists pumping in the air, except for the driver, Clay. Anna shot a quick text to Neal, riding shotgun with Tuck in the Toyota somewhere behind them. He cross-texted before she hit send, "EUREKA!"

Night was falling in the hollow where a smattering of the gran caravan parked in a fairly level field. Anna wondered if their campers would make it out of the mud.

In their entire odyssey across West Virginia, Anna hadn't seen a farm yet prepared for a bad summer. In PA, greenhouses were popping up like mushrooms. Agricultural extension officers manned prominent booths at farm markets, armed with pamphlets and laptops to show plans, and encourage farmers to apply for government hardware kits to secure the crops. PA had the biggest agricultural surplus in the Northeast, and ate high on the hog. Yet PA took the failed spring as seriously as lean Hudson.

West Virginia looked like it gave up long ago. The landscape was much the same, but the roads and buildings looked unloved, with poor upkeep. Anna saw a litter of heroin syringes and oxycontin bottles every time they stopped.

An elderly man with umbrella held them until Tuck caught up, then directed them into downtown Brandywine to 'find the General.'

"People live here?" Clay asked, as they drove on.

"Not many," Ike replied, consulting his laptop. "Used to be two hundred. Looks like less now." Some homes were nice. Mobile homes seemed to outnumber the houses. Gran caravan campers clogged driveways and parking lots all along the downtown strip, which amounted to a block stretched from a school to the post office. A church here, a restaurant there, and an automotive garage seemed to complete the unincorporated hamlet.

Anna added, "The Ohio Army's already been and gone. I think we're following them across the route 33 pass into VA." She'd been concerned about that little cherry on top of their hard trip down West VA – getting to Brandywine only to find the area blocked by an invasion force. But Ohio rolled out this morning. She watched them leave on Tuck's tablet while she took a turn riding in his car.

Rahema asked, "What does a gran caravan have on the Ohio Army? I mean, why would Ohio tolerate them here?"

Ike remained silent. Clay allowed, "Good question."

Anna said, "But you're not going to answer it."

Clay was occupied. He pulled up to an old woman in a bright orange rain parka. "Gas and arms shipment for the caravan. Looking for the General."

"He'll find you," the woman assured him. "Take the trailers back to the school." She pointed back the way they came, then the other way. "That left turn ahead is the road to Virginia."

Annoyed, Clay executed his three-point turn with the unwieldy trailer. He hadn't turned into the school because its parking lot was full, with nowhere to wedge two vehicles with trailers. They spent a half hour in slow negotiations with elderly drivers to move their rigs out of the way. Finally the gas and ammo were detached and deposited in the abbreviated bus lane in front of the school's front door.

They tanked up both cars from the bootleg gas, and claimed their pick of the trade goods screening the gun and ammo shipment.

Then Darcy and the Toyota were free to escape across the street to the wooded back edge of a mobile home park. After ascertaining that no one was home, Anna and Neal rigged a tarp between Darcy and a single-wide to provide them a rain-free living area. Tuck shifted the Toyota to make it three-sided.

"Break time?" Neal called to Clay in enthusiasm. He was eddied out of the camp-making bustle, speaking with Ike.

"Sure," Clay agreed. He shut Darcy's hatchback. "I'm doing office hours, though. Neal, you're up first." Clay opened Darcy's passenger door to usher him in. "Privacy please, the rest of you." Clay went around to the driver's seat and closed them in for their consult.

Fortunately, Anna already pulled out the kitchen gear before Clay shut his 'office.' She cooked supper while he worked his way through one-on-one meetings. Tuck and Rahema were in there together with him for a bit, too.

"What are they doing?" Anna complained to Ike, who helped her turn kebabs on the grill.

"Personnel check, I think," Ike said. "Clay wanted to make sure I hadn't lost my nerve."

Anna considered that. "Now I bet he's trying to convince Rahema to go to Charlottesville with Tuck, instead of to Richmond on her own."

Ike nodded emphatically. "That would be smarter."

Anna smiled at him. "And we haven't lost our nerve? Even though the past couple days were hell?"

Ike nodded more slowly. "I'm reserving judgment until I hear the General's plan to get us to Mount Weather. I'm fine for my op. This travel is daunting, though."

"That's for sure," she agreed.

Clay and Rahema finally emerged from the SUV, and shared a long hug. Anna scowled at all this touching.

After they unlatched, Clay sauntered over to Anna at the stove. "The look on your face," he commented with a flash of smile. He hugged her from behind, and whispered in her ear. "Love you. Supper ready?"

"Do I have something to be jealous about?" she murmured.

"You're too funny. Anna, no one else wants me. I don't want them either. Just you."

"Supper is ready," she allowed. "I don't get a private interview?"

"If you need to tell me something, shoot. Any time. But I'm not your boss."

"Oh, yeah. That."

He chuckled. "Yeah. That. Everybody! Come and get it."

Neal and Tuck had pulled a picnic table under the tarp so they could eat together family-style. Clay raised a toast in fresh pure rainwater. "To making it to the gran caravan!"

They all cheered and drank to that, and dug into the food. As the plates grew bare, the topic of crossing into VA tried to rear its ugly head.

Clay booed it down. "Play time! I want a shower. My car smells like rotten eggs from that refinery. Everybody and their clothes! Bath time!"

Clay rose and started stripping. Tuck looked scandalized as Anna and Rahema followed suit.

Neal whipped him with his rolled T-shirt. "Stare at chicks naked in the showers, and they'll kick you in the nuts."

Once Tuck was bashfully stripping, Neal moved on to Ike, who tried to sit this one out, a middle-aged desk type among young hard-bodies. Neal stole his glasses and stashed them in Darcy for safekeeping. He coaxed Ike into his birthday suit behind the hatchback where the camp's light was dim.

The nude Clay matter-of-factly reached past them to grab soap and shampoo, plus the dish tub, bucket, and detergent. Anna and Rahema headed into the warm heavy rain to rinse their hair. Tuck carried the wad of sulfurous reeking clothes out from the picnic table, then hesitated to put them down and lose his fig leaf.

Clay placed the tub and bucket by Tuck's feet, and squirted a generous helping of shampoo on his hair. "Better lather before that gets in your eyes," he advised. He poured a first dose of detergent over the clothes, too. He moved on to squirt shampoo onto the others.

Tuck dumped the clothes and got with the program. Ike and Neal joined them clicking fingers overhead in the Greek waiter dance until Clay doused them with shampoo.

After that Clay seemed satisfied with group participation. He settled down to wash his own hair and Anna's. Eventually everyone took a turn behind one mobile home or another for a more intimate soaping. Anna and Clay, Ike and Neal stole off in pairs and took their time. Rahema glowered at Tuck when he gallantly offered, but they washed each other's backs in the common driveway where the group frolicked to stay out of the mud.

"That was smooth, right?" Clay asked, as he pinned Anna to the back of the mobile home in the dark.

"Which? Getting everyone to clean? Or stealing me away for sexual favors?"

"Both. I am getting sexual favors, right?" Their cozy home for two was awfully crowded tonight with six.

"I dunno, team leader. Could be considered harassment." She teased a finger along his wet ear. Then she grabbed his shoulders and hopped up, clenching his waist with her knees. "So? Harass me."

They took their time washing up.

Feeling more mellow and relaxed after their private interlude, Anna and Clay were delighted to find Tuck and Rahema had already started the laundry. Everyone's teeth were chattering by the time the sodden mass of clothes smelled better. They wrung the clothes out as best they could, and hung them on a clothesline criss-crossed beneath the tarp. The clothes didn't stand a prayer of drying on a night like this.

Clay liberally sprayed Darcy's interior with air freshener. He tossed the can to Tuck to do likewise to the Toyota. Both cars aired out with the tarp-side doors open.

All inhibitions lost along the way, the group lazed around laughing and chatting in nothing more than a towel, mostly hung around their shoulders. With all the dripping laundry under the tarp, it didn't make sense to don dry clothes until time for bed. By 9:30, Clay was starting to yawn, resting his head on Anna's.

"Aw, did I miss the orgy?"

Six faces swerved to see a heavy-built older man in his 50's, looking amused at the edge of their camp light. Oak leaves glittered from the collar of his modern camouflage uniform. Except, unlike the soldiers of Ohio and Hudson and PA, his arm still bore the U.S. flag.

"Which of you is Clay?" the major asked. "General's ready for you. Walk with me. Put some pants on first, son. I'll wait."

"Can I bring my people?" Clay asked. "I'd like us all to meet the General."

The major's face swerved to Clay in surprise. He'd assumed their leader was Tuck. "I guess they can follow along to the school. I'd like to speak with you privately on the way, though."

28

___

Interesting fact: The Niger Delta held the largest oil reserves in Africa.
Spillage destroyed the environment around the river, including farms and fish.
Guerrillas rose to sabotage the multinational pipelines. They operated bootleg
refineries to benefit the locals.

On arrival at the General's HQ inside the school, the team spread out as per their pre-arranged tasks. On the walk over, Neal asked Anna to study everything to the left, Rahema to the right, Tuck to the center. Neal and Ike would handle electronics, but the others should read every screen.

"It'll be fun!" Neal encouraged. "Like real spy work."

"Just like," Ike muttered. "Memorize all you can."

Clay was already perched on a teacher's desk when the rest arrived, talking to the great man. Clay and Ike looked fairly respectable, in Clay's bright red rain poncho and spare. Tuck wore a more subdued army green poncho. The three proud young West Point graduates wore dumpster chic to meet the boss's boss, ponchos Anna quickly fashioned from black trash bags.

The gran caravan's HQ equipment lay spread out over a half dozen tables, with no techs around to mind the store at this late hour. Or perhaps they'd been sent away for this interview. The major wasn't in there. A projector displayed a map on the classroom whiteboard, showing the latest VA battlefields as well as troop dispositions throughout the East.

Clay stood to introduce his team to the General, who did not acquire a name in the process. Nor was his uniform labeled. Clay ordered the team by age, starting with Ike. Tuck offered a salute instead of a handshake.

"None of that, son," the craggy-faced General told him. "Wrong army." He chuckled. Like the major, his uniform bore the U.S. flag in addition to three stars on each shoulder.

Anna came last to shake his giant paw.

"Good Lord, girl, you're old enough for the Hudson Army?" His accent sounded more Texan than Northeast.

"Eighteen, sir," she told him. "Hudsons are adult from age sixteen. But there's a waiting list for boot camp. Not many younger get in."

"Anna is a superb fighter, sir," Clay assured him. "We survived the Starve together."

"I remember," the General said. "Fascinating background reading, on all of you." He nodded to them. "As I was telling Clay here, I hoped to send you out tonight. He says you're too tired for that. And the other teams are delayed. You made the best time across West Virginia." He smiled, then turned to Clay.

Anna's eyes immediately switched to the left. Rahema was still standing at parade rest, facing the General, so Anna poked her. Rahema took the hint, and forwarded the poke to Tuck, who looked aggrieved, but nodded.

"…Ran out of gas…" the General said to Clay, who listened intently and held the General's eye. Clay resumed his seat on the teacher's desk, and the General perched beside him. Ike and Neal circulated through the hardware. They often looked up in interest at one of the General's points, with sage nods.

Most monitor displays included a logo which Anna mentally dubbed the frosted cabbage – a truncated green hemisphere with a drizzle of icing on top. The first spreadsheet took her a moment's puzzled consideration. *Troop levels,* she decided. *Florida, Carolina, Ken–*

Tenn, Georgia, VA, PA, Ohio, Hudson… After a glance up at the General, she dared to scroll. *And beyond.* The only beyonds she was sure of were *Ark* for Ark–Lou–Sippi, and *TX1, TX2, TX3* for the successors to the Lone Star State. She wondered idly which TX included Austin, where she lived just before New York.

"…Gorey transferred to a hospital in Pittsburgh today," the General continued to his rapt audience of one. "Your backup team took care of it. If you're good to go –"

"Absolutely good to go, sir," Clay said.

Anna *humphed* mentally at that assessment.

"Good. I'll send the backup team along to the Mount Weather pickup for your Ike and Neal…"

Neal, wandering into Anna's zone, whispered, "We'll see about that."

Anna's eyes widened as he plugged an external hard drive into a laptop, hiding his action with his own body. There was a manual lying ajar on the keyboard. After he entered a command, he shifted the manual over the hard drive. He gave her the slightest smile, barely escaping his eyes, then moved on to study something that looked like a plain old printer.

Northern League. Anna finally found text to label the ubiquitous frosted cabbage logo. The item appeared to be a memo from the 'Directorate.' She dared a scroll tap again, and recognized three of seven flags. Next to the logo was a motto, of sorts: *Survival. Sustainable. Sovereign.* The memo content discussed shutting down Incirlik, whatever that was. She committed the words to memory.

"…How's Skully getting on up there?" the General probed. "He's sure enough taken a big bite. I worry about y'all…"

Glad they're bonding, Anna thought, with an amused glance at Clay. He had no skills as a con artist. But Clay could hold someone's attention forever, because he listened with complete and undivided attention and keen intelligence. *And doesn't talk because it makes him look smarter.*

She wished she'd taken center, but Neal was smart to assign that to Tuck. The Ohio lieutenant was studying the map projection in detail. He had the training to understand and remember. Anna noted that the frosted cabbage club had remarkably detailed intel on force movements of VA and all its neighbors. Hudson and PA's forces stayed neatly inside their borders. Ohio moved east as a near-straight sloping line, already crossing the Shenandoah Valley. In contrast, Ken–Tenn, VA, and Carolina were mixing in like a marble cake to the south. *Cakes and cabbages. I must be getting hungry again.*

"...Agreed. The Richmond mission is hopeless. You had a good suggestion, son, to let little Rahema stick with Tucson..." The General forgot Tuck didn't pronounce it like the city in Arizona.

Chairs. Anna counted eight of those, six at workstations and two at the teacher's desk. *Probably for the General and his aide. Maybe six more staff sit in here.*

She stopped short at the whiteboard at the side wall. She hadn't paid attention to the walls, mostly festooned with children's classroom reminders and artwork fading with age. But this board listed eight 'KS teams,' including Snowdon and Tucson and Gilmore, all *'arr 18:00 Weds.'* Anna didn't know Skull's first name, but it began with K. That's where the nickname *Skull* came from, K. Sullivan. She was with Snowdon – Cade – and Tucson, and they arrived around 18:00. So either Rahema or Gorey's real name was Gilmore. Another three teams had X's and a location listed. The remaining two had *'eta,'* expected times of arrival, noon and question mark on Thursday. One of the X teams had the team leader name crossed out, too, Weyland.

She paused to review her memorized items again to make sure her mind hadn't dropped any yet. Fortunately she studied memory tricks along with chemistry in high school. She organized her material by topic, with a count, visual, and verbal mnemonic on each item.

"...You'll be up the Shenandoah like a greased pig. These Ohio boys know what they're doing..."

Anna smiled. She could live with skipping up the Shenandoah Valley to Mount Weather as fast as a greased pig. She couldn't make much sense of the list next to Skull's teams, but decided Garcia's SEAL team was en route.

She noted in passing that Neal plugged flash drives into monitors as well as laptops. These flat screens had easy-access ports on the side. He simply grasped the monitor and pushed the drive in with his thumb, while peering into the display in interest. His portable hard drive was already retrieved. She hoped he didn't clank on the way out of here.

"Ava!" the General hailed her. Clay gave her shoulder a quick squeeze as he headed out of the room.

"Anna," she corrected on automatic, and stepped toward the boss' boss. *Was the General boss of all the death angels? Or of a region?* She didn't have much to go on, but from the screens she'd seen, she suspected the latter. She stopped beside the desk at parade rest, feeling Clay's lazy perch was too presumptuous for a newbie.

"Right, right," the General allowed. "Anna. Cade – Clay – tells me you got interested in the death angels at the same time as him and, um, Neal."

"Yes, sir."

It was just a theory at the time, last summer. As the Apple Zone was released from its borders, aided by its neighbors who bottled them up to die for so long. It was only natural to ask, 'If these Rescos are our saviors, who the hell was killing us?'

Because the two groups wore the same uniform. Who commanded the Apple Zone borders? The same Governor-General Cullen who now ruled the nation in seeming benevolence. But Skull confirmed Cade and Ava's suspicions. Their Resco saviors called in markers to specify where and when the death angels applied their 'treatments' like the poisoned drugs, or riots to be fatally put down.

And who the hell are you, General? Anna's impassive face was on firmly, though. It took over four months, but West Point managed to train her to mind her tongue and expression. When she remembered. Sergeant Calderon taught her, anyway. Ava Panic was not a natural at blank face.

Sharp eyes in a craggy senile face studied her. "The death angels killed your parents," he challenged her.

"Ebola killed my parents, sir," she returned evenly.

Her grandfather, the caretaker of the family, died at home before Ava's eyes, while she was recovering from the disease herself. Deda died bleeding from every orifice, in agony, his skin mottled with purple and greenish bruises everywhere. Her parents were nurses at

Mount Sinai hospital, the largest hospital in New York City. They never stood a chance. They were called in to work for the emergency. Ava never heard from them again.

It wasn't rational. Ava had talked it through during a group session with Gever one night after yoga, back in Basic. But her emotional reality wasn't that the death angels killed Deda. Her gut said she did that. She gave Deda Ebola. And the hospital administrators killed her parents. In their hearts, Cade and Ava didn't blame the death angels. They blamed themselves.

The General frowned at her, searchingly, then looked away. *In shame?* "How do you think Skully's doing? Like having him for a boss?"

"Very much, sir. Skull is overworked. But he's a great boss." She paused. "I'm a little surprised how rough our trip was, coming down from Erie. Most of our arrangements run much smoother."

The General nodded. "Yeah, this whole barrel of monkeys has gone FUBAR. Not Skull's fault. Ohio pulled up their timetable smack dab into ours. Just had to jimmy our way through them."

"Sir." Anna couldn't help pursing her lips a little on that one. Waiting a few days for Ohio to complete its advance would have done wonders to brighten her week. No one needed to die, for instance. She wasn't harmed herself, just scared a little. But she held a grudge over what their hell ride cost Clay.

The General kept nodding, eyes ever narrower. "That's all. Neal!" he barked out.

Anna yielded her place to Neal, who flashed a grin at her as they passed. *Better you than me,* she thought sourly. She didn't listen to the content. But somehow Neal shared some good laughs with the General before Clay returned from his latrine break or whatever.

Another five minutes and they were out of there.

∼

"ARE WE WAITING TO DEBRIEF INSIDE DARCY?" ANNA ASKED, AS THEY crossed the road back toward their camp. Everyone was keeping mum so far. Clay and Neal walked in front, plying their flashlights. The caravan was asleep, it seemed.

"No talking inside Darcy," Clay said, confirming her suspicions. "Or the Toyota. Let Neal and me do the talking to Skull. Success? Ike? Neal?"

"Slam dunk," Neal confirmed.

"Highly illuminating," Ike agreed. "You three? When we get back to camp, I'd like you to sit at the table and write down all you remember, what you saw. Details."

Anna sighed, wishing she could go to bed now instead. But she understood the need to record her memories before they dissipated.

Clay turned to walk backward to address them all, and changed the subject. "We roll out at dawn. Other side of the pass, we join an Ohio convoy headed northeast up the Shenandoah Valley. They'll take us within five miles of Cheeseburger Hill. Tuck, Rahema, you're with us to that point. They'll top up our gas tanks. Then you head south to Charlottesville on the other side of the mountains. No hell ride. No dealing with locals. Piece of cake."

"And you believe this?" Anna groused.

Clay turned his back on her, walking forward again. "I didn't say the ride from Erie would be easy. Skull and I had words over that plan. As you'll remember. This plan is great."

"Great," Anna and Ike and Neal echoed dubiously.

They arrived at their tarp living room out of the rain. Once there, the group naturally tried to break and drift toward separate goals. Clay corralled them together and bade them sit at the picnic table and wait.

"They've been in Darcy," Neal reported from the passenger door.

"Toyota, too," Ike said. "Visible alterations here. Tuck, throw me your keys."

Tuck did so, and rose to see what had been done to his car. The Toyota was his own, not property of the Ohio Army.

Clay pressed him back to his seat. "Let the techs do their job." In a few minutes, Neal handed him some paper and pens. Anna hastened to wipe the picnic table with a damp towel.

"Let's not compare notes until we're done writing," Clay

murmured, taking paper and pen for himself as well. "Keep your voices down."

Four damp heads bent to thoughtfully scratch out everything they could remember from what they saw or learned in the HQ. This took a lot longer than the actual experience. But Neal and Ike seemed busy in the background, working over the car and SUV. Ike wandered around under the tarp for a bit, too, waving some hand-held device.

"Trust between hardened criminals," Anna muttered.

"Anna." Clay silenced her with a word and a frown. He didn't bother to glance up from his note-taking. Tuck requested and received a tablet, so he could annotate a real map instead of drawing the projected map from memory. Anna noted that the tablet was Neal's, not Darcy's. He thoughtfully squirreled it away in a third row seat storage hole with the rest of the geeks' electronics before they followed Clay to HQ.

Anna was done before Clay and Tuck, and sat doodling the frosted cabbage logo and what she could remember of the flags she didn't recognize. Rahema sketched Japanese-style girl comics, with short-bodied chibi figures with big gooey eyes and cascades of hearts. Ike and then Neal joined them at the picnic table with their laptops. They sat transfixed, decanting stolen data off their drives.

"No comms," Clay murmured. "Three copies." He had to rap on their computers to get their attention, and repeat himself.

"Three?" Neal inquired.

"Us. Clay. Rahema," Ike muttered. He was ten miles deep into his data again.

Clay sat back at last. Tuck was still at work, but waved him to go ahead.

"OK. Trainee exercise," Clay said, keeping his voice low, though the cars were shut behind him. "What did you learn about your boss's boss, 'the General?'"

Ike and Neal ignored them. The rest composited their observations.

Anna's coup was the 'Northern League.' She only recognized the flags for the US, Canada, Russia, and UK, but there were seven. Clay vetoed accessing the Internet from here to look up flags of the world.

But Tuck had a memory for flags, and identified one more from her descriptions, Norway.

Tuck also raised eyebrows at Anna's mention of Texas 1, 2, and 3. But that was news to her as well. The spreadsheet said TX3 had the highest troop levels. But that wasn't much use without knowing the partitions inside Texas.

Clay didn't offer much, but answered Anna's question. "The General has a region, not commander of all death angels. I'm sure."

"Hell of a region," Tuck murmured, still poking at his map. "This goes west to two Texases, I think. Damn, I wish I could've scrolled that map west."

"They might not know anything further west," Clay offered. "We don't know which of these super-states are the General's. He'd want troop levels on the neighbors if he can get them. And if he's regional, he's got peers, and they're cooperating. Probably."

"We think Skull and the General cover the same region?" Tuck frowned. "Or is that an assumption?"

Clay sighed. "Assumption. You're right."

"What was that motto again?" Rahema asked Anna.

"Survival. Sustainable. Sovereign."

"So I'm far-fetching here," Rahema said. "But let's say the Northern League is an alliance of nations who are less…inconvenienced…by global warming than their southern neighbors. And the United States reaches too far south. But it's too powerful to ignore, certainly for Canada. And its northern tier is maybe fine."

"Who knows how far south," Anna mused. "The U.S. would want to save all it could. But it wouldn't be able to prove where to draw the line."

"The regions would run north-south," Tuck hazarded. "Each region master would get a cut of the northern tier, and the hopeless south, and the debatable middle."

"Skull's region includes Ohio," Clay added. "And VA, Ken–Tenn, and Carolina. Hudson, New England, and PA, of course."

They lapsed into silent contemplation for a while.

Rahema sighed, and planted her hands on the table. "Doesn't make any difference today. We plan to leave before dawn."

"Yeah, let's hit the sack," Clay agreed, rising. He left his pages on the picnic table, and the others followed his lead. "Don't stay up too late, geeks. Get good stuff?"

"Huh? Incredible," Ike agreed.

"Copies," Clay reiterated. "No comms."

Ike didn't acknowledge that Clay had spoken.

Neal sighed and rose. "Yeah, copies." He bopped a friendly fist onto Ike's head, who ignored him. "I'm the wizard's apprentice. I'll get on that."

Anna pulled Clay aside before entering Darcy. Under cover of a full-body hug, she whispered in his ear. "Are we here to bug Cheeseburger Hill? Or the frosted cabbage?"

"Sh. Yes. Both," Clay whispered back. "Rahema's right. Dawn comes early. Brush teeth."

Tuck wasn't buying the amorous cover act. He waited for them to unclench and leaned in for a word. "What, to my car?"

"You have a dashcam now. Just like mine." Clay smiled at him wanly.

"To Skull? Or the General?"

"Yup."

Anna didn't have much sympathy. She lived with the dashcam all the time. It spied on her love life, for the ones who killed New York City. The Northern League. She worked for them. She wondered what she could ever do to retaliate.

Except, she realized as she drifted off, all six of them, and possibly Skull who sent them, went out on a limb to figure out who the hell they were. *Maybe we all want to take down the Northern League.*

29

Interesting fact: Resco 'markers' were essentially favors owed, and included many favors besides death angel 'treatments.' Markers existed for extra food shipments, attacks, retreats, drone strikes, and the ever-popular 'look the other way while I break the rules.' Resco MacLaren of the Apple held an especially large portfolio of markers, received as gifts during Project Reunion from well-wishers.

The assault on Cheeseburger Hill began with playing dress-up again.

Due to having Rahema and Tuck along, they hadn't discussed the Mount Weather operation in detail until after they traded hugs all around, and waved the Toyota good-bye.

Tuck did all the talking with the Ohio convoy they joined to drive up the Shenandoah Valley. At the end, the convoy topped up their tanks and provided two extra five-gallon gas cans, well-sealed to military spec, for a safety margin. Tuck accepted graciously, then handed them both over to Clay. With luck, that would be enough fuel to carry Darcy all the way back to Jersey at the end of this mission.

Neal provided the Charlottesville-bound pair with a hard drive copy of all the intelligence gained from the gran caravan. But he warned them it was not for transmission, only for safekeeping. If someone needed their backup, it would be hand-carried where it was going.

Anna was sad to see them go. She wondered if she'd ever see them again. She hoped so. She thought they'd make a good team. Tuck had experience in military bureaucracy, and Rahema had the drive to get the job done. Clay and Neal claimed they didn't get too attached to newbies. Ike looked amused. Compared to him, they were all newbies.

Ike's scheme to get into Mount Weather was simpler than Anna expected. The remote facility was at a crossroads on its mountain. On the road approaching from the west lay a local power company branch office, the sort of place they parked trucks for electrical line workers – cherry-pickers to cut back tree branches, utility vans and such. From satellite feeds, the place appeared to be deserted.

By late afternoon Thursday, the same day they left the gran caravan, they rolled in to take a look around. Clay stuck with Darcy to watch the road and discourage anyone who happened by. Anna and the geeks checked out the small office building of NOVEC, the Northern Virginia Electric Cooperative.

NOVEC had already been broken into. The lavatories were the worse for wear. Even driving in a convoy, it was clear that the area was infested with refugees from the coast. Several windows here were shot out. Anna supposed that Cheeseburger Hill security ran off any squatters eventually.

As Ike hoped, the facility provided a locker room for its line workers. Neal selected overalls and toolboxes for himself and Clay. Ike intended to wear his usual clothes, as a supervising engineer. They found nothing small enough for Anna. She'd have to pose as Ike's intern. They picked up nifty matching hard-hats and safety glasses and bright yellow vests for four, and official badges to counterfeit.

Anna found neatly labeled keys for the trucks in the front office, plus the gate key for the razor-topped fence surrounding them. Once she unlocked the gate, Clay drove Darcy in, and parked behind the building, invisible from the road. Presto, they had a building with power, water, and a locked fence for security. Clay declared they were staying the night. A bit of pounding on the locker room door, and Neal opened the back way into the building.

Not all of Anna's keys found a matching vehicle. And of the ones present, not all had gas. But after sifting her way through them, she selected a well-stocked van, and parked it beside Darcy.

The geeks were busy in geek heaven in the office. Anna and Clay took care of camp matters. With luck, their clothes hung in the locker room would be dry by morning. To Anna's amusement, the building's furnace still worked. She cranked up the thermostat to help the clothes along. Outside, the rain lightened to occasional showers and spits. Clay brought the camp stove indoors, and thoughtfully prepared a couple days' worth of ready meals.

None of their activities were visible from the road. From the sky, if anyone looked, there was simply an SUV parked in back as though it belonged there.

Anna and Clay even had time for a full workout and homework.

Around 2 a.m., as they slept comfortably in Darcy, Ike's intermittent power glitches began to travel up the mountain.

The target facility, though capable of being self-powered, was on the grid. Above their Cold War vintage underground bunker, Mount Weather featured extensive training facilities on the surface. They didn't fire up the subterranean power plant to light classrooms for visitors.

In the morning, after the best night's sleep they'd enjoyed since Sunday, they packed up their dry clothes, policed the building, and moved out with both vehicles, locking the gate behind them.

To Anna's disappointment, she didn't enter the Mount Weather compound. Her job was to stay with Darcy a quarter mile down the road. Ike found a control box on a power pole there, and pried it open. The two of them, in their matching hard-hats and yellow dickies and safety glasses, huddled over this. Ike prodded a number of wires, following along with the consequences on his tablet. He found three that yielded interesting symptoms, and labeled them with some masking tape. He taught Anna to use them to generate problems on demand with the probe of an official-looking voltmeter.

"If anyone asks, keep it simple," Clay advised. "You just started as

Mr. Worton's apprentice this week. You have no idea what you're doing."

I can manage that, Anna decided ruefully. She glanced at Ike's name badge. Sure enough – Emmanuel Worton. Her own said Rochelle Greenlaw. Neal was Merle Boyd.

Clay – Abel Hocking for the day – handed her one of the walkie-talkies they lifted from the cop he killed north of Pittsburgh. "We'll keep in touch," he promised. "If you hear three clicks, we're in trouble and can't talk." Safety head gear in the way, he gave her a kiss on the nose. "Stay alert."

And they left her, about 8:30 on a cloudy morning.

Staying alert was easier said than done. Every forty-five minutes or so, Mr. Worton called with an update on their progress. Rochelle generated a power fault for him twice on demand, by stabbing a probe into wire junctions A and C. A grand total of three cars passed on the road.

Her most harrowing moment came when a good Samaritan with a CDC badge stopped to ask if she had car trouble. She assured the nice man she was fine. Her supervisor Mr. Worton was investigating a line problem up the road. Fortunately, he asked no followup questions, just smiled and waved as he drove away.

She killed time writing homework mini-essays on the Byzantine Empire. Left to her own devices, she vowed that she would never, ever take a college subject again on Clay's recommendation. Avicenna, or Ibn Sina, was almost interesting. Medieval Byzantium held no relevance to her life.

The trees were starting to leaf out on this mountain. That mattered. At long last, spring was coming. The day grew warm and muggy. She got a full workout, jogging circles around Darcy. She did strength exercises on the shoulder of the road. She had a leisurely lunch alone with the squirrels.

Anna-Rochelle was bored out of her gourd.

Slightly after 1:00, she got a quick call from Clay-Abel. "Trouble." After a few minutes, this was followed by three clicks.

Boredom vanished. Anna froze. She had no backup plan. Then she realized there was no point to a plan, because she needed to wing it based on current conditions. She was the backup plan. She forced herself to relax and think it through.

She pictured them in a corridor or utility room, somewhere deep in the multi-building complex atop Cheeseburger Hill. They were interrupted being naughty by security. There would be discussion. Security would take them to some other building for further discussion.

Did she want to make a move while everyone was aggravated, and no one was where they were going yet?

Well, that might be a great time to come in guns blazing with a team. Solo against a fortified position, that would land her in detention with them, and deliver Darcy into her captors' hands.

The guys went in with nothing that tied them to the company except a necessary laptop and a tablet. Those were probably set up with push-button simplicity to erase themselves.

Darcy, on the other hand, was a goldmine. The company would want her to get Darcy and her intelligence trove out of there as a top priority. If she called Skull, Anna suspected that's what he would advise. She should proceed to their rendezvous with the backup team. From there, she suspected it was 50-50 whether her new team would go back to retrieve Clay, or proceed to the second MacGuffin mission. Ike was valuable, Clay and Neal maybe dispensable.

They're not dispensable to me. In fairness, Skull probably felt the same. But a lot of lives were riding on the MacGuffin. She didn't need to put Skull in that position. *OK. Calling the boss is a last resort.*

What else could she do? *I'm Rochelle Greenlaw, with the Northern Virginia Electric Cooperative,* she realized. She had a shiny badge to prove it. She could simply drive up to the gate and talk to the guards on duty. *We've lost contact with a work crew. We're afraid their van broke down, and I've come to get them. Have you seen them?*

Even if all three guys had crimed themselves by now, that didn't paint her with the same brush. Maybe they'd stolen the van. She could ask to look them over to see if any were captured NOVEC employees. She could ask the dastardly impostors what they'd done with her coworkers. Maybe she could get one out that way.

Ike was most valuable to the company.

Goody for Ike. Clay is more valuable to me. And the team. Because once

Clay is out, we'll have two people on the outside, and he knows what happened on the inside. Yeah, I can justify choosing Clay.

Should she wait a half hour? An hour? Too soon would be suspicious, she decided, and still catch them in that aggravated milling around stage.

The radio squawked back to life. "False alarm," Clay-Abel reported. "I think we've found the fault. Working on it now."

"Roger that," Anna-Rochelle sent back, then collapsed her head onto her knees. She cracked up laughing in relief. *It was a good rescue plan, though!* she consoled herself. She sat back and gazed at the trees in their yellow-green pointillist glory, brilliant against branches dark from the rain.

Maybe a good plan. Maybe I won't tell Cade what my plan was unless he asks. Maybe I should dream up a better plan in case he does...

At 3:20, an exultant Mr. Worton reported success. They were on their way out. She was to pack up and rendezvous back at the office.

Anna hammered the electrical box shut, took a deep breath, and climbed into Darcy. She'd never driven the SUV alone before. But she took it slow, performed her three-point turn, and proceeded back to the substation. Partway there, Clay came up behind in the van. He gave her a friendly toot on the horn and she swerved. He passed her on the road, laughing no doubt, and slowed enough for her to follow.

Back inside the gate at the NOVEC parking lot, they shed their power company equipment and ID's. Neal and Ike took the time to restore the ID badges to their original contents. They'd already wiped the office for prints. Aside from the bathroom being clean now, the facility was restored to pretty much the condition they found it in, even the coveralls stowed back in their source lockers, and the van parked back in its original spot. Wearing gloves, Anna locked the gate behind them, wiped the key of fingerprints, and left it exactly where she found it.

We were never here. This never happened. This NOVEC site is deserted. The utility crew must have visited from some other office.

Clay had Darcy headed down the mountain before they even paused to tell her how it had gone.

"Perfectly," Ike reported beaming. He kept a souvenir NOVEC

hard-hat, perched on his knee, bright blue with a yellow lightning bolt. "That was a snap."

Hanging on Anna's seat, Neal corrected, "It wasn't that easy. Ike did a brilliant job. We got FEMA. We got CDC. We got Homeland. Grand slam!"

"Well, getting here was the hard part," Ike said modestly.

"Great job, Ike!" Clay praised. "Brave job, too, coming down here."

"Good memory to take home with me," Ike said, deeply gratified. "I've still got it. I can get out here and live!"

"Don't get cocky on the way home," Clay cautioned. "You can still get out here and die, too."

They all laughed.

Ike and Neal fell into technical reminiscences that left Anna lost in the mud. Clay reached over and squeezed her hand with a smile.

"I don't envy you staying outside," he said. "Backup is tough." He frowned, recalling his three-click alarm earlier. "What were you planning, by the way?"

Face burning, she relayed her lame little rescue plan. Walk up to the gate and knock. Please sir, have you seen a NOVEC van? Try to get one of them out who could tell her what was happening inside.

Clay laughed out loud. "Good job, Anna," was all he said.

"What did you do in there?" she asked defensively.

"Stood around ready to spring into action. Doing nothing in the meantime. Just backup, like you." He smiled at her warmly.

Content, she said, "One down, one to go."

"This one's not down until we hand off the geeks," Clay corrected.

"Please, sir," Neal crooned, hanging onto Anna's seat again to stick his head into the front. "I wanna stay and play."

"Huh. What do you say, Ike?" Clay asked.

"Wild horses couldn't drag me to Washington D.C. West Virginia was bad enough."

Neal wheedled, "Mr. Worton is a big boy. He can get home on his own."

Clay grinned. "No, Ike. I'm taking you to your exit ride. What I meant is can you spare us Neal?"

"Easily. Take him. He's yours. Good riddance," Ike replied. "Who's my ride?"

"Matherson leads the backup team."

Fresh from spending all day on backup, Anna reflected that it sucked to be Matherson. His team must be trailing them around through hostile territory, risking their lives to spin their wheels on the off chance Clay's team screwed the pooch and they'd get to step in and save the day. She wondered if that meant Matherson sucked. From the silence in the back seat as Ike digested this news, perhaps he did.

"Yes, you should keep Neal," Ike concluded. He stared out the window in resignation.

"FIND ANYTHING INTERESTING?" ANNA ASKED THE TECH WIZARDS, AS SHE set out dinner at their camp in the Shannondale Springs Wildlife area. They were a few miles north into a spur of West Virginia for the night. Not that it mattered. They were still behind Ohio's line of advance.

While Clay whipped up grilled vegetables in crepes, Ike and Neal stayed glued to their seats, drilling into samples from their illicit data feeds.

"Bad flu outbreak in Chicago," Ike said. Anna recalled that he was from Chicago.

Neal stood and stretched by the tailgate. "They're resettling people from D.C. into the Calvert Hills exclusion zone."

"The company is?" Ike asked sharply.

Neal shook his head. "VA government. Flipping Admiral Sondi O'Hara."

"Calvert Hills?" Anna asked, lost.

"Nuclear plant melted down after the tsunami in February," Neal explained.

Ike offered, "D.C. is a hell-hole, from what we heard in PA."

Clay handed in a plate of crepes for the group. "We'll steer clear of Calvert Hills."

"Hello?" Neal countered. "The meltdown is less than fifty miles from D.C."

"Well, that sucks," Clay allowed. "How far should we keep out of it?"

"Planet B would be good," Ike muttered. But he typed a search into his laptop, still on his lap for dinner. "The Fukushima evacuation area – that's Japan, melted down after the Tohoku tsunami. That was kind of oblong. Must be the prevailing winds off the Pacific. Say twelve to twenty-five miles. But Fukushima was a well-managed disaster. This one not so much."

Neal mused, "Wonder if the river glows at night."

"I don't recommend you go take a look," Ike said, searching for a map next. "I wouldn't go into Chesapeake Bay either if I could help it." He paused, studying the map. "Stay north of I-495 if you can."

Neal and Ava leaned in to look. "But south of Baltimore," Neal suggested. He traced a finger across the Chesapeake from Annapolis to the Delmarva Peninsula. "That's the only way across."

"If it isn't underwater," Ike said. He snapped the laptop shut and traded it for his supper plate. "Mm, this looks delicious as usual, Clay –"

"Don't move!" a hoarse voice demanded behind them. "Give us all your food!"

30

Interesting fact: In the tsunami that year, Hudson and New England safely shut down their coastal nuclear power plants. It was touch and go for a while with the Seabrook facility in New Hampshire. The crisis precipitated Hudson's friendly takeover of New England. Calvert Hills in Maryland was a preventable disaster. Neighboring super-states were unimpressed.

Anna turned her head to see a gaunt, wild-eyed man aiming a pistol at them from the edge of the woods. He dressed not much differently from Ike, save for the stains and tears in his clothes. He looked a little younger, maybe in his mid-thirties.

"You don't need to die tonight," Clay advised him. "Drop your gun and scram."

The man looked irate. "I've got a gun on them! I'll shoot!"

Standing at the cook stove, Clay flipped a crepe into the air. Neal dove left, tackling Ike to the ground. Ava jumped right onto the tailgate, pulling out her pistol along the way. It was a toss-up whether Ava or Clay's shots killed the guy. Ava fired three times into his chest. Clay got him twice through the head. The startled middle-class Virginian didn't get a round off. He never stood a chance.

A wail of woman and children broke out from the trees. Another flurry of rifle shot cut off the woman. High squeals and a crashing through the underbrush spoke of children running away.

"Who's shooting?" Clay demanded.

"Your fucking backup," replied Matherson. "Don't shoot, we're coming in."

A man trudged out of the darkening woods, also in his mid-thirties perhaps, holding an AK-47 at the ready. He wore full camouflage, armor plate, and had the general air of one of the SEALs gone to seed.

Anna found herself not yet motivated to safe and put away her Glock. A second guy, not much older than Clay, emerged similarly dressed and armed. He paused and swallowed uncomfortably at the sight of the dead man.

Clay stuck his Glock back into its holster. "Clay," he said. He pointed and identified the rest of his team in turn by their current names.

"Aw, fuck. You again," Matherson replied. Who he meant was unclear. "I'm Katz. He's Busby. Got extra food? Busby, Clay's no faggot, but he cooks like one."

"Smells good," Busby said.

Anna sighted her pistol at Matherson. "Katz, safe your rifle. Do it now."

"She has a point," Clay said.

Busby promptly complied, and accepted a plate of food from Clay.

Matherson sighted along his rifle at Anna. "Right back ya, bitch! When did we start recruiting midget cunts?"

Clay winged a plate at his shoulder like a Frisbee. "My girlfriend, *Katz*. Stand down, asshole."

"Very rude," Ike commented. "Matherson, put down your gun."

"This is so unreasonable," Neal concurred. "Spoil a girl's dinner, all these homophobic morons around." He dusted himself off and reapplied himself to his supper crepe, glaring at the newcomers.

Matherson, distracted off his aim when hit by Clay's plate, proceeded to safe his rifle and shift it around to his back, lest he lose face. Anna kept a bead on him for another few heartbeats after his gun was away to underline her point. Then she shoved the Glock back in her waistband and hopped down from the tailgate.

"Where's my food?" Matherson demanded. "Busby got some."

"Out of crepe batter," Clay said. "I threw one at the dead guy."

Matherson looked where Clay pointed. He swooped down and grabbed the crepe and dusted it off. He grabbed the plate off the ground, too, and put the crepe on it, then held it out to Clay. "Got filling?"

Clay scraped the last of the filling bowl into the center of his crepe. "Enjoy."

"Where are you taking me, Katz?" Ike asked Matherson.

Matherson had just bitten off a quarter of the rolled crepe, but didn't let that interfere with his talking. "Harrisburg. You and – Neal. You a faggot?" He was looking at Neal at the time.

Ike answered. "No, but of course I'm happy to give you a blow job as soon as Busby falls asleep." He paused. "Just kidding, Busby."

Matherson's complexion purpled. "You're a fag?"

"My ex-wife would say so," Ike deflected. Matherson seemed appeased by that. "How about Gettysburg?" he wheedled. That was closer.

"Orders. You and princess Neal. Harrisburg."

Ike polished off his crepe. "I'll just collect my things. Neal's staying with Clay. I trust you're parked nearby?"

"What, we gonna leave tonight?"

"That'd be good," Clay confirmed. "Thanks, Ike. Neal, why don't you help Ike pack."

Neal stuffed the last of his supper into his mouth and hopped onto the tailgate. He paused to pull his sweatpants down and moon Matherson on the way in.

Anna went around to enter by the passenger door. She quietly collected five hundred Liberty dollars and slipped them to Ike. "In case it helps you escape them quicker. I'm so sorry."

"You have nothing to be sorry about," he assured her. "They're idiots. But I'm a high-value passenger. They'll get me to Harrisburg. Then I go home with my next ride. Thanks for this."

"We'll miss you, Ike. You really were a good time." Anna beamed at him, and they shared a hug.

"I'd say let's do it again. But maybe I've had enough. Nearly had heart failure on that hell-ride through Pittsburgh." They shared a soft laugh.

"Want date rape drugs?" Neal offered practically, shoving the souvenir NOVEC hard hat into Ike's luggage. "Get them to stop the night in Gettysburg, dope them, and slip away."

"Tempting," Ike acknowledged. "But no. Thanks. That's all of it. You keep the camping crap. I'm looking forward to my own bed." Both bent over double in the cramped cargo hold. Ike held out a hand to shake with Neal.

Neal took it and pulled him in for a full hug. "She's right, man. You're a good time. And a great teacher. See ya soon."

"You take care of yourself. You're not as tough as Clay and Anna."

"Way to emasculate a guy, Ike!"

Still chuckling, they piled out of Darcy with Ike's heavy suitcases. Clay hadn't bothered to converse with Matherson-Katz and Busby in their absence. He ate his supper and ignored them, then started cleanup.

Now he took his own turn giving Ike a heartfelt hug. "See you soon, man. You did awesome. Impressed as hell."

"Right back at you," Ike agreed. "Take care of him." He turned to his new and dubious chauffeurs. "You can carry these for me, can't you? I'm afraid they won't roll well through the woods."

"Busby, you carry, I'm on point," Matherson directed. "I should have had your mission, *Clay*. No way your team is tough enough!"

This was his parting shot. Busby obediently grabbed the suitcases, and they headed back into the underbrush.

"Maybe next time," Clay acknowledged. "Bye now. Thanks for backing us up, Katz."

"Yeah, fuck you," drifted back from them crashing through the woods.

Neal waited a few more moments for the sounds of their passage to abate. "Is the boss fucking insane? What was that moron? *That* is our backup team?"

"Peace, Neal," Clay said quietly. "Weyland was our backup. He and his trainee got killed by some hillbillies on Tuesday, coming through West VA. He tried to buy gas from them. They wanted to strip his car.

Then they found his fentanyl and overdosed themselves. By the time the General's guys got there, six dead bodies. They recovered the car."

"Damn. What a waste," Neal agreed.

Clay added, "I wanted Weyland and me together for this mission. Boss didn't want to put the two of us together again. Said if he had two great agents, he wanted one to grab the MacGuffin and the other for backup, and both of us training. My trainee was better than his. So we got the mission. And Weyland got killed. Boss didn't plan to put Matherson on anything in VA. So he was available."

"We got to build this outfit up," Neal said, shaking his head in dismay.

"Trying, man. We got twenty out of your class at West Point. Just not ready yet. Anna's a whole nother league. But she's not ready yet either."

"Hey, hey," Anna interrupted. She raised her water glass. "To Weyland and his partner. Rest in peace."

"To Weyland and his partner," Clay and Neal agreed sheepishly, and drank to that.

"Let's pack and get out of here," Clay said. "I'd feel safer with SEALs around me."

"Cross the Ohio lines tonight?" Anna asked, discouraged. They'd already had a long day.

"Let me ask if it's possible," Clay said, and ducked into Darcy.

With practiced speed, Neal and Anna washed and dried and stowed the kitchen. Anna hung the camp light in the cargo hold to work by, as dusk gave way to night.

"We have a rendezvous," Clay reported, crouched in the hold.

Neal asked, "Think we could salvage Busby?"

"Not too bright," Clay said. "Matherson recruited him. They're alright for what they do, Neal. They run a couple militia outfits that prey on civilians. Southeast PA, south Jersey, northeast Maryland."

Anna headed for the passenger door to climb in, while Neal shut the hatchback. Out of the blue, Anna was grabbed from behind. She took one of the arms so offered and yanked while turning to dislocate it from its unseen shoulder. Turned, she delivered a vicious shin kick to leave her attacker limping. She fought on reflex before her mind registered the fact that her assailant was even slighter than she was.

"Hell," she said in dismay, considering the disabled girl. She still had her in an arm lock. "Do I have to kill her?" she asked Clay.

"No." Clay climbed out to join them, and twisted the girl's slender neck. "But I do," he explained regretfully. "She heard too much. Let's go."

In outrage, Anna dragged the corpse a few feet to get her out of Darcy's way, and dropped her.

Once they were in the SUV and moving again, Anna had to vent. "Three dead bodies, Clay. And orphans scattered in the woods. We had no beef with any of them! They were hungry, desperate. We've been there, done that. She didn't need to die!"

"Anna, shut it," Clay bit out. "She was desperate, yeah. We let her run? She'd take whatever she heard, and try to sell it."

"I thought we were done with that!" Anna yelled. "She was guilty of *nothing* but desperation! Neal! Tell me you're not OK with killing that girl!"

Neal answered slowly. "I never want to screw up like that again. I got emotional and broke op security. I talked company business outside Darcy. So a girl died who shouldn't have. As for whatever you're arguing about, I don't care. The girl was a wannabe looter. We kill looters and rapists. Clay made the right call."

His speech hit Anna like a bucket of cold water. She turned and stared through her side window. They were out of the tiny woods and into paved suburbia, teaming with stressed civilians. She should have been watching for threats.

Eventually Clay said softly, "Just for the record, Neal. While you're feeling guilty? Please don't discourage my trainee. Company has problems. We're working on it."

"You are right," Neal replied. "I apologize, Anna, Clay."

"Apology accepted," Clay said. "Gang, we're tired and cranky. We miss Ike, and Rahema and Tuck. But we're on the same side. Let's cut each other some slack until we put the MacGuffin to bed. The enemies are enough hassle without fighting our friends. Deal?"

"Deal," Anna and Neal echoed softly.

A MILE AFTER THEY ENTERED A LIMITED-ACCESS HIGHWAY, OF NO particular distinction, Clay pulled onto the shoulder and sighed. "Garcia needs a few hours to set up the rendezvous," he explained. "I can't think of anyplace safer to wait."

"OK," Anna agreed. "Get some sleep. You need it most. I'll take watch."

"Two on watch?" Neal asked.

"Let's try one and see how it goes," Clay decided. "Anna, I'll button up Darcy to scream."

"Agreed." Anna grabbed her M4 carbine. Neal didn't bother with bedding. They stepped out to empty their bladders.

And then Anna was alone again by the side of a road. The congestion of VA was a stark contrast to West Virginia and backwoods PA. Even past curfew, a vehicle zoomed by at least once a minute. She wasn't worried about them unless they slowed. But this highway wasn't a proper interstate, inaccessible and deer-proofed. A corrugated steel bumper and an embankment sloping down were all that separated them from the restless teaming crowds beneath.

She perched against the uncomfortable steel railing, hiding from traffic behind Darcy. She figured their first line of defense was to pose as yet another abandoned car.

Tuck had explained what was in store for the new citizens of greater Ohio over the next few days. They would be thoroughly cataloged, identified, resettled, and put to work. Not forced labor, exactly. But if they couldn't prove long-term residency and solvency at their current abode, they'd be added to the indigent roster.

Like Hudson, Ohio did not feed the indigent. They could work or starve. Unlike Hudson, Ohio didn't grant freedom to indigents. They would go to labor camps. These were often made from schools or other unused facilities, such as an empty supermarket. The base labor wages were only eight hundred calories a day in the work camps.

The new citizens, mostly refugees who fled the coast, would be advised in the strongest possible terms to find a more valuable contribution to make to society before they lost too much weight. But these refugees had already tried that for the past three months since the tsunami. In essence, now it was do or die time. They could leave in the morning if selected for a labor call. They had to be back in the camp by nightfall or they would graduate from indigent to convict labor. Along the way, they'd better hope they could convince someone, anyone, that they were worth more than starvation rations in the short months remaining while they still might be.

Darcy wore Ohio plates for the moment. That seemed scant protection from the systematic civilian inventory happening below. Good local Virginians ingratiated themselves with their new overlords during the day. At night they barricaded themselves in their homes while refugees tried to break in to hide from the troops.

In other words, there was a whole lot of shooting going on down below. The super-states manufactured mountains of ammunition.

Anna wondered if it counted as patriotism that she preferred the way Hudson handled its windfall apples. No one expected a survivor like her to be any use when New York City was liberated. They tried to figure out ways for them to become useful, and allowed time for them to heal. The resettled went through a month of quarantine and careful feeding, then were adopted into the hinterlands by communities who committed to make it work. The dregs left behind, like the gang rats, were organized into villes – or not, as they chose. Useful make-work was invented to let them earn their keep.

It was only about a year ago that Anna started getting reliable rations from the Raj, on the days she chose to work for them. The nation of Hudson hadn't even been declared yet. She was no different than that girl Clay had killed a few hours ago. Or rather, she was much worse.

A few young wannabe toughs headed up the embankment. She stood and leveled her rifle at them, letting its red target light do her talking. They took the hint and reversed direction at speed, vanishing into the middle-class subdivision below. She tried sitting on the ground for a bit instead of corrugated steel, and returned to her musing.

The difference was, the citizens below never volunteered to take on the refugees who flooded in. No one wanted them. Hudson felt something was owed to the survivors of the Apple Zone. No one felt that way here. Ava wondered what was different about Hudson to make that so. Clay claimed that it was Public Relations News – another nickname for Project Reunion News. The government mouthpiece was run by Dee Baker, Resco MacLaren's wife, the co-Savior of New York City.

If so, how did that woman get so damned powerful? That she could take a scenario like this and turn it around?

Maybe she didn't turn it around. Maybe she prevented it while it was still preventable. Maybe Ohio was doing all that was possible after prevention failed. Ohio should know, after taking on the collapsed Michigan and Detroit.

Maybe this stupid MacGuffin was worth it, if he could hand over the Delmarva Peninsula as a going concern instead of useless slave labor. Anna would hate to see her old squad mates stuck pacifying Delmarva the way Ohio was treating western VA. If they could even be forced to do it. Anna doubted that. Whole lot of mutiny in store if their commanders tried to force them.

We shoot looters and rapists. Also mutineers, in the Army.

She stilled. Yes, a car was slowing to her position. She rose and cautiously peered through Darcy's windows above the sleeping Neal and Clay.

Damn. Militia. She lay her carbine an arm's length downslope and stood. She walked back to meet the policeman and policewoman as they exited their car, her hands empty and held out slightly from her hips.

"Good evening, officers."

"Ohio ID?" the woman demanded.

Anna dug her laminated card out of her pocket and handed it over. "My friends are asleep in the car. Don't want to cause any trouble. Just need a safe place to get a little shut-eye. We tried to stop in the woods tonight, and got attacked twice. Gave it up and came here."

The truth was worth a shot.

"Youngstown," the policewoman read, and handed Anna back her ID. "Hell of a time to visit VA."

"That's why," Anna allowed. "Trying to fetch a friend. Having some trouble finding him. Is there anything wrong with us parking here?"

"Leave it," the other cop decided, after shining a flashlight down the length of the SUV, peering inside. Anna trusted that Neal hid the AK-47 at his feet. "Let's move on."

"Be out of here by five a.m.," the policewoman ordered, if only to claim the last word. "This is a highway, not a campground. If I were you, I'd get the hell back to Youngstown while the going is good."

"Yes, officer. Thank you, officer," Anna said meekly. *That went well.*

Then the male policeman slapped Darcy's flank.

Darcy screamed bloody murder, of course.

It took another five minutes to talk the cops into leaving again. *Car alarm, just a car alarm...* As soon as they rolled away, Anna took a shaking Neal into her arms and held him a few minutes.

Watch was a lot more fun with Neal to talk to. Neither of them was tempted to talk about anything real. Anna invented a new MacGuffin, a no-good recovering opiate addict brother, who never paid child support for his kids back in Youngstown. Neal claimed a no-good sister, no doubt still prostituting herself for a fix. They one-upped each other, escalating their sibling rap sheets from there, then continually returned to the gender-adjusted refrain, "But he's family, and I love him."

Somehow they ended up laughing all over each other.

Clay declared it time. They drove on toward the Ohio border crossing.

31

Interesting fact: The nuclear meltdown in Carolina was deemed tragic but unavoidable. Florida shut down its nuclear reactors the week before the tsunami. Florida claimed to have no foreknowledge of the catastrophe. No one believed them.

Clay pulled up to park exactly at the marker shown on his map. They were within view of a minor Ohio border crossing.

The peace and quiet of 2 a.m. featured four police SUV's, flashers strobing the narrow state highway. A couple Ohio troop carriers stood nearby on the shoulder. Their border machine gun emplacements were mobile for this phase, mounted on wide-body armored Humvees. They positioned one on each side, then a third and fourth staggered down the road in each direction to stop anyone who got past the two at the border. The westbound backup gun was less than a hundred yards ahead of where Clay parked in the eastbound lane.

Ohio had been very busy beavers. That, or no one stood to fight them. Anna suspected the latter. This border crossing was near Ashburn, only 25 miles from D.C. and their destination. From what

Tuck told her, this was about the extent of Ohio's planned advance this round.

A half-dozen vehicles waited in line ahead of them. Darcy wasn't in line to cross the border yet. It didn't matter. Ohio took their border security seriously. A quartet of Ohio infantry, armed and armored to the teeth, trotted their way, M4 carbines in two-handed ready before them.

"Hide the weapons," Clay murmured. He lowered his window. On second thought, he slowly opened his car door, and exited to stand behind it, hands up by his shoulders.

"Line's over there!" one of the buckeyes barked.

"Not ready to get in line yet, sir," Clay replied. "We have friends coming to meet us."

"Not SOP!" the same one barked, perhaps his only verbal mode while on duty. "Get in line! Or get gone!"

"I'm not sure –"

Clay was interrupted by a fireball *whoompf!* from further east, past the border and to the right of the highway. An impressive red glow emerged, with a column of thick dark smoke rising.

"Get in! Get gone!" the soldier barked again at Clay.

Clay dove back into the car for protection. He hastily raised his window and buckled up. But the soldiers were already trotting away.

"What was Garcia planning?" Anna inquired.

"Didn't say," Clay said. He thoughtfully started the SUV, but didn't move it yet.

Another *whoompf!*, closer this time, rocked Darcy from behind left, again not damaging the highway itself. The border forces, perhaps concluding that they made too juicy a target concentrated as they were, chose to scatter. Some lagged, perhaps to hold the line with a token force. A third explosion nearly upon them tossed a couple off their feet. After that the holdouts boarded transports and retreated into Ohio territory behind them.

Clay gunned Darcy through the open border. Everyone waiting in line for inspection reached the same conclusion, but they didn't drive as fast. Clay claimed the westbound lane for passing, banking on no incoming traffic. Darcy could make it from 0 to 70 mph amazingly fast.

"Clay!" Anna yelled. "Turn right!"

He didn't know why, but he took her word for it. Problem was, Darcy was going entirely too fast to make the 90-degree turn into a residential neighborhood. He braked as best he could. But going wide, he barreled onto a muddy lawn, tires cutting a swath through the turf. Veering out through a flowerbed added a horrible under-car fusillade of decorative gravel. He narrowly avoided a collision with the car parked in the driveway, but scraped Darcy's side against the corner of it. By then, his turn was complete, and his speed bled off enough to proceed down the street.

Testament to the unquiet night, no neighbors dared emerge to look.

At the next block they spotted a big hand-held sign saying 'SEALS X,' by another clump of machine gun bearing Humvees.

"X marks the spot," Anna said.

"How'd you know to turn right?" Clay asked. He brought them to a gradual stop, lips pursed, breathing out. They recognized their old SEAL buddy KT as the one holding the sign.

"They chalked B-E-N across the road, with an arrow," Anna explained. "You missed it because it was in the eastbound lane."

Clay lay his head back and laughed.

"This is so unreasonable," Neal muttered, which set him and Anna to crack up laughing as well.

Clay tried to get out and inspect the damage to Darcy. KT and Anna wouldn't let him.

Anna woke at nearly ten, Clay sound asleep beside her on the air mattress. They were safe for the moment, surrounded by the SEAL camp in an abandoned orchard. Through the moon roof she watched cherry petals spiral down from above, against a cobalt blue sky behind gnarly dark twigs. It was beautiful.

Cherry blossoms came in April in the Apple, when they still had trees in the city. She guessed they were six weeks late here. The team had come down in elevation, but the trees leafing out weren't much more advanced. Long delayed, all the different trees were unfolding at once. She wondered if the cherry fruit would have time to form and ripen, starting this late. But she couldn't worry about that, just enjoyed the delicate white ovals dancing in the breeze. Spring was late, but it still came. Summer would follow.

Neal opened his door and stuck his head in. "Good, you're awake. The SEALs are getting antsy. Want a strategy meeting with Clay. Brought you breakfast."

~

"Took you long enough," Garcia greeted them, when the trio joined the SEALs at a fold-up aluminum picnic table. The orchard spacing provided plenty of room to park Darcy and the SEAL vehicles between rows. The familiar KT and Jamal sat flanking him, all on one side of the table.

"Thanks for letting us sleep," Clay replied, taking a seat across from Garcia. Anna claimed the seat across from KT. Neal sat sideways across from Jamal, enthralled by the orchard's beauty.

Clay continued, "We finished our first mission around seven last night. Handed off Ike – Mike – to his ride home."

"Oh!" Garcia said, taken aback. "I didn't know you had another mission."

Clay vaguely sketched their activities of the past few days. The gran caravan didn't appear in the tale, and Mount Weather only as Cheeseburger Hill. The SEALs were mollified. The young agents needed their little downtime before tackling D.C.

"See you fucked up your precious car," Jamal noted. "Can't hardly see the key scratch anymore –"

"Leave us," Clay demanded.

Simultaneously, Garcia barked, "Walk away, Jamal!"

The state of Darcy's paint job on the driver's side was a fresh wound. Clay first beheld it in broad daylight only minutes before.

Flipping his middle finger at Clay on the way, Jamal sauntered off to join a group of bored guys a row over, attempting to sunbathe draped on a Humvee.

"Jamal has ideas," KT said sunnily. "Want me to go extract them?"

"Thanks, maybe later," Clay said. He folded his arms on the table and got down to business. "So you know the assignment, right? We need to extract this guy – call him Major MacGuffin – from prison in Arlington. Then exit stage north, preferably Jersey."

"And drop off the MacGuffin in Delmarva?" Garcia asked.

"My instructions are to bring him to Hudson," said Cade. "He might expect Delmarva."

Anna provided the tablet map with markers. "Arlington prison, suspected current location of the MacGuffin. Not far from the Pentagon." She scrolled the map. "Chesapeake Bay Bridge, if it's passable." She scrolled again. "Preferred exit Interstate 295 over the Delaware River into Jersey."

Garcia tensed.

"We'll be allowed across I-295," Clay clarified. "We don't need help against the Hudson border forces. Just getting there."

Garcia relaxed, visibly relieved. The Hudson border with VA was absolutely closed, only a few miles long, and trivial to defend. No one crossed the Delaware without Hudson's permission.

"First," Clay said. "Please understand – to us? You guys earn your pay if all you provide is travel escort. That's huge. Until we look, I don't know whether we need you for the prison breakout, too. We definitely need you for the approach and escape."

KT tapped the tablet. "The Chesapeake bridge is underwater. Passable at low tide, if there isn't much chop. But there are low parts."

"No go?" Anna asked. "We hoped to avoid Baltimore."

"You better believe we'll avoid Baltimore," Garcia confirmed. "D.C. is bad enough. In Baltimore they might car-jack a Humvee full of SEALs, even with the machine gun manned."

"Really?" Clay asked.

Neal murmured, "If it could've gotten you out of Manhattan? A few months into the epidemic?"

"Point taken," Clay allowed. "Yeah, we could have taken down this group by then."

"In your dreams," KT scoffed amiably.

"Some reason they're not armed in Baltimore?" Clay suggested gently. "We were. Armed and organized. Rocket launcher would take care of that pesky machine gun. Then you'd be overrun. Anna, we have some of those in Darcy, don't we?"

"Grenade launchers," Anna confirmed. "Only three rounds for the rocket launcher."

KT looked thoughtful at that.

Garcia rallied. "OK, what we've got here is a single platoon. You were right. The others didn't split when they should have. Now I wouldn't trust them. So, ten guys, three armored Humvees. One minivan smaller than yours. We can spare you weapons if you know how to use them."

"Any plate armor my size?" Anna asked. "We've got boots and uniform."

KT and Garcia looked at each other. KT answered. "Maybe a helmet and goggles. That's about it."

"That's fine," Clay said. "Anything needs armor, you guys are far better than we are. I'm glad you've got another minivan."

"What are you thinking?" Garcia asked.

"Step one is to visit that jail in Arlington and make sure our MacGuffin is in it."

A couple hours later, Ava walked up the front steps of Arlington County Corrections alone. The compact grey SUV that dropped her off continued around the block.

The prison surprised her. It looked like an ordinary 12-story white office building, blending comfortably into the commercial neighborhood. The lobby was also bright and clean. They had plenty of captive labor to keep the floors waxed.

"Felicity Kendall, to see my father, Lieutenant Colonel Jack Ekstrom," she told the corrections officer at the front desk. "It is visiting hours, isn't it? I've got to see Daddy!"

Visiting hours were prominently displayed as 9 a.m. to 6 p.m. on Saturday.

Felicity was dressed as the opposite of Eileen today, trying to look as young as possible. Her sports bra under the lavender pin-tucked dress minimized her modest bust. Clashing orange and red and white striped socks topped combat boots. A quarter of her hair was pulled up to fountain from ponytails at her temples. (Clay recoiled, and said she looked like one of those yap-yap dogs.) She added eyeliner, drawn crooked, and baby blue eye shadow on her eyelids only, with no contouring, which failed to enhance her hazel eyes. Her lipstick and blush, metallic pink, harmonized with nothing. Big dangly earrings with feathers tangled in her hair. She cultivated an habitual nervous bounce, even standing at the desk. She bit her lip and looked everywhere except meeting the desk sergeant in the eye.

"ID?" the desk sergeant demanded. His name tag identified him as Sgt. Latham. Unlike most latter-day militia, he wore an old-fashioned police blue uniform instead of army camouflage.

Felicity Kendall was unimpressed by VA's refusal to adapt to the times.

She handed over her photo ID, thoroughly scraped and bent and dirty. She'd gently chewed open a laminated corner and soaked some spit into the paper interior. Only an hour old, Neal's fresh new ID had already suffered a rough life. It advertised that Felicity was 15, and sported a picture of Ava at the beginning of ninth grade, adapted from her Brooklyn Tech high school ID. Her listed address was in Rehoboth Beach, Delaware, an Atlantic oceanside community likely six feet underwater these days.

Sgt. Latham frowned at her sternly. "Do you have a parent with you?"

Felicity bounced harder. "That's the problem. My dad's in here. And my mom – don't get me started on my mom and her latest boyfriend –"

"I have no record here of Colonel Ekstrom having a daughter –"

"Oh!" Felicity started to cry, and bounced harder. "My mom is such a witch! Daddy was in school, and it was an honor violation, and she didn't tell him she was pregnant, and then she sued him for child support, but she wouldn't marry him, and –"

Sgt. Latham handed her a tissue, and bumbled out reassurances, trying desperately to calm her down and shut her up. Not a man experienced with teenage girls, it seemed.

"But I've got to see Daddy!" Felicity wailed. "I've got no place to live! Mom's boyfriend tried to – to – "

"Hormones at that age," another prison guard commiserated with Latham. "Just give her what she wants. It's visiting hours."

"Right, right," Latham allowed. "Just calm down, Miss Kendall. Sit over there. I'll call you when your dad is ready." He kept her ID.

"Thank you!" Felicity wailed. She snatched another tissue from his box to further smear her childish makeup job. Under cover of that, she stuck a little electronic something from Neal on the back of the desk sergeant's computer.

She stepped over to the empty waiting couches and perched at the edge of her seat. She crossed knees and elbows like a pretzel and jounced in agitation, sniveling and miserable.

After a few minutes, Felicity reflected that no one could keep that up forever. She pulled herself together and expressed her agitation by pacing restlessly around the waiting room. She poked at things, riffled through ancient magazines, and was generally unable to settle down. She had time to visit the rest-room. To hunt for money in the couch cushions. Study the view out the windows. Peer through the door windows into the secure parts of the facility.

Sgt. Latham turned on a flat screen TV on the wall, with closed captioning but no sound. Apparently VA had their own state-sponsored media, rather more blatant than Hudson's PR News, called The Voice of the People. Felicity watched it out of the corner of her eye now and then. The news conveyed a pleasant and orderly spring day in greater VA, where nothing was wrong. No crime or riots in D.C. or Baltimore. No mention of the Ohio, Carolina, and Ken–Tenn invasions. The economic situation was looking up, with new job creation. The reassuring woman discussed relocation opportunities for D.C. residents. She showcased the sort of inviting suburban lots being made available near Chesapeake Bay. She didn't mention their proximity to the Calvert Hills nuclear plant meltdown.

In Hudson, you couldn't watch the news for more than 5 minutes before one of the Rescos came up, the personal face of martial law. PR News these days was all about reconstruction from the tsunamis, and public spectacles and events. Here in VA, no Rescos were mentioned, only federal agencies and elected officials Felicity had never heard of. They pretended not to be under martial law. Which seemed pointless to Felicity. No one believed fake news even before the Calm. Three years later, who would bother to watch it?

A couple visitors exited through the security door. A woman with two kids in tow arrived. The brats out-did Felicity in making the waiting room uncomfortable. They went in to visit their father before she did.

After a forty minute wait, Sgt. Latham at last handed Felicity off to another officer to be escorted to the visiting area. She placed her things into a rubber tub that already contained her ID. She dropped in a lipstick and a few crumpled US hundred-dollar bills. VA still used the old currency, though its value was negligible. She had to put her boots in the tub as well. Then they waved an X-ray wand over her.

Fortunately, the wand only looked for metallic weapons.

She followed up the stairs to the second floor, and through another locked door to a windowless cafeteria-style room. As they entered, Ekstrom stood from his otherwise empty table, looking quizzical. The man had fading blond hair, a frame like a bear, and stood well over six feet tall.

Jack Ekstrom should have demanded a DNA test from Felicity's mom.

Felicity's escort had just finished telling her no touching was allowed. So she flung herself into Daddy's arms.

"Oh, Daddy!" she wailed. She pulled his neck down to whisper quickly, "I'm your daughter Felicity Kendall. Getting you out. Don't change clothes." She tucked one tiny RFID tag into his collar and another into his breast pocket before the guard pulled her off and reminded her firmly, no touching.

"Well, Felicity, this is a surprise," Ekstrom said, waving his new nightmare daughter to sit. "How's everything at home?"

"Everybody's worried about you, Daddy! You've got to come home. On Delmarva, we don't know whether to move west or north. Rumors everywhere. Ohio and Ken–Tenn and Carolina have invaded."

"What, all of them?" Ekstrom said with a smile, humoring her.

"Hudson invading too? Now Alabama's got the bomb, who's next?" He half-sang that last part.

"Huh?"

"It's a song from the Cold War. Never mind."

Another officer in camouflage like Ekstrom – they didn't wear the off-white prisoner pajamas – looked them over with lips pursed in disapproval. His wife and pre-teen son behaved as an officer's family ought, posture perfect and hands neatly folded on their laps. Ekstrom returned the major's pursed lips with interest, and stared him down. The lesser officer conceded the point, and turned to mind his own business.

"Your old friend says I should move north with him," Felicity shared. "Uncle Keith? Kevin? Elmire? Elmore?" *Elmira,* was the point she hoped to convey. She was sent by his old pal Major K. Sullivan – Skull – in Elmira. She honestly didn't know what the K stood for.

"Elmore," Ekstrom agreed, eyes narrowing.

"Well, I can't stay with Mom anymore. She's just too crazy. And you're stuck in here, so I have no place else to go!"

Ekstrom leaned forward. "You have to obey your mom, Felicity, just like I obey the commanders above me. But I work for the people below me. I suggest you do the same."

Felicity took this to mean that mom would henceforth stand for Admiral O'Hara, ruler of Greater VA. The meaning of the unsolicited advice escaped her. *There are no people below me.*

He sat back. "Elmore's alright. But my friends down south might be more like we're used to, in Delmarva."

An intriguing point, but Felicity didn't have time to follow it up. She pouted, and said, "So what do you do in here all day?" She pointed to the door. "You live on this floor?"

32

———————

Interesting fact: The Delmarva Peninsula, under the leadership of Resco Lt. Colonel Jack Ekstrom, relocated people at least 10 feet above sea level long before the tsunami. It was the only part of Virginia–Del–Mar (Greater Virginia) to do so, although this basic precaution was in the Resco manual. Tsunami loss of life was still catastrophic in Delmarva.

"Took you long enough," Clay greeted her in front of the steps. He was simply walking past, and she fell in beside him. Her dress bore an RFID tag, too, so he could track when she was coming out. Neal and Ike were fond of the things. They'd stuck them all over the gran caravan's HQ equipment.

Clay handed her the jacket he carried, his, and she hung it over her shoulders. She breathed out relief, feeling the reassuring weight of the Glock in the pocket.

"Was in the waiting room for like forever," Felicity whined.

They didn't talk further on the street. It wasn't bustling, but there were pedestrians, usually in groups and keeping their heads down. Few cars moved except military and police. Civilians used their feet or bicycles.

Past the jail block, they ducked into a defunct coffee shop that advertised free Internet. The minivan was parked by the curb, KT lounging in the back seat looking bored. They didn't acknowledge each other. Judging from the fresh metal scrapes on the door jamb, the guys broke into the coffee shop.

"Hey, hey!" Neal greeted her. "Good job, Felicity. How's Dad?"

"I think he prefers south to north," Felicity replied.

Clay snorted. "We don't always get our wish."

"He said he works for the people below him, not above. He advised me to do the same." She still hadn't figured that one out.

Clay cocked his head. "Is he going to be a problem?"

"I think he wants out," Felicity said. "He cooperated with feeding me details after. I wonder if he really has a daughter."

"She's seven," Neal said, without looking up from his typing. "Lives with her mom. Divorced right before the Calm."

Felicity got down to business. "His cell is on the fourth floor, east. No windows into the cell blocks. He works out in the second floor gym after breakfast, nine to ten. Then Sunday chapel on the ninth floor. Works cleaning detail four hours after lunch. That's all over the building, doesn't know where in advance. Other than that, he's in his cell block."

"I'm tracking his RFID," Neal concurred.

"I told him I'd see him tomorrow."

"One way or the other," Clay agreed. "Do we need to stay here?"

"Just getting…there," Neal replied. "Full maps to the jail house." He considered his screen for a moment, fingers folding his lower lip. "Did you get a cell number?"

"Block 4E, cell 7," Felicity reported. "Were you able to hack into their systems?"

"Yup, the tap you put on the desk sergeant's computer worked a treat. I could maybe use it to glitch their security cameras. Or control their door locks. I'd be here for hours figuring it out, though."

"Can we take it back to the orchard?" Clay asked. Their camp was 15 miles out, but hiding a military unit was nontrivial. Garcia wasn't eager to approach the Pentagon any closer until they made their strike.

"Rather not," replied Neal. "I've got direct Internet here. Satellite from a cherry orchard would draw attention like a beacon."

"The Internet was still on?" Felicity asked Clay.

Clay pointed to the ceiling. "The building is still live. Neal spliced the cafe into someone's office line. The power's live, too. We just turned everything off first. Except the power sockets. Neal's been online for maybe fifteen."

Felicity nodded and started nosing around. Someone had painted the inside of the street windows white to mask what was inside, that being not much besides tables and chairs and a stock of china coffee cups. Felicity couldn't see why they bothered.

She checked out the back, behind the coffee bar. The office and stock room were cramped but serviceable. The office window was barred but unpainted, and overlooked an alley for trash collection. Judging by the state of the dumpsters, trash was no longer collected in Arlington. The alley was deserted, no foot traffic. It ended in a T-intersection across the street from the jail.

She returned to the front and nodded judiciously at Clay. "Not bad, for a base of operations."

"We have the jail schematic on the tablet yet?" Clay asked Neal.

Neal nodded, and unplugged the tablet from his laptop.

Clay handed it to Felicity. "Bring this out to KT? Fill him in. Ask him how they'd go about it."

"Will do," she agreed. She waited inside the front door for some hazy shadows to move past the whitewashed windows. Clay peered out a scratch in the paint, and nodded an all-clear. Then she crossed the sidewalk to join KT in the back seat.

"You really do look fifteen dressed like that," KT greeted her.

Felicity tossed her ponytails and chewed some imaginary gum. "Gee, thanks!" She slouched down to prop her combat boots on the seat back in front of her. "We have a schematic, RFID tracking established, and a prisoner schedule. Oh, and target confirmed. He's in there and knows we're coming for him."

They cozily poured over the map and details, brainstorming ideas.

Some agitated brown guy speaking not-English tried KT's door handle at one point. KT slammed the door into him and made a couple threatening lurches. The brown immigrant fled.

KT took a leisurely look around from his standing vantage before climbing back in. "Street's getting busy. Rush hour in Arlington."

"Wonder what it's like at night," Felicity mused. Deserted, she suspected.

KT shook his head. "Looks like hell on earth. We drove through to check it out on our way to the rendezvous. Gas fires everywhere."

Felicity frowned. "Why? You mean the gas lines under the street?"

"Yeah. They were in crappy repair even before the Calm. Now they're leaking like Swiss cheese. Smell it?"

She sniffed. D.C. smelled awful, but she hadn't analyzed the reek. She'd forgotten that rotten egg smell, the trace chemical added to natural gas, so people would notice a leak. In New York, they turned off the gas lines soon after the epidemic broke out. Project Rebuild only turned them back on after thorough integrity tests on the aged infrastructure. Though to be fair, they were probably more concerned about methane emissions than accidental explosion. Project Rebuild had an awful lot of buildings to demolish. Even now, most structures didn't have an active gas line. Apples were terrified of building fires.

Clay clambered into the front seat. KT closing the car door must have caught his attention. "Getting toward supper time. What have you got so far?"

KT said, "The time window when he's on the second floor is tempting. But I think night buys us more."

Clay nodded. "You're factoring in the tides?"

KT sniffed. "SEAL means Navy, man. Low tide is around five a.m., then five thirty p.m., at the Chesapeake Bay Bridge. Water's a light chop under a southerly five knot breeze."

Felicity asked, "Did you look that up while I wasn't watching?"

"Didn't need to."

Clay smiled. "Got it. So how would you go about this breakout?"

"We'd go in with helos, top and bottom plus two for fire support," KT groused. "Helicopters. But we don't have any. Failing that, we blow holes in a couple walls and fight our way in. Our pigeon isn't in the outside layer. I'm still concerned about collateral damage."

"Don't be," Clay said. "We're not worried about anyone except the pigeon. Major MacGuffin *must* come out alive. Anyone else is an acceptable loss. Dozens if need be."

KT stared at him. Those weren't the operating parameters a SEAL expected in a rescue assault on a civilian facility, least of all their own civilians. "No offense, man, but what exactly does 'agent' mean? What are you guys? I thought it meant spies, like 'secret agent.'"

"Sometimes," Clay agreed. "Agent, like a business agent. I represent my boss's interests. Maybe I have expertise he doesn't have. Or connections. Or time to go meet with people. He's a busy guy. Or places he's too important to risk himself. Like that."

"Huh."

"In this case, it means I make calls like how much collateral damage is acceptable. I know his parameters. We don't want to kill anybody. But we don't worry about it, either. We're good with freeing the prison population, too. That's about a hundred fifty today, by the way. Couple dozen of them military."

"Maximum security prisoners?" KT asked, uncomfortable.

"Nah. This is a county jail. Used to be minor offenders waiting for a court date. Or serving thirty to ninety days. Nobody dangerous in there."

"Oh. OK. Did Neal find any way to hack the systems?"

"He got the outside cameras, so he can mask our approach," Clay said. "Not very fancy, but some."

"*Our* approach?" KT interrupted him. "Don't tell me you're going in."

Clay shrugged. "Ekstrom knows Felicity. She's not going in without me. But we don't have a plan yet," he pointed out. "Anyway, external cameras are on the Internet, Arlington police. Looks like the internal controls are properly hardwired and firewalled. The doors and lockdown controls. Neal isn't optimistic he can hack those."

"I'm good with brute force," KT said.

"What happens," Felicity mused, "if there's a fire in a prison?"

Clay shrugged. "They evacuate or let them die. Before, they certainly would have evacuated. But they'll have sprinkler systems."

"But Neal can hack Arlington systems," Felicity pointed out. "Just not the prison's internal controls. Cut the water, and the sprinklers won't work. And even if they did – KT, got smoke?"

KT grinned. "Got plenty of smoke. You're thinking of blowing a gas main, aren't you?"

"Boom…" Felicity circled her arms above her head to indicate a big cloud of fire, grinning in delight. She adored explosions.

Clay grinned crookedly as well. Terrified as they were of being caught inside a building fire, they loved watching them from safe on the street. "Won't that mobilize the Pentagon, though?"

"No, that would fit right in around here," KT said. "Gas fires are a dime a dozen. Felicity and I were just talking about it. Might attract some firefighters. Might not. And our pigeon would be outside in a crowd instead of where we expect him. But he's tagged for tracking."

"How about both?" Clay asked. "Blow a gas line next to the building, blow a hole in the building. Insert your smoke, however you do that. Then either they come out, or we go in."

"I like it," KT agreed. "Need to talk to my guys. In person." He tipped up the tablet. "Need gas and water line maps. If they run together, might be able to blow both. Save Neal the trouble."

Clay took the tablet. "Back in five." He left to load more maps from Neal.

"You said you had a rocket launcher?" KT asked Felicity.

"We have a bunch of stuff in Darcy. Our car."

"Teargas?"

She smiled. "We do. Couple canisters. That might save us some bullets."

What passed for rush hour died out in Arlington. Felicity headed back to the orchard with KT. Clay stayed behind in the cafe to guard Neal.

 see what KT meant about hell on earth. The sky above Washington D.C. glowed from three active gas fires. Their assault plan would fit right in.

As a Hudson, used to draconian controls on carbon emissions, she was offended that the locals still had gas lines and private heat in their homes, let alone gas to waste. But the fires reflected on the broad Potomac River were glorious.

She rode in the minivan with KT and Garcia. Jamal drove Darcy to the pickup a few blocks away with the rest. They didn't want their getaway vehicles too close to the coming conflagration.

As expected, the streets were deserted at this hour in the commercial district surrounding the jail. They pulled into the trash alley behind the Internet cafe. Low light glowed from the barred office window.

Before Anna exited the car, she reminded the SEALs urgently, "Don't mention what Jamal did to Darcy. Clay will see it soon enough."

She grabbed her gear, plus supper and uniforms for her team. Felicity Kendall was history. Anna wore her Hudson camouflage uniform, combat glasses, and a helmet providing night vision and radio comms with the SEALs. KT carried in headwear for the guys.

A few raps on the back door, and Clay let them in. He looked a bit alarmed at the gift of a high-tech hard hat. "I have no training in this stuff," he murmured, stepping out of the way for them to pile in. Judging by his yawn, he'd been catching a nap.

"Stick close to Neal and me," Anna said.

"OK. Neal's never been in combat," Clay reminded her. "Guys? Protect Neal. High-value asset of the company. And not for his combat talent. More valuable than us, anyway. Second only to the MacGuffin."

The SEALs chuckled. "Keep him with the Humvees?" Garcia suggested.

"Neal is right here," Neal growled from the office, still tapping away at his keyboard. "You need me to track the MacGuffin. Who is in his cell at the moment. Probably asleep."

"You've got control of the external cameras?" Garcia verified. "That was a key assumption in our planning."

They all moved into the tiny office, which seemed a lot bigger without KT and Garcia in it. Anna ducked out from under KT's biceps and sidled next to Neal behind the desk. She set out water and supper for her guys. "Eat."

"Yeah, got cameras," Neal confirmed. "Recording the substitute loop now." He quickly checked progress on that, then dug into his plastic container of hash and beans. "Man, this is salty." He slid half the green salad on top of it from a third container.

Clay poked at his in distaste.

Anna pursed her lips at him. "Clay, a year ago you would have killed for this supper. The SEALs made the hash and beans. I used your verjuice in the salad dressing."

He took her point and started eating.

Neal asked Anna, "Got my throwaway laptop? I can't split for the Humvees without this one."

She slid the spare out of her bag to hand it to him. Neal checked the time and decided he needed to work while he ate.

Garcia put the map tablet on the table. "OK, here's what we're doing. Curtain goes up at zero hours, midnight. I want the camera loops running in fifteen to mask us doing the prep. We move in and wire the gas main to explode here, water main there. And the front of the building here. Side of the building here. Plus cameras to cover approaches on this street. And this alley."

Clay and Neal studied the schematic. Clay pointed at a door. "You're hoping they'll come out this emergency exit?"

Garcia clarified, "They'll come out every exit that isn't blocked."

Neal nodded. "So play camera loops on front and our side until zero hours. Then loops on all sides."

"Can you do that?" Garcia asked.

"Absolutely. Cracked their voice-over-Internet, too. No phone calls out after, say, twenty-three thirty?"

"Sounds good," Garcia confirmed.

"That's land lines," Neal cautioned. "They might have radios, cell phones. Can't block that."

"Where's Darcy?" Clay asked Anna.

"Here." Garcia stabbed the map three blocks away, on their current side of the jail. "All the vehicles wait there. We need to roll out by three hundred latest to make our tidal window on the bridge. Sooner is better."

Clay took a thoughtful gulp of water. "How deep is the water on the bridge?"

Garcia flicked his eyes at Anna. "Nothing Darcy can't handle. All our vehicles will make it except the minivan. We leave that here."

"Got a boat?" Clay asked. "In case we miss our tide window. Pursuit or something."

KT shook his head. "We've got an inflatable and a small engine. But it's 15 miles across the bay. Both sides, you're navigating through drowned residential and commercial districts. Sixteen people. No can do. Don't have the range. We'd be sitting ducks at dawn anyway. And then, no vehicles."

Clay nodded. "OK. Just making sure I understand the exit. What happens in the middle? After the explosions."

33

Interesting fact: Natural gas leaks were not new in Washington D.C. A survey in 2014 found nearly 6,000 of them in the aging pipelines. Desultory repair was discontinued after the Calm.

Anna sprinted for the front of the prison, as fast as she could run given all the stuff in her pack, and her M4 carbine in her hands. The street was empty in the lurid green of her night vision gear. SEALs were to her left and right down the block a bit, rigging the gas and water line charges. Clay, a bit hesitant in the unfamiliar NV green world, was rolling out a spool of wire to her position.

To her delight, Anna got to set the charges on the front of the building. First she glanced in from the edge of the front windows into the waiting room. No one was on duty. If the lobby stayed empty, she'd set charges on the front door as well. She'd cased out the cameras earlier, during her long wait to see Daddy. All but one were on the outer wall, pointed inward. She double-checked her recollection of that single camera that might catch something outdoors. Yes, it matched the caution zone she'd advised the SEALs of earlier.

She stepped in front of the window to check the position of the right interior wall. She wanted her charges to blow out whatever was next to the waiting room as well. She looked back and forth, inside and out, until she'd mentally mapped out the position. Then she got busy gluing bricks of composite explosive to the wall in an array fifteen feet across.

Clay arrived with the spooled wire.

"Stay to my right," Anna whispered. "Camera inside to avoid."

"Got it. Can I help?"

"Measure out sixty arm-lengths of the wire. Like this." She demonstrated looping the wire from hand to elbow and back, feeding from the spool without adding tension to the wire into the street to the right of the entrance. "That's one. I want sixty."

She finished the sides of her array before Clay finished measuring out the wire. Then she started attaching detonators, including to a brick that wasn't attached to the wall yet. "These next two, I want you to put as high up the wall as you can." She put a brick in his hand, detonator side down. Then she applied glue. "Apply glue side to the wall, don't put tension on the wire."

He might have been rusty in algebra, but Clay was no slouch in applied geometry. He got the brick right where Anna wanted it, except higher than she expected.

"OK, next one halfway between that one and this one." They got that done. "Watch for anyone inside, from the edge, while I finish these detonators."

"You really need this much composite?"

"I'm going for overkill," she admitted. "Nobody inside?"

"No one."

"Then we've got a bonus brick. You stay put." She wired its detonator, added glue, and took it as far as her remaining wire allowed, only a foot shy of the front door. She stuck it low to keep the wire off the windows, and returned to Clay.

Over her radio, she reported, "Anna charges set. Waiting for check."

Clay asked, "Is Neal back at the cars yet?" He asked her, not the radio. Anna had given him the quick basics of radio control, and set his to listen to the chatter. But she told him not to talk, and spent their limited training time on the night vision gear instead.

"Is Neal in location?" Anna relayed.

"Neal en route," Neal replied.

KT trotted up to them to check her wiring. "Good, good...glue gun." He added a dab to the highest brick. "Good, good, and...good." He cut the wire spool from the final composite brick and picked it up. "Jesus, Anna, you really want to break a building. Let's go."

They trotted behind him, down the block, around the corner, and into the alley. The minivan was gone as per plan. Another one of the SEALs crouched waiting with the controls, in relative safety from the blasts.

"Gas good, front windows good," KT advised him.

"Eight minutes," the other replied.

KT and Anna reviewed next steps for Clay, what to do after the explosions. Both of them fitted attachments to their rifles. Garcia reported the water main was set over the radio. Assorted other reports came as people moved into zero hour position, ending with Garcia, who had to move to the far corner.

"Three explosions," the SEAL on the detonators reminded them. "Move on my call."

"Yeah. Check your earplugs," KT advised Anna and Clay. The plugs were supposed to seal themselves automatically at incoming noise above a certain decibel level, but they covered their ears anyway. They crouched down behind a dumpster. Several walls and plenty of rubbish shielded them from the coming shock waves.

The first explosion was the worst, the gas main, knocking Anna back onto her butt. She wished she could have seen the beautiful blast. The front wall came next, and sent flying glass and chips of building even into the alley around two corners to rain on them. That left her feeling better about not seeing the gas main explosion. The third explosion was nearly a block away, and no rain of debris could reach them.

"Clear," the detonator man said. He picked up his rifle and headed right at the alley mouth. KT led Anna and Clay toward the front. A geyser of flaming gas lay in front of them.

"Shit," KT said at the corner near the front. The flames lapped awfully close to the building for comfort. His hand landed on Clay's shoulder. "Clay, stay put."

"I'm good," Anna insisted. She already had her smoke round loaded in her grenade launcher.

KT loaded his, glanced at her, and nodded. He jogged along the building front, Anna close at his heels. It was hard to recognize the planned holes in the facade by the yawning wreckage left behind. But the waiting room was certainly blasted open, plus the anonymous rooms to its right. Some of the furniture was on fire.

No need to get fancy. They fired their grenades, KT left at the front desk, Anna to the right into the next corridor. As their enhanced plumes of deep smoke added to the mix, KT declared it enough, and they rejoined Clay.

"Can everyone hear?" KT yelled, as they trotted down the side street by their original alley. Their next position was at the far end of this block, at the back of the prison.

"I'm good," Anna reported.

"Door's opening," Clay said. They'd just passed the prison emergency exit across from the alley.

They'd hoped that wouldn't happen quite so fast. KT radioed in the fact, and urged them on to skim the wall across the street.

Clay spun and shot his AK-47 at a prison guard who aimed a pistol at him, then picked off the guard next to him as well. A few prisoners with leg manacles fell over trying to escape this, clogging the orderly exit from the building.

"Who's shooting?" Garcia demanded over the radio.

"Clay fired, self-defense," KT responded. "Is our pigeon on this side?"

"That's a negative," Neal reported. "Headed for rear door."

"KT, get them out of there," Garcia barked.

Clay didn't seem to be paying attention to the radio. Crouched low, Anna beside him, he studied the lurid green moving things in the night vision tableau before him. He decided where another couple guards were, and picked them off. The mass of prisoners, caught dithering between an active shooter and a towering wall of flame, finally made the right choice. They surged toward the alley, leaving more than four bodies on the pavement in their wake.

"Prisoners took guns off the guards," Clay commented to KT. "These guys didn't move like military."

"Don't shoot without orders next time?" KT requested.

"Someone aims at me or my girlfriend, I shoot," Clay replied with finality.

"Point," KT allowed. "Let's move."

Before they made it to the back cross-street, Neal got on the radio again. "Dammit! Two pigeons. Anna, confirm. Two RFID's on the pigeon?"

"Confirmed," Anna replied.

"Well, they're out of the building. One went left, the other went right."

"Tracking on your mobile," the SEAL communications tech said. He was back at the Humvees with Neal.

KT crouched at the wall about fifteen feet from the corner. Anna and Clay squatted beside him. He pulled out a handheld. After a moment's study, he confirmed, "One's headed toward us. Hold. Wait for it."

There were indeed a crowd of people moving toward them. But green vision and a rather indirect map screen didn't make it easy to single out one man among dozens. KT didn't bother to explain. He just looked up suddenly. "One of them."

Anna put hands to mouth for a small megaphone. "Daddy! Over here!" Felicity's voice rang out. The correctly bear-shaped tall man detached from the throng and jogged toward them. No one had shackled his legs.

Several others, following some herd instinct, headed after him. Anna fired several shots above their heads. They changed their minds.

"The fuck did you do, Felicity?" Ekstrom demanded, diving in to take a knee beside them.

"Got one," Garcia reported over the radio before KT could report. "He's black, though. Wasn't our pigeon white?"

"Bring him," Ekstrom and Clay demanded, closely echoed by KT over the radio. "Both pigeons acquired," KT added. "Running for home."

"All units, head home," Garcia agreed. "All objectives secured. Watch your friendly fire."

"Call me Anna, Dad," she said, levering herself up from the pavement before offering a hand. "Big guy is KT. My boyfriend is Clay. You're MacGuffin."

He barked a short laugh.

"Let's go," KT prompted. He motioned the other three ahead of him and to the right on the cross-street.

"Teargas?" Anna offered.

"Nah, they're milling around fine," KT decided. "Go, go, go!"

The MacGuffin didn't have night vision gear, and Clay was new to his, and KT was their best firepower. Anna claimed the colonel's arm to lead him along.

They jogged up the block, KT covering their six. Anna wasn't supposed to, but couldn't help glancing back. Most of the prisoners headed up a side street to vanish into the night for their freedom. But a few kept coming their way, with guards yelling and following. Once they put another intersection behind them, KT shot a few rounds over their heads to encourage them to vacate this street. A few continued behind them. But from their silhouettes, they were in the SEAL platoon. After that, KT stopped covering their rear, and Anna's team ran faster.

"This left," Anna called out. "Half block up."

"Clay, I'm driving Darcy," KT informed him as they neared the vehicles. "MacGuffin, Anna, in Darcy with us."

"What the fuck did you do to my car?" Clay demanded as its shape individuated from the hulking wide bodies around it, all parked ready to roll out.

"Later, Clay," Anna insisted.

They clambered in. Neal already sat in his usual second row seat. KT took the wheel, Clay beside him. Anna guided Major MacGuffin to sit on Clay's bed.

"Who did you give the other RFID tag to?" she demanded. "Or did someone take it?"

"Major Willick," the MacGuffin replied. "I wanted him out, too. Who do you work for?"

"I told you," said Anna. She held up a wait finger for a moment as radio status reports passed her ears that he couldn't hear. "We call him the boss for security. So is Willick Delmarva, too? Regular army officer? Resco?"

"Resco. Charlottesville," the colonel replied. "You know, they saw you were military, and we're like five miles from the Pentagon. We need to move!"

"Agreed," Anna said. "Sit tight." She moved forward and hung on the back of Clay's seat. "You heard that?"

Clay nodded.

KT said, "Jamal hasn't reported in. Three minutes for the retrieval team."

"I heard," Clay acknowledged. "Willick. Give him the minivan. Does it have gas?"

"Keys," Neal said, offering them dangling from his fingers. "Half tank."

"Good enough." Clay grabbed the keys and exited the car. KT radioed Garcia to deliver Willick to the minivan.

"You're using Willick as a diversion?" the MacGuffin said, irate.

"We're going the opposite direction," Neal told him sharply. "We gave the man wheels. Can it."

"I need to talk to him!"

"No," the other three chorused.

Clay jumped back in. "Everyone's accounted for? Besides Jamal. Everyone in this vehicle."

"We planned to move out together," KT said. "Taking different surface routes."

"Bad plan," Clay said. "Go fast, go through. Space the cars." As though to underscore his point, the minivan peeled out from the back of the line and passed them.

"But –"

"That's an order," Clay clarified. "Up ahead take a right on Clarendon, and then radio Garcia. Go."

KT pulled out without headlights, driving by his NV gear. Anna bit her lip. NV driving wasn't ideal.

Once they were moving, and Garcia notified, Clay provided further directions. Essentially, they'd follow the Potomac River southeast past a couple other bridges, then cross on I-395 and follow it as it bent north, until they could escape east on route 50.

KT asked, "You want everyone to do this?"

"I don't care how anyone else reaches route 50. The bridge is on route 50."

"Good. That's an equivalent plan," KT allowed. "But Clay, that leaves us without concentration of force. Man, Garcia showed you the plan, and you didn't argue."

"Still not arguing," Clay said. "It's bad for our health to clump up. Also bad to go slow on surface roads. KT, for the mission to succeed, we don't need all the Humvees to cross to Delmarva. Just Darcy. The others might scatter, go to ground. Or rejoin as planned."

Anna added, "Pentagon, KT. They could send drones after us. It's not good for Darcy to be associated too soon with the Humvees that just knocked over the jail. Might even want to turn the headlights on when you get a chance."

KT thoughtfully relayed the new parameters to Garcia. Then, hesitantly, he broached the sore point. "Clay, it's not clear Darcy can get across that bridge. I mean, the modifications will help –"

"Hold that thought," Clay interrupted. He turned and grasped Anna's hand. He pulled her around for a kiss between the front seats. "That was awesome, Anna. I had no idea you could do all that. Neal, impressed as hell, man. KT, you too. Fantastic work. My compliments to your whole team. Relay that to everyone, please."

"You can be sweet at the damnedest times," Anna said, stroking his jaw.

"Priorities," Clay replied. "You're mine. Everyone in Darcy. No offense to your buddies, KT. Did they retrieve Jamal yet?" He'd been talking and ignoring the radio chatter. The radio conversation was in Navy-speak anyway, and hard for Clay to follow.

"Yeah. Took a shot, messed up his radio. His Humvee is rolling now, and the medic is working on him. Everyone's rolling."

"Think he's going to make it?"

"Haven't heard otherwise. I assume so."

"Good." Clay reluctantly let Anna go, and sighed. "My car is ten inches taller."

"More like four inches taller after you lot climbed in," Neal said. "It was higher without you."

KT slowed the car as they veered onto the George Washington Memorial Parkway. The helmet and NV goggles came off, and the headlights came on. Anna removed her own helmet and helped Clay to do the same but keep the radio in his ear.

"This used to be land?" Anna asked, looking at the wide sheet of water spreading beneath the parkway.

"Yeah," KT agreed, subdued. He pointed. "Arlington National Cemetery to the right."

"Sorry, man," Clay said softly. "That's gotta suck."

"The cemetery isn't all underwater," KT clarified. "This island drowned, though. Lady Bird Johnson Park. Used to be a narrower river. Tidal, though."

The highway itself was high and dry. They passed between soaring ramps and under two stretches of interstate, to finally reach the ramp leading their way.

Anna was grateful they weren't doing a repeat of Pittsburgh at this overly complicated interchange. Even at 1:00 a.m., fires reflected across the extra broad Potomac. She couldn't tell anymore which of the towers of flame and smoke was theirs. The complex nest of roadways – it was worse on the east side – looked all kinds of wrong footed in water instead of land. She wondered how long the roads could last this way, footed in mud. Large low buildings crested the riffled water off to the right. The map tablet glowing in Clay's hands showed they were passing another drowned island.

KT stayed to the right of many complicated lanes. Anna breathed a sigh of relief as they passed onto fairly dry land. They were in Washington D.C. now. If Clay had routed them across a previous bridge, they could have followed alongside the Lincoln Memorial and the National Mall. No doubt that's why he chose a different bridge, to avoid the surface roads. KT veered to follow I-395 north to reach route 50. A loud array of orange warning signs and barricades sent him to jump onto the surface roads.

"Tunnel," he commented. "Flooded."

Clay zoomed in his map in a hurry. "Hell. Sorry."

"No worries," KT said. "I know the way."

So Anna got to see the National Mall and Capitol from street level after all. In a city without streetlights, the Capitol Dome was lit blindingly bright off to their right. The lights down the National Mall to the left trailed off into the bloated river.

"They still use the Capitol?" she asked.

"Greater VA has a Congress," KT said. "Still calls itself the United States Congress. Three states and D.C. Part of them, anyway."

"Delusions of grandeur," Neal commented. He was as entranced by the view as Anna and Clay were, though.

Over the radio, Anna heard that police took after one of the Humvees, who was leading them in a merry chase across the Potomac. It seemed far away and unrelated to her, as she watched the federal buildings of D.C. slide by. They jogged left onto a broad avenue, and the first residential section emerged, high end apartments. Their route wouldn't take them through the predominantly poor black neighborhoods of D.C., except safe above them on a freeway.

They all breathed a sigh of relief as they joined route 50 and headed east toward Chesapeake Bay.

"How did Jamal make my car taller?" Clay finally asked.

Anna had hoped Clay wouldn't realize it was Jamal who modified Darcy. No such luck.

"Jacked it up with blocks in the suspension?" KT hazarded. "Something about a torsion bar? I'm no mechanic. Added a snorkel, too."

"Snorkel," Clay echoed.

Anna held her breath expecting a blowup. Fortunately, her beloved cracked up laughing.

"Incoming priority message," Darcy said.

Skull spoke right over her. "Clay, you've got a drone on you."

34

Interesting fact: The southern bridge across Chesapeake Bay, the Chesapeake Bay Bridge Tunnel, was 23 miles long, including four high bridges, two mile-long tunnel segments, plus causeways. This was destroyed in the tsunami.

Clay froze from his laughter at the news of the drone. He tapped Darcy's dashboard three times, thinking.

"KT, nothing on the radio for a few minutes," he said.

"We're out of range," KT confirmed bitterly.

"Take the next exit. See if we can park under a tree and look innocuous."

"What about my guys?"

"We're stopped, they're moving," Clay explained. "Closest will close the gap. Then we'll relay the message to them."

"Stop on the highway?"

"No, then we're sitting ducks." Clay turned and stuck his head between the seats. "Neal, you have any way to get through to them? Or track the drone?"

"Once we're stopped, I might be able to extend our radio range. That's about it."

With deep reluctance, KT said, "This car has all the high-value prizes. The Humvees are the more obvious targets. We could just run."

"I can't sacrifice this car," Clay agreed. "But we owe your team more than that. We'll do what we can, KT. Warn them at least."

KT nodded relief. "Exit."

Clay waited until they entered the exit lane, and said, "Darcy, switch RFID."

Neal exclaimed, "You've got electronically switchable ID on this car? How most excellently awesome!"

"Yeah. Anna, did you get that tracker off the MacGuffin?"

Anna had already dove into the back to fetch it from him. She started to roll down the window.

"Stop!" Neal yelled urgently. "Don't throw it! Give it to me." He tucked it away in a pouch. "Faraday cage. I keep all my RFID chips in it."

Anna looked at him blankly.

"Black box pouch. Nothing transmits from inside."

"Ah. Got it," Anna agreed.

This stretch of Virginia wasn't as lushly forested as Pennsylvania and Up Finger. The present landscape looked like some kind of bluegrass horse heaven. KT made for a house up a low hill with some stately trees by its driveway.

"Does Garcia have a satellite phone?" Clay asked, still brainstorming.

"I don't know the number," KT replied. "Your boss? He must have a way to contact Garcia."

Clay drummed his fingers again. "Not yet. Other ideas, gang?"

KT pulled under a giant weeping willow tree by a sleeping household and cut the lights. A dog barked from out back. Neal jumped out with some wire.

Clay leaned around his seat and held Anna's eye for a moment. His eyes were lit with amusement, but he kept his face straight. "So how do we take down a drone?"

Anna broke into a grin. "We have rocket launchers." *We don't have a snowball's chance in hell of sighting the drone to aim at it. But yes, we could fire rockets into the sky. If we were really, really stupid.* "They'd backtrack the trajectory and fire at us. Kind of advertises where we are," she explained apologetically.

Clay smiled.

What are you up to? Anna thought, and frowned a question at him.

Neal climbed back into the car. He attached a wire to KT's ear set. "Is that any better?"

KT tested it. "No joy. Still out of range."

"Once we've got radio communications," Anna said, "we could have four different locations shooting at the drone. That would be safer." *In our dreams. But yeah, theoretically safer. Assuming the drone can only shoot one of us at a time.*

"What are we doing?" Neal asked in disbelief.

"Figuring out how to shoot the drone out of the sky," Clay replied, deadpan.

"Awesome!" Neal replied, barely missing a beat. Only Anna and Clay could see his face well enough to read, *How stupid is that?* written all over it.

Good, Neal understood the game. Probably better than Anna did, though she continued to play along.

Ekstrom finally piped up from the back. "You're insane! You cannot take down a drone! Just drive!"

"I don't like being called insane," Clay shared. "It worries me."

"Yeah, Daddy! Don't be mean!" Anna shot into the back. "Clay's my boyfriend, and he is not crazy!"

Neal offered, "I think Clay's wild and crazy in the best possible sort of way. In fact, I think we're all kind of nuts. And I like us!"

Clay smiled, eyes alight, and pointed toward Ekstrom.

Markers, Anna finally realized. *Rescos hold markers on each other! Like they call in favors for death angel services, drugs and attacks and stuff.*

"Daddy?" she asked. "Do you have a marker that could get that drone recalled?"

"I can't waste a marker for that!" Ekstrom the MacGuffin objected. "Those markers are to defend my people, not myself! Stop calling me Daddy. Freak."

"Hey!" Clay barked at him. "Don't call my girlfriend a freak."

"Yeah, because that's what's important here," Ekstrom countered. "We're free and clear, in a civilian vehicle. You even changed the RFID. Just *drive*, dammit!"

"I'm not willing to give up the SEALs yet," Clay said.

"Incoming priority message –" Darcy attempted.

Skull spoke right over her. "Clay, MacGuffin is right. Just go, dammit."

"Duly noted," Clay acknowledged coolly. "Please keep this channel clear unless you have new information."

"A direct order *is* new information," Skull claimed.

"You're not here, boss. I am. My call. Don't make me muzzle the channel. Clay *out*." He turned back to the conversation. "How low do drones fly, anyway?"

"Pretty low," Anna replied. "Oh, I know, I have a laser pointer. And the targeting lasers on our rifles! If we hit just the right place on the drone, we can blind it."

"Yeah!" Neal agreed with enthusiasm. "There was that kid, before the Calm! He brought down a drone with a laser by accident. The Feds tried him as an adult. Got laughed out of court!"

"That *cannot* work!" Ekstrom objected. "Look. The rocket launcher was a billion to one chance. A laser pointer is a *trillion* to one. Listen to Skull. *Drive!*"

"Use a marker, Daddy," Anna said.

"No!"

"Your suggestion is duly noted," Clay said to Ekstrom. "Anna, get your rocket launcher ready for when we've got radio contact re-established. Neal, KT, the three of us will use the laser targeting on our rifles."

"Alright, dammit!" Ekstrom said. "I'll give you a goddamned marker!"

Clay held up his satellite phone between the front seats. "Phone number, please?"

"I – Hell," Ekstrom said. "Um…"

"Incoming message –"

Skull rattled off a string of digits, followed by, "MacLaren."

Clay entered the numbers, and said, "MacGuffin, get up here. I don't hold any markers. He's not going to do it for me."

The phone was on speaker. It rang a couple times, followed by a sleepy, "MacLaren," with audible yawn. It wasn't 2:00 a.m. yet.

"Ekstrom," the MacGuffin said. "Emmett, I need to call in a marker, and I don't have my phone. A drone is hunting me in an SUV, and three Humvees. Drone over Arlington, D.C., and route 50 east to the Chesapeake Bay Bridge."

Fresh from sleep, MacLaren's hillbilly drawl was more noticeable than usual. "Wait. What? I thought you were in jail."

"This is my jailbreak," Ekstrom admitted, embarrassed as hell. "I've got the marker, Emmett. You know I'm good for it."

"Those markers are for Delmarva, Ekstrom. Not your own sorry ass." MacLaren's yawn was audible over the phone. "Good luck with the hide and seek."

"Alright! A second marker for you. Bonus food shipment."

"Why, thank you kindly," MacLaren drawled. "A pleasure doing business." He disconnected.

"Does that mean he'll do it?" KT asked.

"He'll do it," Ekstrom said. He didn't sound too sure of that.

The radio finally crackled back to life, barely. KT told the closest trailing Humvee, Garcia, to stop moving and wait on further news. Drone in the sky hunting them. Most of what Garcia said was garbled, but that much got through.

"Incoming message –"

Skull reported, "Drone is out of your sky. Recalled to base with equipment failure. Estimated time to repair eight hours. Maybe twelve."

"No other drones?" Clay asked.

"Pentagon has only the one left. The rest belong to the Air Force in PA. PA will not cooperate. Recommend you resume driving."

"Thank you, boss," Clay said.

"Clay…"

"Yes, boss?"

"Never mind. Happy trails."

"Sleep sweet, boss."

"Thank you, Daddy," Anna said, and dropped a chaste kiss on Ekstrom's cheek. He was still bent over double between her and Neal in the second row.

Ekstrom recoiled and squat-shuffled back to the air mattress. He looked like a bear trapped in a doll-house.

"Bio break. Then let's roll," Clay declared. "My turn to drive?"

"Sure, if you want," KT agreed. "We need to stop for rendezvous before the bridge, though." He seemed a little doubtful whether Clay would obey that plan. But it was his car and mission, after all.

Anna broke out more snacks.

"I'm driving Darcy," Anna said softly. "Alone." She swallowed.

Clay cast his gaze over the dark waters lapping the approach to the sunken bridge. They didn't need to rendezvous at some secret location and come in guns blazing. There was no guard here blocking the bridge. That was unnecessary. The highway was blocked off with orange sawhorses and a big sign.

BRIDGE OUT. ROAD CLOSED.

The SEAL Humvees caught up to Darcy at the roadblock and parked alongside. They'd been here over an hour, resting and shifting gear between the vehicles. But the tide was now a half hour from dead low, giving them an hour at dead slow to cross the worst 13 miles while the water was at low ebb.

Not that the tides here were very deep – only about a foot difference separated high and low, significantly less tide than on the familiar Hudson shores.

Strange but true, military Humvees were capable of driving through nearly five feet of water. Civilian models weren't normally kitted out for it, though they could also handle a few feet. The diesel engine operated fine underwater. The exhaust was no problem because it pushed out air with enough pressure. The engine just needed its air intake clear. Military Humvees were equipped with a snorkel on the air intake to keep it above water.

Darcy now sported a snorkel herself, tucked inside the hood. She did not, however, have a diesel engine, or anywhere near the modifications required to seal or drain all the necessary engine compartments to keep her spark plugs and fuel dry. The new snorkel gave her an extra couple feet leeway on the air intake, which normally was just above the front bumper. But to keep her engine compartment dry, she had to ride as high as possible.

With the removable seats and all the cargo transferred to the Humvees, she now rode about 13 inches higher than normal. And she was as light as she could get, minus the driver.

Clay shook his head slowly. "No. Ava, you don't have to do this," he whispered. "How much difference can it make? Fifty pounds?"

Cade was lean, but he was solid muscle, and 9 inches taller than Ava. His weight was perfect for his trim build. Ava, on the other hand, had lost a few pounds the past few days. She was back under the 100 pounds she'd fought so hard to achieve to enter Army Basic.

She put her hand on his chest. "I'm a stronger swimmer. Cade, no matter how well she's driven, Darcy might not make it. If she floats away – better me than you. I'll get out. Swim to a Humvee. We're surrounded by SEALs. No way I'll drown. You wouldn't be safe enough."

Cade swallowed uncomfortably, and pulled her into his arms, tucking her head under his chin. "There's an island halfway across. If you want to bail –"

"I won't give up," Ava insisted. "Failure is not an option. I want to save Darcy for you."

"Fuck Darcy," Cade said.

"No. I can do this." She pushed out of his arms and looked him in the eye. "It isn't highway driving. Cade, I'll be going like four miles per hour. Following KT's tail-lights the whole way. Just like when you walked me down the highway to that stupid rock, the first day I drove. I can do this."

He raised an open hand and dropped it, to acquiesce. "You want me on the radio? Keep you company?"

"Yeah. But I want KT on the radio even more. He knows what we're doing."

They both chuckled, and Cade lay his forehead on hers. "Thank you. You're right. You can do this. And Darcy gives us an edge. But let her go if you have to. Right? Just a car. You're everything to me."

"Yeah. You, too."

KT cleared his throat a few paces away, then approached as the young couple separated with a squeeze of hands. "Even my flotation belt is too big for you. But it's the best I've got."

Amused, Anna tried on the waterskiing belt. Its two ends met with enough room left over to easily step out, her hips included. She let out a little on the strap, then overlapped the foam and snapped it closed at her back. "Perfect."

"Heller and Tobin are in wet suits," KT told Clay. "Ready for rescue if need be."

"Thanks, KT," Clay said. "You've been awesome. Hey, how's Jamal?"

"He'll be alright. Lost some blood, but they gave him a transfusion. Stable."

"You carry blood for transfusions?" Anna asked.

"Yeah, we store it inside brother SEALs. Nice and fresh."

"I should learn to do that," Anna grumbled.

"Time to go," KT said.

He walked with them to see Clay into Garcia's Humvee. Neal was in there guarding his electronics, plus Ekstrom and one of the wet suit men.

Ekstrom took one look at Anna in the float belt, and said, "No. No, that's insane. You need to leave the SUV behind!"

"Shut up, MacGuffin," Clay said. "You're spoiling the moment." He gave Anna a wordless kiss, then climbed in the back with their prize senile.

KT took Anna by the elbow to lead her to Darcy. "Steady spacing. If you have any trouble seeing me, you tell me on the radio, and I'll slow up. But not too close. Your brakes will barely work. You can't accelerate much or you'll create a bow wave that gets into the engine. Just slow and steady. The hard part is staying on the road. We can't see it very well. Some places the guard rail is likely underwater. The second you feel yourself going off the road bed, turn back toward the middle, not too hard."

"Got it." Anna swallowed. She climbed into Darcy. She'd already adjusted the seat. She pulled on her radio headset, and tested it with KT as he walked to board his own Humvee. The lead vehicle rolled into the water.

35

Interesting fact: The kid who took down a military drone was flying a simple consumer model bearing a disco ball to light a party. He was aiming his laser pointer at the disco ball, unaware of the multi-million dollar hardware beyond.

It felt strange driving Darcy from so high above the road. The height didn't last. Anna advanced to water's edge, and waited to duplicate the spacing between the lead Humvee and KT. Then she waded Darcy in.

The first mile or so had only a few inches of water on the roadbed, with the edges clearly visible. She could even see the lane lines painted on the asphalt just below her headlights, at first. Seawater lapped peacefully through the drowned shoreline, roofs sticking up. Loops of exit and entrance ramps came and went to the sides. Anna blew out softly and focused on right this moment, at one with KT's taillights and gently spreading wake before her. Darcy was responsive, and little steering or accelerating was involved.

"Dip, and about to reach open water," KT reported over the radio. "Anna, you'll start to get waves coming in from the right. Not too big. Just be aware of it. They'll try to push you to the left. Keep adjusting. Slow and steady."

"You're doing great, baby," Clay said. "I'm so proud of you."

Tears prickled her eyes. "Clay, cut that out. No mushy stuff."

Soft laughter came over the radio. KT and Clay bandied cheerful insults instead. KT's taillights suddenly sank much closer to the red water surface. Much more, and they'd be in the water. Another minute, and she could see waves begin to wash between them, only a few inches tall at first. Darcy was pushing much harder now. Anna gently increased her pressure on the accelerator. And she breathed out into the anxiety.

"Concrete guard rail is going under," Tollman reported from the lead car. "I see the suspension cables ahead, in high beams. I hope this stretch of road is straight."

"Gentle bend to the left," Clay reported.

"OK. Yeah, I see it," Tollman said. "Just went through the deepest point. Starting to climb."

"Slowing through the deep, Anna," KT said. "Mind your spacing."

Then KT's taillights plunged underwater. Ava could still see their glow, barely, and could see him. The waves had risen to a foot and definitely pushed to the left. She steered into them, and pushed harder on the accelerator as Darcy started plowing ocean with the front bumper. She scraped a little on the right on a concrete guardrail, and corrected. But it slowed her down. Darcy struggled to push so much water.

Suddenly, Darcy lurched forward. Her bumper cleared the low point, and she had too much acceleration. She eased off. But KT was pulling ahead.

"Don't speed up, KT. Please." She swallowed. He'd reached the suspension bridge portion, soaring up out of the water, high and dry. The land approaches to this bridge were drowned, not the bridge itself.

"That's affirm," KT replied. "Tollman, we prefer max five knots for the whole trip."

"Empty interstate, clear sailing next three miles," Tollman said. "Oh, alright. Let me know if you change your mind. I feel like an idiot tooling along this slow."

Anna didn't feel that way at all. The high suspension bridge, with its arcing cables, didn't inspire her to speed up in the slightest. It made her nervous. She'd never driven on a suspension bridge before. It swayed a little.

"Shit!" Tollman yelled.

KT slowed, and Anna followed suit. "Tollman, report," KT said mildly.

"Yeah, use the left lane. Hug the divider. Fucking section of the road fell out. Five knots is good."

In a few minutes, Anna could see the hole for herself. A stretch over a hundred feet long was simply missing, its cables snapped. She was grateful that Darcy was narrower than the Humvees. KT really did hug the left divider, even to scraping his side. His tires only cleared the hole by a few inches. A fresh piece broke off the gaping edge.

"Garcia," Anna said. "Hole is growing in KT's wake. Recommend your left tires climb onto the divider."

"Good to know," Garcia acknowledged.

Anna hugged the divider as best she could, the sides of the tires scraping it, but didn't climb it. And in a couple minutes she was past and breathing out.

Fortunately that was the last bit of excitement on the high miles of the bridge, designed for boats to pass beneath.

"Coming up on Kent Island," Tollman reported. "Could be swimming the rest of the way."

Technically, they were past the bridge. But there was another short bridge from the island to the mainland of the Delmarva peninsula. And the island was a whole lot smaller than it used to be. Both island and mainland were drowned for the next 11 miles, so far as they could tell, and possibly the short bridge between them as well.

"You know," Tollman said, "there was a guy who used to charge twenty-five bucks to drive people across that bridge in their own cars. Made a mint doing it. One of the top ten scariest bridges in the world."

"Ha, ha," Anna replied.

"Stow it, Tollman," Garcia ordered.

"Dammit!" Tollman yelled. "All stop. I think the road washed out in the tsunami. Driving on mud. Hunting for a path now."

The convoy held up for 20 minutes waiting for Tollman to find a viable route by trial and error. The team waded out with sticks at one point.

"OK, this is going to be deep," Tollman finally reported. "The Humvees will make it. Fifty-fifty on the SUV."

"Will I degrade it going through?" KT said.

"Yeah, send the SUV through first."

"If I get stuck, I'll block the way," Anna objected.

Garcia decided. "KT and Garcia going through first. Anna, pull over."

Past the gully there was apparently a high point, where the Humvees were in only eight inches or so of water. Dawn was gathering. The water lightened to steel grey, and the sky grew noticeably lighter by the minute. Since they were headed east, sunrise would not be entirely welcome for their visibility. Garcia's Humvee swam through with water partway up its doors.

"OK, Anna," said Tollman. "Garcia was too far right. Correct three feet to the left. And just gun it. Try to reach the deep point with momentum."

From a dead stop. In a foot and a half of water. Anna didn't say anything. She just grimaced and put Darcy back in gear. She breathed out, and plunged the accelerator to the floor. She reached a lofty seven miles per hour before the front bumper took a nosedive.

"I'm not moving," she radioed after a minute, going ever slower. Water seeped in by her feet.

"You are moving, Anna," KT said. "Just keep going. Don't let up."

Darcy's engine strained mightily. It felt like mud was churning away and dissolving under her tires. One tire, and then another, dropped with a sickening lurch, but only one at a time, so she was still in business. And then suddenly, both tires on the right dropped. The wheels spun, and her momentum was gone.

Anna didn't dare turn the wheel to the right to seek traction, only left, but that didn't work. Waves rocked the SUV slightly, but not enough for her to get the right wheels out of their hole. *But maybe...*

"Only have left tires working. Bailing out to investigate," Ava reported. "Going off radio."

"Sending Heller and Tobin to help you," KT advised, just before she pulled off her headset. *Too bad I don't have a – yes!* Ike had left a walking stick in Darcy's cargo hold. Not his fancy Renaissance Faire stick with the dragon head, just one he'd fashioned from a tree branch during a rest stop. Ava paused to grab that.

With difficulty, she climbed out the upward-leaning driver's door, leaving Darcy running in neutral, steering wheel hard to left. She landed in cold water up to KT's flotation belt, and realized that wouldn't help. She needed to wade, not swim. She stowed the stick and stripped the belt, and reattached it by its straps to her upper arm. That way it could float around with her, without getting in the way.

Damn, that water was cold. She took the stick again to poke around, doubling the testing reach of her feet. She stepped forward to go around the front of Darcy on automatic, then paused.

The way up that I know of was behind, not ahead. First the right front wheel had dropped, then the right rear. She waded out to the left of the driver's door, feeling around with her feet and poking with Ike's stick. It wasn't much, only a couple inches, but the bottom did rise slightly about 10 feet to the left. It was slippery, like asphalt rose to drowned lawn.

Heller and Tobin arrived, and she explained her thinking. Tobin took over the stick and followed her slight rise, to see if it would lead back to the road. Heller handed her a welcome wool sweater, which she hastily donned. Her teeth were starting to chatter. The wool would keep her warm even when wet.

They rounded the back of the SUV, and found where Darcy had fallen into the hole. Heller didn't think she could find enough purchase to reverse, though.

"Can we rock it?" Anna suggested. "Use a wave, and us pushing, just to get the front tire out of the hole?"

They hailed Tobin back for manpower. In relief, Anna swam back to the driver's seat one-armed, sweater off and held above her head. She was sick of walking ribs-deep while feeling around with numb toes and sneakers.

In the end, the two SEALs, aided by the water's buoyancy, held up Darcy's right side, while Ava steered, walking along to the left. They coaxed Darcy back to the new path Tobin had proved out. They told her to hop in and drive, while they continued to push from behind, to make up for Darcy's lost momentum. It was a hard slog.

And then suddenly Anna was past the worst. Darcy picked up speed and left the SEALs behind. Finally back on the road, the bumper slurped clear of the water, just as an eye-searing shoulder of sun crested the horizon. Anna stopped to pick up the wet suit men for a lift to the Humvees. Darcy was able to start moving again from a stop here.

"Good job, Anna," KT told her. "Fall in again after me. Tollman, let's increase spacing."

"Good move," Tollman agreed.

Crossing Chesapeake Bay took nearly two hours. But they got through it, Darcy included. They climbed a slight hill and stopped. Anna threw open the car door and just sat for a moment, breathing deep. She gazed back over the road they'd come in the dawn's early light. They'd just emerged from a trackless sheet of water, marked only by a few roofs and random telephone poles. Visibility didn't stretch far enough to spot the spans of the suspension bridge above the gleam of the water. The Chesapeake was swallowing back its own.

Anna tiredly unbuckled the float belt as Clay reached her. He folded her into his arms and kissed the crown of her head.

"Good job, Ava," he murmured. "It's been a terror and a privilege watching you grow up, girl. Proud of you."

"Thank you," she breathed. After a moment puzzling it out, she added, "You were already grown up, before the epidemic. You haven't grown up this year. You just finally had a chance to calm down. I didn't realize before. The only place you could blow off steam, was with me. Running the gang, you were always acting."

"I shouldn't have taken it out on you," Cade whispered. "I'm so sorry for that."

She shook her head, snuggled against his chest. "You didn't have much choice. No outlet." She chuckled. "You know the best thing I learned in the Army? Was how much I antagonized people. I was a brat."

"Not really. Sort of. Yeah." They both chuckled. Then he kissed her deep.

"We can't be everything for each other like that," Ava said. "That was too intense."

"Yeah. But we can be all we can be," Cade said. "Sort of next to each other. Some of the time anyway."

Ava frowned. *Some of the time?*

But he gave her another quick peck, and said, "I need to go plan the next leg of the trip with the SEALs. Take a break. You've earned it."

"Need to reload Darcy," she objected. "Her carpet's kinda squishy. Sorry."

"Never mind. Neal and I can get the gear. Any gas left?"

They poured the spare gas cans into the tank before the bridge. The ones she thought they wouldn't need, because the tank would get them to Jersey. "Eighth of a tank, almost," she reported. "Darcy, you get lousy mileage pushing water."

Curiosity dragged her to her feet to follow him, though her knees wobbled a bit. There were houses and stuff above water here, though their lawns were full of sand and seaweed. The high water marks reached the first floor.

Clay bent heads quietly with KT and Garcia. So Anna hung back with Ekstrom and Neal.

"No people here," she said to Ekstrom. "Evacuated?"

"Yeah. This whole headland is condemned, to Hickory Ridge, another few miles up the road," the colonel replied. "That's how I ran afoul of O'Hara. She didn't want the populace 'alarmed.' I enforced mandatory evacuation to twenty feet elevation this side, fifteen on the Atlantic side of Delmarva."

Hudson went with 20 feet everywhere along its coast. Twenty feet starting from the newly risen sea level, that is, rounded up – 30 feet above where sea level used to be.

"Why unequal?" Neal asked with a frown. His native Long Island was hit hard by the tsunami, though with surprisingly low loss of life compared to Jersey and old Rhode Island and Cape Cod, the new state of Narragansett. The ecotopian regime on Long Island took its storm surge planning seriously. Long Island and Delmarva wouldn't last forever. Maybe not even for their lifespans.

"The Chesapeake Bay area is sinking," Ekstrom explained. "Geology. Add more water, makes it heavier, so it sinks faster."

"Colonel," Clay interrupted. "We need to re-fuel. Close as possible. Diesel for the Humvees, gas for Darcy. We're also concerned about pursuit. Any way you could get the locals to ignore a small convoy? Up to Delaware Bay, if you could. The I-295 bridge. We need to continue north."

Military bio-diesel was a commonplace. Fortunately, they used plenty of gas, too, and had some about 10 miles up the road toward Dover, Ekstrom's HQ in mid-peninsula. Using the satellite phone Clay offered him, the colonel called ahead.

O'Hara had indeed sent out an all-points bulletin on three renegade Humvees and a blue SUV, wanted for arson and terrorism. Darcy was green. O'Hara had no IDs on any of them, and described the renegades as Army special ops, not Navy.

Ekstrom clarified to his militia that their 'act of terrorism' was springing him out of jail. He neglected to mention the damage they'd done to street and prison. He took time to talk to his subordinate Rescos. Both were new, the tsunami having killed their predecessors.

Clay and Anna and Garcia stood by Ekstrom's side through the whole negotiation. Clay finally intervened. "Sir? You'll have plenty of time to talk to them soon. I need some battery left on my sat phone."

Clay caught Anna's eye in warning.

After filling their tanks to the brim up the road, they thanked the military gas station profusely and drove away.

"Time. Tie him up," Clay directed in Darcy.

"What? What the hell?" Ekstrom demanded, as KT and Neal wrestled him.

"General Hoffman in Jersey wants to speak to you, sir," Clay clarified. "You're not going to Dover."

"You came to kidnap me for Hudson?"

"Kidnap is a strong word," Clay said. He was driving again for the moment. He nodded and waved to every militia vehicle they passed. The militia waved back, some with victory signs, glad to have their rightful Resco back on the job. "I'm sure they just want to talk."

"I demand to speak with Sullivan!"

"Yes, sir. I'll see if he's available," Clay said. "Darcy, record. Hey, boss, just turned left for home. Our guest wishes to speak to you. All is well. Bringing home some fish. Darcy, end." He added for Ekstrom's benefit, "Now we wait for his reply, sir."

Anna, seated beside him, noted that none of those commands actually sent a message to Skull. She smiled out the window.

"What names for Jersey?" Anna asked, yawning, as they waited politely before an assertive maze of concrete dividers just before the I-295 bridge across the Delaware River. A pushy sign in orange advised *HUDSON BORDER. WAIT HERE. DO NOT ENTER UNTIL SUMMONED FORWARD.* The machine gun towers were none too subtle, either.

"Our own names," Cade replied. "We're Hudson citizens, returning from abroad."

Ava looked pointedly back at Ekstrom and KT. Ekstrom was snoring. Maybe she shouldn't have dosed him with the second antihistamine. But he was getting annoying.

"GREEN SUV. ADVANCE TO POINT A," an especially loud speaker instructed. "HUMVEES. DO NOT ADVANCE OR YOU WILL BE FIRED UPON." Blackened chunks bitten out of the concrete dividers gave credence to this warning.

"Ah, warm Hudson hospitality!" Neal quipped. The announcer had a strong Queens accent and everything. "They won't do a body cavity search, will they?"

"Don't give them ideas," Cade returned, and added, "PA would."

Darcy was a trifle long for the jogs in the passenger vehicle maze. Cade had to back and forth around one corner. But they made it to point A. Ava noted signs for points B, C, and D. The gauntlet for trucks included points E through J, that she could see.

Point A featured a speaker grill, like the ones once used to order burgers at a drive-through. "State your names and business."

"Special agent Cade Snowdon, Hudson military intelligence. Returning from a mission in Virginia. Plus two more Hudson agents.

We have two VA military prisoners for General Pete Hoffman. Resco light colonel Jack Ekstrom. Navy SEAL specialist Keenan Tannhauser. The SEAL Humvees behind us would like to either defect to join military intelligence, or rejoin the Navy in Hudson."

The fact that Cade was a Hudson military intelligence agent would have been news to Ava, if she believed it. She didn't.

"Advance to point B." There was a fork in the maze. A hard right led to point B. The generous express lane to the left said, *RETURN TO VA. And never come back*, was merely implied.

At Point C they graduated to actual soldiers manning the position. "Get out," they instructed. "Everybody." Six troopers hung back, weapons trained on them, while two stepped forward to check ID. Cade and Ava were easy – they had their phones. They could walk into a Hudson cafeteria and order a skimpy meal right now.

Daneel wasn't about to hand over his phone to a border flunky. "Daneel U. Snoodegrass," he said, and helpfully spelled it out for them. Like Ava and Cade, his legal name was fictitious. Ava only changed her surname Panic to Pawic. Cade used Frosty Supreme Snowman.

"From?" Romberg demanded. His uniform was labeled.

"Um. Patchogue, on the Island?" Daneel hazarded.

"Guess again, genius," the burly white soldier said, studying his own phone. Romberg showed it to his companion, a lean black guy.

"Come on, man," Daneel wheedled. "I was working in Ronkonkoma before I split for Army Basic. You guys class of April, like us?"

"I knew it! Panic, right?" the black soldier said. *Blooie*, advised his uniform, likely his street handle. "Romberg, you remember them, right? They were ringleaders in the Lard Belly Mutiny!"

Romberg scowled and shook his head. "This says you're a voter in Ronkawonkabonkafog. That some kind of joke?"

Daneel pointed at him in triumph. "I would have guessed that next!"

"Romberg's from Albany," Blooie excused his cranky partner. "Arrived the day before the mutiny. Didn't understand what was going down."

"You should have been shot," Romberg grumbled.

"Hey, were you in Carella's battalion?" Blooie asked Daneel.

"Smith." Daneel shrugged modestly. "Hey, somebody's got to be worst, right? We really had you going at the start, though, when we outweighed you." The three fat camp alumni laughed together.

Romberg glowered at them. "So mutineers and fuck-ups get booted into flashy jobs in intelligence. While we're stuck here on the bridge to nowhere. God, the Army sucks."

Check. Ava blinked in realization. No, there had never been a snowball's chance in hell of Daneel or herself being accepted into the regular Army. Not after their roles in the mutiny. Her sergeant Calderon had even told her as much. *Panic, you're a walking insurrection.* She was just too tunnel-visioned at the time to accept it, too focused on achieving her goal, still in denial over not being selected.

"– Cunt like her," Romberg said, disrupting her reverie. Blooie had been shooting the breeze with Daneel about how little traffic they allowed through here.

"What did you call me?" Ava demanded sharply.

"Man, that's not cool," Blooie muttered.

Cade had ignored the banter up til now. Glittering blue eyes fixed on Romberg in icy fury. "I demand to speak to your commanding officer. Now!"

This appeal to irrelevant authority made the tired morning a half hour longer. But Ava enjoyed serving the yutz a reprimand. Romberg would never get away with calling Blooie a nigger, especially not since his lieutenant was black, too. The few 'female men' who survived Basic deserved the same respect. And a border guard using language like that on a citizen was uncool.

So that bit of retribution was fun. But any interest she might have had in the proceedings, a job she might have held if she made Army, died long before the process ground to a halt at Point D, a parking lot spanning two highway lanes under a machine gun tower. They sat around yawning in Darcy while the three SEAL Humvees gradually rejoined them.

Lieutenant Sesay returned to Cade's driver's window. Ava didn't get her hopes up. He'd been back and forth three times already.

"You are cleared to proceed to the Resco Mansion in Brooklyn Prospect."

Cade blinked at him stupidly. "What?"

Lt. Sesay unpacked his instructions. "You are to deliver Colonel Ekstrom to General Hoffman. The general is in the city for a meeting. He's expecting you at the Resco Mansion, in Brooklyn Prospect. If you need fuel, stop at the gas station across the bridge."

"All of us?" Cade indicated the Humvees with a wave of his hand.

"This vehicle only. Move out. Now." Sesay retreated to his communications booth, brooking no further inquiry regarding the fate of the other SEALs. Soldiers opened the exit gate in the razor-wire topped fence that enclosed the Point D waiting pen.

"I can drive," Daneel offered. Cade and KT and Ava took him up on it, and soon fell asleep.

36

Interesting fact: Delmarva was 60% of the land area of old New Jersey, and by this point had a seventh the population. It was culturally southern, closer to Carolina than Jersey. Its highest elevation was about 90 feet.

Hours later, the car stopped moving. Ava's nose awoke before her eyes opened, reporting the familiar complex scent of home. She uncurled from the passenger seat, stretched and yawned, and finally registered the view of the Brooklyn Bridge before her. The dashboard said it was nearly four in the afternoon.

Daneel was in the back, collecting his stuff. Ava roused herself to clamber past Cade and KT, still asleep in the second row. "You're not coming with us?"

"Resco Mansion? No," Daneel replied. "Colonel Cameron might be there. I can catch a bus here to the train station, and head back to Elmira." His stuff actually took unpacking, rather than packing. He'd already transferred it to a Humvee and back this morning. He extracted Ava and Cade's electronics from his own, including their copy of the downloads from the gran caravan.

"Stay," Ava urged. "Meet the Rescos. We'll drop off Ekstrom, then crash with friends in Chelsea. I hope to see my old squad before we leave the city. You remember them."

Daneel paused, solemn for once. "Downside of being a con artist, Panic. I'm not one of them. Blooie and Romberg at the bridge showed me that." He sounded sad. "Colonel Cameron – I admire the hell out of him. He set me up with an internship on the meshnet team. Got me into the Army. And I conned him."

"You're one of us," Ava insisted. "Team." She reached over to wake Cade with a gentle hand on his belly. "Daneel is leaving."

"Oh, yeah?" Cade roused, stretching like Ava. He scrubbed his face with his hands, and took in his surroundings with a yawn. He nodded. "Cool. Take KT?"

"Could do," Daneel agreed, brightening.

Ava woke the SEAL and carried out his stuff, also pre-packed.

They parted with heart-felt hugs and mutual assurances that they were impressed as hell, and looked forward to another mission together.

"You're our team, Daneel," she whispered in his ear. Judging by his quiet warm smile, he was grateful. Ava served KT the same treatment. Cade followed up with his own private words of bonding.

Ava and Cade climbed back into Darcy's front seat, and waved as Daneel and KT walked away.

"Thanks for that," Cade said. "Company needs all the team-building we can get. Not a lot of pride in the work."

Ava smiled agreement and squeezed his hand.

"Darcy, record message," Cade said. "Hey, boss. Clown fish split to take the train. Headed to palace to deliver the package. Then hope to visit friends in Chelsea to catch some Z's. OK if we take a couple days off? We're exhausted. Darcy, send message to boss."

"Incoming message –"

"Hey, Cade, welcome home," Skull said. "Wait on Chelsea. You'll stay at MacLaren's house. Brief the Rescos tomorrow."

"Brief them? On what?"

"Anything they want to know."

Cade hesitated, frown deepening toward horror. *"Anything?"*

"You will cooperate fully. And secure us increased funding. Don't worry. MacLaren and Hoffman have your back."

Apparently Ekstrom in the back wasn't asleep, just lying doggo. "Skull has a death wish," he commented.

~

CADE PULLED UP IN FRONT OF THE GREAT RESCO MANSION. AVA GAZED AT the double-wide four-story brownstone, mouth open in awe. Cade glanced at her and smiled, as though silently laughing at her.

"What?" she demanded.

"It's a brownstone, Ava." He squeezed her hand. "And they're just guys, like Daddy back there." The mirth drained from his eyes, probably recalling their new bonus mission of 'briefing' the Hudson Resco Raj.

"I wish you'd stop calling me Daddy," Jack Ekstrom grumbled. He was sitting up now, studying Brooklyn Prospect in interest.

Ava wondered if the other Rescos would hold it against them for rough handling on Daddy. "Yes, sir, Colonel Ekstrom sir."

Ekstrom snorted. "That's almost worse."

Decisively, Cade climbed out of Darcy. He walked to the back hatch to help Ekstrom out and let him stretch his legs.

Ava clambered into the cargo hold. "What should we bring with us? Tablet? Laptop?"

"You risked your lives getting me out of that prison," Ekstrom said gruffly. "Thank you."

"Sorry about the high-handed treatment, sir," Cade offered. "Orders. Also just kinda tired."

"Understood," Ekstrom allowed, pursing his lips. "That's on Hoffman, not you."

"Is there like an officer's parole or something?" Cade inquired. "I untie you, you cooperate with delivery to this Hoffman guy?"

That surprised a laugh out of the colonel. "Yes. Please. I am happy to meet with my counterparts in Hudson. I will not attempt escape. You have my word of honor."

Cade dug out some scissors and cut the zip-tie fastening Ekstrom's hands. By then, a couple local militia approached to inquire what they thought they were doing. The police headquarters was next door to the Resco Mansion. Ekstrom politely explained that they were expected. One of the cops headed up the half-story front steps to announce their arrival. The other peered into the SUV at Ava and Cade.

Ava flipped the cop her middle finger. He returned the gesture, but took her point and left.

"Business manners, Eileen," Cade murmured.

"Jack!" Colonel MacLaren called out. He jogged down his front steps with a huge grin. A few other officers disgorged from the front door behind him. Ava recognized them all. Emmett MacLaren of the Apple, and Carlos Mora of Connecticut, she'd spoken with at West Point. Cam Cameron of Long Island, and Ash Margolis, in the Apple for months on Project Rebuild but now back Upstate, she'd seen in person but hadn't spoken with.

Ava might be star-struck, but the Rescos weren't reticent in the least.

"Emmett! Great to see you again!" Ekstrom called back. The two colonels met with handshake and hug, not salutes. "Thanks for the assist on the drone. Sorry I missed your wedding. Boss kept me tied up."

MacLaren laughed. "Uh-huh. Hey, Jack, you've met Ash Margolis, right? I ought to see to my other guests." Ekstrom proceeded to greet the rest of the officers.

This wasn't quite the prisoner delivery Ava envisioned. More than a little intimidated, she exited the back side door after Cade, away from the Ekstrom reception.

MacLaren stepped around to greet them, hand extended for a shake. Low-voiced, he inquired, "Cade Snowdon and Ava Panic, right?" After they nodded agreement, his voice returned to normal volume. "Good to see you both again! Thank you, sincerely, for retrieving Jack for us. Hell of a job."

"Yes, sir," Ava agreed, shaking his hand after Cade.

"None of the sir stuff, Panic," the colonel advised. "Call me Emmett. First name basis at my house. Or street handle. Yours was… Frosty, right?" he asked Cade. "The Snowman?"

"Just Cade, s– I left Frosty behind with the gang."

Emmett nodded. "When was the big jailbreak?"

"About sixteen hours ago," Ava said. "Long drive since then."

"Travel does suck these days, doesn't it," Emmett said. "I want to hear all about it. We all do. But you must be exhausted. I need to take Ekstrom to see the brass at the hotel now. You're staying with us. Go on in and make yourselves comfortable. I'll see you at dinner." Returning to a lower voice, he added, "Skull's an ally. I've got your back. Save details for the briefing."

Colonel Carlos Mora approached from behind Darcy with a warm smile. A full-bird colonel now, outranking the lieutenant colonels MacLaren and Ekstrom, Carlos was older, with a stocky build and Native American complexion. "Panic! Great to see you again!" he greeted her, offering a hand-shake.

"Carlos, I have to –" Emmett excused himself. "Could you –?"

"No problem," Carlos assured him. Ava introduced Carlos to Cade, as Emmett and Margolis headed up the street with Ekstrom instead of back into the mansion.

"Cam!" Carlos called across the car. "Help carry."

With much bustle, the friendly martial law rulers of Connecticut and Long Island toted the two young death angels and their luggage up gleaming hardwood floors to their bedroom. The beautiful room with queen-sized bed took up a front quarter of the third floor. A pass-through bathroom led to a room dedicated to an indoor kitchen garden, with a staircase to the roof. Cam pointed out his room at the top of the stairs as they passed.

Along the way, Emmett's housekeeper, Gladys, approached briefly for an introduction. She took one sniff of them, then returned with a giant basket to collect their laundry. While Cade claimed the shower first, Gladys climbed the stairs yet again to deliver a plate of snacks to tide them over until supper.

"We should stay in here until then?" Ava inquired nervously.

"Go wherever you want," Gladys replied, surprised. "Or, well, no. Stay out of other people's bedrooms. And the office. And the basement is mine. But my hot tub is fired up out back. The pool is heated, too. The roof garden is nice. Dinner's probably around seven."

Ava wasn't sure what she expected at the Resco Mansion. But this wasn't it.

~

"Maisie's doing great," Carlos told Ava, at the dining room table. Ava had shown Carlos' fifteen-year-old daughter Maisie around West Point when they visited in December. "Has a new boyfriend. Kind of a loser, but improvable. I'm sure she'd love to hear from you."

"I'm sorry!" Ava blurted. "On a mission, I wasn't allowed to –"

Carlos waved that off. "No worries. You're busy."

"Clearly," Cam agreed, glancing up from his laptop with a smile. The tall blond officer wasn't as handsome and charismatic up close as he seemed on the news, where he often served as spokesman for the Raj. But then, he wasn't trying to charm anyone at the moment. He was answering email at a friend's house, cooling his heels until supper.

Though the bed was tempting, after their showers Ava and Cade succumbed to curiosity and set off to explore the house instead. The roof garden was indeed nice, though the sheltered crops were young yet. The greenhouse room, blindingly bright and gurgling with hydroponics, had ripe offerings of every salad vegetable, plus trays of seedlings for both indoors and outdoor transplant. The second floor housed the master bedroom. They stuck their heads in and retreated. A posh guest room stood empty on the opposite end of the landing, and another with closed door.

Their snooping ended abruptly as they were spotted on the stairway down to the main floor. They peered briefly into the other side of the staircase. That held a sparsely furnished vast living room. A big office at the back was partitioned off with glass French doors. Then they joined Carlos and Cam kibitzing in the open floor plan expanse of dining room plus kitchen. Gladys prepared supper back there.

Cade returned from a foray into Gladys' realm to admire the kitchen. He handed Ava a hard-boiled egg. "They have chickens in the backyard," he told her in delight. "Think I could keep chickens? A cage for them in Darcy?"

"Ew." Ava turned back to Carlos. "Darcy is the SUV. Named for a previous girlfriend."

Cam Cameron barked a laugh at that.

"Word of advice, son," Carlos said, eyes crinkling. "Save some mystique for after the wedding."

"I heard that," Gladys called. Her raucous accent spoke of Queens, the Apple borough wrapping north and east of Brooklyn.

Carlos tilted his head toward Gladys, with a bashfulness adorable in a man in his forties. "We're dating. So how was Delmarva? Or no, you would have driven up past Baltimore, right?"

Cameron frowned and pulled up a map on his laptop.

"No, Delmarva," Cade replied. "Seemed less risky. The bridge is underwater, though. Ava drove that part." He ran a hand down her back and smiled at her. "Proud of you."

"I'll say," Cam said. "That must have been a hell of a drive. I'm impressed, Ava."

"Thanks," she said softly.

The officers casually drilled for details on Delmarva while reminding each other not to hassle the kids, their briefing was tomorrow. They didn't ask about the mission itself or operational details. But they were deeply interested in anything Ava and Cade could tell them about Delmarva itself. The young agents conferred and agreed that they could probably extract some good footage from Darcy's hood camera to illustrate their trip for the presentation.

Carlos asked Cam, "Do we expect Delmarva to last as well as Long Island?"

"Not really," Cam murmured. "I can pull it up. No." He closed his laptop and picked it up. "Let me show you on the big screen."

They trailed him to the modest conversational grouping of nice grey leather furniture in the middle of the enormous wood-floored living room. Sock-footed in deference to the gorgeous floors, Cam got a running start and slid halfway there. Grinning, Ava and Cade followed his lead. They overshot and happily slid back.

On the wall was one of the largest flat screen monitors Ava had ever seen. With a smooth familiarity that spoke of long practice, Cam plugged a dongle from a control tablet into his computer. In moments, he had up a map of Long Island as Ava had never seen it before, diminished by losses to sudden sea level rise after the tsunami, drowned land shaded in lavender against the ocean blue. The famous barrier islands to the south, like Jones Beach and Fire Island, were gone. Without the barriers to protect it, the south side of the main island looked like it was being chewed on as well. The northern coast wasn't much changed. Cam zoomed out a bit to include the western end, Brooklyn and Queens, where they now stood.

"This is now?" Ava asked.

She walked to the monitor to find Manhattan Beach, the part of the Brooklyn waterfront where her boot camp squad searched for survivors just after the tsunami. It was underwater.

"Yeah," Cam agreed. He adjusted an on-screen control to increase sea level from plus-three meters to plus-nine. Over half of Brooklyn and Queens sank beneath the waves, including incursions on the north side. Ava's eye was naturally drawn to the Apple, though they were here to compare Cam's Long Island and Ekstrom's Delmarva. Where they stood in Brooklyn Prospect was still on dry land on this flooded map, and most of her home turf of Manhattan as well, and even the Brooklyn Bridge between them. Unsurprisingly, the new villes of Project Rebuild remained dry. Beyond a narrow strip of Jerseyborough, a huge bay swallowed Newark and other cities of urban North Jersey.

The Apple was Emmett's problem, not Cam's. He scrolled briefly up to Carlos' Connecticut for orientation – mostly high and dry – then panned down the less fortunate Jersey coast. He fit the screen to show Philadelphia at the top, above the broadened Delaware Bay, with Norfolk at the bottom, sunken by the southern mouth of Chesapeake Bay.

Long Island might have lost a tenth of its land area at 9 meters of sea level rise. On Delmarva, it looked like a quarter. And unlike Long Island, Delmarva didn't have a rocky high side, just the narrow isthmus where the peninsula met Pennsylvania. It wouldn't meet Jersey at all anymore. The Delaware River grew as wide as the drowned bridge across Chesapeake Bay that Ava traversed this morning. It stayed broad past Philadelphia, and another 50 miles northeast to Trenton. The ocean seeped deeply into Delmarva in lavender from both sides.

Ava pointed to the long narrow southern tail of Delmarva, shown in speckled white and lavender. "What happens when it's like this? Can you keep it dry land?"

"No," Cam replied. "Too exposed. If Ekstrom's doing his job, that's already condemned. Should turn into marsh. New barrier islands if they're lucky."

"He was doing his job," Carlos said. "So O'Hara threw him in jail." Admiral O'Hara ruled the failed Greater Virginia.

Cam gave a disgusted nod. "This understates the land loss. Without the barrier islands to the east, this will all crumble." He used the tablet to draw a line paring off any speckled bits to the east. "But the worst part is the west, because Chesapeake Bay is sinking." He sketched in a wider margin on that side. What was left of Delmarva grew significantly smaller than the more cohesive chunk of South Jersey above it.

"How are the water tables?" Carlos asked, hand to his jaw in thought.

"Roof cisterns work –" Cam began.

His cell phone rang and he answered it, turning away from the group with a glance of apology. "Hey, baby. Nothing much. My proposal got pushed to tomorrow. Or never, you know how it goes. Oh, hey! We have a surprise guest today. You remember that dance thing you did at West Point?"

Cam turned to smile at Ava. She'd mentioned that she'd seen him before in person, just the once. Cam's husband led an event during fat camp, before Basic Combat Training began. Dwayne, the Resco of eastern Long Island under Cam, did a dance workout for all the recruits to get their endorphins sky high. Then he held a talk for those who wanted to come, about processing bad memories regarding sex, sex work, and rape. He focused on gay sex, being gay himself. But everyone was invited to dump their issues.

Ava grinned back at Cam. The 'gay sex talk' was one of the infamous highlights of her time at the Point. Her friends Puño and Doc emulated Dwayne all the time. His event was a major hit. Those were the happy memories that came to mind.

"Ava. Tiny girl, ash brown hair. I'll put you on speaker."

"Hi, Ava!" Dwayne said. "Ava, Ava… Not ringing a bell. Did you share something?" Not many girls had spoken up at the gay sex talk.

"Panic," Ava corrected. "Yeah, I shared…" A moment too late, she remembered what she shared. And she froze.

"Panic! Now I remember you!" Dwayne said triumphantly. "You and your ex were gang-raped, right in front of each other. I wondered whether –"

Cam saw their young faces at the moment of impact. His thumb hung up on his husband while he inserted himself bodily between Cade and Ava.

"*You – !*" Cade gasped at Ava, eyes wide. Ava stepped backward, and dropped to a defensive fighting crouch.

37

____

Interesting fact: The so-called 'Resco Mansion' embarrassed its occupant Emmett MacLaren. He accepted the luxurious brownstone to help persuade his then-girlfriend Dee to move into the city. Once New England joined Hudson, the house was too small to house Resco summit meetings.

"**W**alk away," Cam ordered Cade, in the command voice of a highly capable combat officer. "You do not look at her. You look at me. *Walk. Away.*"

Carlos crowded in from the other side, arms folded, further blocking Cade from Ava.

Cade gave a wordless scream of rage, then wheeled. He launched a roundhouse kick into the triangular wall under the staircase. That left a hole in the drywall about a yard wide. Then he ran out of the house, leaving his sneakers behind and the door hanging open. Ava automatically moved to follow. Carlos caught her.

"No," he said gently but firmly. "Panic, you can't talk to him now."

Cam peered out over the Prospect green, then closed the front door. He pulled out his phone again. Ava expected him to call his husband Dwayne back to explain, but instead he called Emmett on speaker. The militia would be warned that the blond gang rat in crisis was highly

365

dangerous, but belonged to Emmett. The Rescos wanted him back undamaged. But don't let him harm anyone else either.

"Sorry, Emmett," Cam ended softly. He stowed the phone and turned to Ava. "I'm sure Dwayne will be sorry, too. I imagine he just thought 'ex,' you know?"

Ava swallowed. "We got back together."

"Of course," Mora murmured. "No one meant any harm, Ava. But from a guy's perspective…"

Early in the Epidemic – the same week their parents died, in fact – the couple was jumped by a dozen black guys. They were raped and cut on in front of each other. Ava wasn't sure how clearly Cade remembered that night. Not well, she suspected. Her own nightmares revolved around failing to defend Cade. But he was mortified at having been raped.

Ava said, "I should never have told that to anyone. That was beyond humiliation. From a guy's perspective."

"No," Cam agreed softly.

"He'll never forgive me," Ava breathed, on the brink of tears. "Dammit…" Her hands clenched and unclenched. She hadn't fully risen from her fighting stance. She breathed out. *Just breathe out. Your lungs breathe in by themselves.* Cade's voice in her mind.

"Both of them," Carlos commented to Cam, though he turned his face to speak toward the staircase.

"Calisthenics," Cam barked. "Attention! Jumping jacks for ten! Ten! Nine! Eight!"

Ava's reflexes took hold from Basic Combat Training. She automatically stood up straight when he called attention. She performed jumping jacks on command, following Cam and Carlos. She performed the push-ups, squats, and lunges that followed. Until at last, coming up from a series of sit-ups, she hugged her knees to her chest, hid her face in her arm, and cried silent heaving sobs.

Carlos and Cam finished the exercise set, and another besides, and let her cry. Then Cam went away. Carlos cautiously sat beside her, leaving a foot of glossy floor between them. He rested a hand on her back companionably.

When her sobs died down a little, he offered, "When you love somebody, you make yourself vulnerable. When that trust is betrayed, it hurts like hell. That doesn't mean it's unforgivable, Panic. In truth, it's inevitable." He paused. "How is Cade at handling stuff like this?"

"I thought he'd kill me. And I deserved it."

"Mm, no. He should never hit you. You know that, right?"

Ava wiped her nose on her knee. Carlos dryly handed her a clean handkerchief. "We're karate black belts. We hit each other all the time."

"In anger?"

"I hit him in anger all the time," she admitted. "His control is better. But he hits a lot harder when he loses it."

Carlos laughed softly. "I bet he does. Guy looked fairly deadly."

"So am I," she hissed in self-defense. "He's just bigger."

"How'd he get the scar on his face?"

Ava honked her nose out on the handkerchief in dismay. "That night. The night we were..."

"Ouch. Sorry." Carlos was silent a moment, thinking. "Ava, I don't need to hear it. But if you need to tell it, I'm here to listen. By now, Maisie has told me most of what she went through."

Ava recoiled, and shook her head in revulsion. "Thanks. No." She rubbed her face and dried it with the handkerchief. "You think the Rescos would like video with the briefing tomorrow? Picture show? Snapshots of our fun-filled vacation in Virginia?"

"We'd love it. Pictures make it breathe. Especially Delmarva. We're not eager to absorb Delmarva. Penn. New England. All within a few months."

Carlos walked her out to Darcy to retrieve the hood cam hard drive, in case Cade lurked nearby. But she didn't spot him on the green. Then the colonel helped her with the tech setup to sift through video on the big monitor in the living room. Ava's memory for time of day was fairly good. Counting on her fingers worked for back-figuring the dates. And Cade's tablet had that recognition software to help sift through structures. The work was mechanical and soothing. Carlos left her in peace with it.

Ava had worked up a nice collection of the low-lights of West Virginia and the Shenandoah Valley, when the doorbell rang. Cam answered the door, but Ava looked up, heart pounding. She half expected to see a bleeding and hand-cuffed Cade dragged between battered and irate militia officers.

"Butch, here to see Panic," announced a gruff girl's voice. "Mac-Laren sent me, while the guys hunt down Frosty."

Butch? Ava leapt to her feet. Butch took over her old job as 'queen bitch' of the White Supreme gang when Ava split nine months ago. The tough lesbian gang queen had attended Ava's graduation from West Point last month. She sauntered in like she owned the place, gazing around in cool amusement. Ava envied the way Butch had 'saunter' down to an art form. The bigger-framed girl could carry off giant chunky studded leather collar, piercings, and a rainbow-colored two-inch shag of hair. Warmer weather bared upper-body tribal tattoos worthy of a Japanese mobster.

Ava flew to her in delight, nearly tackling her. "Butch, you bitch!"

Butch easily deflected Ava's weight into a spinning hug. "Hey, asshole!" Her eye caught on the gaping hole in the wall, and she grinned. "Frosty do that? Lucky he didn't break a stud."

Ava sniffed. "Wasn't wearing shoes. Lucky a stud didn't break his foot."

Butch shook her head in dismissal. "Men. Idiots. What can you do?"

Ava laughed, a little too hard. "Yeah. I really effed up, Butch."

"You have that knack," Butch agreed judiciously. "Man, Frosty? No one else can get a rise out of him. Stone cold. But you?" She laughed and swiped one hand against the other and launched the fingers high in the air. "Phwup! You set him off like a bottle rocket! Shit, girl, good thing you can fight so good!"

Gladys stuck her head cautiously around the stairs. "Ava? Would your friend like something to eat?"

"Hey, senile bitch!" Butch greeted Gladys. "Love to eat you! Yum, yum!"

Ava shoved Butch hard enough for her to stumble. "Yes, please, Gladys. Play nice, turkey, we're in a class joint. Speaking of, what are you doing here?"

"I said, dumb-ass," Butch replied. "MacLaren sent a car to pick us up. Maz, Elon, me. To come visit youse. The guys are out hunting

Frosty." She crouched and slunk to pantomime stalking with a shot-gun, like something out of an old cartoon. They laughed at the image.

Maz was Frosty's best friend from way back, age thirteen or so. He ruled White Supreme these days. Elon led Libre, the Puerto Rican gang next door. These days they collaborated with other gang leaders to make Chelsea an official ville like Brooklyn Prospect, but run by and for the gangs. They also favored a libertarian regime rather than the socialist democratic town meetings that held sway in the senile villes. The gang leaders ruled with an iron fist. There were no soft jobs, and any commerce was fair game. They sought to maintain their gangs, yet participate fully in the food distribution and other benefits the Raj offered its citizens.

More to the point, if anyone could take down Frosty, it was his best friend Maz. And not just in a fight – Maz could make Frosty laugh his way out of his upset, too. That's where Frosty and Panic were headed that night they were jumped and raped. They were walking to Maz's house, to team up if they found him still alive. Though the event replayed elsewhere in her nightmares. Her least favorite dream version had them pinned at the edge of a roof ten stories up.

The girls fell to the couch giggling. Ava killed the video. She couldn't tell Butch anything about her job, where she'd been, or why she was at the Resco Mansion. So she extracted salacious gossip from Butch about the old gang. As despot of the female contingent, Butch had the dirt on everyone. The jaw-dropping news was that Maz had a steady girlfriend for nearly two weeks now. Historically, Maz didn't even do one-night stands. He favored nooners.

Elon kept a harem of three girls and played them against each other as joint queen bee. No wonder he had cat scratches on his face all the time. Cade claimed Elon only slept with his most recent. But when Elon broke up with his original queen bee, the other girls tore her limb from limb. After that, Elon kept his exes around to share power. Ava wasn't sure whether to believe this generous interpretation of Elon's motives.

Gladys thumped a plate of cheese and crackers and veggies down on the coffee table with a scowl. Butch flicked her tongue out at her like a lizard, flirting. Gladys harrumphed and stalked away. Ava hit

Butch with a backhand punch. A little while later, a gaggle of officers filed in the door. Ava glanced over wistfully, but Cade wasn't among them. Butch drew her back in with the lowdown on the soaring prostitution trade in Chinatown now that the Navy had moved into the Apple.

Emmett MacLaren and his wife Dee Baker stepped in and stood before them as Butch completed her thought. Dee's welcoming smile grew increasingly abstract. Emmett's expression was closer to amused incredulity.

"Sorry to interrupt," he interrupted, "but we're about to serve dinner. Would you rather wait for Cade and your friends?" He appeared uncertain whether that was a good idea. But he brought in gang rat expertise to solve his gang rat problem. He was prepared to take their lead.

"I want to eat," Butch pounced. "I'm willing to eat twice."

Dee smiled. "Good choice. Um, out here? So you girls can...? Maybe I could join you."

"Awesome!" Butch said, brown eyes glowing.

Ava had profound reservations about that expression. "Out here might be best," she allowed. "We'd enjoy your company." She doubted that, but it seemed the thing to say. She considered Dee's business casual attire, a study in navy blue.

"So, Butch," Dee attempted. "What do you do for work?"

"I boss bitches around," Butch replied with a quick smile.

Ava intervened. "Butch took over my old job as queen bee. Gang leader for the female membership." Her smile was a little less predatory than Butch's. "That's still cleaning and sanitation plus, um..."

"Income-generating activities, yes," Butch agreed. "Such as servicing the Navy. And salvage, of course."

"Queen bee mostly makes sure everyone is doing her part on group priorities," Ava explained. "Resolve disputes."

Emmett wheeled in a serving cart bearing their supper plates, salad bowls, and water goblets. Apparently he decided to join them. Dee helped him set everything out on the coffee table. She forbid the girls to help, as they were guests.

Ava and Butch leaned shoulders together in disbelief and solidarity as the Apple's Royal Couple served them supper.

"What?" Dee asked.

"Nothing. Smells great!" Ava assured her.

"Smells like –" Butch began.

"Shut up, Butch," Ava instructed. "Manners."

Butch glared at her. "Look, princess. You and Maz and the Frost-king, you come from money. I come from the streets. And proud of it! I *am* using my manners!"

"Uh-huh," Emmett agreed, calmly sitting to eat. "We're glad you could make it, Butch. Ava, I apologize for taking advantage of you like this. But Dee and I wanted to have some gang rats over. Get to know y'all better. This is awesome for us. Just be yourselves."

Ava's eyes danced to the gaping hole under the staircase. "Maybe some manners. Sorry about your wall. Um, we can pay for that."

"Not a problem," Emmett said. "Cam and I knocked a hole there a couple months ago. Darlin', we should put a couch there."

Dee nodded with an extra bland glance in his direction. Ava pictured Cam Cameron and Emmett MacLaren, heroes of Hudson, wrestling in the living room and bashing a hole in the wall. She tamped down a smile and applied herself to an excellent salad. She'd seen Gladys come down the stairs with the produce fresh-picked.

"We found this new ingredient," Ava offered. "Verjuice." She prattled away about Cade's experiments with verjuice, especially in salad dressing and mushrooms. Butch was bowled over to learn that Frosty could cook.

From there the awkward conversation began to flow. It turned out the chickens in the back yard were Emmett's. He'd always kept chickens except when he was stationed overseas. The indoor vegetable jungle and downstairs planters were Dee's domain. Gladys ruled the roof gardens.

They'd strayed onto talking clothes when Cade and the guys showed up at last. No one was bleeding. Maz might end up with a bruise on his cheekbone, but probably not a black eye. They were in boisterous high spirits.

Cade caught sight of Ava in the living room, and leveled her an icy glare. Elon shouldered him aside and made some caustic comment that caused Cade to chuckle darkly.

Emmett excused himself to host the boy party with the men (and Gladys) in the dining room. Ava tried not to be insulted that he was worried about what damage the guys might inflict. She consoled herself that she and Butch were perfectly capable of reducing the mansion to rubble. As girls they simply didn't choose to. And they certainly wouldn't do it by accident.

"Must suck to be testosterone-poisoned," Butch said, possibly thinking along the same lines.

"Oh, I don't know," said Dee. "Looks like a lot of fun. Believe you're immortal. No worries. No goals except getting laid. Such a simple-minded, exuberant existence."

The dress, of course, was next on the girls' agenda. Yes, Dee's dress from the Royal Wedding was shoved in the back of a closet, along with steampunk and other whimsical clothing.

Dee hadn't realized before that gang rats didn't treat clothes as personal property. Butch and Ava filled her in on the system. Laundry was a major hassle. So kids often joined laundry-and-clothes-boutique clubs. You brought in your dirty laundry, left it to be washed for its next wearer, and picked out your wardrobe for the coming week. Since people had favorite outfits and styles, they tended to frequent the same shop on a subscriber basis. Butch belonged to Dyke Duds on West 22nd. Ava favored Evil Elves on Bleeker before she left for Basic.

Thundering elephants bounded up the stairs past Dee's bedroom. Maz stuck his head in, jaw-length honey-blond hair tamed by a backwards red baseball cap as usual. "Hot-tub! Be there!" He pounded the door for emphasis, a bit too hard. Fortunately, the bedroom door was solid maple instead of hollow core, and the doorstop held firm. He didn't pause to check for damage before he took off up the stairs, two at a time, after Cade and Elon.

"Um," said Butch, gauging Ava's tiny build. Not that Ava had a spare bathing suit to offer. Ava's own bathing suit and towel landed outside the door, tossed from above.

"Here, Butch," Dee offered, stepping to a bureau. "I have lots of bathing suits. Or a dark T-shirt?" Her bedroom even included decorative oriental screens to change behind. Dee used the vast en suite master bath.

The elephants charged back down. Elon and Maz landed loud, having slid down the banisters. Frosty told them to mind the walls. Maz pointed out helpfully that the handyman would come anyway to fix the hole Frosty left in the living room. Judging by the sound effects, the best friends wrestled and rolled and thudded down the next flight of stairs.

"Frosty's not usually like this," Butch offered to Dee, from behind her black screen, festooned with dragons. "Maz either. They know how to act. Hell, you should have seen Maz's brownstone. Put even this place to shame. Trust fund baby, old money. Tonight Maz is cheering Frosty up."

Ava was grateful and touched, that Butch would defend Frosty and Maz.

"Sounds like it's working!" Dee said gamely.

The pool party out back was a lot of fun. Carlos and Gladys prudently chose to observe from chairs on the back deck with a glass of wine, and stayed dry. Colonels Margolis, Cameron, and MacLaren, however, were determined to keep up with the tough youths. Mostly the girls stuck to the hot tub while the guys lowered the water level in the lap pool by splashing it across the back yard. But Ava and Butch mounted Elon and Maz's shoulders for a chicken fight in the pool. Occasionally the guys would cannonball into the hot-tub for a few minutes to warm up. It was only about 60 degrees out, and cooling.

Any time Frosty and Ava got too close to each other, one of the guys butted in to distract him. Bruises were blooming on Frosty and Maz, on legs and torso, but Elon appeared unscathed. Possibly his darker skin just hid the damage better. All of them had plenty of old scars.

They didn't mind. Fighting was their way of life. That went for the colonels, too. The officers weren't even particularly brainier than the younger guys – Frosty and Maz and Elon were brilliant as well as deadly, and masters of leadership. The colonels had wider experience. And probably a whole lot less testosterone at their age, but they still led young men. Cam, particularly, still played hard. He and his husband Dwayne were renowned for their beach parties. *So what if we're poor. Long Island has great beaches!*

Despite burning off a generous meal, eventually lips started to turn blue. Everyone sluiced off under the garden hose, dried themselves, and got dressed. Their host Emmett started to yawn uncontrollably. Curfew was long gone. A militia car was called, and Ava and Cade's gang friends took their leave.

"Do you need to talk?" Dee offered Ava in the dining room. "Me, or Carlos?" Cam had steered Cade into the living room for a similar quiet word.

"I'm good," Ava assured her on automatic. It wasn't that she didn't expect a nasty conversation once she and Cade were alone together. She just honestly believed that if he hit her, she deserved it on this one. That was what sucked most when Cade hit her. She'd earned it. "Just really tired. We knocked off a prison, um, 22 hours ago."

Cade claimed the empty bedroom next to Cam, without talking to Ava first. She tried to worry about that. But when her head hit the pillow, sleep dragged her under immediately.

She sat bolt upright as a scream split the night. *Frosty.*

38

Interesting fact: The propaganda campaign in Delmarva began days before Ekstrom arrived in Brooklyn. Hudson hackers hijacked Internet communications to start pushing special Project Reunion News bulletins to the peninsula. The Calvert Hills nuclear disaster, and Admiral O'Hara jailing Ekstrom during disaster recovery, were presented among the evidence of gross negligence and mismanagement.

Cade stumbled out of his room in decent-enough pajamas – a wife-beater and baby blue plaid dorm pants. Cam provided those when he steered Frosty to bed in the unfamiliar room. Cade. Ben. Whoever.

None of this was familiar, and it veered sickeningly. He swallowed trying to control his nausea.

Everything about these nightmares sucked, but the room swimming around him was his least favorite. And the memory of being raped. And the ringing in his ears. And the memory of Ava screaming, being raped. He couldn't remember what was worst, where he was, or why he was worrying about what was worst. It all sucked.

Out! I want out!

Cam was at his elbow, urgently steering him onto the stairs that yawned and shrunk and tilted. The mouth of an oaken shark rose to swallow him with a zillion sawing brown teeth, gleaming wet with air. The older man said something, but Cade couldn't hear. Or maybe he could hear but couldn't make anything make sense. A door opened a crack at the far end of the landing, and oh-so-familiar eyes peeked out. *Ava's safe. Good.* Cam waved her away.

Cade tripped on the slippery moving stairs and too-long dorm pants, Cam's. Agile as a ballerina, even on this heaving ship, he spun and landed well on hands and toes, his fingers gripping a stair several down from where his feet had been.

Cam hustled by and got a shoulder under his armpit. That was better. Everything visual swam, but Cade's body sense was outstanding. The officer's supporting body became a stable point in Cade's spinning perceptions, as they worked their way down more stairs. Cade simply closed his eyes. He walked better blind.

Other doors and people happened on the next landing. Cade wasn't looking, couldn't hear, didn't care. *Out!*

He was sitting on the comfortable leather couch in Emmett MacLaren's living room, a mug of hot milk in his hands. He'd blacked out since the second floor landing. No one guided his hands on the plain sturdy white mug. Cam and Carlos were both there. C's. Everyone's name began with C. *Who am I?*

Who are you who asks? That made his head hurt worse. He took a sip of the hot milk, laced with maple sugar and vanillin. "Vanillin is made from wood pulp," Cade said aloud. "I miss real vanilla."

"I did not know that," Carlos acknowledged.

Cam grinned. "Welcome back. Has the room quit spinning?"

"Did I say that?" Cade asked. He couldn't remember saying that. That was the worst thing about these nightmares, the black outs and phase ins. He was losing his mind. And that was the worst thing. He wasn't afraid he was going insane. He was insane. Just like Mom.

Mom didn't want to die. She hung on, bleeding from her eyes, her nose, her mouth, bleeding under her skin, turning yellow and purple and white. He wished so hard she would just let go. There was no way for her to live. Yet she held on forever.

Cam relieved Cade of his mug as he face-dived into his palms. If only the AK-47 on the damned laundromat would let up for a minute, so he could get his guys out of here! Then the damned tank swiveled its gun and blew up the laundromat, with Cade and his team pinned beneath it. And Cade was up and flying through the air.

And the worst thing about these nightmares was that even the goddamn flashback wouldn't stand still. It morphed. There were so many damned nightmares. He couldn't fight them all.

"…Xanax?" Carlos suggested.

"No drugs," Cam ruled. "Cade, try to drink the milk." He held onto the mug this time, helping Cade hold it steady. "Cade, where are you?"

"Keeps shifting," Cade reported. "Living room. MacLaren's house. North Jersey a second ago. Fucking Chet from Midtown. Pardon my French. Aimed a fucking cannon at me and my guys. Sent me flying through the air."

"Do you remember landing?" Cam asked.

Cade frowned. "No. No, I blacked out a long time. Weaved in and out. Rode on an APC most of the way back. Maz held me on. God, the headache. Panic went mental when I got home. And my temper. Out of the blue. I had no idea what got me angry. Just – *bam!*" The warm milk was helping, though. He was tracking this conversation. He thought he was tracking. Maybe he'd be wrong again.

"Was this during the Starve, son?" Carlos asked. The other C, the Native American.

"Yeah. October," Cade said. "A month before Project Reunion. Before we heard about it, anyway. I always remember it beginning with Thanksgiving dinner. Out of nowhere. Invitations fluttering on the breeze. You're invited to Thanksgiving dinner. Christ."

Cam pressed him to drink more milk. It helped. Maybe Panic was right. He got weird with that low blood sugar thing. But he was never hungry. He got so tired of being hungry that he decided not to feel that anymore. Scared, too. Fear sucked and never ended. Glad to be rid of that. Why bother to feel anything at all, when it all sucked.

"How did you treat the concussion?" Carlos asked.

"Huh? Oh, after Chet blew me up. Um, Panic gave me aspirin and put cool washcloths on my head. Kept the room dark. Quiet. Cleaned up the other wounds. Not much we could do. You survive. Do it again."

"Cade, would you be willing to see a psychiatrist?" Cam asked.

"I've tried. *He* gave me Xanax. Ton of other crap. Anti-psychotics. Couldn't decide if I was borderline or schizophrenic –"

"Cade, are you listening?" Cam interrupted. "You had a traumatic brain injury – a TBI. And you have PTSD from all the other crap you went through. You're not psychotic. Not borderline. Not schizophrenic."

"I'm not getting better, either," Cade said. "Panic got better. My mother went insane. Maz says it's OK. When I finally lose it, come home to Chelsea. He'll take me in. Take care of me for the rest of my life. Just don't kill Panic."

"Killing Panic wouldn't help," Carlos agreed.

"Protect Ava," Cade said, squeezing his eyes shut. A tear leaked out. "Have I lost it this time?"

"Cade, you had a nightmare, after a major trigger," Cam said firmly. He forced more milk on the younger man. "You were perfectly rational. You just led a dangerous, highly successful mission into VA. You've got triggers. You need to see a psychiatrist to disarm the triggers. You're too dangerous to go around half-cocked like this. You know that."

"I tried."

"Yes, I heard you. You tried," Cameron said. "Carlos, see? This is why I'm so strict about shrinks who claim they can treat apples. Most of them are total quacks. Cade, I can get you a *good* psychiatrist. One I know can do the job. Experienced with combat vets like us. Are you willing to talk to him?"

"Yeah. I always was. I tried on my own. Books. Sk– My boss tried to help."

Cam shook his head. "It's the brain injury, Cade. I had the same thing. One of my purple heart collection. Car bomb in Jordan. Met my husband that time. He scraped me off the pavement and carried me to a hospital. What you're describing, on the APC? Yeah. Been there. Done that. The headache hurt like a sonofabitch. The rages out of nowhere? Nearly throttled my room-mate. You don't need a shrink who treats suburban angst. You need a guy with a proven track record on combat brain injury. I'll get you the right guy."

"Takes time," Carlos added. "Parts of your brain were damaged. Other parts learn to take over. Confusing and scary from what I've heard."

"That was a long time ago," Cade argued.

"Year and a half?" Cam estimated. "You've only been eating well for what, six months?"

"About that," Cade allowed. That reminded him to finish his milk. It helped. His head was clearing. He could think. But the clawing worry remained. "Ava is safe?"

"Ava is safe upstairs," Carlos agreed. "And Cade, she had a lot of help, for five months, at West Point. To work on her PTSD."

"And she didn't have that brain injury," Cam said. "That makes it harder. But you can heal. Just, don't compare your progress to Ava, or anyone else. OK?"

"OK. She's safe upstairs?"

"You need to see her?"

Cade was torn on that one. *Hell, yes!* He wanted to see her. *Hell, no!* He was afraid he'd hurt her. He swallowed. "Yeah."

"I'll come with you," Cam said. "I'm going your way. Good night, Carlos."

At Ava's door, Cam opened it a crack in lieu of knocking. Cade slipped in and kneeled beside the bed. Ava pulled him in to hide his face in her breasts and hold on for dear life around her hips, the way he always needed after that nightmare.

"You're safe?" Cam asked her. "You're sure?"

"Sure," Ava replied. "Next time we should sleep in the car. Not cause everyone so much trouble." She cuddled Cade tight.

"No worries. See you in the morning."

She waited until Cam's door closed across the landing. "Cade, I am so sorry."

"Don't talk. Please."

She was safe. He was safe and holding her. That's all that mattered. She tried to make stuff so damned complicated with emotional crap. Cade didn't want complicated. He couldn't control all the rest, so to hell with it all. He just wanted to hold her and sleep.

~

AVA AND CADE BOTH FROZE A LITTLE COMING DOWN TO THE DINING ROOM for breakfast. Mercifully, the house's folk were old hands at dealing with apple survivors and their quirks.

Everyone smiled and said good morning. No one mentioned last night. Gladys offered them French toast and hot herb tea.

After breakfast, Ava joined the runners, then swam a few laps with Dee. Cade stuck with Carlos. They jogged too, but only a little, favoring strength training. Then the colonels headed out to a meeting at the hotel where they'd taken Ekstrom. Ava and Cade's briefing would be after lunch, back here.

Ava was sorry to hear that. It meant they had hours to prepare a proper presentation. She'd hoped to just wing it and answer questions.

They put their heads together and organized the material. Cade liked the low-lights of West VA video she'd started. Working together, they gleaned enough interesting footage from Virginia and Maryland and Delmarva to extend the video to about 20 minutes, then spliced in maps to extend it to a half hour, plus captions to make it self-explanatory. They could run it in the background and not dwell on it unless they were asked.

Skull sent a ready-made presentation for his financial pitch. Ava was glad she'd seen what it cost for spare parts for cell towers. The numbers were astronomical. The labels for outlays were rich in euphemism.

Skull included staffing levels. There were casualties on the VA missions. He included a page showing their faces, but no names. Cade pointed out Weyland and his trainee for Ava, their intended backup team who died in West VA trying to buy gas.

Ava blew Cade's mind by knowing how to put together an after action report. Expository writing and creative writing were Cade's forte, along with anything to do with English grammar, punctuation, and spelling. The facts, organized and indexed for a Resco to browse quickly then dig deeper, Ava had done before, with tutoring sergeants at her elbow.

Which was just as well. The doorbell rang just before 10:00. A middle-aged psychiatrist, Dr. Keillor, arrived and swept Cade away upstairs. They were closeted for a couple hours. Ava was glad she fed Cade a midmorning snack first. And she was happy for Cade, if this guy was any good compared to the quack who prescribed him a shelf worth of mind-numbing drugs, then left him still terrified he was schizophrenic and would only get worse. But she was stuck writing the rest of the presentation on her own.

Or was she? Skull was her boss, not Cade.

She decided to prepare it piecemeal and email each part to Skull for review. The first section came back beautifully formatted, with smooth animation tricks. He even added extra details and backup pages.

She used Skull's format, and the rest came together fairly quickly. This wasn't a report, it was a presentation. Bullet points only needed a few words for orientation.

Ava didn't know what to say about the General and the gran caravan. She wasn't even sure Skull authorized them to spy on the General's HQ. Maybe Cade instigated it, maybe not. Maybe Ike and Neal were just being subversive. Less said the better, she decided. Besides, she never learned what the techs found out.

Skull provided backup screens to highlight the intelligence gained from Mount Weather. Ava and Cade were too busy running at the time to care.

Cade came down with Dr. Keillor, looking as though some of the weight of the world was lifted from his shoulders. But Cade left to drive the doctor to his next appointment.

Emmett dropped in to tell Ava to freeze changes to her presentation. He helped her email it to Pete Hoffman for review before the meeting at thirteen hundred.

Cade returned to gobble his lunch and go upstairs with Ava to change. He only had time to skim what they were about to present.

39

———————

Interesting fact: The invasion of Delmarva became a textbook case for the Hudson Army. Not for military prowess, though it was well executed. The moral of the story was that Hudson pacified an area the size of Long Island in under two weeks by winning over hearts and minds before they invaded.

"Nice suit!" Lt. Col. Cameron called out, as Cade and Ava descended the stairs into the living room. The young couple wore Dean and Eileen's outfits, minus Eileen's pancaked makeup and heels.

Cade grinned crookedly and struck a couple male model poses. "I have an excellent tailor in Philadelphia."

Cameron appreciated the show, but advised him to stick to his current career. Carlos Mora reminded Cam that an army officer had no earthly use for a suit. Dee Baker assured Ava that her outfit was just as impressive as Cade's.

Ava appreciated Dee's attempt to put her at ease. Cade was comfortable in his suit and public speaking. Ava felt intimidated by the audience. She blew out to calm the jitters.

Generals Pete Hoffman and Ivan Link, along with Emmett MacLaren and Ash Margolis, conferred in the office beyond closed glass French doors. The brownstone's beautiful oaken library opened off the back of the living room. Now it was a bit crammed with utilitarian tables, cables, office chairs, and networked peripherals.

Ava was surprised the meeting didn't convene on time. Weren't officers supposed to be sticklers for that? Preferring action to the alarming prospect of chitchat with colonels, she set her video to play on the giant living room monitor.

The small group coalesced, riveted by maps and views of West Virginia. By the time the bootleg refinery rolled on screen, several were jotting notes. Cade and Ava hadn't been formally introduced yet, and stood at the back. The half dozen or so Rescos saved their questions for later.

Emmett stuck his head out the office door. "Cade? Ava? Join us in the office?" He ushered them in to present to General Hoffman, and Ivan Link, once the Governor-General of New England before it merged with Hudson. Hoffman was the older man, though only recently promoted to general rank. He was somewhat big and frumpy and comfortable looking. The younger and trimmer Link sat erect and cool.

Hoffman rose to shake their hands. "Deeply impressed," he assured them. "You've done Hudson a great service, and Delmarva. With Ekstrom to direct our invasion, you've saved thousands of lives. That was a tough mission. Carried out brilliantly. " He met their eyes to underscore his sincere appreciation.

Then he stepped back and waved a hand to indicate his computer. "I've decided to cancel your presentation. It's very good. Fascinating reading. But this summit is about Delmarva." He indicated his handful of lead Rescos in the living room. "I need my people focused on that. For your boss's...proposal...I need a different group of people in the room. After Delmarva. I understand why Sullivan tried now. But I won't permit it."

Hoffman paused for a quick disarming smile. "No reflection on you whatsoever. Great work. I'll follow up with Sullivan directly."

Ava was miffed. But Cade looked relieved as he steered her back into the living room. Hoffman followed and told his people to head back to the hotel. The gathering morphed into the familiar format of an army receiving line. Cade and Ava shook each Resco's hand as they queued up to exit the brownstone, and offered their congratulations on a daring rescue.

Dee and Carlos Mora hung back to argue Pete Hoffman into letting them use Cade and Ava's adventure in their PR campaign in Delmarva. PR News could use a lurid story to whet Delmarvan appetites for Hudson propaganda. Pete ruled that Cade and Ava and the SEALs were off limits, plus the prison breakout in Arlington.

Emmett joined the couple when the rest were gone. "I see why Skull speaks so highly of you. Well done." He offered a hand to shake like all the others.

Emmett continued, "I apologize for being scarce during your visit. I'm your host. But we invade VA in 40 hours. I'm helping my wife with the PR again." He smiled at Ava.

"That fast," Cade said.

"We were waiting on you," Emmett replied. "Ekstrom, anyway. Thank you. Anything I can do, let me know. Think of me as your company backup in the city."

Ava's eyes widened.

Cade said, "Thank you, sir. Your hospitality has gone above and beyond. Especially with my outburst last night. I apologize."

Emmett shook his head. "Always hard to come down off a mission. We know that. I should thank you for last night. Truly. We don't understand your generation too well. We're trying to build a new nation. We care what your generation thinks. What you want for your lives. But what that looks like to young apples, I don't have a clue."

"Sure you do," Cade replied softly. "Eat rage. And not much else. For a couple years." Glittering cold blue eyes met Emmett's warm hazel ones.

"Uh-huh," Emmett said, holding Cade's eye unflinching. "That part I caught. How to channel that rage, what you want, that's still a mystery."

Ava flashed him her model-quality wide smile. "When we figure it out, we'll let you know. We like you. And Dee. Cam and Carlos. We owe you."

Cade wasn't that warm. "Skull considers you an ally. Good enough for me."

After that prickly interchange, Cade and Ava took their leave with grace and appreciation for their host.

~

"TONIGHT AT THE DOJO?" AVA SUGGESTED, FOR A REUNION WITH HER Army Basic squad mates. She dabbed Eileen's makeup off her face with some cold cream that reeked of camphor and menthol.

Cade had already changed into jeans and a short-sleeved Oxford shirt. Now he was packing their gear. He looked awfully preppy for the Chelsea ganglands, in Ava's opinion. He paused, then dropped to a seat on the bed.

"Cade?" she prompted. He didn't reply. She quickly sluiced off her face, then joined him on the bed.

He was just staring. She took his hand and squeezed. "Where are you?" she asked softly.

"Oh, I'm tracking," he replied. "I…"

"You're not up to visiting my squad," Ava suggested. She brushed the hair over his temple with her fingertips. His hair was softer. He used to bleach it nearly white, then mousse it upward. Now it was a natural blond, darkening toward her own light brown, and touchable. Frosty the Snowman didn't do vulnerable if he could help it. Cade Snowdon was vulnerable today.

"No," he agreed. "I'm sorry. You deserve to see your friends. And I should support you. I just…"

"You want to go home to Elmira," Ava concluded. "Safe."

Home wasn't Chelsea with Maz anymore. If he hadn't seen Maz last night, there would be no hesitation now. They'd be headed straight to Manhattan, despite the prospect of being mobbed and welcomed by the gang he used to rule. That would suck. Trying to invent a Cade persona to meet with Ava's friends would suck, too. For Cade, simply being himself on display wasn't an option right now. He needed to hide.

"You could stay. Take the train tomorrow," he offered desperately.

"No, it's OK. Everybody's probably busy with the invasion, anyway. You're more important to me." *You need me today.*

Cade scowled. "It's not a choice. Me or your friends."

"It's a choice what to do today. Let's get you home."

He turned to crush her in a hug. He buried his face in her hair. "Thank you. I'm sorry."

"You're welcome. Always. I smell like cold cream."

"You smell clean and healthy and safe," Cade countered. "That's a miracle. We made it."

SPRING HAD WROUGHT GREAT CHANGES AT THE CAMPGROUND COMPOUND in Elmira. Leaves unfurled at last, all species, all at once. The unnerving cold dry windy stasis had given way to quick-passing fronts of torrential rain and muggy sun, sometimes several rounds in the same day.

Little crop plants visited outdoors to harden in the harsh conditions, safely tucked into their greenhouses at night. Hudson dared not lose any more seed to freak frosts. Even the company grew some crops, tended by whoever happened to be in residence.

Daneel stayed. He could collaborate with Art Walsh – Ike/Mike's real name – just as easily online. Daneel needed full Internet capability, of course, of the highest bandwidth. He spoofed it so that Internet traffic originating from the campground was automatically routed to bounce all over Up Finger and beyond, untraceable.

Ava could text with her friends in the city and the Army from the comfort of home. Cade could continue treatment with Dr. Keillor by video.

Art Walsh was home safe in Binghamton. He claimed to be happy to lose Daneel as a room-mate.

KT stayed. Skull intended to make him a field agent, like Cade. But Skull sorely needed a top-level aide. Cade had been doing that, but only when he was home. He hoped the two of them would take turns, and perhaps Daneel as well.

Garcia and Jamal and the other SEALs were still working their way through Navy exit interviews. Skull hoped to hire most of them.

The agents held a memorial dinner for Weyland and his trainee one night in the campground clubhouse. That was Cade's original backup team on this mission, the pair killed in West Virginia trying to buy gas. Skull and Cade, bolstered by several beers, recounted their life stories, and some memorable Weyland missions. Weyland survived the Starve in Yonkers, a tough suburb of the Bronx. His trainee, a girl called Ballzer, hailed from Secaucus in Jersey. They didn't get the chance to know her well, though Skull recounted some of her funnier bonehead moves during her weeks with Weyland. Skull liked her. So did Weyland.

Skull told them Gorey, Rahema's partner, was making a full recovery. He was also sentenced to inpatient drug rehab for a few months in Pittsburgh. Skull declined to extract him. The message was loud and clear to the agents in Elmira. The boss had a low tolerance for drug abuse on the job.

Cade and Skull had a long private one-on-one in the hot tub, with beer. Skull decided Cade would stay home next to give him time for treatment and to finish his GED.

Besides, Darcy was in the shop for repairs and cleaning. And a paint job – she couldn't return to PA wearing forest green. Cade made Ava pick out a loaner car for use in the meantime, something she thought looked fun to drive.

He promptly amended his criteria when she chose a two-seater red Smart Fortwo. He required that the vehicle seat four adults with room for groceries. She ended up with a blue hybrid Toyota like Tuck's. She drove KT and Daneel to go shopping that very Thursday at the Sayre farm market.

Each painted a scarf at the water troughs. KT and Daneel's designs evoked waves and beach. Ava marbled one for Skull in black and white and swirling shades of grey, with just one drop of blood red dye for accent.

Skull liked it a lot.

~

"YOU NEED ME," AVA SAID. SHE WAS ALONE WITH CADE IN THEIR CABIN, her last night at the campground. "I'm sorry to leave you."

Skull had broken through her denial at last, when they had their one-on-one. She was a full-blown field agent in her own right. She wouldn't always be partnered with Cade. The company contractors needed quarterly visits. Weyland was due to tour Cleveland and Detroit. Ohio had been his beat. But Weyland was gone, and Ava was ready. Tomorrow she'd take KT and two new hires and show them the ropes.

Cade pulled her to him, to sit on his lap on the hard little couch. "I do need you," he agreed thoughtfully. "But I'm OK here, Ava. Now, I am. In December, alone here, after seeing you leave for Basic? I thought I'd lose my mind. Skull should have sent me back to Maz as a basket case. But instead he helped me get my act together. I liked the work."

Cade paused to tuck Ava's hair behind her ear. "Dr. Keillor is helping. Each time we defuse a trigger, it's like my mind stops fracturing on things. Skittering away. I want to finish this, and get better."

"No argument there," Ava said, resting her fingers on his chest. "The treatment is helping. I'm just afraid you need me here to hold you while you go through it." She kissed him. "Don't you?"

He hugged her close. "Nah. You'll be safe with KT. And your newbs look promising. Train up the three of them, be back in a few weeks. Daneel's moving into the cabin with me. Keep me company. Ava, we'll go out in the field together again. Just not this time."

"I love you. I'll miss you." She ran her hand down his arm. He felt so good. He smelled of hot tub chlorine, and the steak and mushrooms he'd served for her farewell supper. She'd miss him fiercely.

"You, too. But we're building something here."

"Yeah? Have you figured out what that is yet?"

Cade smirked. "No, but it's coming along nicely. I like the team we're building. Especially with you on it."

"We had a gang," Ava hazarded. "It worked for us. This is our new gang?"

"Better one this time." Cade snuggled his nose to hers. "Ava, your idea last summer, joining Soho Ville? That was good. But I hated being locked in that city with the seniles. Maz and Elon's plan, youth gang rule, control the Chinatown sex trade? That makes me sick. Join the Army and obey orders? Baby, you couldn't make it. Me?" He huffed a laugh. "They'd put me in front of a firing squad. No. Because of the gang, all my opportunities are organized crime. The company is a leader in my field."

"Freedom to travel," Ava mused. "Money and great food. You even help pick our new members. Taking any kid just because he was white, that wasn't great criteria."

"Death selected them," Cade quibbled. "By and by."

Ava couldn't argue with that. The kids who lasted weren't just white. They were strong, cunning, and flexible as a weasel. "You're not the boss now, though."

"I like leaning on Skull. It's orgasmic. Like the food. I learn a lot from him. Better role model than the senile gang leaders. Less pressure on me. And the backup? Baby, it's not all on us to protect thousands anymore. Someone covers our asses, too. That's awesome."

She held his face to gaze into his eyes. She nodded, satisfied with what she saw there. He was happy here with the death angels. "You deserve less pressure. You done good, Cade. Too bad this outfit doesn't need a queen bee."

"Don't be too sure," Cade said. "You always figure out what needs doing, and do it. And I need you."

"I need you, too."

"Time to grow now," Cade said, as he had five months before. "Give each other space for that again."

He said that to her at the beginning of Army Basic. He said they shouldn't keep in touch because they couldn't see each other and it hurt too much. Ava took it well. She cried her eyes out all afternoon. Then at supper she started the Lard Belly Mutiny. But that was all five months ago. She was ever so much more mature now.

Good, she thought. They were on the same wavelength. She replied as she had then, "Five foot one *forever!*"

Enough talking with words. Talking with their bodies was more fun.

∾

KT chose an upscale Chevy Suburban rather than Cade's Ford Expedition. He named her Rosa. He invested long hours and loving care into equipping her with pet toys to rival Cade's. The new trainees had arrived eager and ecstatic to hit the road.

Ava left with them the next morning to see what wonders Ohio had in store.

KT made her drive.

Eager for more? Ava Panic continues in *Feral Courier*.

From gang rat to diplomat.

Ava Panic prefers a simple mission. If it bothers her, shoot it.

But with her partner benched, tiny Ava gets no respect from the supplier low-lifes in Ohio. Then she makes a chance discovery – Canada has advanced new cell phones.

In a crumbling world, this tech is a game-changer. The Northeast can't produce the microchips. Neither can Canada. Where did they come from?

To find out, Ava has to cross the continent alone, slip into the Pacific Northwest undetected, and figure out whom to contact.

Canada holds the only route through the Dust Bowl, a single train. Under false pretenses, Ava is on it. Along with secret police, counter-agents, troops, and a lost defector from home.

And a whole lot of trouble.

ALSO BY GINGER BOOTH

Calm Act Feral America: Ava Panic

Feral Recruit

Feral Agent

Feral Courier

Feral Carolina

Short Prequels

Ebola Day (Ava & Cade)

*Civilly Disobedient (Dee) ***

*Dust of Kansas (Emmett) ***

Road to Humble Texas (Kayden)

*** free for reader group*

Calm Act, Books 1-4 : Dee Baker

End Game

Project Reunion

Martial Lawless

Tsunami Wake

The Calm Act Books 1-3 (box set)

Thrive Space Colony Adventures

Skyship Thrive

Spaceship Thrive (~April 2019)

Nonfiction:

Indoor Salad: How to Grow Vegetables Indoors

ACKNOWLEDGMENTS

I'm deeply grateful to my test readers. My beta readers put up with reading the manuscript while I'm still writing it. The hard-working team for *Feral Agent* included Bee Gentry, Jim Hunt, Brett Jarman, Ron Kaminski, Bonne Kelley, Karen Reinertsen, Mike Ryan, Suella Tucker, and WMH Cheryl. Thank you so much for your time and insights, and most importantly for your friendship, and urging me on.

I offer my newsletter subscribers the chance to be Tuckerized – donate their names for characters. This time the Tuckerized were: farmer Ron Kaminski, Sixers chief Fred Oelrich, and returning characters Frosty, gang leader Maz, and death angel Skull. Thank you for playing! Of course the characters bear no resemblance to the people who offered their names.

Thanks as well to the advance review copy readers, who read the almost-final manuscript, ready to write reviews for book launch.

And thank you, for reading my book. Without you, I couldn't do what I do, so I really appreciate that you give my work a chance. Drop me a line! I personally respond to all messages. Books take a long time to write. Feedback is the fuel that powers the next story.

Ginger Booth

Made in the USA
Middletown, DE
19 May 2022